This book is a work of fiction. All characters, names, locations, and events portrayed in this book are fictional or used in an imaginary manner to entertain, and any resemblance to any real people, situations, or incidents is purely coincidental.

MANSFIELD PARK AND MUMMIES:
Monster Mayhem, Matrimony, Ancient Curses, True Love, and Other Dire Delights

Jane Austen and Vera Nazarian

Cover Art Details:
"Miss Pinkerton's Academy" by George Goodwin Kilburne (1839-1924); "Malvern Hall" by John Constable (1809); "Grabkammer der Nefertari, Gattin des Ramses II., Szene: Der Gott Re-Harakleti und Amentit, die Göttin des Okzidents"; "Photo from Egyptian Gallery, British Museum" by Steve F. E. Cameron (2006-2007).

Interior Illustrations:
"Appendix," courtesy of Pearson Scott Foresman.
"After Mummification," Copyright © 2009 by Vera Nazarian

ISBN-13: 978-1-60762-047-1
ISBN-10: 1-60762-047-2

FIRST EDITION
Trade Paperback

November 16, 2009

A Publication of
Norilana Books
P. O. Box 2188
Winnetka, CA 91396
www.norilana.com

Printed in the United States of America

Mansfield Park and Mummies:

Monster Mayhem, Matrimony, Ancient Curses, True Love, and Other Dire Delights

Curiosities

an imprint of

Norilana Books

www.norilana.com

For Janet Chui
My thanks for the mummies!

Mansfield Park

and

MUMMIES

Monster Mayhem, Matrimony, Ancient Curses, True Love, and Other Dire Delights

Jane Austen

and

Vera Nazarian

With Scholarly Footnotes and Appendices

Chapter I

About three thousand years ago, an Ancient Egyptian Pharaoh, with infinite riches of his kingdom surrounding him, had the bad luck to die, be embalmed, mummified and then sealed up in his great tomb among the sands of Lower Egypt, and to be thereby raised to the rank of eternity and, quite possibly, deity.

About thirty years ago, Miss Maria Ward, of Huntingdon, with only seven thousand pounds and nary a kingdom or sand granule in sight, had the good luck to captivate Sir Thomas Bertram, of Mansfield Park, in the county of Northampton, and to be thereby raised to the rank of a baronet's lady, with all the comforts and consequences of an handsome house and large income.

With the former, all Egypt mourned. With the latter, all Huntingdon exclaimed on the greatness of the match, and her uncle, the lawyer, himself allowed her to be at least three thousand pounds short of any equitable claim to it. The deceased Pharaoh had two royal siblings who immediately benefited from his elevation to the Afterlife. Miss Maria Ward had two sisters to be benefited by her elevation—not to the Afterlife, to be sure, but to the even grander state of AfterEngagement—and such of their acquaintance as thought Miss Ward and Miss Frances quite as handsome as Miss Maria, did not scruple to predict their marrying with almost equal advantage. But whether three thousand or merely thirty years ago, there certainly are not so many men of large fortune in the world as there are pretty (and decidedly unmummified) women to deserve them.

While the venerable Pharaoh mummy continued to desiccate in secret splendor for thousands of years, far into the future, our Maria's one sister, Miss Ward, at the end of half a dozen years, found herself obliged to be attached to the Rev. Mr. Norris, a friend of her brother-in-law, with scarcely any private fortune, and the other, Miss Frances, fared yet worse. Miss Ward's match was indeed not contemptible: Sir Thomas happily gave his friend an income in the living of Mansfield. And Mr. and Mrs. Norris began their career of conjugal felicity with very little less than a thousand a year. But Miss Frances married, in the common phrase, to disoblige her family, and by fixing on a lieutenant of marines, without education, fortune, or connexions, did it very thoroughly. Short of marrying the mummy of a deceased ancient Egyptian pharaoh, she could hardly have made a more untoward choice. But, speaking of mummies, dear Reader, we are getting somewhat ahead of ourselves—

Sir Thomas Bertram had every intention to gladly assist Lady Bertram's sister in her relative destitution. But her husband's profession was such as no interest could reach. And before Sir Thomas could devise another method of aid, an absolute breach between the sisters had taken place. It was a breach of tremendous proportions, a crevasse, a grand canyon, or possibly, a pyramid of sorts—a truly monstrous and rather angular coldness, or maybe a heat, but most likely a thing lukewarm and therefore utterly indifferent, as though brought forth out of the grave, spurred on by royal dead ancients. It was the natural result of the conduct of each party—such as a very imprudent marriage almost always produces.

To save herself from useless remonstrance, Mrs. Price never wrote to her family on the subject till actually married.

Lady Bertram, who was a woman of very tranquil feelings, and a temper remarkably easy and indolent—one might say, placid to the point of being simultaneously deceased and yet walking upright—would have contented herself with merely giving up her sister, and thinking no more of the matter. But Mrs. Norris had a spirit of activity, not to mention a vaguely wolfish streak, which could not be satisfied till she had written a long and angry letter to Fanny, to point out the folly of her conduct, and threaten her with all its possible ill consequences—palsy, the poor house, rabid creature bites, the cut complete. Mrs. Price, in her turn, was injured and angry; and her bitter answer to her sisters put an end to all intercourse[1] between them for a considerable period.

Their homes were so distant, and the circles in which they moved so distinct—Lady Bertram, for instance was always surrounded by Egyptologists, famous exotic doctorate-endowed visiting scholars *du jour,* and attended instructional lectures that would have bored the other to tears—as almost to preclude the means of ever hearing of each other's existence during the eleven following years. Or, at least, it seemed unlikely to Sir Thomas that Mrs. Norris should ever have it in her power to tell them, as often as she did (in her angry *wolfish* voice), that Fanny had got another child and it was neither bitten by anything wild nor stunted in limb or brain development.

By the end of eleven years, however—a mere blink of an instant to a drying mummy, but quite a different matter to a robust living female; but oh, mustn't get ahead of ourselves—Mrs. Price could no longer afford to cherish pride or resentment, or to lose one connexion that might possibly assist her. A large and still increasing family, an husband disabled for active service (except for his mouth, decidedly still deployed on multiple vessels in the East Indies), but not the less equal to company and good liquor, and a very small income—all made her eager to regain the friends she had so carelessly sacrificed.

---

[1] Ahem!

Thus, she addressed Lady Bertram in a letter of contrition and despondence, a superfluity of children, a fair mention of Egyptology, and a want of almost everything else. This could not but dispose them all to a reconciliation. Mrs. Price was preparing for her ninth lying-in; and after bewailing the circumstance, and imploring their countenance as sponsors to the expected child, she could not conceal how important they might be to the future maintenance of the eight already in being.

Her eldest was a boy of ten years old, a fine spirited fellow, who longed to be out in the world, sailing the seas or perchance digging up Egypt (the latter being a strong hint to Lady Bertram to put her in favor of the boy) or seeking treasure in the New World; but what could she do? Was there any chance of his being hereafter useful to Sir Thomas in the concerns of his West Indian property? No situation would be beneath him; or what did Sir Thomas think of Woolwich?

The letter was not unproductive. It re-established peace and kindness. Sir Thomas sent friendly advice and professions, sanguine Lady Bertram dispatched money and baby-linen and Egyptian grave-robbed trifles, and Mrs. Norris wrote the letters.

And within a twelvemonth a more important advantage to Mrs. Price resulted from it. Mrs. Norris often observed to others that she could not get her poor sister and her family out of her head—especially on bright moonlit nights when her head felt rather giddy and almost not her own but, shockingly, one with the field vermin in the countryside—and that, much as they had all done for her, she seemed to be wanting to do more. Finally she admitted her wish that poor Mrs. Price should be relieved from the charge and expense of *one* of her children.

"What if they were among them to undertake the care of her eldest daughter—a girl now nine years old, of an age to require more attention than her poor mother could possibly give? The trouble and expense of it to them would be nothing, compared with the benevolence of the action."

Lady Bertram agreed with her instantly. “I think we cannot do better,” said she; “let us send for the child. Is she hale and ruddy-cheeked, do you think? Are her teeth all in? Will she be able to handle papyrus?”

Sir Thomas could not give so instantaneous and unqualified a consent. He debated and hesitated—it was a serious charge. A girl so brought up must be adequately provided for, or there would be cruelty instead of kindness in taking her from her family. He thought of his own four children, of his two sons, of cousins in love, etc.;—but no sooner did he try to object, than Mrs. Norris interrupted him with a near-howl—a matronly cough, surely, the weather was dreadful and the moon close to full—and a reply to all objections, stated or not.

“My dear Sir Thomas, I perfectly comprehend you, and do justice to the generosity and delicacy of your notions. I entirely agree with you as to the propriety of fully providing for a child one had taken into one’s own hands. Having no children of my own, I look to the children of my sisters! Do not let us be frightened from a good deed by a trifle. Give a girl an education, by all means, then send her off to harvest Egypt if it pleases—” (with a look at her sister) “You are thinking of your sons forming a possible *tendre* for a female cousin—but *that* is the least likely to happen. They would be brought up like brothers and sisters. It is, in fact, the only sure way of preventing the connexion. Suppose her a pretty girl, and seen by Tom or Edmund for the first time seven years hence—I dare say there would be mischief. The very idea of her having been suffered to grow up at a distance from us all in poverty and neglect, would be enough to make either of the dear, sweet-tempered boys in love with her. But breed her up with them from this time, and suppose her even to have the beauty of an angel, she will never be more to either than a sister.”

"There is a great deal of truth in what you say," replied Sir Thomas, "I only meant to observe that it ought not to be lightly engaged in. To make it really serviceable to Mrs. Price, and creditable to ourselves, we must secure to the child the provision of a gentlewoman."

"I thoroughly understand you," cried Mrs. Norris, "you are everything that is generous and considerate. So, if you are not against it, I will write to my poor sister tomorrow, and make the proposal. And, as soon as matters are settled, *I* will engage to get the child to Mansfield, with no trouble to *you*. I will send Nanny to London on purpose, and the child be appointed to meet her there. They may easily get her from Portsmouth to town by the coach, under the care of any creditable person."

Sir Thomas no longer made any objection, and a more respectable, though less economical rendezvous being substituted, everything was considered as settled. But while Sir Thomas was fully resolved to be the patron of the selected child, Mrs. Norris herself had no intention of being at any expense whatever in her maintenance. As far as talk, she was thoroughly benevolent; verily, nobody knew better how to dictate liberality to others. But her love of money was equal to her love of directing—she saved her own and spent that of her friends.

Having married on a narrower income, Mrs. Norris had fancied a very strict line of economy necessary. And with no children to provide for, she had nothing to impede her frugality. Under this principle, with no real affection for her sister, she could only take credit for *arranging* so expensive a charity. Though, perhaps, after this conversation, she might walk home to the Parsonage (in the delightful moonlight that simply begged for a full-throated howl) in the happy belief of being the most liberal-minded sister and aunt in the world.

When the subject was brought forward again, her views were more fully explained. In reply to Lady Bertram's calm inquiry of "Where shall the child come to first, sister, to you or to us?" Sir Thomas heard with some surprise that it would be totally out of Mrs. Norris's power to take any share in the personal charge of her. He had been considering her as a particularly welcome addition at the Parsonage, as a desirable companion to an aunt who had no children of her own; but he found himself wholly mistaken. Mrs. Norris was sorry to say that the little girl's staying with them was quite out of the question. Poor Mr. Norris's indifferent state of health made it an impossibility: he (and his gout) could no more bear the noise of a child than he could fly; poor Mr. Norris took up every moment of her time.

"Then she had better come to us," said Lady Bertram, with the utmost composure, scraping away with patience and futility—and a poultice of apricot jam—some caked-on sand from a clay tablet once belonging to a servant of Ramses III.

After a short pause Sir Thomas added with dignity, "Yes, let her home be in this house. We will do our duty by her. She will have companions of her own age, her own artifacts, and a regular instructress."

"Very true," cried Mrs. Norris, "which are all very important considerations. It will be just the same to Miss Lee whether she has three girls to teach, or only two. I only wish I could be more useful; but you see I do all in my power. I am not one of those that spare their own trouble; and Nanny shall fetch her, however it may put me to inconvenience to have my chief counsellor away for three days. I suppose, sister, you will put the child in the little white attic, near the old nurseries. It will be the best place for her, so near Miss Lee, not far from the girls, and close by the housemaids, who could help to dress her, and take care of her clothes. For I suppose you would not think it fair to expect Ellis to wait on her as well as the others. Indeed, I do not see that you could possibly place her anywhere else."

Lady Bertram made no opposition. It was indeed a fine excuse to visit the attic more often. The little white attic—oh, if only they knew what *treasure* reposed just next door—

"I hope she will prove a well-disposed girl," continued Mrs. Norris, "and be sensible of her uncommon good fortune."

"Should her disposition be really bad," said Sir Thomas, "we must not, for our own children's sake, continue her in the family. But there is no reason to expect so great an evil. We shall probably see much to wish altered in her. We must prepare ourselves for gross ignorance, some meanness of opinions, and very distressing vulgarity of manner. But these are not incurable faults. Nor, I trust, can they be dangerous for her associates. Had my daughters been *younger* than herself, I should have considered the introduction of such a companion as a matter of very serious moment. But, as it is, I hope there can be nothing to fear for *them,* and everything to hope for *her,* from the association."

"That is exactly what I think," cried Mrs. Norris, "and what I was saying to my husband this morning. It will be an education for the child. Merely being with her cousins; if Miss Lee taught her nothing, she would learn to be good and clever from *them.*"

"I hope she will not tease my poor pug," said Lady Bertram; "I have but just got Julia to leave it alone. She must also be very careful of the Egyptian items of my fine collection, taking great care not to touch or smear with unclean fingers, or, Heaven forbid, drop and break anything so precious and costly."

"There will be some difficulty in our way, Mrs. Norris," observed Sir Thomas, thinking in the meantime that an Egyptian thing or two dropped and broken would not be such a bad thing, "as to the distinction proper to be made between the girls as they grow up. How to preserve in the minds of my *daughters* the consciousness of what they are, without making them think too lowly of their cousin. And how, without depressing her spirits too far, to make her remember that she is not a *Miss Bertram*. I should wish to see them very good friends, and would not authorise in my girls the smallest degree of arrogance towards their relation. But still they cannot be equals. Their rank, fortune, rights, ability to catalogue entrails extraction tools from Luxor, and expectations will always be different. It is a point of great delicacy, and you must assist us in chusing exactly the right line of conduct."

Mrs. Norris agreed with him as to its difficulty but encouraged hope that it would be managed.

It will be readily believed that Mrs. Norris did not write to her sister in vain. Mrs. Price seemed rather surprised that a girl should be fixed on, when she had so many fine boys. But she accepted the offer most thankfully, assuring them of her daughter's being a very gentle, good-humoured girl, and trusting they would never have cause to throw her off. She spoke of her as somewhat delicate and puny, but was hopeful of her being materially better for change of air. Poor woman! she undoubtedly thought change of air might agree with many of her children—unlike what it might do to the vestments of a newly exhumed and exposed to the elements ancient mummy.

Chapter II

The little girl performed her long journey in safety; and at Northampton was met by Mrs. Norris, who immediately sniffed her behind the ears, in an unexpected bit of behavioral oddity, but gladly took credit of being first to welcome her and recommend her to the rest of the family.

Fanny Price was at this time just ten years old, and though there might not be much in her first appearance to captivate, there was, at least, nothing to disgust her relations. She was small for her age, with no glow of complexion, nor any other striking beauty. She was exceedingly timid and shy, and shrinking from notice. But her air, though awkward, was not vulgar, her voice was sweet, and when she spoke her countenance was pretty.

Sir Thomas and Lady Bertram received her very kindly; and Sir Thomas, seeing how much she needed encouragement, tried to be all that was conciliating: but he had to work against a most untoward gravity of deportment. Lady Bertram, without half so much trouble, by the mere aid of a good-humoured smile, became immediately the less awful character of the two.

The young people were all at home, and handled the introduction very well, with much good humour, and no embarrassment, at least on the part of the sons, who, at seventeen and sixteen, and tall of their age, had all the grandeur of men in the eyes of their little cousin. The two girls were more at a loss from being younger and in greater awe of their father, who addressed them on the occasion with rather an injudicious particularity. But they were too much used to company and praise to have anything like natural shyness. Their confidence increased from their cousin's total lack of it, and they examined her face and frock in easy indifference.

They were a remarkably fine family, the sons very well-looking, the daughters decidedly handsome, as though heirs to an ancient dynasty, and all of them well-grown and forward of their age, which produced as striking a difference between the cousins in person, as education had given to their address. There were but two years between the youngest and Fanny. Julia Bertram was only twelve, and Maria but a year older.

The little visitor meanwhile was as unhappy as possible. Afraid of everybody, ashamed of herself, and longing for the home she had left, she knew not how to look up, and could scarcely speak to be heard, or without crying. Mrs. Norris had been talking to her the whole way from Northampton of her wonderful good fortune, and the extraordinary degree of gratitude and good behaviour which it ought to produce, and Fanny's misery was only increased by the idea of its being a wicked thing for her not to be happy.

The fatigue, too, of so long a journey, became soon no trifling evil. And the constant sidelong glances at Mrs. Norris in the bright moonlight accorded her peculiar, even grotesque, momentary hallucinations of lupine scowling jaws which were of course not there. In vain were the well-meant condescensions of Sir Thomas, and all the officious prognostications of Mrs. Norris that she would be a good girl. In vain did Lady Bertram smile and make her sit on the sofa with herself and pug and a medium-sized First Dynasty oil jug that took up much of the seating space. And vain was even the sight of a gooseberry tart towards giving her comfort.

Fanny took one look to the right and saw a crocodile, to the left, a replica of the Sphinx, and, right before her, what appeared to be a very deceased and frightful face of an upright golden god with eyes shut—a minor blessing—and a serpent coming out of its chin. No wonder she could scarcely swallow two mouthfuls before tears interrupted her!

Sleep seeming to be her likeliest friend, she was taken to finish her sorrows in bed. There she dreamed of strange never before imagined ghouls—some bloodless, others shriveled, all walking upright, shreds of desiccated linen wrappings, the howling of wolves, and everywhere, bright sun-lit sand. In short, rather ghastly and unwarranted stuff.

"This is not a very promising beginning," said Mrs. Norris, sitting down next to the oil-jug on the other side of Lady Bertram, when Fanny had left the room. "After all that I said to her as we came along, I thought she would have behaved better; I told her how much might depend upon her acquitting herself well at first. I wish there may not be a little sulkiness of temper—her poor mother had a good deal; but we must make allowances for such a child—and I do not know that her being sorry to leave her home is really against her. For, with all its faults, it *was* her home, and she cannot as yet understand how much she has changed for the better. But then there is moderation in all things." And Mrs. Norris pushed herself somewhat against the jug to make room on the sofa for her own person.

It required a longer time, however, than Mrs. Norris was inclined to allow, to reconcile Fanny to the novelty of Mansfield Park, a maze of rooms and people and crocodile-headed statuary and Osiris artifacts, and the separation from everybody she had been used to. Her feelings were very acute, and too little understood to be properly attended to. Nobody meant to be

unkind, but nobody put themselves out of their way to secure her comfort. It was confusing for the child to watch Lady Bertram move about silently when she did not lie on the sofa or sort amulets in small caskets, and to disappear frequently upstairs near her own room, while strange frightful noises were often heard in the night. And oh, that pug! That strange little dog ran about like a miniature wolf cub, or possibly a very large cat, and made sounds the like of which Fanny had never heard in her life.

The holiday allowed to the Miss Bertrams the next day, on purpose to afford leisure for getting acquainted with, and entertaining their young cousin, produced little union. They could not but hold her cheap on finding that she had but two sashes, and had never learned French. And when they perceived her to be little struck with the duet they were so good as to play, they could do no more than make her a generous present of some of their least valued toys (primarily of Egyptian origin), and leave her to herself, while they adjourned to whatever might be the favourite holiday sport of the moment, making artificial flowers or wasting gold paper or pulling ostrich feathers out of oversized fans from Cairo.

Fanny, whether near or far from her cousins, whether in the schoolroom, the drawing-room, or the replica-of-the-Nile shrubbery, was equally forlorn, finding something to fear in every person and place, even the shadows, for it seemed that Mansfield Park was—oddly enough, an entity unto itself—*alive*. Or, better yet, *undead.*

She was disheartened by Lady Bertram's sepulcral silence interspersed with abrupt references to archeological digs and the latest acquisitions of Egyptian Goddess Bast and crocodile-headed Sobek figurines on her bed chamber mantel, awed by Sir Thomas's grave looks and severe distress upon each utterance of "Egypt," or "cat," or "crocodile-headed," or "papyrus," and quite overcome by Mrs. Norris's wolfish admonitions and her tendency to shuffle about like a lumbering thing when she thought no one else was looking in her direction.

Fanny's elder cousins mortified her by reflections on her size, and abashed her by noticing her shyness: Miss Lee wondered at her ignorance, and the maid-servants sneered at her clothes. And when to these sorrows was added the idea of the brothers and sisters among whom she had always been important as playfellow, instructress, and nurse, the despondence that sunk her little heart was severe.

The grandeur of the house astonished, but could not console her. The rooms were too large and cluttered for her to move in with ease: whatever she touched she expected to injure. She crept about in constant terror of something or other related to ancient burial; often retreating towards her own chamber to cry. And the little girl who was spoken of in the drawing-room when she left it at night as seeming so desirably sensible of her peculiar good fortune, ended every day's sorrows by sobbing herself to sleep.

Lady Bertram's visits to a nearby locked room did not help, since they seemed to occur in the middle of the night. Fanny passed the room on the way downstairs, and she wondered with a strange dread born of instinct, what was within—some gothic mystery of Udolpho, and yet no doubt, something likely quite harmless and imported from Luxor. A week had passed in this way, and no suspicion of it conveyed by her quiet passive manner, when she was found one morning by her cousin Edmund, the youngest of the sons, sitting crying on the attic stairs, next to a Cairo crate.

"My dear little cousin," said he, with all the gentleness of an excellent nature, "what can be the matter?" And sitting down by her, he was at great pains to overcome her shame in being so surprised, and persuade her to speak openly. Was she ill? or was anybody angry with her? or had she quarrelled with Maria and Julia? or was she puzzled about anything in her antiquities lesson that he could explain? Did she, in short, want anything he could possibly get her, or do for her? For a long while no answer could be obtained beyond a "no, no—not at all—no, thank you"; but he still persevered; and no sooner had he begun to refer to her own home, than her increased sobs explained to him where the grievance lay. He tried to console her.

"You are sorry to leave Mama, my dear little Fanny," said he, "which shows you to be a very good girl. But you must remember that you are with relations and friends, who all love you, and wish to make you happy. Let us walk out in the park, and you shall tell me all about your brothers and sisters. And I will be sure to tell you all about mine. After I am all done, you will be quite shocked, I dare say, possibly terrified, and even astounded out of your misery. You see, dear Fanny, Mansfield Park is under a Dreadful Ancient Curse. But it's quite all right, because, you see, I have it all quite under control."

"I beg pardon, cousin," Fanny inquired, "did I hear you speak correctly, a—Curse?"

"Yes, dearest Fanny, and it is tremendously exciting!"

"What do you mean?"

At which point Edmund proceeded to relate a tale that took Fanny's mind quite off her homesickness and her beloved siblings and family back home and fixed her attention firmly to the present spot, sitting as they were on the attic stairs.

"Mansfield Park," spoke Edmund, " is quite infested with all manner of Wonder. Some might not call it such, and some would call it Abomination, but I believe—firmly, with all my faith in the Lord's will—that it is all here for a reason. To test me maybe, the depths of my moral character and veracity, my integrity and inner peace—"

"Pray, cousin, enough, speak!" cried Fanny, beginning to tremble somewhat, but trying to conceal any semblance of such unfortunate weakness or palsy, "tell me of this!"

"Indeed, tell it I must, else you will never understand the hoary depth of us, this house, or this family, Fanny. Now then— It started about five years ago, when I was rather younger than I am now—"

"Were you a suckling infant, cousin?" said Fanny, considering his present considerable youthfulness.

Edmund laughed. "No, not quite so young. It was then that my dear mother attended a series of exhibitions and lectures at the grand museum in London, presented by a visiting gentleman, a doctor of Egyptology or other some such, one Georg Ebers, and a team of his associates. They were deep in the process of Digging up all of Egypt, you know, and were responsible probably for more discoveries and more holes in the sandy landscape of that fair and sun-drenched distant land than anyone else in Europe or Asia or the Americas put together—or so it seemed. Mother was bewitched by Ancient Egypt, by the gold and the mystery and the ritual glamour, struck up a correspondence with the whole lot of them, and started acquiring mementoes of their Egyptian adventures: at first, discreetly, then with complete abandon and disregard for cost or normalcy—as you can see by the state of the large drawing room which now resembles the great temple at Karnak more than it does a British parlor."

"I see," said Fanny. "But—a Curse? Pray, continue."

And Edmund did.

"At some point, Fanny, when various large boxes began to arrive by post on a daily basis, it seemed, and mother spent more time upstairs in the attics than she did grooming her pug, I took it upon myself to observe things closer, and this is what I learned—"

"How brave of you, cousin!"

"Not courage was involved, but desperation. I heard—indeed, all of us heard, peculiar noises in the night, shufflings, flickering of candlelight or even torches and the faint whiff of exotic incense—in short, something was happening all the time, and the house had been changed. Aunt Norris, ascended the stairs one evening and was gone for quite a long time. The moon was full that night, and I had hidden myself near a flight leading to the upper corridor, and suddenly, a strange shadow came, a wolf-like *thing* sped by, howling—*howling* right as it passed, so that my heart nearly burst with unholy terror, and I prayed silently—and in the praying I knew that *thing* for what it was, none other than my dear Aunt Norris, transformed into a—monster! Another shriek and howl, and she leapt through an open window on the flight of stairs, and raced off into the night, to hunt. Yes, Fanny, she was a creature no longer human, an unholy *wolf*."

Fanny listened to her cousin, unblinking, her gentle mien with its unwavering expression frozen in a mixture of wonder and disbelief. "I believe, cousin Edmund," she said at last in a barely audible voice, "you are trying to frighten me, and being cruel, playing some manner of mean jest—"

"Oh Heaven knows, not I, Fanny!" exclaimed Edmund, his eyes more serious and earnest than anyone she knew. And he took her by the hand, pulling her, so that Fanny could not help but follow him, and they indeed walked outside, as Edmund originally intended.

"Now then, I am not done," he spoke. "You must allow me to finish and do not interrupt until I am done, and then you may ask me any questions you wish—for I know you will have many questions, my gentle cousin—"

She nodded. Her hand was still clutched in his, and she did not for a moment recall it, nor that they were outside and it was a sunlit time of day and a time for lighthearted banter, not dark recollections.

"The next thing I observed, Fanny, was that since that one fateful night Aunt Norris became a bit peculiar, more crude and lumbering in posture, and every full moon she would be gone at nights; they said livestock disappeared and was later found torn to shreds. That was bad enough, but then I kept my watch on them all, and there was now a difference in my mother, too. Not a werewolf, no . . . But she ate almost nothing and grew very pale, and her silences and distraction grew deeper. The only thing that seemed to matter was the latest arriving Egyptian trinkets and boxes. I observed her wear a very special necklet on her person, practically always—an antique gold thing shaped like an eye of a beast god with lapis and inlaid stones and twisted wings of a bird flared wide. She would fondle it with her fingers and mutter, words that seemed to be of another tongue. My poor father tried to avert his eyes whenever her mutterings grew too overt, but even he could no longer shut himself to the obvious: mother was either mad as a hatter, seriously ill, or possessed by devil's minions. Or in the least, cats, birds, and crocodiles."

"Oh!" said Fanny. "Poor Lady Bertram! Which was it?"

"I would say all three. That is, wait—are we talking about creatures or ailments? In which case, all six. Maybe even more—it is likely I am forgetting to catalogue a number of other items of mother's interest. In any case, at least, one thing seemed to become the other, and as time went on, and a London doctor was brought in to call upon her regularly, it seemed not to make a difference. They tried different diets upon her, leeches and sunshine, and plein air walks, and medicinal herb elixirs. Mother did not respond. The parson was called upon to spend time and deliver sermon upon sermon, and there was some minor responses akin to cringing and even one shriek, I am told, but all came to naught. Father then tried to forbid the artifact purchases and a few of the boxes were returned to sender, but mother had a fit of hysterics that lasted a fortnight, and Aunt Norris had the ghastliest of vapors—seriously, one dared not take a breath of air in the same room, it was so dire—Maria and Julia hid away in closets, Tom left the house, Lord only knows where, and, in short, Mansfield Park became Bedlam."

"And so you think for certain, cousin, it's a Curse?"

"I don't think," Edmund said. "I *know*. Because once when no one else was in the living room, I stole up to mother, pretending to act in jest as she was reposing on the divan, and ripped the necklet from her—it had come loose and started to slip around her collar—and in that moment, a stifling hot dark wind tore through the room when all the windows were shut and it was a cool day. And my mother turned to me, and her eyes had grown dark without pupils and red as coals in the center, and her dear, normally smiling mouth parted, and there were long feline teeth! I felt a presence gather in the room, a swirling maelstrom and the sting of sand, and I could not help but cry out. As the worst of cowards I dropped the necklet, and it landed in her lap. Upon which, immediately, the room became light again, the *presence* of the burning dark receded, and my mother's face became normal as though nothing had happened. While my lips still moved in prayer, mother took the necklet and calmly tied it around her neck once more. And she said to me, 'Whatever is the matter, dear boy? You look as though you've seen a ghost!' In that moment I realized she honestly did not recall the strange several moments of hell that had just come to pass between us."

"What—what was that necklet, then?" Fanny said, faintly. "Was it the Curse, or a thing that contained it?"

"Edmund looked at her with an expression that spoke many things. "How remarkably wise you are, little cousin! how insightful! Your question is brilliant—for to this day I do not know for certain if that necklet, infernal as it might be, is my mother's bane or salvation. In truth, I—do not *dare* find out."

After walking some time in silence, they returned inside.

"There's more to this story," whispered Edmund, "But I leave it for another day. I've frightened you enough—for which

I am truly sorry, but it had to be said—and now it is time to think of happier things: your sweet sisters, dear brothers!"

Fanny was more than glad to change the subject. Not only had she been terrified out of her gloom by Edmund, but he now brought her to the most joyful topic possible, thereby succeeding in a perfect engagement of mental faculties that took her mind off any inner personal sorrow.

On pursuing the happy subject, Edmund found that, dear as all these brothers and sisters generally were, there was one among them who ran more in her thoughts than the rest. It was William whom she talked of most, and wanted most to see—especially now, after the frightful talk of Curses. William, the eldest, a year older than herself, her constant companion and friend; her advocate with her mother (of whom he was the darling) in every distress. "William did not like she should come away; he had told her he should miss her very much indeed." "But William will write to you, I dare say." "Yes, he had promised he would, but he had told *her* to write first." "And when shall you do it?" She hung her head and answered hesitatingly, "she did not know; she had not any paper. Only papyrus."

"If that be all your difficulty, I will furnish you with paper and every other non-Egyptian material, and you may write your letter whenever you choose. Would it make you happy to write to William?"

"Yes, very."

"Then let it be done now. Come with me into the breakfast-room, we shall find everything there, and be sure of having the room to ourselves."

"But, cousin, will it go to the post? What, with all the boxes being delivered, will it be in the way—"

"Yes, depend upon me it shall: it shall go with the other letters; and, as your uncle will frank it, it will cost William nothing."

"My uncle!" repeated Fanny, with a frightened look.

"Yes, when you have written the letter, I will take it to my father to frank. He will be rather pleased to have some outgoing mail for a change. Indeed, he might be happy to provide a box for you to mail out. Does William like cats? Figurines, that is? Or mayhap, crocodiles?"

Edmund's mouth was firm and yet mayhap there was some trembling, some shadow of suppressed jocundity at the corners—

Fanny thought it a bold measure, but offered no further resistance; and they went together into the breakfast-room, where Edmund prepared her paper, and ruled her lines with all the goodwill that her brother could himself have felt, and probably with somewhat more exactness. He continued with her the whole time of her writing, to assist her with his penknife or his orthography, as either were wanted; and added to these attentions a kindness to her brother which delighted her beyond all the rest. He wrote with his own hand his love to his cousin William, and sent him half a guinea under the seal. And despite his previous threat, no ancient feline statuette was blessedly included.

Fanny's feelings on the occasion were such as she believed herself incapable of expressing. But her countenance and a few artless words fully conveyed all their gratitude and delight, and her cousin began to find her an interesting object. He talked to her more, and, from all that she said, was convinced of her having an affectionate heart, and a strong desire of doing right. And he could perceive her to be further entitled to attention by great sensibility of her situation, and great timidity.

In the abrupt revelation of the Curse, he had never knowingly given her pain, but he now felt that she required more positive kindness not to mention a better explanation. And with that view Edmund endeavoured to lessen her fears, despite all things. He gave her a great deal of good advice as to avoiding

Aunt Norris, treading with care around Lady Bertram's archeological items, playing with Maria and Julia, and being as merry as possible despite strange noises in the night.

From this day Fanny grew more comfortable. She felt that she had a friend, and the kindness of her cousin Edmund gave her better spirits with everybody else. The place, despite its unraveling secrets and *strangeness* became less strange, and the people less formidable—even the tediously nagging fanged ones, even during a full moon. And if there were some amongst them whom she could not cease to fear, she began at least to know their ways, and to catch the best manner of conforming to them. He own little rusticities and awkwardnesses necessarily wore away, and she was no longer materially afraid to appear before her uncle, nor did her aunt Norris's howlish voice make her start too much.

To her cousins she became occasionally an acceptable companion. Though unworthy, from inferiority of age and strength, to be their constant associate, their pleasures and schemes were sometimes of a nature to make a third very useful, especially when that third was of an obliging, yielding temper. They had to admit—when their aunt inquired into her faults, or their brother Edmund urged her claims to their kindness—that "Fanny was good-natured enough."

Edmund was uniformly kind himself; and Fanny had nothing worse to endure on the part of Tom than that sort of merriment which a young man of seventeen will always think fair with a child of ten. He was just entering into life, full of spirits, and with all the liberal dispositions of an eldest son, who feels born only for expense and enjoyment. His kindness to his little cousin was consistent with his situation and rights: he made her some very pretty presents, and laughed at her.

As her appearance and spirits improved, Sir Thomas and Mrs. Norris thought with greater satisfaction of their benevolent plan. It was pretty soon decided that, though far from clever, she showed a tractable disposition, and seemed likely to give them little trouble.

A mean opinion of her abilities was not confined to *them.* Fanny could read, work, and write, but she had been taught nothing more. As her cousins found her ignorant of many things with which they had been long familiar, they thought her prodigiously stupid, and for the first two or three weeks were continually bringing some fresh report of it into the drawing-room. "Dear mama, only think, my cousin cannot put the map of Europe together—or my cousin cannot tell the principal rivers in Russia—or, she never heard of Asia Minor or the Great Pyramid of Giza—or she does not know the difference between water-colours and crayons and burial chamber paint!—How strange!—Did you ever hear anything so stupid?"

"My dear," their considerate aunt would reply, "it is very bad, but you must not expect everybody to be as forward and quick at learning as yourself."

"But, aunt, she is really so very ignorant!—Do you know, we asked her last night which way she would go to get to Ireland; and she said, she should cross to the Isle of Wight. She thinks of nothing but the Isle of Wight, and she calls it *the Island*, as if there were no other island in the world. I cannot remember the time when I did not know a great deal that she has not the least notion of yet. How long ago it is, aunt, since we used to repeat the chronological order of the pharaohs of Egypt, with the dates of their accession, order of their Dynasties, and most of the principal events of their reigns!"

"Yes," added the other; "and of the Roman emperors as low as Severus; besides a great deal of the heathen mythology, and all the metals, semi-metals, planets, and distinguished philosophers. And, yes—Egypt! All of it, from head to toe, Lower and Upper, ancient to the beginning of time, filled with the overflowing fertility of the Nile, with kings and pharaohs and princes and princesses and priests and hieroglyphics and strange gravesites and *mummification*—"

"Very true indeed, my dears, but you are blessed with wonderful memories, exposed to Egypt on a daily basis, thanks to my dearest sister and her—*tendre,* and your poor cousin has probably none at all. There is a vast deal of difference in memories, as well as in everything else, and therefore you must make allowance for your cousin, and pity her deficiency. And remember that, if you are ever so forward and clever yourselves, you should always be modest; for, much as you know already, there is a great deal more for you to learn."

"Yes, I know there is, till I am seventeen. But I must tell you another thing of Fanny, so odd and so stupid and tedious. Do you know, she says she does not want to learn either music or drawing? She says she'd rather decipher hieroglyphics!"

"To be sure, my dear, that is very stupid indeed, and shows a great want of genius and emulation. But, all things considered, I do not know whether it is not as well that it should be so, for, though you know (owing to me) your papa and mama are so good as to bring her up with you, it is not at all necessary that she should be as accomplished as you are;—on the contrary, it is much more desirable that there should be a difference."

Such were the counsels by which Mrs. Norris assisted to form her nieces' minds. It is not very surprising that, with all their promising talents and early information, they should be entirely deficient in the less common acquirements of self-knowledge, generosity and humility. In everything but disposition they were admirably taught. Sir Thomas did not know what was wanting; he was not outwardly affectionate—the reserve of his manner repressed all the flow of their spirits before him.

To the education of her daughters Lady Bertram paid not the smallest attention. She had not time for such cares. She was a woman who spent her days in sitting, nicely dressed, on a sofa, going through newly arrived boxes and cataloguing her new treasures, doing some long piece of needlework with Egyptian patterns and motifs, thinking more of her pug and her overflowing attic than her children, but very indulgent to the latter when it did not put herself to inconvenience, guided in everything important by distinguished Egyptologists, Sir Thomas, and in smaller concerns by her sister.

Had she possessed greater leisure for the service of her girls, she would still have supposed it unnecessary, for they were under the care of a governess, with proper masters, and could want nothing more. As for Fanny's being stupid at learning, she could only say "it was very unlucky, but some people *were* stupid, and Fanny must take more pains: she did not know what else was to be done; and, except her being so dull, she saw no harm in the poor little thing, and always found her very handy and quick in carrying messages, and fetching whatever burial implement she required."

Fanny, with all her faults of ignorance and timidity, was fixed at Mansfield Park, and, learning to transfer in its favour much of her attachment to her former home, grew up there not unhappily among her cousins. There was no positive ill-nature in Maria or Julia; and though Fanny was often mortified by their treatment of her, she thought too lowly of her own claims to feel injured by it.

From about the time of her entering the family, Lady Bertram, in consequence of her peculiar ill-health, a whiff of supernatural possession, and a great deal of indolence, gave up the house in town (which she used to occupy every spring), and remained wholly in the country, leaving Sir Thomas to attend his duty in Parliament, with whatever increase or diminution of comfort might arise from her absence. In the country, therefore, the Miss Bertrams continued to exercise their memories with hieroglyphics, practise their duets, ignore the drawing room museum clutter, and grow tall and womanly.

Their father saw them becoming in person, manner, and accomplishments, everything that could satisfy his anxiety. His eldest son was careless and extravagant, and had already given him much uneasiness with decidedly idiotic schemes; but his other children promised him nothing but good. His daughters, he felt, while they retained the name of Bertram, must be giving it new grace, and in quitting it, he trusted, would extend its respectable alliances. And the character of Edmund, his strong good sense and uprightness of mind, bid most fairly for utility, honour, and happiness to himself and all his connexions. He was to be a clergyman.

"My dear cousin Fanny," Edmund took her aside at one point, to better explain his future position, "as you recall, our discussion of the—ahem—early days, when I mentioned a certain Curse. I had, in that day, used the word Wonder alongside the word Abomination. And that is because my firmness of faith and my purpose in life have been clarified and ultimately decided for me, and I knew even then what I must do—I must serve God with all my heart, and in that service I will find a way to rid my mother, my family, all of Mansfield Park, of this evil that is secretly upon us, leeching away my mother's strength and will to live, my brother's wits and common sense, and making my sisters shallow and insensitive to the plight of yourself and so many others. As a member of God's Holy Clergy, in His Great Name, I shall overcome, and I shall Exorcise the devil from this house. Pray, tell no one of this, of my true reasons, Fanny, I beg you. Nay, I know I need not beg, no need to ask, for your heart is true and you feel with all of your being, and you know what must be done indeed."

"I understand, Edmund," she replied. And then she took a deep breath, and with all her resolve and inner strength, and because she had looked into his dear eyes, she offered: "If you must have assistance in this, you can count on me, every day, you know."

"I know." Edmund leaned forward and placed his large warm hands around her own trembling fingers—for a moment, only. And then he stepped away.

And that instant Fanny would not forget.

In the meantime, amid the cares and complacency of his own children, Sir Thomas did not forget to do what he could for the children of Mrs. Price. He assisted her liberally in the education and disposal of her sons as they became old enough for a determinate pursuit. And Fanny, though separated from her family, had the truest satisfaction in hearing of any kindness towards them, or of any improvement in their situation or conduct.

Once only, in the course of many years, had she the happiness of being with William. Of the rest she saw nothing—nobody seemed to think of her ever going amongst them again, even for a visit, nobody at home seemed to want her. But William, determining, soon after her removal, to be a sailor, was invited to spend a week with his sister in Northamptonshire before he went to sea. Their eager affection in meeting, their exquisite delight in being together, their hours of happy mirth, and moments of serious conference, may be imagined; as well as the sanguine views and spirits of the boy even to the last, and the misery of the girl when he left her, loaded with well wishes and gifts of small concealed Egyptian trinkets—as Sir Thomas would have it, "for good luck." Luckily the visit happened in the Christmas holidays, when the household was a bit agitated in particular, and she could directly look for comfort to her cousin Edmund. He told her such charming things of what William was to do, and be hereafter, in consequence of his profession, as made her admit that the separation might have some use.

Edmund's friendship never failed her: his leaving Eton for Oxford did not change in his kind dispositions, and only afforded more frequent opportunities of proving them. Without any display of doing more than the rest, or any fear of doing too much, he was always true to Fanny's interests, and considerate of her feelings, making her good qualities understood and more apparent; giving her advice, consolation, and encouragement, as well as discussing—in somewhat delightful clandestine moments that Fanny came to treasure—various aspects of the family Curse.

Kept back as she was by everybody else, his single support could not bring her forward. But his attentions were of the highest importance in improving her mind. He knew her to be clever, to have a quick apprehension as well as good sense, and a fondness for reading, which, properly directed, must be an education in itself. Miss Lee taught her French and introductory hieroglyphics, and heard her read the daily portion of history. But Edmund recommended the books which charmed her leisure hours and incidentally referenced Exorcisms. He encouraged her taste, and corrected her judgment. He made reading useful by talking to her of what she read, and heightened its attraction by judicious praise.

In return for such services she loved him better than anybody in the world except William—her heart was divided between the two.

Chapter III

The first event of any importance in the family was the death of Mr. Norris—some suggested it was due to a dire and unfortunate infection resulting from a wild *animal* bite—which happened when Fanny was about fifteen, and necessarily introduced changes. Mrs. Norris, on quitting the Parsonage, removed first to the Park, and afterwards to a small house of Sir Thomas's in the village. She consoled herself for the loss of her husband by deciding she could do very well without him; and for her reduction of income by the evident necessity of stricter economy.

The living was hereafter for Edmund. Had his uncle died a few years sooner, it would have been duly given to some friend to hold till he were old enough for orders. But Tom's extravagance and folly had been so great as to render a different disposal of the next presentation necessary, and the younger brother must help to pay for the pleasures of the elder.

There was another family living actually held for Edmund. But though it eased Sir Thomas's conscience, he could not but feel it to be an act of injustice, and he earnestly tried to impress his eldest son with the same conviction, in the hope of its producing a better effect.

"I blush for you, Tom," said he, in his most dignified manner; "I trust you pity you brother. You have robbed Edmund for ten, twenty, thirty years, perhaps for life, of more than half the income which ought to be his, by wagering to raise miniature ponies. After they grew to be full size horses, you sold them back for half their initial price and purchased a large mechanical *object* for which I have no name, that is at present sitting behind the stables and being used by hens as a roost. Next, there were the ostrich-versus-man jumping wagers, the rare duck supposedly from Peking but really from Brighton—ah, how you loved that duck, until it flew in your mother's face with murderous intent. . . . The expedition to the Welsh moors in search of spotted *banshees!* You kept a mermaid secreted away in a tub and *she* turned out to be a large rotted log dressed in petticoats. Need I go on? It may hereafter be in my power, or in yours, to procure Edmund better preferment. But it must not be forgotten that nothing can be adequate recompense for the advantage which he is now obliged to forego through the urgency of your moronic debts."

Tom listened with some shame and some sorrow. But escaping as quickly as possible, he soon, with cheerful selfishness reflected, firstly, that he had not been half so much in debt as some of his friends (one of whom, a Mr. Yates, had bought a small rowboat that he was told was Noah's Ark—but even Tom knew that was daft; Noah's Ark had to be at least as large as a sloop); secondly, look what Her Ladyship his own mother and her extravagant archeological eccentricities was doing to the family estate; thirdly, that his father had made a most tiresome piece of work of it; and, finally, that the future incumbent, whoever he might be, would, in all probability, die very soon.

On Mr. Norris's death the presentation became the right of a Dr. Grant, who came consequently to reside at Mansfield; and on proving to be a hearty man of forty-five, seemed likely to disappoint Mr. Bertram's calculations. But "no, he was a short-necked, apoplectic sort of fellow, and, plied well with good things, would soon pop off."

Dr. Grant had a wife about fifteen years his junior, but no children; and they entered the neighbourhood as very respectable, agreeable people.

The time was now come when Sir Thomas expected his sister-in-law to claim her share in their niece. The change in Mrs. Norris's situation, and the improvement in Fanny's age, seemed to do away any former objection to their living together. And as his own circumstances were rendered less fair than heretofore, by some recent losses on his West India estate, in addition to his eldest son's extravagance, and of course, the dear wife's chronic pursuit of Egyptology, it became not undesirable to himself to be relieved from the expense of her support, and the obligation of her future provision. He mentioned this to his wife; with Fanny present, and Lady Bertram calmly observed to her, "So, Fanny, you are going to leave us, and live with my sister. How shall you like it?"

Fanny was too much surprised to do more than repeat her aunt's words, "Going to leave you?"

"Yes, my dear; why should you be astonished? You have been five years with us, and my sister always meant to take you when Mr. Norris died. But you must come up and help me with the artifact cataloguing and tack on my patterns all the same."

The news was as disagreeable to Fanny as it had been unexpected. She had never received kindness from her aunt Norris, and could not love her.

"I shall be very sorry to go away," said she, with a faltering voice.

"Yes, I dare say you will; *that's* natural enough. I suppose you have had as little to vex you since you came into this house as any creature in the world."

"I hope I am not ungrateful, aunt," said Fanny modestly.

"No, my dear; I hope not. I have always found you a very good girl. Very good at polishing gold surfaces, too. And you always bring me the proper adze[2] and knife when I am practicing ritual on poultry."

"And am I never to live here again?"

"Never, my dear; but you are sure of a comfortable home. It can make very little difference to you, whether you are in one house or the other."

Fanny left the room with a very sorrowful heart; she could feel the difference to be rather approaching the size of the Nile Delta during the fertile flood season. And the possibility of living with her aunt inspired dread rather than satisfaction. As soon as she met with Edmund she told him her distress.

"Cousin," said she, "something is going to happen which I do not like at all; and though you have often persuaded me into being reconciled to things that I disliked at first, you will not be able to do it now. I am going to live entirely with my aunt Norris."

"Indeed!"

"Yes; my aunt Bertram has just told me so. It is quite settled. I am to leave Mansfield Park, and go to the White House, I suppose, as soon as she is removed there."

"Well, Fanny, and if the plan were not unpleasant to you, I should call it an excellent one."

"Oh, cousin!"

"It has everything else in its favour. My aunt is acting like a sensible woman in wishing for you. She is choosing a friend and companion exactly where she ought, and I am glad her love of money does not interfere. You will be what you ought to be to her. I hope it does not distress you very much, Fanny?"

"Indeed it does: I cannot like it. I love this house and everything in it—no matter how peculiar or Cursed—even the

---

[2] An ancient metal thing. Seriously, thou needst google it.

Egypt: I shall love nothing there. You know how uncomfortable I feel with her."

"I can say nothing for her manner to you as a child; but it was the same with us all, or nearly so. She never knew how to be pleasant to children, even before the inception of the Unholy *affliction.* But you are now of an age to be treated better. I think she is behaving better already. And when you are her only companion, you *must* be important to her. Just be sure to mark the calendar for the full moons and lock yourself in tightly at night. I dare say no harm shall occur."

"I can never be important to any one. And oh, how is one to endure the wolfish thing?"

"What is to prevent you?"

"Everything. My situation, my foolishness and awkwardness. My own lack of sharpened incisors."

"As to your foolishness and awkwardness, my dear Fanny, believe me, you never have a shadow of either, but in using the words so improperly. There is no reason in the world why you should not be important where you are known. You have good sense, a sweet temper, and a grateful heart. I do not know any better qualifications for a friend and companion, especially one as gentle-toothed as you."

"You are too kind," said Fanny, colouring at such praise; "how shall I ever thank you as I ought, for thinking so well of me? Oh! cousin, if I am to go away, I shall remember your goodness to the last moment of my life. Even as my aunt is tearing me into shreds, I will continue to think well and gloriously of you."

"Why, indeed, Fanny, I should hope to be remembered at such a distance as the White House, but I beg you, without the sanguinity. You speak as if you were going two hundred miles off instead of only across the park. But you will belong to us almost as much as ever. The two families will be meeting every day in the year. The only difference will be that, living with your aunt, you will necessarily be brought forward as you ought to be. *Here* there are too many whom you can hide behind; but with *her* you will be forced to speak for yourself."

"Rather you mean I will be forced to forage the countryside. Oh! Do not say so."

"I must say it, and say it with pleasure. No! That is—not the countryside! Mrs. Norris is much better fitted than my mother for having the charge of you now. Except for those few nights a month, she is of a temper to do a great deal for anybody she really interests herself about, and she will force you to do justice to your natural powers."

"She will corner me one of those few nights and take my head right off! Surely there's some truth to the rumors as to what really happened to poor Mr. Norris!"

"Oh, fie, cousin! she'll do no such thing. She takes only field and garden vermin of the lesser variety, no more. Besides, you wear the silver Lord's cross that I've given you, to ensure safety."

Fanny sighed, thinking how little good it did to the departed Mr. Norris, who was undoubtedly *vermined,* to put it delicately, despite being surrounded as he was with all things Godly, and said, "I cannot see things as you do; but I ought to believe you to be right rather than myself, and I am very much obliged to you for trying to reconcile me to what must be. If I could suppose my aunt really to care for me, it would be delightful to feel myself of consequence to anybody. *Here,* I know, I am of none, and yet I love the place so well."

"The place, Fanny, is what you will not quit, though you quit the house. Indeed, as you are one of the family, the Curse transforms to a Blessing of sorts, and reaches us all and will keep you bound and localized as surely as anything. You will have as free a command of the park and gardens as ever. You will still witness the daily exotic crates delivery by post at the gates. Even *your* constant little heart need not take fright at such a nominal change. You will have the same walks to frequent, the same library to choose from, the same crocodile and cat statuary and clay tablets to avoid smashing at every turn, the same people to look at, the same horse to ride."

"Very true. Yes, dear old grey pony! So much like a tiny camel, says my aunt, your mother, but I never quite saw that—Ah! cousin, when I remember how much I used to dread riding, what terrors it gave me to hear it talked of as likely to do me good, and then think of the kind pains you took to persuade me out of my fears, and convince me that I should like it after a little while, and feel how right you proved to be, I am inclined to hope you may always prophesy as well."

"Indeed! Did anyone ever mention, you now ride like an Amazon, cousin? Splendid seat! And I am quite convinced that your being with Mrs. Norris will be as good for your mind as riding has been for your health, and as much for your ultimate happiness too."

So ended their discourse, which might as well have been spared. For Mrs. Norris had not the smallest intention of taking Fanny. It had never occurred to her but as a thing to be carefully avoided. To prevent its being expected, she had fixed on the smallest habitation which could rank as genteel among the buildings of Mansfield parish, the White House being only just large enough to receive herself and her servants, and allow a spare room for a friend (not to forget, a place to lock herself up during the full moon, for the *thing* which shall not be spoken of). The spare rooms at the Parsonage had never been wanted, but the absolute necessity of a spare room for a "friend" was now never forgotten. Not all her precautions, however, could save her from being suspected of something better. Perhaps, her very display of the importance of a spare room might have misled Sir Thomas to suppose it really intended for Fanny. Lady Bertram soon brought the matter to a certainty by carelessly observing to Mrs. Norris—

"I think, sister, we need not keep Miss Lee any longer, when Fanny goes to live with you."

Mrs. Norris almost started. "Live with me, dear Lady Bertram! what do you mean?"

"Is she not to live with you? I thought you had settled it with Sir Thomas."

"Me! never. I never spoke a syllable about it to Sir Thomas, nor he to me. Fanny live with me! Good heaven! what could I do with Fanny? Me! a poor, helpless, forlorn widow, unfit for anything, my spirits quite broke down; what could I do with a girl of fifteen? the very age to need most attention and care, and put the cheerfullest spirits to the test! Sir Thomas could not seriously expect such a thing! How came Sir Thomas to speak to you about it?"

"Indeed, I do not know. I suppose he thought it best."

"But what did he say? He could not say he *wished* me to take Fanny. I am sure in his heart he could not."

"No; he only said he thought it very likely; and I thought so too. We both thought it would be a comfort to you. But if you do not like it, there is no more to be said. She is no encumbrance here."

"Dear sister, if you consider my unhappy state, how can she be any comfort to me? Here am I, a poor desolate widow—" Mrs. Norris went on at length, finishing with: "If I could wish it for my own sake, I would not do so unjust a thing by the poor girl. She is in good hands. I must struggle through my sorrows and difficulties as I can."

"Then you will not mind living by yourself quite alone? Particularly considering your—ahem—delicate and chronic monthly *condition?*"

"Lady Bertram, I do not complain. I know I cannot live as I have done, but I must retrench where I can—" (after much more of this, Lady Bertram started to nod off) "—to be able to lay by a little at the end of the year."

"I dare say you will," said Lady Bertram, jolting awake.

"My object, Lady Bertram, is to be of use to those that come after me. It is for your children's good that I wish to be richer. I have nobody else to care for, but I should be very glad to think I could leave a little trifle among them."

"You are very good, but do not trouble yourself about them. They are sure of being well provided for. Sir Thomas will take care of that."

"Why, you know, Sir Thomas's means will be rather reduced if the Antigua estate is to make such poor returns."

"Oh! *that* will soon be settled. Sir Thomas has been writing about it, I know. And there is the—ahem—" Lady Bertram went silent, thinking of what was up in the attic—

"Well," said Mrs. Norris, moving to go, "I can only say that my sole desire is to be of use to your family. If Sir Thomas should ever speak again about my taking Fanny, you might say that my health and spirits put it quite out of the question. Besides, I really have no bed to give her, for I must keep a spare room for a friend."

Lady Bertram repeated enough of this conversation to convince her husband how much he had mistaken his sister-in-law's views. From that moment Mrs. Norris was perfectly safe from all expectation. He could not but wonder at her refusing to do anything for a niece whom she had been so forward to adopt. But he grew reconciled to being better able to provide for Fanny himself.

Fanny soon learnt how unnecessary her fears had been. Her resulting happiness conveyed much consolation to Edmund on her behalf. Mrs. Norris took possession of the White House, its vermin soon fled, the Grants arrived at the Parsonage, and these events over, everything at Mansfield went on for some time as usual.

We are come, dear Reader, very close to the beginning of the introduction of a certain much anticipated subject—namely, mummies—close but not quite there, so patience, all in due course—

The Grants, disposed to be friendly and sociable, gave great satisfaction among their new acquaintance. They had their faults, and Mrs. Norris soon found them out. The Doctor was very fond of eating, and would have a good dinner every day. And Mrs. Grant, instead of contriving to gratify him at little expense, gave her cook as high wages as they did at Mansfield Park, and was scarcely ever seen in her offices. Mrs. Norris could not speak with any temper of such grievances, nor of the quantity of butter and eggs that were regularly consumed in the house. "Nobody loved plenty and hospitality more than herself; the Parsonage had never been wanting in comforts of any sort, had never borne a bad character in *her time,* but this was truly incomprehensible. A fine lady in a country parsonage was quite out of place. *Her* store-room might have been good enough for Mrs. Grant. Inquiries produced that Mrs. Grant never had more than five thousand pounds."

Lady Bertram listened without much interest to this sort of invective. Fully submerged in Ancient mysteries and indeed drowning in Egyptology, she only felt all the injuries of beauty in Mrs. Grant's being so well settled in life without being handsome, and expressed her astonishment on that point almost as often as Mrs. Norris discussed the other.

These opinions had been hardly in place a year before another event arose of great importance in the family. Sir Thomas found it expedient to go to Antigua himself, for the better arrangement of his affairs, and he took his eldest son with him, in the hope of detaching him from some bad connexions at home, and from all further thoughts of the Brighton Duck (of which Tom still mused fondly). They left England with the probability of being nearly a twelvemonth absent.

This event was the momentous Ancient Sign that Lady Bertram—and indeed a certain ancient desiccated pharaoh—was waiting for.

But first—the necessity of this remote travel and its effect upon his son, reconciled Sir Thomas to quitting the rest of his family, and of leaving his daughters to the direction of others at their present most interesting time of life. He could not think Lady Bertram quite equal to supply his place with them, or rather, to perform what should have been her own; but, in Mrs. Norris's watchful attention, and in Edmund's judgment, he had sufficient confidence to make him go without fears for their conduct.

Little did Sir Thomas know that Egypt will take his absence to manifest full force in Mansfield Park. . . .

Lady Bertram did not at all like to have her husband leave her, on some fundamental affectionate level of her psyche. But, being the Conduit—at long last—for Ancient Egyptian Deity, she was beyond thrilled; she was enraptured.

She was not disturbed by any alarm for his safety, or solicitude for his comfort, being one of those persons who think nothing can be dangerous, or difficult, or fatiguing to anybody but themselves. And she reveled in the new freedom to finally Act.

And here it can be said, at last:—those crates, those endless shipments from the East, those exotic boxes that arrived on a daily basis for so many years, that were greeted with such obsessive delight by Lady Bertram—these were not merely artifacts, cat and crocodile-headed statues, tablets, jars, trinkets, and rolls of papyrus.

They were *mummies*.

Boxes and boxes upon crates of whole embalmed, mummified long-dead Egyptians, of all ranks and excavations; whole bodies and pieces and organ parts in some cases bound in linen, dried with salt and natron, soaked in perfumed oils, and always, a shadow of the hot wind blowing sand and a brilliant sun-lit sky of the land of Amen-Ra. . . .

The mummies, packed firmly in their crates, were stored everywhere on the property, filling the attics to overflowing, in spare rooms, in corridors, stairwells, in the cellars, in the sheds, kitchens, everywhere.

And there were enough of them to form a regiment, a series of squadrons; nay, a whole army.

An army of mummies.

You might ask, gentle Reader, how this firecracker-barrel of a disaster-waiting-to-happen came about? how a proper high-ranking British aristocrat family and respectable grand estate got embroiled in such a peculiar Cursed, dreadful, and dangerous situation?

Well indeed, you might ask. And the answer to this mystery is:—

There was among them one mummy, or rather, a Mummy, the grandest of them all, in a splendid golden sarcophagus, stored in the little room right next to Fanny's tiny bedroom. It had been the very first of the many acquisitions, and has been in fact the only *item* that Lady Bertram did not order and pursue herself. A distinguished Egyptologist, with a slew of references, including a glowing letter from her absolute authority of authorities, Georg Ebers, had asked if he could take up her one-time casual and kind offer of storage in order to temporarily house a splendid *find* destined for the collection of the British Museum, that was to be sorted and catalogued in due time, but for the moment it needed a discreet and clandestine place to stay, and what lovelier than the loveliest Mansfield Park? He was in the neighborhood, one could see, and it was terribly obliging of Her Ladyship to offer generous hospitality to the venerable bit of the Ancient Past in her very own safe and dry and secure attic.

Charmed and flattered into immediate acquiescence, Lady Bertram agreed. The shipment of a great crate followed. It was dutifully taken upstairs. The Egyptologist was wined and dined, and then made his excuses and soon disappeared, with an abundance of promises of contacting her as soon as progress was made with the museum bureaucracy, at which point the precious find would be relocated to its final destination. But—that was the last they heard of the Egyptologist.[3]

And thus the Mummy came to inhabit Mansfield Park.

And with it came the Curse.

Lady Bertram discovered, in a stash of items belonging with the sarcophagus, a particular lovely amulet. She innocently placed it around her neck and became mesmerized, enthralled by the emanations coming from the royal undead creature bound in precious rotting linen underneath the ancient layers of gold—sleeping and dreaming and calling out to her in its own dreams, calling for Egypt. *All things Egypt.* From grand pyramids to the smallest shrunken cat mummy. The pharaoh's otherworldly longing manifested full force in the sensitive lady and translated into her conscious daily obsession. Lady Bertram started to make more and more purchases of imported Egyptian items; at first a quite charming and innocent hobby, then more and more peculiar, until even Sir Thomas could see something was amiss—with his wife, he thought.

Little did Sir Thomas know. . . .

The subtle influence of the Mummy grew and grew. With time, as it dreamed of its ancient beloved land, and the house came to be filled with the very items that surrounded him three thousand years ago, it began to *call* upon others of its kind, and hence, more crates, more deliveries, more other mummies. A certain other minor amulet liberated from its supernaturally

---

[3] In fact, detained on an extensive Dig in the Valley of the Kings, the poor Egyptologist by the name of J—— had fallen through a secret underground chamber into a pit of snakes and scorpions, miraculously escaped unscathed but badly frightened, took a brief sabbatical to recover his composure, and was not heard of again for at least a decade.

protected case unleashed a rather unrelated local beast spirit—local to Britain and of the lupine variety—which immediately took possession of the first unoccupied human being who happened to be Mrs. Norris, creeping up the stairs to the attic where Lady Bertram (occupied by the Mummy's powerful influence and therefore not an option herself) stood mesmerized, opening and activating items at random, including that fateful amulet.

At the time of our narrative, when Fanny was witness to the departure of Sir Thomas to take care of business in Antigua, the situation with the mummies and the grand Mummy was ripe, shall we say—ripe for an explosion of sorts.

The household was being left to their own devices. The Miss Bertrams were much to be pitied on the occasion: not for their sorrow, but for their want of it. Their father was no object of love to them; he had never seemed the friend of their pleasures, and his absence was unhappily most welcome. They were relieved by it from all restraint; and without aiming at one gratification that would probably have been forbidden by Sir Thomas, they felt themselves immediately at their own disposal, and to have every indulgence within their reach.

Fanny's unconscious relief was quite equal to her cousins'. But a more tender nature suggested that her feelings were ungrateful, and she really grieved because she could not grieve. "Sir Thomas, who had done so much for her and her brothers, and who was gone perhaps never to return! that she should see him go without a tear! a shameful insensibility."

He had said to her, moreover, on the very last morning, that he hoped she might see William again in the course of the ensuing winter, and had charged her to write and invite him to Mansfield as soon as the squadron to which he belonged was in England. "This was so thoughtful and kind!"

Had he but smiled upon her, and called her "my dear Fanny," every former frown or cold address might have been forgotten. But he had ended his speech in a way to sink her in sad mortification, by adding, "If William does come to Mansfield, I hope you convince him that your years here have not been spent entirely without improvement. Though, I fear, he must find his sister at sixteen in some respects too much like his sister at ten."

She cried bitterly over this reflection when her uncle was gone; and her cousins, on seeing her with red eyes, set her down as a hypocrite.

Chapter IV

Tom Bertram had spent so little of his time at home that he could be only nominally missed. Lady Bertram was soon astonished to find how very well they did even without his father, how well Edmund could supply his place in carving, talking to the steward, writing to the attorney, settling with the servants, directing the placement of Egyptian crates, and equally saving her from all possible fatigue or exertion in every particular but that of directing her letters.

The earliest intelligence of the travellers' safe arrival at Antigua, after a favourable voyage, was received; though not before Mrs. Norris had indulged in very dreadful fears, even without a pending full moon, and tried to make Edmund participate in them whenever she could get him alone. As she depended on being the first person made acquainted with any fatal catastrophe, she had already arranged the manner of breaking it to all the others. However, Sir Thomas's assurances of their both being alive and well made it necessary to set aside her agitation and affectionate preparatory speeches for a while.

While the crated mummies continued lying dormant every which way underfoot, the winter came and passed without their being called for—the speeches, that is, not mummies. The accounts continued perfectly good; and Mrs. Norris, in promoting gaieties for her nieces, assisting their toilets, displaying their accomplishments, and looking about for their future husbands, had so much to do (in addition to interfering in her sister's affairs, and overlooking Mrs. Grant's wastefulness), that it left her very little occasion to be occupied in fears for the absent.

The Miss Bertrams were now fully established among the belles of the area. Joined to beauty and brilliant acquirements was a naturally easy, civil manner, so that they possessed the neighborhood's favour and admiration (as well as its grand total share of mummified long-dead Egyptians). Their vanity was in such good order that they seemed quite free from it. They gave themselves no airs; while the praises attending such behaviour, coming from their aunt, served to strengthen them in believing they had no faults.

Lady Bertram did not go into public with her daughters. On the surface, she was too indolent even to accept a mother's gratification in witnessing their success at the expense of any personal trouble. In reality she was in the process of accelerating her Egyptological endeavors to a fever pitch, readying all things for a Momentous Occasion. Thus, the charge was made over to her sister.

Mrs. Norris desired nothing better than a post of such honourable representation. She thoroughly relished the means it afforded her of mixing in society without having horses to hire or dealing with any more sorting of papyrus and tablets and—to be honest—quite infernal beast-headed statuary: infernal indeed, and decidedly *non-lupine*.

Fanny had no share in the festivities of the season. But she enjoyed being useful as her aunt's companion when they called away the rest of the family. As Miss Lee had left Mansfield, she naturally became everything to Lady Bertram during the night of a ball or a party. She talked, listened, read to her. The tranquility of such evenings, her perfect security in such a *tête-à-tête* from any sound of unkindness, was unspeakably welcome to a mind which had seldom known a pause in its alarms or embarrassments.

"You are quite an amiable girl," said Lady Bertram in a rare endearing mood, on one such cozy evening, "and you are ready, I am certain. I must soon take you to a certain room in the attic near your own, and you shall make acquaintance of—"

"I thank you, aunt," replied Fanny, putting aside a scholarly excavations journal from which she had been reading. She had a very good notion of what her aunt was hinting at, since she could hear the noises every night and they were getting more prominent. Besides, Lady Bertram was in a new habit of sleepwalking and talking, in what sounded like foreign tongues. And this notion put Fanny in a momentary state of dread. So far, in all her myriad errands, she had managed to avoid accompanying her aunt *there*.

"Later, then. Later, when the Nile rises and overflows its banks. But, do go on now, read."

Thus, for the moment, a visit to the dark *unknown* was averted, with or without the threat of a flood.

As to her cousins' gaieties, Fanny loved to hear an account of them, especially of the balls, and whom Edmund had danced with. She thought too lowly of her own situation to imagine she should ever be admitted to the same, and listened without personal aspirations. Upon the whole, it was a comfortable winter to her—though it brought no William to England, the never-failing hope of his arrival was worth much, and the Cursed mysteries remained dormant.

The ensuing spring deprived her of her valued friend, the old grey pony. For some time she was in danger of feeling the loss in her health as well as in her affections. For in spite of the acknowledged importance of her riding on horse-back, no measures were taken for mounting[4] her again, "because," as it

[4] Not in the Biblical sense.

was observed by her aunts, "she might ride one of her cousin's horses at *any time* when they did not want them."

Since the Miss Bertrams wanted their horses every fine day, and had no idea of carrying their obliging manners to the sacrifice of any real pleasure, that time, of course, never came. They took their cheerful rides in the fine mornings of April and May. Fanny either sat at home the whole day with one aunt, or walked beyond her strength at the instigation of the other: Lady Bertram holding exercise to be as unnecessary for everybody as it was unpleasant to herself, unless it involved unpacking postal boxes; and Mrs. Norris, who was walking all day (and often running in tongue-lolling, saliva scattering frenzy all night), thinking everybody ought to walk as much.

Edmund was absent at this time, or the evil would have been earlier remedied. When he returned, to understand how Fanny was situated, and perceived its ill effects, there seemed with him but one thing to be done. "Fanny must have a horse" was the resolute declaration with which he opposed whatever was voiced by the supineness of his mother, or the economy of his aunt. Mrs. Norris could not help thinking that some steady old equine thing might be found among the numbers belonging to the Park that would do vastly well; or that one might be borrowed of the steward; or that perhaps Dr. Grant might now and then lend them the pony he sent to the post.

"Hah!" exclaimed Edmund to Fanny, taking her aside upon that occasion. "A pony taken from the post? A pony denied the privilege of transporting Cursed Egyptian treasures? Never, not in all Creation!"

"Something is afoot, cousin," Fanny said meanwhile. "While you've been away, your mother has taken to reading hieroglyphics—out loud! As though she knows their meaning. And she promised to have me visit *whatever* is in that room."

"Stand firm, dearest Fanny," he replied. "Your faith will be fixed and strong, and no Curse will have power over it. But—

do try to make any excuses possible with mother *not* to visit that room. And if needed, promise me you will run—"

"Edmund, I will do as you say."

In the meantime the no-riding situation persisted. Mrs. Norris could not but consider it as absolutely unnecessary, and even improper, that Fanny should have a regular lady's horse of her own, in the style of her cousins. She was sure Sir Thomas had never intended it. To be making such a purchase in his absence, and adding to the great expenses of his stable, at a time when a large part of his income was unsettled, seemed to her unjustifiable. "Fanny must have a horse," was Edmund's only reply. Mrs. Norris could not see it in the same light. Lady Bertram did: she entirely agreed with her son as to the necessity of a beast of transportation—though, she continued to ask whatever happened to the little camel Fanny used to ride—and as to its being considered necessary by his father; she only pleaded against there being any hurry; she only wanted him to wait till Sir Thomas's return, and then Sir Thomas might settle it all himself. He would be at home in September, and where would be the harm of only waiting till September? So many things might happen before then—

Though Edmund was much more displeased with his aunt than with his mother, as evincing least regard for her niece, he could not help paying attention to what she said. At length he determined on a solution which would not upset his father yet procure for Fanny the immediate means of exercise which he could not bear she should be without. He had three horses of his own, but not one that would carry a woman, not even one who rode like an Amazon, or so he thought. Two of them were hunters; the third, a useful road-horse which he resolved to exchange for one that his cousin might ride, and it was settled.

The new mare, decidedly un-camel-like, proved a treasure. With very little trouble she fit the purpose, and Fanny was then put in almost full possession of her. She had not supposed that anything could ever suit her like the old grey pony. But her delight in Edmund's mare was far beyond any former pleasure of the sort. And his kindness remained beyond her ability to express. She regarded her cousin as an example of everything good and great, as possessing worth which no one but herself could ever appreciate, and entitled to perfect gratitude. Her sentiments towards him were compounded of all that was respectful, grateful, confiding, and tender.

As the horse continued in name, as well as fact, the property of Edmund, Mrs. Norris could tolerate its being for Fanny's use. And had Lady Bertram ever thought about her own objection again, he might have been excused in her eyes for not waiting till Sir Thomas's return in September.

For, when September came Sir Thomas was still abroad, and without any near prospect of finishing his business. Unfavourable circumstances had suddenly arisen at a moment when he was beginning to turn all his thoughts towards England. The great uncertainty convinced Sir Thomas to remain by himself and wait out the unfortunate business, while sending home his woeful idiot son—Tom had managed to procure in the local market a round-bellied rock that he thought a priceless statue of an Antigua fertility deity, so there went another £100.

Tom arrived safely, bringing an excellent account of his father's health, and the said rock—but to very little purpose, as far as Mrs. Norris was concerned (very little purpose *not* as to the rock, but to as far as Tom's safe return—to ahem—oh, criminy, whatever! gentle Reader, the meaning is apparent, and authorial words twist around and fail miserably at this juncture).

Furthermore, Sir Thomas's sending away his son seemed to her so like a parent's care, under the influence of a foreboding of evil to himself. Indeed, she could not help but feel dreadful presentiments. As the long evenings of autumn came on, Mrs. Norris was so terribly haunted by these ideas, in the sad solitariness of her cottage, as to be obliged to take daily refuge in the dining-room of the Park, even dangerously close to the times of a full moon.

The return of winter engagements, however, was not without its effect. In the course of their progress, her mind became so pleasantly occupied in superintending the fortunes of her eldest niece, as tolerably to quiet her nerves. "If poor Sir Thomas were fated never to return, it would be peculiarly consoling to see their dear Maria well married," she very often thought; always when they were in the company of men of fortune, and particularly on the introduction of a young man who had recently succeeded to one of the largest estates and finest places in the country.

Mr. Rushworth was from the first struck with the beauty of Miss Bertram, and, being inclined to marry, soon fancied himself in love. He was a heavy young man, with not more than common sense; but as there was nothing disagreeable in his figure or address, the young lady was well pleased with her conquest. Being now in her twenty-first year, Maria Bertram was beginning to think matrimony a duty. Since a marriage with Mr. Rushworth would give her the enjoyment of a larger income than her father's, a way to escape a domicile filled with exotic statuary and crates (as well as ensure her a fine house in town clear of all things Egyptian, which was now a prime object), it became, by the same rule of moral obligation, her evident duty to marry Mr. Rushworth if she could.

Mrs. Norris was most zealous in promoting the match, by every suggestion and contrivance likely to enhance its desirableness to either party. Among other means, she sought an intimacy[5] with the gentleman's mother, who at present lived with him, and to whom she even forced Lady Bertram to set aside the unwrapping of papyrus and go through ten miles of indifferent road to pay a morning visit. It was not long before a good understanding took place between this lady and herself.

---

[5] Not in the Biblical sense.

Mrs. Rushworth acknowledged herself very desirous that her son should marry, and declared that of all the young ladies she had ever seen, Miss Bertram seemed, by her amiable qualities and accomplishments, the best adapted to make him happy. Mrs. Norris accepted the compliment, and admired the nice discernment of character which could so well distinguish merit. Maria was indeed the pride and delight of them all—perfectly faultless—an angel. And, of course, so surrounded by admirers, she must be difficult in her choice. Yet, as far as Mrs. Norris could allow herself to decide on so short an acquaintance, Mr. Rushworth appeared precisely the young man to deserve and attach her.

So perfectly suitable was Mr. Rushworth indeed, to Mrs. Norris's notions of ideal matrimony that she forgot herself a certain full moon, and shared a short carriage ride with the young gentleman, while singing praises to Maria, and managed to just barely miss a certain break in the clouds and the revelation of a certain bright nocturnal celestial object that had such a regular and dire *effect* on her.

Mr. Rushworth never knew what hit him. Indeed, he never remembered the incident, but the bite was there, on his forearm, right through the fine linen shirtsleeve, and things got a bit sanguined and rather dizzy, from there on. He was certain, out of nowhere there had been a monstrous big dog, or maybe a wolf, in the carriage; it growled and bit him, then bounded outside, and he barely managed to get home and retell the tale to his mother, forgetting all about the presence and indeed, role, of the venerable Mrs. Norris in the whole incident.

Mrs. Norris may have been forgotten that night, but the impression of her *transformed* teeth remained in a certain portly young gentleman's forearm. And though it healed well and soon enough, unfortunately Mr. Rushworth was never to be his former self again. . . .

After dancing with each other at a proper number of balls, Maria and Mr. Rushworth justified everyone's expectant opinions, and an engagement (with a due reference to the absent Sir Thomas) was entered into, much to the satisfaction of their respective families, and of the general lookers-on of the neighbourhood, who had, for many weeks past, felt the expediency of Mr. Rushworth's marrying Miss Bertram—especially considering how restless the young gentleman seemed to become lately, and how much additional vermin turned up dead, and how much domesticated small livestock went missing in the surrounding countryside.

It was some months before Sir Thomas's consent could be received. But, in the meanwhile, as no one felt a doubt of his most cordial pleasure in the connexion, the intercourse[6] of the two families was carried on without restraint, much Egyptian stuff was transferred over to the Rushworths' (despite Maria's gentle pallor at the sight of each moving box) and no other attempt made at secrecy than Mrs. Norris's talking of it everywhere as a matter not to be talked of at present.

Edmund was the only one of the family who could see a fault in the business. No representation of his aunt's could induce him to find Mr. Rushworth a desirable companion. He could allow his sister to be the best judge of her own happiness, but he was not pleased that her happiness should centre in a large *income*. Nor could he refrain from often saying to himself, in Mr. Rushworth's company—"If this man had not twelve thousand a year, he would be a very stupid fellow. Indeed, a rather wolfish fellow, too." For, being sensitized to such things by long-term observation, Edmund could see the signs of a supernatural *something* or other in Mr. Rushworth, and it boded of nothing good and a goodly amount of the idiotic.

---

[6] Oh dear! Such thoughts are worthy of Ancient Rome, not a civilized modern drawing room.

"Just what we need, Fanny," Edmund muttered, in her hearing alone, "another unholy Curse in the family—though I do believe Aunt Norris had a hand in this one—"

"More like a tooth—" finished Fanny, biting her lip immediately afterward, seeing how Edmund was in a dire and serious mood.

"Thou must not mock their affliction, gentle cousin!" exclaimed Edmund, looking her in the eyes with his dear own, blazing with zeal. "I am afraid the struggle of Good and Holy on this family's behalf will have a harder time of it, now. Especially since, as you say, something terrible is afoot. I am not ready—oh, this Servant of the Lord is not ready yet to face the evil, the darkness surrounding us here in Mansfield Park! Oh, if only I were ready—"

"Well, ready or not, cousin, you do have me. Always. I will do whatever it is you need of me, to help you in the struggle to come—"

Thus, Edmund continued to question the union. Sir Thomas, however, was truly happy in the prospect of an alliance so unquestionably advantageous, and of which he heard nothing but the perfectly good and agreeable. It was a connexion exactly of the right sort, and his most hearty concurrence was conveyed as soon as possible. He only conditioned that the marriage should not take place before his return, which he was again eagerly looking forward to. He wrote in April, and had strong hopes of settling everything to his entire satisfaction, and leaving Antigua before the end of the summer.

Learning this, Lady Bertram naturally became agitated with a combination of spousal joy and supernatural urgency. She dropped a gilded Horus figurine which fell on top of a clay tablet which splattered all over the floor, frightening the pug into a fit of yapping. And then Lady Bertram tore two rolls of papyrus in the process of unwrapping them before Fanny gently took the third from her trembling fingers and called for a bit of tea to calm the Egypt into its normal reposing state.

Such was the state of affairs in the month of July; and Fanny had just reached her eighteenth year, when the society of the village received an addition in the brother and sister of Mrs. Grant, a Mr. and Miss Crawford, the children of her mother by a second marriage.

They were young people of fortune. The son had a good estate in Norfolk, the daughter twenty thousand pounds. As children, their sister had been always very fond of them. But, as her own marriage had been soon followed by the death of their common parent (which left them to the care of a brother of their father, of whom Mrs. Grant knew nothing), she had scarcely seen them since. In their uncle's house they had found a kind home. Admiral and Mrs. Crawford, though agreeing in nothing else, were united in affection for these children, and each had their favourite. The Admiral delighted in the boy, Mrs. Crawford doted on the girl; and it was the lady's death which now obliged her *protégée*, after some months' further trial at her uncle's house, to find another home.

Admiral Crawford was a man of vicious conduct, who chose, instead of retaining his niece, to bring his *mistress* under his own roof (the mistress being a beautiful but equally vicious woman with a freezing gaze, a strange pallid manner about her coupled with a "medical" aversion to sunlight, and a peculiarly insistent ownership of a long wooden crate of her own that she ordered to be stored in the cellar). To this intolerable situation Mrs. Grant was indebted for her sister's coming to her, for Mrs. Grant, having by this time run through the usual resources of ladies residing in the country without a family of children—having more than filled her favourite sitting-room with pretty furniture, and made a choice collection of plants, poultry, and Egyptian overflow generously brought over from the main house—was very much in want of some variety at home. The arrival, therefore, of a well-loved sister, was highly agreeable; and her chief anxiety was lest Mansfield should not satisfy the habits of a young woman who had been mostly used to London.

Miss Crawford was not entirely free from similar apprehensions, though they arose principally from doubts of her sister's style of living and tone of society (and most recently, an excess of possible exposure to countryside sunlight). It was not till after she had tried in vain to persuade her brother to settle with her at his own country house, that she could resolve to hazard herself among her other relations. To anything like a permanence of abode, or limitation of society, Henry Crawford had, unluckily, a great dislike: he could not accommodate his sister in an article of such importance; but he kindly escorted her into Northamptonshire, and as readily engaged to fetch her away again, at half an hour's notice, whenever she were weary of the place.

The meeting was very satisfactory on each side. Miss Crawford found a sister without preciseness or rusticity, a sister's husband who looked the gentleman, and a house commodious and well fitted up, though, to be sure, quirky in décor. And Mrs. Grant received in those whom she hoped to love better than ever a young man and woman of very prepossessing appearance.

Mary Crawford was remarkably pretty—striking, indeed, with a rare delicacy of pale skin and deep rose lips that were near the sanguine shade of midnight. Henry, though not handsome, had air and countenance. The manners of both were lively and pleasant, and Mrs. Grant immediately gave them credit for everything else. She was delighted with each, but Mary was her dearest object. And having never been able to glory in beauty of her own, she thoroughly enjoyed the power of being proud of her sister's.

It must be pointed out that Mary was a changed young woman, it seemed, from the last time Mrs. Grant had seen her, and there was something about her that was hard to put a finger on, something deep and primeval and rather profound, akin to night. . . . Mrs. Grant truly had no notion of the strange Egyptian goings on at Mansfield Park, but even she discerned something vaguely but equally uncanny in Mary Crawford. Goodness, whatever was it?

But no matter the oddity; she had not waited her arrival to look out for a suitable match for her: she had fixed on Tom Bertram. The eldest son of a baronet was not too good for a girl of twenty thousand pounds, with all the elegance and accomplishments which Mrs. Grant foresaw in her; and being a warm-hearted, unreserved woman, Mary had not been three hours in the house before she told her what she had planned.

Miss Crawford was glad to find a family of such consequence so very near them, and not at all displeased either at her sister's early care, or the choice it had fallen on. Matrimony was her object—one of her objects—provided she could marry well. And having seen Mr. Bertram in town, she knew that objection could no more be made to his person than to his situation in life. While she treated it as a joke, therefore, she did not forget to think of it seriously. The scheme was soon repeated to Henry.

"And now," added Mrs. Grant, "I have thought of something to make it complete. I should dearly love to settle you both in this country; and therefore, Henry, you shall marry the youngest Miss Bertram, a nice, handsome, good-humoured, accomplished girl, who will make you very happy."

Henry bowed and thanked her.

"My dear sister," said Mary, "if you can persuade him into anything of the sort, it will be a fresh matter of delight to me to find myself allied to anybody so clever, and I shall only regret that you have not half a dozen daughters to dispose of. If you can persuade Henry to marry, you must have the address of a Frenchwoman. All that English abilities can do has been tried already. I have three very particular friends who have been all dying for him in their turn; and the pains which they, their mothers (very clever women), as well as my dear aunt and myself, have taken to reason, coax, or trick him into marrying, is inconceivable! He is the most horrible flirt that can be imagined. If your Miss Bertrams do not like to have their hearts broke, let them avoid Henry."

Mary did not voice the notion that she herself was to be avoided likewise by eligible gentlemen willing to keep their hearts (and more) intact—but not for the same reasons.

"My dear brother, I will not believe this of you."

"No, I am sure you are too good," retorted Henry. "You will be kinder than Mary. You will allow for the doubts of youth and inexperience. I am of a cautious temper, and unwilling to risk my happiness in a hurry. Nobody can think more highly of the matrimonial state than myself. I consider the blessing of a wife as most justly described in those discreet lines of the poet—'Heaven's *last* best gift.'"

"There, Mrs. Grant, you see how he dwells on one word, and only look at his smile. I assure you he is very detestable; the Admiral's lessons have quite spoiled him."

"I pay very little regard," said Mrs. Grant, "to what any young person says on the subject of marriage. If they profess a disinclination for it, I only set it down that they have not yet seen the right person."

Dr. Grant laughingly congratulated Miss Crawford on feeling no disinclination to the state herself.

"Oh yes! I am not at all ashamed of it. I would have everybody marry if they can do it properly: I do not like to have people throw themselves away; but everybody should marry as soon as they can do it to advantage." And saying this, Miss Crawford flashed a sudden brilliant smile that managed to charm the Grants at the same time as it hid some rather unnaturally sharp upper teeth.

Chapter V

The young people were pleased with each other from the first. On each side there was much to attract, and their acquaintance soon promised as early an intimacy as good manners would warrant. The exotic clutter of Mansfield Park and the chronic dazed expression of Lady Bertram elicited a moment of silent astonishment from Miss Crawford and Mr. Henry Crawford. But then there was a blink, an indrawn breath, an exchange of gazes with one another, and Mary Crawford smiled knowingly, while Henry's expression remained composed but covering something delicate and rather *wicked.*

Miss Crawford's beauty did her no disservice with the Miss Bertrams. They were too handsome themselves to dislike any woman for being so too, and were almost as much charmed as their brothers with her lively dark eye, clear brown complexion marred only by an excessive odd pallor, and general prettiness. Had she been tall, full formed, and fair, it might have been more of a trial: but as it was, there could be no comparison; and she was most allowably a sweet, pretty girl, while they were the finest young women in the country.

Her brother was not handsome: no, when they first saw him he was absolutely plain, black and plain; but still he was the gentleman, with a pleasing address. The second meeting proved him not so very plain: he was plain, to be sure, but then he had so much countenance, and his teeth were so good, and he was so well made, that one soon forgot he was plain. And after a third interview, after dining in company with him at the Parsonage, he was no longer allowed to be called so by anybody. He was, in fact, the most agreeable young man the sisters had ever known, and they were equally delighted with him.

"What a pretty young man he is," Lady Bertram was heard to mutter, "almost Egyptian. Indeed, once the Mouth is Opened, he might look very much like—" Her cryptic words were hardly analyzed however by anyone except Edmund and Fanny, who consulted in secrecy in the corridor.

"What does mother mean, I wonder, Fanny," mused Edmund, leaning on a large sealed wooden crate stacked upon another in the hallway. "If it has something to do with the goings on upstairs, I dread to think what she might have planned. Something *ritualistic.*"

Fanny was almost afraid to venture this, but, absentmindedly peeling a wooden shaving from the corner of the same crate, she said: "What if, cousin, what if Lady Bertram plans to *initiate* the gentleman and the lady into whatever plans she has? Plans related to the Cursed situation?"

"Of that I have little doubt, dear Fanny. But my question is, specifically for *what?*"

"Did you happen to see how odd Miss Crawford looked as she first noticed the condition of the parlor?"

Edmund seemed to change color slightly, and he hurried to say, "Odd? Whatever do you mean? Miss Crawford is admittedly very lovely, I see nothing odd—"

Fanny sighed. Behind her, planted in a round-bottomed Memphis jar stood an anchored fan—palm frond-shaped, lapis and ostrich, and newly arrived from Cairo. If not for its bulky presence, she would have found herself shrinking against the wall in sorrow.

It must be said about Henry Crawford that Miss Bertram's engagement made him in equity the property of Julia, of which Julia was fully aware. And before he had been at Mansfield a week, she was quite ready to be fallen in love with.

Maria's notions on the subject were more confused and indistinct. "There could be no harm in her liking an agreeable man—everybody knew her situation—Mr. Crawford must take care of himself."

Mr. Crawford did not mean to be in any danger. Both Miss Bertrams were worth pleasing, and were ready to be pleased; and he began with no object but of making them like him. He did not want them to *die* of love. But with sense and temper which ought to have made him judge and feel better, he allowed himself great latitude on such points.

"I like your Miss Bertrams exceedingly, sister," said he, as he returned from attending them to their carriage after the said dinner visit; "they are very elegant, agreeable girls. Such *healthy* girls. And their mother—the dear Lady Bertram seems to be quite taken with me, in the brief moments that she finds herself away from—papyrus."

"So they are indeed, and I am delighted to hear you say it. But, despite the mother's charming hobby, you do like Julia best." said Mary, with a dark *wicked* twinkle in her eye.

"Oh yes! I like Julia best."

"But do you really? for Miss Bertram is in general thought the handsomest."

"So I should suppose. She has the advantage in every feature, and I prefer her countenance; but I like Julia best. Miss Bertram is certainly the handsomest, and I have found her the most agreeable, but I shall always like Julia best—because you order me. And because it seems to please everyone in this charmingly quaint private *museum* of antiquities, including Her Egyptian Ladyship."

"I shall not talk to you, Henry, but I know you *will* like her best at last."

"Julia or Her Ladyship? You must mean Julia. Do not I tell you that I like her best *at first?*"

"And besides, Miss Bertram is engaged. Remember that, my dear brother. Amid the splendor of antiquities, her choice is made."

"Yes, and I like her the better for it. An engaged woman is always more agreeable than a disengaged. She is satisfied with herself. Her cares are over, her papyrus rolled and stacked, so to speak, and she feels that she may exert all her powers of pleasing without suspicion. All is safe with a lady engaged: no harm can be done."

"Harm can always be done, you know so very well," said Miss Crawford, allowing her lips to rise at the corners. "Ah, delicious harm! This place, this grand madhouse, puts me rather in the mind of it. And the poor engaged spouse . . . oh dear."

Henry's dark eyes appeared even darker, wickedly sweetly so. "Why, as to that, Mr. Rushworth is a very good sort of young man, and it is a great match for her. Did you observe the delightful manner in which he sniffs her neck when he thinks they are unwatched? I daresay my hounds can do no better."

"Sniffs her neck? How scandalous! whatever do you mean?" Mrs. Grant interrupted in some confusion, since she was quite unaware of the fine nuances being discussed.

Maria subtly ignored her gentler sister. "But Miss Bertram does not care three straws for him; *that* is your opinion of your intimate friend. *I* do not subscribe to it. I am sure Miss Bertram is very much attached to Mr. Rushworth, with and without neck sniffing. I could see it in her eyes, when he was mentioned. I think too well of Miss Bertram to suppose she would ever give her hand without her heart."

"Mary, how shall we manage him?"

"We must leave him to himself, I believe. Talking does no good. He will be taken in at last."

"But I would not have him *taken in*; I would not have him duped; I would have it all fair and honourable."

"Oh dear! let him stand his chance and be taken in. It will do just as well. Everybody is taken in at some period or other."

"Not always in marriage, dear Mary," said Mrs. Grant.

"In marriage especially. With all due respect to such of the present company as chance to be married, my dear Mrs. Grant, there is not one in a hundred of either sex who is not taken in when they marry. Look where I will, I see that it *is* so; and I feel that it *must* be so, when I consider that it is, of all transactions, the one in which people expect most from others, and are least honest themselves."

"Ah! You have been in a bad school for matrimony, in Hill Street."

Mary thought she had been in much worse, but that was not to be announced. . . .

"My poor aunt had certainly little cause to love the state. But, speaking from my own observation, it is a manoeuvring business. I know so many who have married in the full expectation and confidence of some one particular advantage in the connexion, or accomplishment, or good quality in the person, who have found themselves entirely deceived, and been obliged to put up with exactly the reverse. What is this but a take in?"

"My dear child, I beg your pardon, but I cannot quite believe you. Depend upon it, you see but half. You see the evil, but you do not see the consolation. There will be little rubs and disappointments everywhere, and we are all apt to expect too much. But then, if one scheme of happiness fails, human nature turns to another; if the first calculation is wrong, we make a second better: we find comfort somewhere—and those evil-minded observers, dearest Mary, who make much of a little, are more taken in and deceived than the parties themselves."

"Well done, sister! I honour your *esprit du corps*. When I am a wife, I mean to be just as staunch myself; and I wish my friends in general would be so too. It would save me many a heartache."

"You are as bad as your brother, Mary; but we will cure you both. Mansfield shall cure you both, and without any taking in. Stay with us, and we will cure you."

The Crawfords, without wanting to be cured, into ham or otherwise, or even mummified, were very willing to stay. Lady Bertram indeed seemed to have taken a grand liking to them both, particularly Henry. Mary was satisfied with the Parsonage as a present home, and Henry equally ready to lengthen his visit. He had come, intending to spend only a few days with them; but Mansfield promised well, and there was nothing to call him elsewhere. It delighted Mrs. Grant to keep them both with her, and Dr. Grant was exceedingly well contented to have it so: a talking pretty young woman like Miss Crawford is always pleasant society to an indolent, stay-at-home man; and Mr. Crawford's being his guest was an excuse for drinking claret every day.

The Miss Bertrams' admiration of Mr. Crawford was more rapturous than anything which Miss Crawford's habits made her likely to feel. She acknowledged, however, that the Mr. Bertrams were very fine young men—that two such young men were not often seen together even in London—and that their manners, particularly those of the eldest, were very good. *He* had been much in London, and had more liveliness and gallantry than Edmund, and must, therefore, be preferred; and, indeed, his being the eldest was another strong claim. She had felt an early presentiment that she *should* like the eldest best. She knew it was her way.

Tom Bertram must have been thought pleasant, indeed, at any rate. He was the sort of young man to be generally liked—once his tendency to be duped by utter nonsense was reconciled with. His agreeableness was of the kind to be oftener found agreeable than some endowments of a higher stamp (such as a full measure of wit), for he had easy manners, excellent spirits, a large acquaintance, and a great deal to say. And the reversion of Mansfield Park, and a baronetcy, did no harm to all this.

Miss Crawford soon felt that he and his situation might do. She looked about her with due consideration, and found almost everything in his favour: a park, a real park, five miles round, a spacious modern-built house, so well placed and well screened as to deserve to be in any collection of engravings of gentlemen's seats in the kingdom—and wanting only to be completely new-furnished and purged of the ancient fruits of the Nile—pleasant sisters, a quiet though obviously *strange* mother, a metaphysically fascinating *situation*, and an agreeable man himself—with the advantage of being tied up from much gaming and idiot schemes at present by a promise to his father, and of being Sir Thomas hereafter. It might do very well; she believed she should accept him. And she began accordingly to interest herself a little about the black and white striped "horse" from the African Continent which he was readying to run at the B—— races.

These races were to call him away not long after their acquaintance began (indeed, sparing him an unspeakable fate). As the family did not, from his usual goings on, expect him back again for many weeks, it would be prudent to bring his passion to an early proof. Much was said on his side to induce her to attend the races and "see his little striped African marvel win," schemes were made for a large party to attend them, but it was only talk.

And Fanny, what was *she* doing and thinking all this while? and what was *her* opinion of the newcomers? Few young ladies of eighteen could be less called on to speak their opinion than Fanny. In a quiet way, very little attended to, she paid her tribute of admiration to Miss Crawford's beauty, coupled with a measure of caution and suspicion, for she could sense something different about her. But as she still continued to think Mr. Crawford very plain, in spite of her two cousins repeatedly insisting the contrary, she never mentioned *him*. The notice, which she excited herself, was to this effect.

"I begin now to understand you all, except Miss Price," said Miss Crawford, as she was walking with the Mr. Bertrams. "Pray, is she out, or is she not? I am puzzled. She dined at the Parsonage, with the rest of you, which seemed like being *out;* and yet she says so little, that I can hardly suppose she *is*."

Edmund, to whom this was chiefly addressed, replied, "I believe I know what you mean, but I will not undertake to answer the question. My cousin is grown up. She has the age and sense of a woman, but the outs and not outs are beyond me."

"And yet, in general, nothing can be more easily ascertained. The distinction is so broad. Manners as well as appearance are, generally speaking, so totally different. Till now, I could not have supposed it possible to be mistaken as to a girl's being out or not."

And then Miss Crawford proceeded to impart her vigorous opinion on the subject at some great length, discussing the fine delicacies of the female condition of being out in society, with examples of scandalous behavior and drastic change in personality before and after the fact.

"But now I must be satisfied about Miss Price," she concluded. "Does she go to balls? Does she dine out every where, as well as at my sister's?"

"No," replied Edmund; "I do not think she has ever been to a ball. My mother seldom goes into company herself, and dines nowhere but with Mrs. Grant, and Fanny stays at home with *her*."

"Oh! then the point is clear. Miss Price is not out."

Chapter VI

Mr. Bertram set off for ——— with his striped champion-to-be, and Miss Crawford was prepared to find a great chasm in their society, and to miss him decidedly in the meetings which were now becoming almost daily between the families. On their all dining together at the Park soon after his going, she retook her chosen place near the bottom of the table, right next to the gilded and nearly life-size statue of Isis, fully expecting to feel a most melancholy difference in the change of masters.

It would be a very flat business, she was sure. In comparison with his brother, Edmund would have nothing to say. The soup would be sent round in a most spiritless manner, wine drank without any smiles or agreeable trifling, and the venison cut up without supplying one pleasant anecdote of any former haunch, or a single entertaining story, about "my friend such a one" or even the latest arrived Cairo crate on the part of Lady Bertram. She must try to find amusement in what was passing at the upper end of the table, and in observing Mr. Rushworth, who was now making his appearance at Mansfield for the first time since the Crawfords' arrival. He had been visiting a friend in the neighbouring county, and that friend having recently had his grounds laid out by an improver. Mr. Rushworth was returned with his head full of the subject.

He was very eager to be improving his own place in the same way. He could talk of nothing else, punctuated by occasional near-howls that, no matter how beastly odd, elicited no expression of surprise from anyone present. The subject had been already handled in the palm frond-shadowed drawing-room; it was revived in the dining-parlour which was noticeably crowded due to several new long imported crates lined up in a perimeter against the walls next to the already resident oil jars from the Middle Kingdom. Miss Bertram's attention and opinion was evidently his chief aim; and though her deportment showed rather conscious superiority than any solicitude to oblige him, the mention of Sotherton Court, and the ideas attached to it, gave her a feeling of complacency, which prevented her from being very ungracious.

"I wish you could see Compton," said he; "it is the most complete thing! Argh! Grrowl! Ahem—I never saw a place so altered in my life. I told Smith I did not know where I was. The approach *now,* is one of the finest things in the country: you see the house in the most surprising manner. I declare, Ayyyy! Ahem, when I got back to Sotherton yesterday, it looked like a prison—quite a dismal old prison. Grrr! Arghrowwl!"

"Oh, for shame!" cried Mrs. Norris, ending on a bit of a nasal snarl herself. "A prison indeed? Sotherton Court is the noblest old place in the world."

"It wants improvement, ma'am, beyond anything. I never saw a place that wanted so much—Argh!—improvement in my life. It is so forlorn that I do not know what can be done with it."

"I am happy to part with some of my fine *objects d'art* from the batch that just came in from Karnak," murmured Lady Bertram.

Mr. Rushworth was quick to reply with a very extremely modulated "*No!* Argh! Grr! I mean, no, thank you."

"No wonder that Mr. Rushworth should think so at present," meanwhile said Mrs. Grant to Mrs. Norris, with a smile; "but depend upon it, Sotherton will have *every* improvement in time which his heart can desire."

"I must try to do something with it," said Mr. Rushworth, "but I do not know what. Ayyywrrrooowl! Ahem. I hope I shall have some good friend to help me."

Lady Bertram took hold of a crocodile-headed salt shaker and opened her mouth, then appeared to enter a daze.

"Your best friend upon such an occasion," said Miss Bertram calmly, "would be Mr. Repton, I imagine."

"That is what I was thinking of. Grr! As he has done so well by Smith, I think I had better have him at once. His terms are five guineas a day."

"Well, and if they were *ten,*" cried Mrs. Norris, "I am sure *you* need not regard it. The expense need not be any impediment. If I were you, I would have everything done in the best style, as nice as possible. Such a place as Sotherton Court deserves everything that taste and money can do. You have space to work upon there, and grounds that will well reward you. For my own part, if I had anything within the fiftieth part of the size of Sotherton—" And Mrs. Norris went on at length about acres, garden walls, plantations, and apricot trees, ending with: "we put in the apricot against the stable wall, which is now grown such a noble tree, and getting to such perfection, sir," addressing herself then to Dr. Grant.

"The tree thrives well, beyond a doubt, madam," replied Dr. Grant. "The soil is good; and I never pass it without regretting that the fruit should be so little worth the trouble of gathering."

"Sir, it is a Moor Park, we bought it as a Moor Park, and it cost us—that is, it was a present from Sir Thomas, but I saw the bill—and I know it cost seven shillings, and was charged as a Moor Park. Argh! Ayyrooowwl! *Ahem.*"

"You were imposed on, ma'am," replied Dr. Grant: "these potatoes have as much the flavour of a Moor Park apricot as the fruit from that tree. It is an insipid fruit at the best; but a good apricot is eatable, which none from my garden are."

"The truth is, ma'am," said Mrs. Grant, ignoring the howling and pretending to whisper across the table to Mrs. Norris, "that Dr. Grant hardly knows what the natural taste of our apricot is: he is scarcely ever indulged with one, for it is so valuable a fruit; and ours is such a remarkably large, fair sort, that what with early tarts and preserves, my cook contrives to get them all."

Mrs. Norris, who had begun to redden and growl to match Mr. Rushworth, was appeased. And, for a little while, other subjects took place of the improvements of Sotherton, while the wolfish baying had settled down. Dr. Grant and Mrs. Norris were seldom good friends; their acquaintance had begun in dilapidations, and their habits were totally dissimilar, in particular on moonlit nights.

After a short interruption Mr. Rushworth began again. "Smith's place is the admiration of all the country; and it was a mere nothing before Repton took it in hand. I think—Grr!—I shall have Repton."

"Mr. Rushworth," said Lady Bertram, "if I were you, I would have a very pretty shrubbery. One likes to get out into a shrubbery in fine weather. We are fortunately situated as to resemble the fertile Nile river valley here in Mansfield. Indeed, only last night I thought I saw an ibis standing on one foot, very pretty—"

"I believe that was a goose, mother," Edmund put in, clearing his throat. No one seemed to pay any note, except for Fanny who lifted a napkin to her lips and pressed very tight.

Mr. Rushworth was eager to assure her ladyship of his acquiescence, and tried to make out something complimentary. But, between his submission to *her* taste, his growls and grunts, and his having always intended the same himself, with the superadded objects of professing attention to the comfort of ladies in general, and of insinuating that there was *one* only whom he was anxious to please, he grew puzzled in his own flow of verbiage, and Edmund was glad to put an end to his speech by a proposal of wine.

Mr. Rushworth, however, though not usually a great talker, had still more to howl—ahem—say on the subject next his heart. "Smith has not much above a hundred acres altogether in his grounds, which is little enough, and makes it more surprising that the place can have been so improved. Ayyyeee! Now, at Sotherton we have a good seven hundred, without reckoning the water meadows; Grrrrowwrawl! Arghoowieee! HOOOWL! OH, BLASTED H—! *Ahem,* pardon—" (at this point everyone at the table had paused eating, to stare at Mr. Rushworth, who thunderously cleared his throat in an attempt to mask the irrevocably escaped scandalous utterance; then continued, unperturbed) "—so that I think, if so much could be done at Compton, we need not despair. There have been two or three fine old trees cut down, that grew too near the house, and it opens the prospect amazingly—Ayyyyrrroww!—which makes me think that Repton, or anybody of that sort, would certainly have the avenue at Sotherton down: the avenue that leads from the west front to the top of the hill, you know," turning to Miss Bertram particularly as he spoke. But Miss Bertram thought it most becoming to reply—

"The avenue! Oh! I do not recollect it. I really know very little of Sotherton."

"It is rather hard to see the Nile, not with all the river reeds and palms and bamboo lining the edge of the property on that side," mused Lady Bertram, forgetting momentarily that they were not talking about Mansfield Park, or for that matter, the African Continent.

Fanny, who was sitting on the other side of Edmund, exactly opposite Miss Crawford, and who had been attentively listening, now looked at him, and said in a low voice—

"Cut down an avenue! What a pity! Does it not make you think of Cowper? 'Ye fallen avenues, once more I mourn your fate unmerited.'"

He smiled as he answered, "I am afraid the avenue stands a bad chance, Fanny. Unless someone manages to convince my mother it is of Egyptian origin, then she will personally stand up to defend it before the falling axe and saw—"

"I should like to see Sotherton before it is cut down, to see the place as it is now, in its old state; but I do not suppose I shall."

"Have you never been there? No, you never can; and, unluckily, it is out of distance for a ride, even for a little Amazon such as yourself. I wish we could contrive it."

"Oh! it does not signify. Whenever I do see it, you will tell me how it has been altered."

"I collect," said Miss Crawford, "that Sotherton is an old place, and a place of some grandeur. In any particular style of building?"

"The pyramid shape is an excellent design in architecture," said Lady Bertram. "Though, I do not believe Sotherton has a pyramid."

With filial civility, Edmund ignored the comment. "The house was built in Elizabeth's time, and is a large, regular, brick building;" he said, "heavy, but respectable looking, and has many good rooms. It is ill placed. It stands in one of the lowest spots of the park; in that respect, unfavourable for improvement. But the woods are fine, and there is a stream, which, I dare say, might be made a good deal of. Mr. Rushworth is quite right, I think, in meaning to give it a modern dress, and I have no doubt that it will be all done extremely well."

Miss Crawford listened with submission, and said to herself, "He is a well-bred man; he makes the best of it."

"I do not wish to influence Mr. Rushworth," he continued; "but, had I a place to new fashion, I should not put myself into the hands of an improver. I would rather have an inferior degree of beauty, of my own choice, and acquired progressively. I would rather abide by my own blunders than by his."

"*You* would know what you were about, of course; Argh! but that would not suit *me*. Grrooowr! HOOOOWL! Ah, blimey, *pardon me!* I have no eye or ingenuity for such matters, but as they are before me; and had I a place of my own in the country, I should be most thankful to any Mr. Repton who would undertake it, and give me as much beauty—Arrrooowwee!—as he could for my money; and I should never look at it till it was complete."

"It would be delightful to *me* to see the progress of it all," said Fanny, using her handkerchief to discreetly wipe the flying projectile droplets of Mr. Rushworth's spittle that had reached her all the way across the table.

"Ay, you have been brought up to it," said Miss Crawford. "It was no part of my education; and the only dose I ever had, being administered by not the first favourite in the world, has made me consider improvements *in hand* as the greatest of nuisances. Three years ago the Admiral, my honoured uncle, bought a cottage at Twickenham for us all to spend our summers in; and my aunt and I went down to it quite in raptures. But being excessively pretty, it was soon found necessary to be improved, and for three months we were all dirt and confusion, without a gravel walk to step on, or a bench fit for use. I would have everything as complete as possible in the country, shrubberies and flower-gardens, and rustic seats innumerable: but it must all be done without my care. Henry is different; he loves to be doing."

Edmund was sorry to hear Miss Crawford, whom he was much disposed to admire, speak so freely of her uncle. It did not suit his sense of propriety, and he was silenced, till induced by further smiles and liveliness to put the matter by for the present.

"Mr. Bertram," said she, "I have tidings of my harp at last. I am assured that it is safe at Northampton; and there it has probably been these ten days, in spite of the solemn assurances we have so often received to the contrary." Edmund expressed his pleasure and surprise. "The truth is, that our inquiries were too direct; we sent a servant, we went ourselves: this will not do seventy miles from London; but this morning we heard of it in the right way. It was seen by some farmer, and he told the miller, and the miller told the butcher, and the butcher's son-in-law left word at the shop."

"I am very glad that you have heard of it, by whatever means, and hope there will be no further delay."

"I am to have it to-morrow; but how do you think it is to be conveyed? Not by a wagon or cart: oh no! nothing of that kind could be hired in the village. I might as well have asked for porters and a handbarrow."

"You would find it difficult, just now, in the middle of a very late hay harvest, to hire a horse and cart."

"If the harp resembled a crocodile, were over a millennium in age and hailed directly from Egypt, there would be no problem whatsoever in transporting it here," said Miss Julia Bertram coolly. "Indeed, you might suggest to mother—"

"Why, Julia!" spoke Edmund in soft reproach.

"I was astonished to find what a piece of work was made of it!" continued Miss Crawford. "To want a horse and cart in the country seemed impossible, so I told my maid to speak for one directly. As I cannot look out of my dressing-closet without seeing one farmyard, nor walk in the shrubbery without passing another, I thought it would be only ask and have, and was rather grieved that I could not give the advantage to all. Guess my surprise, when I found that I had been asking the most unreasonable, most impossible thing in the world; had offended all the farmers, all the labourers, all the hay in the parish! As for Dr. Grant's bailiff, I believe I had better keep out of *his* way. Even my brother-in-law himself, who is all kindness in general, looked rather black upon me when he found what I had been at."

"You could not be expected to have thought on the subject before; but when you *do* think of it, you must see the importance of getting in the grass. The hire of a cart at any time is not so easy as you suppose. Our farmers are not in the habit of letting them out. But in harvest, it is quite out of their power to spare a horse."

"I shall understand all your ways in time; but, coming down with the true London maxim, that everything is to be got with money, I was a little embarrassed at first by the sturdy independence of your country customs. However, I am to have my harp fetched to-morrow. Henry, who is good-nature itself, has offered to fetch it in his barouche. Will it not be honourably conveyed?"

Edmund spoke of the harp as his favourite instrument, and hoped to be soon allowed to hear her. Fanny had never heard the harp at all, and wished for it very much.

"I shall be most happy to play to you both," said Miss Crawford; "at least as long as you can like to listen: probably much longer, for I dearly love music myself. Now, Mr. Bertram, if you write to your brother, I entreat you to tell him that my harp is come: he heard so much of my misery about it. And you may say, if you please, that I shall prepare my most plaintive airs against his return, in compassion to his feelings, as I know his little striped—*horse* will lose."

"If I write, I will say whatever you wish me; but I do not, at present, foresee any occasion for writing."

"No, I dare say, nor if he were to be gone a twelvemonth, would you ever write to him, nor he to you, if it could be helped.

The occasion would never be foreseen. What strange creatures brothers are! You would not write to each other but upon the most urgent necessity in the world. When obliged to write that a horse is ill, or a relation dead, it is done in the fewest possible words. But one style among you, and I know it perfectly. Henry, who is in every other respect exactly what a brother should be, who loves me, consults me, confides in me, and will talk to me by the hour together, has never yet turned the page in a letter. Very often it is nothing more than—'Dear Mary, I am just arrived. Bath seems full, and everything as usual. Yours sincerely.' That is the true manly style; that is a complete brother's letter."

"When they are at a distance from all their family," said Fanny, colouring for William's sake, "they can write long letters."

"Miss Price has a brother at sea," said Edmund, "whose excellence as a correspondent makes her think you too severe upon us."

"At sea, has she? In the king's service, of course?"

Fanny would rather have had Edmund tell the story, but his determined silence obliged her to relate her brother's situation. Her voice was animated in speaking of his profession, and the foreign stations he had been on. But she could not mention the number of years that he had been absent without tears in her eyes. Miss Crawford civilly wished him an early promotion.

"Do you know anything of my cousin's captain?" said Edmund; "Captain Marshall? You have a large acquaintance in the navy, I conclude?"

"Among admirals, large enough; but," with an air of grandeur, "we know very little of the inferior ranks. Post-captains may be very good sort of men, but they do not belong to *us*. Of various admirals I could tell you a great deal—their flags, the gradation of their pay, their bickerings and jealousies. But, in general, I can assure you that they are all passed over, and all very ill used. Certainly, my home at my uncle's brought me acquainted with a circle of admirals. Of *Rears* and *Vices* I saw enough. Now do not be suspecting me of a pun, I entreat."

Edmund again felt grave, and only replied, "It is a noble profession."

"Yes, the profession is well enough under two circumstances: if it make the fortune, and if there be discretion in spending it. But in short, it is not a favourite profession of mine. It has never worn an amiable form to *me*."

Edmund reverted to the harp, and was again very happy in the prospect of hearing her play.

Lady Bertram came out of her doze to hear the end of it and exclaimed "A harp! The divine and dulcet instrument of the Pharaohs!"

The subject of improving grounds, meanwhile, was still under consideration among the others. Mrs. Grant could not help addressing her brother, though it was calling his attention from Miss Julia Bertram.

"My dear Henry, have *you* nothing to say? You have been an improver yourself, and from what I hear of Everingham, it may vie with any place in England. Its natural beauties, I am sure, are great. Everingham, as it *used* to be, was perfect in my estimation: such a happy fall of ground, and such timber! What would I not give to see it again!"

"Nothing could be so gratifying to me as to hear your opinion of it," was his answer; "but I fear there would be some disappointment: you would not find it equal to your present ideas. In extent, it is a mere nothing; and, as for improvement, there was very little for me to do—too little: I should like to have been busy much longer."

"You are fond of the sort of thing?" said Julia.

"Excessively; but what with the natural advantages of the ground, which pointed out, even to a very young eye, what little remained to be done, and my own consequent resolutions, I had not been of age three months before Everingham was all that it is now. My plan was laid at Westminster, altered at Cambridge, and at one-and-twenty executed. I am inclined to envy Mr. Rushworth for having so much happiness yet before him. I have been a devourer of my own."

"Those who see quickly, will resolve quickly, and act quickly," said Julia. "*You* can never want employment. Instead of envying Mr. Rushworth, you should assist him with your opinion."

Mrs. Grant, hearing the latter part of this speech, enforced it warmly, persuaded that no judgment could be equal to her brother's. And as Miss Bertram caught at the idea likewise, and gave it her full support, declaring that it was infinitely better to consult with friends and disinterested advisers, than immediately to throw the business into the hands of a professional man, Mr. Rushworth was ready to request the favour of Mr. Crawford's assistance. And Mr. Crawford, after properly depreciating his own abilities, was quite at his service.

Mr. Rushworth then began to howl and redden with excitement and propose Mr. Crawford's doing him the honour of coming over to Sotherton, and taking a bed there. It was then that Mrs. Norris, as if reading in her two nieces' minds their little approbation of a plan which was to take Mr. Crawford away, interposed with an amendment.

"There can be no doubt of Mr. Crawford's willingness; but why should not more of us go? Why should not we make a little party? Here are many that would be interested in your improvements, my dear Mr. Rushworth, and that would like to hear Mr. Crawford's opinion on the spot, and that might be of some small use to you with *their* opinions. As for my own part, I could go and sit a few hours with your dear mother, Mrs. Rushworth, while the rest of you walked about and settled things. Then we could all return to a late dinner here, or at

Sotherton, however is most agreeable to your mother, and have a pleasant drive home by moonlight. I dare say Mr. Crawford would take my two nieces and me in his barouche, and Edmund can go on horseback, you know, sister, and Fanny will stay at home with you."

Lady Bertram made no objection, for unbeknownst to all she had some very Grand Plans to initiate.

Meanwhile, everyone interested in the outing expressed their concurrence, excepting Edmund. He heard it all and said nothing.

Chapter VII

"Well, Fanny, and how do you like Miss Crawford *now?*" said Edmund the next day, after thinking some time on the subject himself. "How did you like her yesterday?"

"Very well—very much. I like to hear her talk. She entertains me; and she is so extremely pretty, that I have great pleasure in looking at her."

"It is her countenance that is so attractive. She has a wonderful play of feature! But was there nothing in her conversation that struck you, Fanny, as not quite right?"

"Oh yes! she ought not to have spoken of her uncle as she did. I was quite astonished. An uncle with whom she has been living so many years, and who, whatever his faults, is so fond of her brother, treating him quite like a son. I could not have believed it!"

"I thought you would be struck. It was very wrong; very indecorous."

"And very ungrateful, I think."

"Ungrateful is a strong word. I do not know that her uncle has any claim to her *gratitude.* His wife certainly had. Her warm respect for her aunt's memory misleads her here. She is awkwardly circumstanced. With such warm feelings and lively spirits it must be difficult to do justice to her affection for Mrs.

Crawford, without throwing a shade on the Admiral. I do not pretend to know who was most to blame in their disagreements, though the Admiral's present conduct might incline one to the side of his wife. But it is natural and amiable that Miss Crawford should acquit her aunt entirely. I do not censure her *opinions;* but there certainly *is* impropriety in making them public."

"Do not you think," said Fanny, after a little consideration, "that this impropriety is a reflection itself upon Mrs. Crawford, as her niece has been entirely brought up by her? She cannot have given her right notions of what was due to the Admiral. Surely some *other* female had a modicum of shaping of her nature."

"That is a fair remark. Yes, we must suppose the faults of the niece to have been those of the aunt, then the *other woman.* And it makes one more sensible of her disadvantages. But I think her present home must do her good. Mrs. Grant's manners are just what they ought to be. She speaks of her brother with a very pleasing affection."

"Yes, except as to his writing her such short letters. She made me almost laugh; but I cannot rate so very highly the love or good-nature of a brother who will not give himself the trouble of writing anything worth reading to his sisters, when they are separated. I am sure William would never have used *me* so, under any circumstances. And what right had she to suppose that *you* would not write long letters when you were absent?"

"The right of a lively mind, Fanny, seizing whatever may contribute to its own amusement or that of others; perfectly allowable, when untinctured by ill-humour or roughness. There is not a shadow of either in Miss Crawford: nothing sharp, or loud, or coarse. She is perfectly feminine, except in the instances we have been speaking of. There she cannot be justified. I am glad you saw it all as I did."

"She is indeed perfectly lovely," said Fanny quietly. "Though I cannot help but wonder why in some moments she appears so cold and pale and, frankly, *Cursed* somehow, in some secret manner of her own. Cursed, maybe, with a void in the spot where there ought to be her heart."

But Edmund did not hear.

Having formed her mind and gained Fanny's affections, there was a good chance of her thinking like him. But on this subject, there began now to be some danger of dissimilarity. For he was in a line of admiration of Miss Crawford, which might lead him where Fanny could not follow.

Miss Crawford's attractions did not lessen. The harp arrived, minus any crocodile embellishments, and rather added to her beauty, wit, and good-humour; for she played with the greatest obligingness, with an expression and taste which were peculiarly becoming, and there was something clever to be said at the close of every air. Edmund was at the Parsonage every day, to be indulged with his favourite instrument. One morning secured an invitation for the next.

A young woman, pretty, lively, with a harp as elegant as herself, and both placed near a window, cut down to the ground, and opening on a little lawn, surrounded by shrubs in the rich foliage of summer—it was enough to catch any man's heart. The season, the scene, the air, were all favourable to tenderness and sentiment. Mrs. Grant and her tambour frame were not without their use: it was all in harmony. And as everything will turn to account when love is once set going, even the sandwich tray, and Dr. Grant doing the honours of it, were worth looking at.

Without knowing what he was about, Edmund was beginning, at the end of a week of such intercourse,[7] to be a good deal in love. And to the credit of the lady it may be added that, without his being a man of the world or an elder brother, without any of the arts of flattery or the gaieties of small talk, he began to be *agreeable* to her. She felt it to be so, though she had

[7] How improper! Please, do think, rather, of the sandwich! for it is far more nourishing, body and soul, than such impurity of thought.

not foreseen, and could hardly understand it. He was not pleasant by any common rule: he talked no nonsense. He paid no compliments, his opinions were unbending, his attentions tranquil and simple. There was a charm, perhaps, in his sincerity, his steadiness, his integrity, which Miss Crawford might be equal to feel, though not equal to discuss with herself. She did not think very much about it, however: he pleased her for the present; she liked to have him near her; it was enough.

Enough, for the moment. . . .

Fanny could not wonder that Edmund was at the Parsonage every morning. She would gladly have been there too, to hear the harp. Neither could she wonder that, when the evening stroll was over, and the two families parted again, he should attend Mrs. Grant and her sister to their home, while Mr. Crawford was devoted to the ladies of the Park. But she thought it a very bad exchange. If Edmund were not there to mix the wine and water for her, she would rather go without it.

She was a little surprised that he could spend so many hours with Miss Crawford, and not see more of the sort of fault which he had already observed, and of which *she* was reminded by a something of a *dark* nature whenever she was in her company. But so it was. Edmund was fond of speaking to her of Miss Crawford (apparently the Admiral had not been mentioned again). Fanny scrupled to point out her own remarks to him, lest it should appear like ill-nature.

The first actual pain which Miss Crawford occasioned her was the consequence of an inclination to learn to ride, which the former caught, soon after her being settled at Mansfield, from the example of the young ladies at the Park. As Edmund's acquaintance with her increased, it led to his offer of his own quiet mare for the purpose of her first attempts. No hurt was intended by him to his cousin—*she* was not to lose a day's exercise by it. The mare was only to be taken down to the Parsonage half an hour before her ride were to begin. Fanny, on its being first proposed, so far from feeling slighted, was almost over-powered with gratitude that he should be *asking* her leave for it.

Miss Crawford made her first riding attempt with great credit to herself, and no inconvenience to Fanny. Edmund, who had taken down the mare and presided at the whole, returned with it in excellent time, before either Fanny or the steady old coachman, who always attended her when she rode without her cousins, were ready to set forward.

The second day's trial was not so guiltless. Miss Crawford's enjoyment of riding was such that she did not know how to leave off. Active and fearless, and though rather small, strongly made, she seemed formed for a horsewoman. And to the pure genuine pleasure of the exercise (often lowering her face to press her cheeks close to the mare, to hug the horse about the neck in unabashed excitement), something was probably added in Edmund's attendance and instructions, and something more in the conviction of very much surpassing her sex in general by her early progress, to make her unwilling to dismount. Fanny was ready and waiting, and Mrs. Norris was beginning to scold her for not being gone, and still no horse was announced, no Edmund appeared. To avoid her aunt, and look for him, she went out.

The houses, though scarcely half a mile apart, were not within sight of each other. But, by walking fifty yards from the hall door, she could look down the park, and command a view of the Parsonage and all its demesnes, gently rising beyond the village road. In Dr. Grant's meadow she immediately saw the group—Edmund and Miss Crawford both on horse-back, riding side by side, Dr. and Mrs. Grant, and Mr. Crawford, with two or three grooms, standing about and looking on. A happy party it appeared to her, all interested in one object: cheerful beyond a doubt, for the sound of merriment ascended even to her.

It was a sound which did not make *her* cheerful. Fanny wondered that Edmund should forget her, and felt a pang. She could not turn her eyes from the meadow, could not help seeing all that passed. She even noticed a somewhat odd-looking figure[8] walking, in what appeared to be large aimless circles, with a dead-stiff lumbering gait, off in the distance; probably an additional groom.

At first Miss Crawford and her companion made the circuit of the field, at a foot's pace. Then, at *her* apparent suggestion, they rose into a canter. To Fanny's timid nature it was most astonishing to see how well she sat. After a few minutes they stopped entirely. Edmund was close to her; he was speaking to her; he was evidently directing her management of the bridle. He had hold of her hand; Fanny saw it, or the imagination supplied what the eye could not reach. She must not wonder at all this; what could be more natural than that Edmund should be making himself useful, and proving his good-nature by any one? She could not but think, indeed, that Mr. Crawford might as well have saved him the trouble; that it would have been particularly proper and becoming in a brother to have done it himself. But Mr. Crawford, with all his boasted good-nature, and all his coachmanship, probably knew nothing of the matter, and had no active kindness in comparison of Edmund. She began to think it rather hard upon the mare to have such double duty; if she were forgotten, the poor mare should be remembered.

Her feelings for one and the other were soon calmed somewhat by seeing the party in the meadow disperse. Miss Crawford still on horseback, but attended by Edmund on foot, passed through a gate into the lane, and so into the park, and made towards the spot where Fanny stood. She began then to be afraid of appearing rude and impatient; and walked to meet them with a great anxiety to avoid the suspicion.

---

[8] Aha! At last, pay attention, gentle Reader, this is Important!

"My dear Miss Price," said Miss Crawford, her face less pale than usual and her lips unusually ruddy even for her own stark complexion, as soon as she was at all within hearing, "I am come to make my own apologies for keeping you waiting; but I have nothing in the world to say for myself—I knew it was very late, and that I was behaving extremely ill. Therefore, if you please, you must forgive me. Selfishness must always be forgiven, because there is no hope of a cure."

Fanny's answer was extremely civil, and Edmund added his conviction that she could be in no hurry. "For there is more than time enough for my cousin to ride twice as far as she ever goes," said he, "and you have been promoting her comfort by preventing her from setting off half an hour sooner: clouds are now coming up, and now she will not suffer from the heat. I wish *you* may not be fatigued by so much exercise and saved yourself this walk home."

"No part of it fatigues me but getting off this horse, I assure you," said she, as she sprang down with his help; "I am very strong. And now that the lovely clouds are coming up, I dare say I feel *invincible*. Nothing ever fatigues me but doing what I do not like. Miss Price, I give way to you with a very bad grace; but I sincerely hope you will have a pleasant ride, and that I may have nothing but good to hear of this dear, delightful, beautiful animal."

The old coachman, who had been waiting about with his own horse and glancing about him somewhat gruffly and suspiciously, now joined them. Fanny was lifted on hers, and they set off across another part of the park; her feelings of discomfort not lightened by seeing, as she looked back, that the others were walking down the hill together to the village. Nor did her attendant do her much good by his comments on Miss Crawford's great cleverness as a horse-woman, which he had been watching with an interest almost equal to her own.

"It is a pleasure to see a lady with such a good heart for riding!" said he, after complaining a bit about strange-looking fellows stumbling about the property and how young ladies must take care. "I never see one sit a horse better. She did not seem to have a thought of fear. Very different from you, miss, when you first began, six years ago come next Easter. Lord bless you! how you did tremble when Sir Thomas first had you put on!—Oh, look! there, miss, there he goes again, that odd fellow, or maybe that is some other one—"

Fanny glanced to look in the direction he pointed, but there appeared to be no one there. "But now, though I no longer tremble, it does not make one bit of difference," she thought.

In the drawing-room Miss Crawford was also celebrated. Her merit in being gifted by Nature with strength and courage was fully appreciated by the Miss Bertrams. Her delight in riding and her early excellence in it was like their own, and they had great pleasure in praising it.

"Indeed, it was as though the horse itself was enthralled by the splendid ability of the rider!" said Edmund, adding, "Which reminds me, I thought I saw a bit of sanguined foam at the side of its neck. Poor beast, it must have grazed a tree branch. So enthralled was I in observation that I forgot to mention to the groom to check it."

"I was sure she would ride well," said Julia; "she has the make for it. Her figure is as neat as her brother's."

"Yes," added Maria, "and her spirits are as good, and she has the same energy of character. I cannot but think that good horsemanship has a great deal to do with the mind."

When they parted at night Edmund asked Fanny whether she meant to ride the next day.

"No, I do not know—not if you want the mare," was her answer.

"I do not want her at all for myself," said he; "but whenever you are next inclined to stay at home, I think Miss

Crawford would be glad to have her a longer time—for a whole morning, in short. She has a great desire to get as far as Mansfield Common: Mrs. Grant has been telling her of its fine views, and I have no doubt of her being perfectly equal to it. But any morning will do for this. She would be extremely sorry to interfere with you. It would be very wrong if she did. *She* rides only for pleasure; *you* for health."

"I shall not ride to-morrow, certainly," said Fanny; "I have been out very often lately, and would rather stay at home. You know I am strong enough now to walk very well."

Edmund looked pleased, which must be Fanny's comfort, and the ride to Mansfield Common took place the next morning. The party included all the young people but herself, and was much enjoyed. A successful scheme of this sort generally brings on another; and the having been to Mansfield Common disposed them all for going somewhere else the day after. There were many other views to be shewn; and though the weather was hot, there were shady lanes wherever they wanted to go. At some point one of them pointed out a distant lumbering figure seen moving oddly among the trees, walking stiffly like clockwork, with arms semi-raised and slightly extended forward.

"Must be some drunken lout," said Miss Crawford with a breezy laugh, her lips very red in the sunlight, and her eyes somehow very, very dark.

"A nearby villager, no doubt. Though, it is far too early in the day to have imbibed quite that much. Look how he lumbers along, like a wooden scarecrow, an acrobat on stilts!" said Henry.

Before anything else could be speculated, soon enough the unusual figure disappeared in the distance and was forgotten.

Four fine mornings successively were spent in this manner, in shewing the Crawfords the country. Everything was gaiety and good-humour, the heat only a minor inconvenience—till the fourth day, when the happiness of one of the party was exceedingly clouded. Miss Bertram was the one. Edmund and Julia were invited to dine at the Parsonage, and *she* was excluded. It was meant and done by Mrs. Grant, with perfect good-humour, on Mr. Rushworth's account, who was partly expected at the Park that day; but it was felt as a very grievous injury, and her good manners were severely taxed to conceal her vexation and anger till she reached home. As Mr. Rushworth did *not* come, due to some beastly indisposition, the injury was increased, and she had not even the relief of shewing her power over him; she could only be sullen to her mother, aunt, and cousin, and throw as great a gloom as possible over their dinner and dessert.

Between ten and eleven Edmund and Julia walked into the drawing-room, fresh with the evening air, glowing and cheerful, the very reverse of what they found in the three ladies sitting there, for Maria would scarcely raise her eyes from her book, and Lady Bertram was half-asleep over a roll of papyrus. Even Mrs. Norris, discomposed by her niece's ill-humour, asked one or two questions about the dinner, and then said no more. For a few minutes the brother and sister were too eager in their praise of the night and their remarks on the stars, to think beyond themselves. But when the first pause came, Edmund, looking around, said, "But where is Fanny? Is she gone to bed?"

"No, not that I know of," replied Mrs. Norris with a stifled growl; "she was here a moment ago."

Fanny's own gentle voice speaking from the other end of the room told them that she was on the sofa. Mrs. Norris began scolding.

"That is a very foolish trick, Fanny, to be idling away all the evening upon a sofa. Why cannot you come and sit here, and employ yourself as *we* do? If you have no work of your own, I can supply you from the poor basket. There is all the new *faience* and unsorted tomb items from that small crate marked "Luxor 21," and I dare say even non-Egyptian calico, that was bought last week, not touched yet. I am sure I almost broke my back by cutting it out after I nigh-destroyed my fingers on the brittle pottery. You should learn to think of other people; and, take my word for it, it is a shocking trick for a young person to be always lolling upon a sofa."

Before half this was said, Fanny was returned to her seat at the table, and had taken up her work again; and Julia, who was in high good-humour, from the pleasures of the day, did her the justice of exclaiming, "I must say, ma'am, that Fanny is as little upon the sofa as anybody in the house."

"Fanny," said Edmund, after looking at her attentively, "I am sure you have the headache."

She could not deny it, but said it was not very bad.

"I can hardly believe you," he replied; "I know your looks too well. How long have you had it?"

"Since a little before dinner. It is nothing but the heat and the dust and sand on these antique items."

"Never mind the imported sand and dust—that would be nothing out of the ordinary for *this house*—but did you go out in the heat?"

"Go out! to be sure she did," said Mrs. Norris: "would you have her stay within such a fine day as this? Were not we *all* out? Even your mother was out to-day for above an hour, after she quitted the examination of the hieroglyphics on that tiny pot-bellied vase."

"Yes, indeed, Edmund," added her ladyship, who had been thoroughly awakened by Mrs. Norris's sharp reprimand to Fanny; "I was out above an hour. I sat three-quarters of an hour in the flower-garden, perusing the ancient script of the great Amenhotep—a truly delightful pastime, indoors or out—while Fanny cut the roses; and very pleasant it was, I assure you, but very hot, just as it ought to be in Thebes. It was shady enough in the alcove, but I declare I quite dreaded the coming home again."

"Fanny has been cutting roses, has she?"

"Yes, and I am afraid they will be the last this year. Indeed, I am considering replacing some of the rose bushes with lotus plants—would that work, or does one require a river current or pond? But oh yes, Fanny—Poor thing! *She* found it hot enough; but they were so full-blown that one could not wait. Lotus, on the other hand, would not require such upkeep—"

"There was no help for it, certainly," rejoined Mrs. Norris, in a rather softened voice; "but I question whether her headache might not be caught *then,* sister. There is nothing so likely to give it as standing and stooping in a hot sun; but I dare say it will be well to-morrow. Suppose you let her have your aromatic vinegar; I always forget to have mine filled."

"She has got it," said Lady Bertram; "she has had it ever since she came back from your house the second time."

"What!" cried Edmund; "has she been walking as well as cutting roses; walking across the hot park to your house, and doing it twice, ma'am? No wonder her head aches."

Mrs. Norris was talking to Julia, and did not "hear."

"I was afraid it would be too much for her," said Lady Bertram; "but when the roses were gathered, your aunt wished to have them, and then you know they must be taken home."

"But were there roses enough to oblige her to go twice?"

"No; but they were to be put into the spare room to dry. Unluckily, Fanny forgot to lock the door of the room and bring away the key, so she was obliged to go again."

Edmund got up and walked about the room, saying, "And could nobody be employed on such an errand but Fanny? Upon my word, ma'am, it has been a very ill-managed business."

"I am sure I do not know how it was to have been done better," cried Mrs. Norris, unable to be longer deaf; "unless I had gone myself. But I cannot be in two places at once. And I was talking to Mr. Green at that very time about your mother's dairymaid—" in this she went on for some time, finally—"but really I cannot do everything at once, and oh, not with these tedious giant crates underfoot everyplace! And as for Fanny's just stepping down to my house for me—it is not much above a quarter of a mile. How often do I pace it three times a day, early and late, ay, and in all weathers too, with the moon full and gone, and say nothing about it?"

"I wish Fanny had half your *preternatural* strength, ma'am."

"If Fanny would be more regular in her exercise, she would not be knocked up[9] so soon. She has not been out on horseback now this long while, and when she does not ride, she ought to walk. If she had been riding before, I should not have asked it of her. But I thought it would rather do her good after being stooping among the roses; for there is nothing so refreshing as a walk after a fatigue of that kind; and though the sun was strong, it was not so very hot. Between ourselves, Edmund," nodding significantly at his mother, "it was cutting the roses, and dawdling about in the flower-garden, that did the mischief."

"I am afraid it was, indeed," said the more candid Lady Bertram, who had overheard her; "I am very much afraid she caught the headache there, for the heat was enough to kill anybody, and moreover, enough to dry them out something awful, so that they lie in a dreadful desiccated condition for many, many, many years. . . . It was as much as I could bear myself. Lying there dry as a stick of leather for two, nay three thousand years—that is, sitting and calling to pug, or is it Amen-Ra, and trying to keep him from the flower-beds, was almost too much for me. Gracious! That is, I do not intend to imply *Amen-Ra* be kept from the flower-beds—"

Edmund said no more to either lady; but going quietly to another table, on which the supper-tray yet remained, brought a glass of Madeira to Fanny, and obliged her to drink the greater

[9] Gentle Reader, I dare say, your thoughts are again rather unseemly.

part. She wished to be able to decline it; but the tears, which a variety of feelings created, made it easier to swallow than to speak.

Vexed as Edmund was with his mother and aunt, he was still more angry with himself. His own forgetfulness of her was worse than anything which they had done. Nothing of this would have happened had she been properly considered. But she had been left four days without any choice of companions or riding exercise, and without any excuse for avoiding whatever her unreasonable aunts might require. He was ashamed, and very seriously resolved, however unwilling he must be to check a pleasure of Miss Crawford's, that it should never happen again.

Fanny went to bed with her heart as full of Edmund's unexpected kindness as on the first evening of her arrival at the Park.

Chapter VIII

Fanny's rides recommenced the very next day. And as it was a pleasant fresh-feeling morning, Edmund trusted that her losses, both of health and pleasure, would be soon made good. While she was gone Mr. Rushworth arrived, growling randomly in his usual manner—which the rest of the fine company made a delicate point of ignoring as one might overlook the unfortunate liberties of Bedlam, if Bedlam were to possess a fine estate such as Sotherton.

In addition, Mr. Rushworth escorted his mother (who did not growl even once, though she seemed to start in abject distaste at each instance of her son's *affectation*). Mrs. Rushworth came to be civil and to shew her civility in supporting their grand plan to visit Sotherton. Mrs. Norris and her nieces were all well pleased with its revival, and an early day was named and agreed to, provided Mr. Crawford should be disengaged. On a hint from Miss Bertram, Mr. Rushworth discovered that the properest thing to be done was for him to walk down to the Parsonage directly, and call on Mr. Crawford, and inquire whether Wednesday would suit him or not.

Before his return Mrs. Grant and Miss Crawford came in. Having been out some time, and taken a different route to the house, they had not met him, seeing instead only some lumbering fellow going around in circles in the distance—such shoddy clothing he had on, and remarkably bad skin—one might almost say it was peeling. . . .

Comfortable hopes were given that Mr. Rushworth would find Mr. Crawford at home. The Sotherton scheme was mentioned of course. It was hardly possible, indeed, that anything else should be talked of, for Mrs. Norris was in high spirits about it, making occasional yapping noises. And Mrs. Rushworth, a well-meaning, pompous woman, who thought of nothing but her own and her son's concerns, had not yet given up pressing Lady Bertram to be of the party.

Lady Bertram continuously declined it, vehemently insisting she had things to do in the attic that day. But her placid and dreamlike manner of refusal made Mrs. Rushworth still think she wished to come, till Mrs. Norris's more numerous words and louder yapping tone convinced her of the truth.

"The fatigue would be a great deal too much for my sister, I assure you, my dear Mrs. Rushworth. Ten miles there, and ten back, you know. What with all the household duties that must be carried out in regards to the deliveries—we get them nigh twice a day, as you know, all of an Egyptian nature. You must excuse my sister on this occasion, and accept of our two dear girls and myself without her. Sotherton is the only place that could give her a *wish* to go so far, but it cannot be, indeed. She will have a companion in Fanny Price, so it will all do very well. And as for Edmund, as he is not here to speak for himself, I will answer for his being most happy to join the party. He can go on horseback."

Mrs. Rushworth, obliged to yield to Lady Bertram's staying at home, could only be sorry. "The loss of her ladyship's company would be a great drawback, and she should have been extremely happy to have seen the young lady too, Miss Price, who had never been at Sotherton yet, and it was a pity she should not see the place."

"You are all kindness, my dear madam," cried Mrs. Norris; "but as to Fanny, she will have opportunities in plenty of seeing Sotherton. She has time enough before her; and her going now is quite out of the question. Lady Bertram could not possibly spare her."

"Oh no! I cannot do without Fanny. She is the *one among the reeds and the lotus blossoms*—oh, that is, she—"

Mrs. Rushworth next proceeded, under the conviction that everybody must be wanting to see Sotherton, to include Miss Crawford in the invitation. And though Mrs. Grant civilly declined it on her own account, she was glad to secure any pleasure for her sister. And Mary, properly pressed and persuaded, accepted her share of the civility.

Mr. Rushworth came back from the Parsonage successful. And Edmund made his appearance just in time to learn what had been settled for Wednesday, to attend Mrs. Rushworth to her carriage, and walk half-way down the park with the two other ladies, to be sure they were safe—since peculiar *strangers* have been seen lately lurking on the property.

On his return to the breakfast-room, he found Mrs. Norris trying to make up her mind as to whether Miss Crawford's being of the party were desirable or not, or whether her brother's barouche would not be full without her. The Miss Bertrams laughed at the idea, assuring her that the barouche would hold four perfectly well, independent of the box, on which *one* might go with him.

"But why is it necessary," said Edmund, "that *only* Crawford's carriage should be employed? Why is no use to be made of my mother's chaise? I could not, when the scheme was first mentioned the other day, understand why a visit from the family were not to be made in the carriage of the family."

"What!" cried Julia: "go boxed up three in a postchaise in this weather, when we may have seats in a barouche! No, my dear Edmund, that will not quite do."

"Besides," said Maria, "I know that Mr. Crawford depends upon taking us. Indeed, he would claim it as a promise."

"And, my dear Edmund," added Mrs. Norris, "taking out *two* carriages when *one* will do, would be trouble for nothing. And, coachman is not very fond of the roads between here and Sotherton. He always complains bitterly of the narrow lanes scratching his carriage. Indeed, one should not like to have dear Sir Thomas, when he comes home, find all the varnish scratched off. And especially now, says Wilcox, there are some strange louts seen mulling about, who might be up to no good—"

"Louts? Varnish? That would not be a very handsome reason for using Mr. Crawford's," said Maria; "but the truth is, Wilcox is a stupid old fellow, and does not know how to drive. I will answer for it that we shall find no inconvenience from narrow roads on Wednesday. Not if all the vagrant populace of the county descends upon us in an attempt to rob or loot or even merely remove precious varnish with branches ripped from trees for just such an occasion!"

"There is no hardship, I suppose, nothing unpleasant," said Edmund, "in going on the barouche box."

"Unpleasant!" cried Maria: "oh dear! I believe it would be generally thought the favourite seat. There can be no comparison as to one's view of the country. Probably Miss Crawford will choose the barouche-box herself."

"There can be no objection, then, to Fanny's going with you. There can be no doubt of your having room for her."

"Fanny!" repeated Mrs. Norris; "my dear Edmund, there is no idea of her going with us. She stays with her aunt. I told Mrs. Rushworth so. She is not expected."

"You can have no reason, I imagine, madam," said he, addressing his mother, "for wishing Fanny *not* to be of the party, but as it relates to yourself, to your own comfort and arcane *schemes*. If you could do without her, you would not wish to keep her at home?"

"To be sure not, but I *cannot* do without her. Especially not this one day, when so much is to transpire—"

"You can, if I stay at home with you, as I mean to do. Indeed, I would very much like to know what is about to *transpire,* as you say."

There was a general outcry at this. "Yes," he continued, "there is no necessity for my going, and I mean to stay at home. Fanny has a great desire to see Sotherton. I know she wishes it very much. She has not often a gratification of the kind, and I am sure, ma'am, you would be glad to give her the pleasure now?"

"Oh yes! very glad, if your aunt sees no objection." Lady Bertram spoke in a dreamy manner, as though her tremulous insistence of moments before had meant nothing.

Mrs. Norris was very ready with the only objection which could remain—their having positively assured Mrs. Rushworth that Fanny could not go, which seemed to her a difficulty quite impossible to be got over. Mrs. Norris had no affection for Fanny, no wish of procuring her pleasure at any time. But her opposition to Edmund *now,* arose more from partiality for her own scheme, because it *was* her own, than from anything else.

Edmund told her that she need not distress herself on Mrs. Rushworth's account. He had taken the opportunity, as he walked with her through the hall, of mentioning Miss Price as one who would probably be of the party, and had received a very sufficient invitation for his cousin. Mrs. Norris was too much vexed to submit with a very good grace, and would only say, "Very well, just as you chuse, settle it your own way, Grrrr! Ayyy! Ahem—I am sure I do not care about it."

"It seems very odd," said Maria, "that you should be staying at home instead of Fanny."

"I am sure she ought to be very much obliged to you," added Julia, hastily leaving the room as she spoke, from a consciousness that she ought to offer to stay at home herself.

"Fanny will feel quite as grateful as the occasion requires," was Edmund's only reply, and the subject dropt.

Fanny's gratitude, when she heard the plan, was, in fact, much greater than her pleasure. She felt Edmund's kindness with all the sensibility which he, unsuspicious of her fond attachment, could be aware of. But that he should forego any enjoyment on her account gave her pain, and her own satisfaction in seeing Sotherton would be nothing without him.

The next meeting of the two Mansfield families produced another alteration in the plan, and one that was admitted with general approbation. Mrs. Grant offered herself as companion for the day to Lady Bertram in lieu of her son, and Dr. Grant was to join them at dinner. Lady Bertram was very well pleased to have it so, and the young ladies were in spirits again. Even Edmund was very thankful for an arrangement which restored him to his share of the party. And Mrs. Norris thought it an excellent plan.

Wednesday was fine, and soon after breakfast the barouche arrived, Mr. Crawford driving his sisters. Since everybody was ready, there was nothing to be done but for Mrs. Grant to alight and the others to take their places. The place of all places, the envied seat, the post of honour, was unappropriated. To whose happy lot was it to fall? While each of the Miss Bertrams were meditating how best (and with the most appearance of obliging the others) to secure it, the matter was settled by Mrs. Grant's saying, as she stepped from the carriage, "As there are five of you, it will be better that one should sit with Henry. As you were saying lately that you wished you could drive, Julia, I think this will be a good opportunity for you to take a lesson."

Happy Julia! Unhappy Maria! The former was on the barouche-box in a moment, the latter took her seat within, in gloom and mortification; and the carriage drove off amid the good wishes of the two remaining ladies, and the barking of pug in his mistress's arms—

And, a somewhat unusual creaking of wooden crates stored all around the estate, and the consequent *stirring* of their mummified occupants. . . .

It was indeed the Moment.

Lady Bertram immediately came up with a scheme to occupy Mrs. Grant in the drawing room with some needlework and excused herself, saying "she will be away for just a moment or two." She then left the chamber.

Finding herself at last *truly* all alone, but for the pug and the bounty of Egypt, Lady Bertram betoke herself upstairs immediately, rushing rather breathlessly, and then walked in the dimness of the attic corridor, past Fanny's little room and paused before another—the door of the mysterious chamber that she visited so often. She turned the lock and then opened it.

And at last, dear Reader, we may follow Lady Bertram inside.

Within the room, was darkness. The windows were shaded by thick curtains against the bright morning, and Lady Bertram went to it and drew one of the curtains aside in a narrow slit, to give herself some illumination.

What the light of day revealed was no less than the innards of a burial chamber in the grandest pyramid of Egypt. In the center, upon a slab, lay a long sarcophagus, decorated with lapis and precious gold. All around stood various statuary of gods bearing the heads of crocodile, falcon, cat, ibis, and other unnamed creature-beasts; there were precious jars, vases, pots, chests and boxes, containing all the household goods of an unnamed pharaoh who had walked the earth three thousand years ago. Leaning in the corners were great gilded spears, bows and arrows, swords and axes of the guardians of the pharaoh, life-sized wooden figures who sat in stooped positions all around the perimeter, interspersed with occasional mummified baboons, cats and canines. Oh, and a crocodile—the long crocodile mummy lay in the deepest corner on top of a golden chest.

Lady Bertram took in the splendid and terrifying sight without batting an eyelash, and then took steps that drew her just at the foot of the sarcophagus. She slowly picked up a nearby small casket that spanned two arms at most, and removed a number of sacred amulets, including a forked dagger, a serpent-headed dagger and something that might have been a stunted crooked poker, but was instead a censer bearing the remote resemblance of a human hand and arm. In a momentary daze she stood, holding the items without comprehension. Then she laid them out on a small side table that appeared to be just for such a purpose, and already contained an unopened book scroll.

And only then did Lady Bertram use both hands to lift the heavy golden lid of the sarcophagus and drag it aside with a horrendous scrape.

Within, lay a human figure wrapped from head to foot in flimsy decaying fine linen the color of yellow and rust, and obscured with a layer of dust.

It was still, unmoving, dead to the world, as only a thing of three thousand years could be.

"The Opening of the Mouth Ceremony is started!" exclaimed Lady Bertram. She took up the hand-shaped crooked amulet and raised it before her, waving it through the air and then resting it gently on the area where would be the mummy's lips. Then with the other hand she took up the book scroll—none other than the *Book of the Dead*—and began to read the words of awakening:

My lips are parted by bright Ptah,
My mouth is opened by the god who rules my birth.
Thoth defeats Seth to control my movement of lips.
Aten gives strength and motion to my—Achoo!

—my arms—

Lady Bertram sneezed, coughed delicately to clear her throat, then continued:

My mouth is bestowed by the ones who guard me.
With the metal of his making Ptah fills my mouth,
The same metal that opened all mouths.
Sekhmet-Wadjet from the west, Sahyt rules all souls.
I am ruled by them, my mouth is mine.
My Dream is broken and I Rise and Speak and Live.
Rise! Speak! Live!

And as the last words slithered from Lady Bertram's somewhat mumbling lips, she then said a sentence or two in a completely foreign tongue, and waved the various amulets about like cutlery at suppertime.

The attic room began to rumble and shake.

The Mummy's sunken chest rose and fell. And then it sat up, slowly, until it was upright. Linen bits went flapping all around, and dust arose, as the Mummy then slowly lifted one desiccated wrapped leg over the side of the sarcophagus, then the other. And then it stood up, teetering, and raised one arm, and underneath the linen its mouth moved and rounded into a concave circular orifice.

It seemed the Mummy strove to speak, but yet could not.

"Oh dear, well then," said the brave lady, trying to make the Mummy feel more comfortable, all things considered. Then she continued in a much firmer tone. "Well, I do bid you welcome to the world and to our splendid isle of Majesty's Great Britain, My Lord, O Great Pharaoh. 'Tis truly a veritable delight, a rare pleasure to have you here under my roof, you must be—ahem—*parched* and famished. The world has certainly changed since oh-so-many years ago, and naturally you might have questions. May I offer you a gooseberry tart? Fanny does harbor a liking of them and so does Julia—"

The Mummy apparently found its voice at last.

Out came the most horrid bellow that Lady Bertram had ever had the misfortune of hearing.

But the lady was rather nonplussed. "Oh dear," she said. "I don't suppose I ought to have some tea brought up instead?"

"RWAH! RWAHARRR!" said the Mummy, now raising both hands.

"A rack of lamb? Beg pardon?"

"ARRWAW WAY WARRRTH!"

"Oh dear!" Lady Bertram wrung her hands. "Does your Mummyship perchance mean to request—"

"AWRAW WOWW WAUTH!"

"Oh dear! Oh dear! Whatever does that signify? Perchance—*a rat gone south?* No? Goodness, I do not think we have rats. That is, I am certain we do not allow them on the premises. Verily, I must insist, that no matter the customs of your own dear bygone Egypt, here we do not consume vermin, particularly not in this household—my dear sister Norris, being the one exception, of course. Or, is it arcane pharaonic code for some other particular royal need—"

"UMWAWP MAH WOUTH!"

"A whap of vermouth? Whatever could that be? I *am* sorry—"

"AAAAAAAAAARGH!" The Mummy shook its upraised hands, howling mightily. It appeared to be in frustrated distress.

"UNWAWP MY WOUTH!"

"Oh! Oh! Yes! Indeed, now I understand, *unwrap my mouth!* Why, by all means I shall." And Lady Bertram hurried to oblige.

The Mummy lowered both arms in sudden relief and nodded its head slowly, while the good lady worked on its facial area with a sharpened tool, ripping ancient cotton to make a proper hole as though it were nothing more than embroidery, all the while making soothing cooing noises, as though talking to pug.

"There you are!" she added, when the gruesome task was done. "All nice and comfortable, so your Lordly Mummyship might speak properly."

And the Mummy spoke indeed. Its chest made a motion to bellow its lungs, with the sound of a hiss in old sails.

"I am free," it finally said, speaking the English tongue with odd peculiarity, in a voice hollow and gravelly and sounding like a faraway wind from an ancient desert.

"I am free and *I hunger.*"

Their road was through a pleasant country; and Fanny, whose rides had never been extensive, was very happy in observing all that was new, and admiring all that was pretty. She was not often invited to join in the conversation of the others, nor did she desire it. Her own thoughts and reflections were her best companions. And, in observing the appearance of the country, the bearings of the roads, the difference of soil, the state of the harvest, the cottages, the cattle, the children, the occasional lumbering figures walking in circles, she found entertainment that could only have been heightened by having Edmund to speak to of what she felt.

That was the only point of resemblance between her and the lady who sat by her—in everything but a value for Edmund, Miss Crawford was very unlike her. She had none of Fanny's delicacy of taste, of mind, of feeling. She saw inanimate Nature, with little observation. Her attention was all for men and women, her talents for the light and lively (and in other ways still hidden, for the *dark)*. In looking back after Edmund, however, when there was any stretch of road behind them, or when he gained on them in ascending a hill, they were united, and a "there he is" broke at the same moment from them both, more than once.

"Oh no, that is decidedly not Edmund, but some odd fellow—there, did you see how he just walked directly into the shrubbery? How odd! Oh, there he goes again, as though banging against a wall—well, never mind. He is gone now—"

For the first seven miles Miss Bertram had very little real comfort: her prospect always ended in Mr. Crawford and her sister sitting side by side, full of conversation and merriment. To see only his expressive profile, as he turned with a smile to Julia, or to catch the laugh of the other, was a perpetual source of irritation. Her own sense of propriety could barely smooth it over. When Julia looked back, it was with a countenance of delight, and whenever she spoke, it was in the highest spirits: "her view of the country was charming, she wished they could all see it," etc. But her only offer of exchange was addressed to Miss Crawford, as they gained the summit of a long hill, and was not more inviting than this: "Here is a fine burst of country. I wish you had my seat, but I dare say you will not take it, let me press you ever so much;" and Miss Crawford could hardly answer before they were moving again at a good pace.

When they came within the influence of Sotherton associations, it was better for Miss Bertram, who might be said to have two strings to her bow. She had Rushworth feelings, and Crawford feelings, and in the vicinity of Sotherton the former had considerable effect. Mr. Rushworth's consequence was hers. She could not tell Miss Crawford that "those woods belonged to Sotherton," she could not carelessly observe that "she believed that it was now all Mr. Rushworth's property on each side of the road," without elation of heart. And this pleasure only increased with their approach to the capital freehold mansion, and ancient manorial residence of the family, with all its rights of court-leet and court-baron.

"Now we shall have no more rough road, Miss Crawford; our difficulties are over. The rest of the way is such as it ought to be. Mr. Rushworth has made it since he succeeded to the estate. Here begins the village. Those cottages are really a disgrace. That fellow over there, stumbling around disgracefully—merely ignore him. The church spire is reckoned remarkably handsome. I am glad the church is not so close to the great house as often happens in old places. The annoyance of the bells must be terrible. There is the parsonage: a tidy-looking house, and I understand the clergyman and his wife are very decent people. Those are almshouses, built by some of the family. To the right is the steward's house; he is a very respectable man. No, that is not the steward himself—looks like another lumbering fellow, also very odd looking, raggedy, with unsightly skin—do please ignore him. Now we are coming to the lodge-gates; but we have nearly a mile through the park still. It is not ugly, you see, at this end; there is some fine timber, but the situation of the house is dreadful. We go down hill to it for half a mile, past those two oddly staggering ruffians—whatever is with so many peculiar drunks? Look, there goes one, walking right into the other as though he were a post! —and it is a pity, for it would not be an ill-looking place if it had a better approach and fewer rabble."

Miss Crawford was not slow to admire. She pretty well guessed Miss Bertram's feelings, and made it a point of honour to promote her enjoyment to the utmost. Mrs. Norris was all delight and volubility and yelps. Even Fanny had something to say in admiration, and might be heard with complacency. Her eye was eagerly taking in everything within her reach. And after being at some pains to get a view of the house, and observing that "it was a sort of building which she must look at with respect," she added: "Now, where is the avenue? The house fronts the east, I perceive. The avenue, therefore, must be at the back of it. Mr. Rushworth talked of the west front."

"Yes, it is exactly behind the house; begins at a little distance, and ascends for half a mile to the extremity of the grounds. You may see something of it here—the more distant trees. It is oak entirely."

Miss Bertram could now speak with decided information of what she knew nothing about when Mr. Rushworth had asked her opinion. And her spirits were in as happy a flutter as vanity and pride could furnish, when they drove up to the spacious stone steps before the principal entrance.

In the meantime, back at Mansfield Park, we return, dear Reader, to Lady Bertram and the ancient newly resurrected Mummy, conversing politely in the attic.

"I hunger!" repeated the great Lord of Egypt, and it took one step closer toward Her Ladyship.

Her Ladyship took one petite step back, wrung her skirts with both hands, but held her ground.

"I shall fetch the cook immediately!" she exclaimed. "What would you prefer, My Great Lord? We have partridges and pheasant in the larder, and I believe there has been a nice front portion of beef sent from the butcher's—"

"I hunger!" repeated the Mummy for yet another time, and Lady Bertram used a bell pull to summon the servant.

Minutes later a young maid was curtsying at the doors, not daring to center this normally forbidden attic chamber.

"Come in, come in, Galston. Now, the gentleman, our noble guest, would like a bite to eat, so you must hereby inform cook we need—"

But Lady Bertram's words were cut off by a piercing shriek as poor Galston peered inside and saw the monstrous figure of the undead Mummy.

"Oh, stop that. How ungracious, girl. Get in here and beg pardon of His Mummified Lordship!" Lady Bertram pushed her poor serving maid inside and closed the door behind them.

The Mummy turned, raising its arms forward, and beckoned to the maidservant. "Yes! Come!" it spoke, its mouth orifice moving akin to a pit of darkness, "I will feed upon your life."

"If you please, only just a tad, Your Mummyship," muttered Lady Bertram. "Galston is required for later, for the laundering tasks—"

The young girl approached, suddenly mesmerized, taking tottering steps toward the Mummy. No longer afraid, she heard only sweet music from a distant land, and a voice of her beloved, calling her. . . .

"Ahem!" said Lady Bertram. "Now then, that's settled. Though, wouldn't Your Lordship rather have a nice steak or a rack of lamb?"

The Mummy put its swaddled hand upon the maid's forehead and suddenly there was a crackle of energy, bluish lightning in the air. The girl shuddered under the touch, and in a matter of seconds collapsed and fell.

"Oh, dear . . ." Lady Bertram muttered. "Whatever was that? Are you all right, Galston? What are you doing on the floor? Why is she on the floor? Will she be able to do laundry?"

"She has given me life," replied the Mummy.

"Not all of it, I hope! She is, as I dare say, required. Begging all pardon of your Pharaonic Lordship, of course."

But the Mummy regarded Lady Bertram in momentary silence. He was *changing.*

His voice was much stronger and the echoes of remote ages past was less prominent. While, at the same time he seemed to stand up with more solidity and the outlines of his figure under the linen had gained bulk. "I have taken much but not all. Fear not, My Servant, this one still lives and will recover. But I must have more. Bring me—others. Many others, such as herself. For now that I am free, my children are also waking and must feed vicariously through me, until we have all regained true life."

"Goodness, a large dinner party, then," muttered Lady Bertram. "Oh!" And then, just for one instant, regaining a bit of her real self, her eyes grew round, and she suddenly fainted, landing directly upon the motionless figure of Galston.

The Mummy stepped over them both with stiff creaking steps, approached the door, and exited the chamber.

Chapter IX

Mr. Rushworth was at the door to receive his fair lady; and the whole party were welcomed by him with due attention. In the drawing-room they were met with equal cordiality by the mother, and Miss Bertram had all the distinction with each that she could wish.

After the business of arriving was over, it was first necessary to eat, and the doors were thrown open to admit them through intermediate rooms into the appointed dining-parlour, where a collation was prepared with abundance and elegance. Much was said, and much was ate, and all went well. The particular object of the day was then considered. How would Mr. Crawford like, in what manner would he chuse, to take a survey of the grounds? Mr. Rushworth mentioned his curricle. Mr. Crawford suggested the greater desirableness of some carriage which might convey more than two. "To be depriving themselves of the advantage of other eyes and other judgments, might be an evil even beyond the loss of present pleasure."

Mrs. Rushworth proposed that the chaise should be taken also. But this was scarcely received as an amendment: the young ladies neither smiled nor spoke. Her next proposition, of shewing the house to such of them as had not been there before, was more acceptable, for Miss Bertram was pleased to have its size displayed, and all were glad to be doing something.

The whole party rose accordingly, and under Mrs. Rushworth's guidance were shewn through a number of rooms, all lofty, and many large, and amply furnished in the taste of fifty years back, with shining floors, solid mahogany, rich damask, marble, gilding, and carving, each handsome in its way.

"Ah what a true delight, sister!" whispered Julia to Maria, "to see nary a crocodile-headed entity nor a roll of papyrus in sight. You will be very fortunate indeed to abide here and not stumble upon crates underfoot."

"One couldn't agree more."

Of pictures there were abundance, and some few good, but the larger part were family portraits, no longer anything to anybody but Mrs. Rushworth, who had been at great pains to learn all that the housekeeper could teach, and was now almost equally well qualified to shew the house. On the present occasion she addressed herself chiefly to Miss Crawford and Fanny, but there was no comparison in the willingness of their attention. Miss Crawford, who had seen scores of great houses, and cared for none of them, had only the appearance of civilly listening. Fanny, however, to whom everything was interesting and new, attended with unaffected earnestness to all that Mrs. Rushworth could relate of the family in former times, its rise and grandeur, regal visits and loyal efforts. She was delighted to connect anything with history already known, or warm her imagination with scenes of the past.

The situation of the house excluded the possibility of much prospect from any of the rooms. While Fanny and some of the others were attending Mrs. Rushworth, Henry Crawford was looking grave and shaking his head at the windows. Every room on the west front looked across a lawn to the beginning of the avenue immediately beyond tall iron palisades and gates.

Having visited more rooms than could only contribute to the window-tax, and find employment for housemaids, "Now," said Mrs. Rushworth, "we are coming to the chapel, which properly we ought to enter from above, and look down upon. But as we are quite among friends, I will take you in this way."

They entered, and Miss Crawford went last, after a moment of inexplicable hesitation.

Fanny's imagination had prepared her for something grander than a mere spacious, oblong room, fitted up for the purpose of devotion. There was nothing striking or solemn other than the profusion of mahogany, and the crimson velvet cushions appearing over the ledge of the family gallery above.

"I am disappointed," said she, in a low voice, to Edmund. "This is not my idea of a chapel. There is nothing awe-inspiring here, or melancholy, or grand. Here are no aisles, no arches, no inscriptions. No banners, cousin, to be 'blown by the night wind of heaven.' No signs that a 'Scottish monarch sleeps below.'"

"You forget, Fanny, how recently all this has been built, and for how confined a purpose, compared with the old chapels of castles and monasteries. It was only for the private use of the family. They have been buried, I suppose, in the parish church. *There* you must look for the banners and the achievements."

"It was foolish of me not to think of all that; but I am disappointed. I suppose that with an imagination accustomed to hoary wonders and Curses of Mansfield Park, all else pales in comparison."

"Hush! Speak not of the Unmentionable," retorted Edmund, but he wore a fleeting smile.

Mrs. Rushworth began her relation. "This chapel was fitted up as you see it, in James the Second's time—"

But before the dear lady could speak another word, came a sudden and rather dire interruption—a horrendous flutter of wings and a sound of screaming fowl, rude and terrifying.

Something came forth from beyond the pews in the back . . . something large and casting violent beating shadows about the chapel, the shadows of rapidly beating furious wings.

Maria gave a small scream, Julia exclaimed, while a few of the gentlemen instinctively put their hands up to protect themselves from the aerial assault.

The thing, flying like a hawk from heavens, large and of an indeterminate color—for it was moving too fast to tell—was neither an angel nor demon of hell, in this holy abode. However, this thing, this *creature,* made its way directly at none other than Miss Crawford.

With viciousness unbounded, indeed unexhibited by any normal fowl, it screeched, low and horn-like, and beat itself, threw itself, *hurled* itself like a banshee into Miss Crawford's face.

"Oh dear God!" said Edmund. "No, it cannot be! Not Tom's—not his own—not here—"

Miss Crawford however was undaunted, and she moved very fast (almost preternaturally so) to beat the attacking creature away from her, using her bonnet as a shield to cover her features, and raising her elbow in a crook to extend the protection around the rest of her person.

"Oh yes! Yes, it is, it must be!" cried Fanny. "Cousin, you are correct to surmise, I see the same dove-grey markings on its plumage, the white tips of feathers, yes—"

"*What?* What is it?" exclaimed Mr. Crawford in frustration, too stunned to come to his sister's aid.

"It cannot be," continued Edmund, "but surely it is indeed Tom's—duck! The *duck* from Brighton! The one that had viciously flown into our mother's face! I remember, father told him to get rid of it immediately, of course, but Tom had no heart to put it down. . . . Thus, if I recall correctly, he set it loose somewhere in the back of the stables, next to his mechanical contraption with all that steam and gears and—"

"Why yes, I remember too, cousin!" said Fanny. "The duck was rather beastly, the terror of the hens, and then, I believe it went wild, and, I suppose, was not seen again—"

"Not until now! You are absolutely right, Fanny, this is it," exclaimed Julia, joining their reminiscences, "this is none other than the Brighton Duck! Silly Tom and his wild schemes!"

"Well yes," said Maria, recovering her composure, "I also see it now, the resemblance—it must be the horrid creature. But—whatever is it doing here? So far away from Mansfield Park? How did it get here?"

"I can only venture to guess," said Edmund, "it must have followed us, by perching on the barouche just now. Or possibly it took a ride during another one of the trips between our households—

"Is it possible it *flew?*" said Julia.

"Oh, for heaven's sake, does it matter?" hissed Mrs. Norris, beginning to make urgent yelping noises.

Miss Crawford meanwhile continued to beat off the attacking duck that had relentlessly chosen her for its target, and was flying around in circles, dive-bombing her.

"My dear! Oh!" exclaimed Mrs. Rushworth at last, putting a hand to her heart. "Upon my word, would someone *please* assist Miss Crawford in her struggle? Get this foul creature out of here! Immediately! This is, after all, designed to be a House of God—James, *do* something!"

Mr. Rushworth, taking control of the situation indeed, in particular to show his masterly nature to his bride-to-be, took up a cane and used it to swat wildly in the direction of the flying duck—but, to little effect, it must be admitted. He was holding himself back—his wolfish growls and the hunter instinct—altogether too much to be of any use as a civilized defender and combatant.

The Brighton Duck meanwhile gave a series of terrifying loud honks, the sound of which echoed and resounded through the stillness of the chapel. And then, making another final pass at Miss Crawford, it rose higher, circling, and then, faster than a swallow, it betook itself out the open door and out of the chapel.

It was gone without a sound.

There were several long moments of stunned silence.

Then, everyone let out a sigh of relief.

"My dear Miss Crawford!" said Edmund at last, still stupefied from the indescribable *occurrence*. "Are you unhurt, I pray?"

Miss Crawford calmly shook off the front of her dress, and plucked a loose duck feather from her sleeve, then cleared her throat. Then, with a little smirk, she replied. "Yes, I do believe I am perfectly well and rather undisturbed, all things considered. Well! that was a lovely interlude. By Jove! The things one sees out in the country!" And turning to Mrs. Rushworth, she said, "My *very* dear Mrs. Rushworth, I beg all pardons for this outrageous silliness; but please, do go on with your story."

"Well, if you are certain you are well, my dear," said Mrs. Rushworth. Then, clearing her throat, she resumed her lecture. "As I was saying, this fine chapel was fitted up as you all see it now, in James the Second's time. Before that period, the pews were only wainscot. And there is reason to think that the linings and cushions of the pulpit and family seat were only purple cloth—"

"And yet, I wonder why the duck chose Miss Crawford?" Fanny could not rest her curiosity, and whispered to Edmund, while Mrs. Rushworth was speaking. "Why chuse *her,* and only her, of all of us here present—"

"Heaven only knows, Fanny, Heaven only knows," he replied in a like whisper. "It has proven to be a vicious creature. There is no accounting for its madness."

Mrs. Rushworth was saying, "It is a handsome chapel, and was formerly in constant use both morning and evening.

Prayers were always read in it by the domestic chaplain, within the memory of many; but the late Mr. Rushworth left it off."

"Every generation has its improvements," said Miss Crawford, with a fixed smile, to Edmund. She seemed to be well recovered from the extremely odd incident of moments earlier and now stood a bit farther away than everyone else from the pulpit. Other than the one smile she put on for Edmund, during other moments she had a closed, tight-lipped expression, as though suffering a tad of vaporous indigestion.

Mrs. Rushworth was gone to repeat her lesson to Mr. Crawford.

Edmund, Fanny, and Miss Crawford remained in a cluster together, considering the chapel history. There was an unspoken decision from that point forward, to no longer make mention of the *duck*.

"It is a pity," cried Fanny, "that the prayer custom was discontinued. It was a valuable part of former times. A whole family assembling regularly for the purpose of prayer is fine!"

"Very fine indeed," said Miss Crawford, laughing. "It must do the heads of the family a great deal of good to force all the poor housemaids and footmen to leave business and pleasure, and say their prayers here twice a day, while they are inventing excuses themselves for staying away."

"*That* is hardly Fanny's idea of a family assembling," said Edmund. "If the master and mistress do *not* attend themselves, there must be more harm than good in the custom."

"At any rate, it is safer to leave people to their own devices on such subjects. Everybody likes to go their own way—to chuse their own time and manner of devotion. Nobody likes the obligation of attendance, the formality, the restraint, the length of time. If the good people who used to kneel and gape in that gallery could have foreseen that the time would ever come when men and women might lie another ten minutes in bed, when they woke with a headache, without danger of reprobation, because chapel was missed, they would have jumped with joy and envy. Cannot you imagine with what unwilling feelings the former belles of the house of Rushworth did many a time repair to this chapel? The young Mrs. Eleanors and Mrs. Bridgets—starched up into seeming piety, but with heads full of something very different—with no sudden flying fowl to relieve them of their long moments of stupor—or especially if the poor chaplain were not worth looking at—and, in those days, I fancy parsons were very inferior even to what they are now."

For a few moments she was unanswered. Fanny coloured and looked at Edmund, but felt too angry for speech. He too needed a little recollection before he could say, "Your lively mind can hardly be serious even on serious subjects. You have given us an amusing sketch, and human nature cannot say it was not so. We must all feel *at times* the difficulty of fixing our thoughts as we could wish. But if you are supposing it a frequent thing—a weakness grown into a habit from neglect—what could be expected from the *private* devotions of such persons? Do you think the minds which suffer, which are indulged in wanderings in a chapel, would be more collected in a closet?"

"Yes, very likely. There would be less to distract the attention from without, and it would not be tried so long."

And Miss Crawford looked sideways and with an inexplicable *something* or other, in the direction of a crucifix.

"The mind which does not struggle against itself under *one* circumstance, would find objects to distract it in the *other*. The influence of place and example may often rouse better feelings eventually. However, the greater length of the service, I admit to be sometimes too hard a stretch upon the mind. One wishes it were not so; but I have not yet left Oxford long enough to forget what chapel prayers are."

While this was passing, the rest of the party being scattered about the chapel, Julia called Mr. Crawford's attention to her sister, by saying, "Do look at Mr. Rushworth and Maria, standing side by side, exactly as if the ceremony were going to be performed. Have not they completely the air of it?"

Mr. Crawford smiled his acquiescence, and stepping forward to Maria, said, in a voice which she only could hear, "I do not like to see Miss Bertram so near the altar."

Starting, the lady instinctively moved a step or two, but recovering herself in a moment, affected to laugh, and asked him, in a tone not much louder, "If he would give her away?"

"I am afraid I should do it very awkwardly," was his reply, with a look of meaning.

Julia, joining them at the moment, carried on the joke.

"Upon my word, it is really a pity that it should not take place directly, if we had but a proper license. For here we are altogether, and nothing in the world could be more snug and pleasant." And she talked and laughed about it with so little caution as to catch the comprehension of Mr. Rushworth and his mother, and expose her sister to the whispered gallantries of her lover, while Mrs. Rushworth spoke with proper smiles and dignity of its being a most happy event to her whenever it took place.

"If Edmund were but in orders!" cried Julia, and running to where he stood with Miss Crawford and Fanny: "My dear Edmund, if you were but in orders now, you might perform the ceremony directly. How unlucky that you are not ordained; Mr. Rushworth and Maria are quite ready."

Miss Crawford's countenance, as Julia spoke, might have amused a disinterested observer. No vicious flying demon fowl-spawn from hell could ever do the damage that a single spoken line of information could accomplish. Miss Crawford looked almost aghast under the new idea she was receiving. Fanny pitied her. "How distressed she will be at what she said just now," passed across her mind.

"Ordained!" said Miss Crawford; "what, are you to be a clergyman?"

"Yes; I shall take orders soon after my father's return—probably at Christmas."

Miss Crawford rallied her spirits, and recovered her complexion—yet for the second time in one half hour. "If I had known this before, I would have spoken of the cloth with more respect," she said, and changed the subject.

The chapel was soon afterwards left to the silence and stillness which reigned in it. Miss Bertram, displeased with her sister, led the way, and all seemed to feel that they had been there long enough.

The lower part of the house was now entirely shewn. Mrs. Rushworth, never weary in the cause, would have proceeded towards the principal staircase, and taken them through all the rooms above, if her son had not interposed with a doubt of there being time enough. "For if," said he, "we are *too* long going over the house, we shall not have time for what is to be done out of doors. It is past two, and we are to dine at five. Grroooowwwrrrgh! Ahem."

Mrs. Rushworth submitted. The question of surveying the grounds, with the who and the how, was likely to be more fully agitated, and Mrs. Norris was beginning to arrange by what junction of carriages and horses most could be done, when the young people, meeting with an outward door—temptingly open on a flight of steps which led immediately to turf and shrubs, and all the sweets of pleasure-grounds—as by one impulse, one wish for air and liberty, all walked out.

"Suppose we turn down here for the present," said Mrs. Rushworth, civilly taking the hint and following them. "Here are the greatest number of our plants, and the curious pheasants."

"Query," said Mr. Crawford, looking round him, "whether we may not find something to employ us here before we go farther? I see walls of great promise. Mr. Rushworth, shall we summon a council on this lawn?"

"James," said Mrs. Rushworth to her son, "I believe the wilderness will be new to all the party. The Miss Bertrams have never seen the wilderness yet. I trust you to—ahem—*handle* yourself. And if you run into the horrid duck creature that attacked Miss Crawford, pray, handle *it*."

No objection was made, but for some time there seemed no inclination to move in any plan, or to any distance. All were attracted at first by the plants or the pheasants, and all dispersed about in happy independence.

Mr. Crawford was the first to move forward to examine the capabilities of that end of the house. The lawn, bounded on each side by a high wall, contained beyond the first planted area a bowling-green. And farther yet, a long terrace walk, backed by iron palisades, and commanding a view over them into the tops of the trees of the wilderness immediately adjoining.

It was a good spot for fault-finding. Mr. Crawford was soon followed by Miss Bertram and Mr. Rushworth. When the others began to form into parties, these three were found in busy consultation on the terrace by Edmund, Miss Crawford, and Fanny, who seemed as naturally to unite, and who, after a short participation, left them and walked on.

The remaining three, Mrs. Rushworth, Mrs. Norris, and Julia, were still far behind. Julia, whose happy star no longer prevailed, was obliged to keep by the side of Mrs. Rushworth, and restrain her impatient feet to that lady's slow pace. Meanwhile her aunt, having fallen in with the housekeeper, who was out to feed the pheasants, was lingering behind in gossip.

Poor Julia, the only one out of the nine not tolerably satisfied with her lot, was now in a state of complete penance—as different from the Julia of the barouche-box as could be imagined. The politeness with which she had been brought up made it impossible for her to escape; while the lack of consideration of others (never an essential part of her education), made her miserable under it.

"This is insufferably hot," said Miss Crawford, appearing almost morbidly grey-complexioned in the bright sunlight, when they had taken one turn on the terrace, and were drawing a second time to the door in the middle which opened to the wilderness. "Shall any of us object to being comfortable? Here is a nice little wood, if one can but get into it. What happiness if the door were unlocked! but of course it is. In these great places the gardeners are the only people who can go where they like."

The door, however, proved not to be locked, and they were all agreed in turning joyfully through it, and leaving the unmitigated glare of day behind. A considerable flight of steps landed them in the wilderness, which was a planted wood of about two acres. Though chiefly of larch and laurel and beech cut down and laid out with too much regularity, it was darkness and shade, and natural beauty, compared with the bowling-green and the terrace.

In the group behind them, Mr. Rushworth forgot himself momentarily and started to growl and sniff the air in the enthusiastic manner of a hound who's scented prey—so loudly that he could be heard miles away. They all felt the refreshment of it—not as hounds, of course, but in a more civilized fashion—and for some time could only walk and admire.

At length, after a short pause, Miss Crawford who had recovered considerably in the shadows, began with, "So you are to be a clergyman, Mr. Bertram. This is rather a surprise to me."

"Why should it surprise you? You must suppose me designed for some profession, and might perceive that I am neither a lawyer, nor a soldier, nor a sailor."

"Very true; but, in short, it had not occurred to me. And you know there is generally an uncle or a grandfather to leave a fortune to the second son."

In that instant, elsewhere, Mr. Rushworth made an enthusiastic yelp at the sight of a squirrel racing on a tree branch, then pretended to be clearing his throat, while Maria gave him a long withering look, and Mr. Crawford gallantly made a point of not noticing.

"A very praiseworthy practice," said Edmund, ignoring Mr. Rushworth's spectacle being played out in back of them, "but not quite universal. I am one of the exceptions, and *being* one, must do something for myself."

"But why are you to be a clergyman? I thought *that* was always the lot of the youngest, where there were many to chuse before him."

"Do you think the church itself never chosen, then?"

Elsewhere, came a very wolfish, very unrestrained howl.

"*Never* is a black word. But yes, in the *never* of conversation, which means *not very often,* I do think it. For what is to be done in the church? Men love to distinguish themselves, and in either of the other lines distinction may be gained, but not in the church. A clergyman is nothing."

There was a loud crashing of shrubbery. This time both Miss Bertrams turned from their variably distant vantage points to see Mr. Rushworth make a very sudden move, despite his portly figure, in the direction of a pair of other squirrels, and break off a large portion of a low-hanging branch.

Edmund, grave in demeanor, completely ignored it.

"The *nothing* of conversation has its gradations, I hope," he said, "as well as the *never*. A clergyman cannot be high in state or fashion. He must not head mobs, or set the ton in dress. But I cannot call that situation nothing which has the charge of all that is of the first importance to mankind, individually or collectively considered, temporally and eternally, which has the guardianship of religion and morals. No one here can call the *office* nothing. If the man who holds it is so, it is by the neglect of his duty, by foregoing its just importance, and stepping out of his place to appear what he ought not to appear."

"*You* assign greater consequence to the clergyman than one has been used to hear given, or than I can quite comprehend," said Miss Crawford, while in back of them came sounds of Mr. Rushworth battling shrubbery like a locomotive derailed. "One does not see much of this influence and importance in society, and how can it be acquired where they are so seldom seen themselves? How can two sermons a week, even supposing them worth hearing, do all that you speak of? govern the conduct and fashion the manners of a large congregation for the rest of the week? One scarcely sees a clergyman out of his pulpit."

"*You* are speaking of London, *I* am speaking of the nation at large."

With an unholy growl, Mr. Rushworth had his prey at last. He emerged proudly from the greenery, with a bushy-tailed critter in his teeth. However, regaining a modicum of human reason, he immediately released it, and, wiping his mouth with his coat sleeves, attempted to whistle nonchalantly, then choked on a bit of fur.

"The metropolis, I imagine, is a pretty fair sample of the rest," continued Miss Crawford, ignoring the beastly choking sounds Mr. Rushworth made many feet away, as he doubled over from coughing and sent ringing echoes over the otherwise quiet countryside.

"Not, I should hope, of the proportion of virtue to vice throughout the kingdom. We do not look in great cities for our best morality. A fine preacher is followed and admired; but it is not in fine preaching only that a good clergyman will be useful in his parish and his neighbourhood. In London, the clergy are lost in the crowds of their parishioners. They are known to most only as preachers. And with regard to their influencing public manners, Miss Crawford must not misunderstand me, or suppose I mean to call them the arbiters of good-breeding, the regulators of refinement and courtesy. The *manners* I speak of might rather be called *conduct,* perhaps, the result of good principles."

"Certainly," said Fanny, with gentle earnestness, then turned around with concern, in the direction of the distant Mr. Rushworth.

"There," cried Miss Crawford, "you have quite convinced Miss Price already.

"I wish I could convince Miss Crawford too."

"I do not think you ever will," said she, with an arch smile; "I am just as much surprised now as I was at first that you should intend to take orders. You really are fit for something better. Come, do change your mind. It is not too late. Go into the law."

"Go into the law! With as much ease as I was told to go into this wilderness."

Mr. Rushworth was of course having no problem going into the wilderness as they were speaking, but Miss Crawford was not about to use such an argument with Edmund.

"Now you are going to say something about law being the worst wilderness of the two, but I forestall you."

"You need not hurry to prevent my saying a *bon mot,* for there is not the least wit in my nature. I am a very matter-of-fact, plain-spoken being, and may blunder on the borders of a repartee for half an hour together without striking it out."

Nearly a mile away, Mr. Rushworth stopped coughing, and now wheezed a bit as he shook leaves and grassy twigs off his coat.

A general silence succeeded at last. Each was thoughtful. Fanny made the first interruption by saying, "I wonder that I should be tired with only walking in this sweet wood. But the next time we come to a seat, if it is not disagreeable to you, I should be glad to sit down for a little while. Also, perhaps Mr. Rushworth would like to sit down for a bit also, when he catches up with us."

"My dear Fanny," cried Edmund, immediately drawing her arm within his, "how thoughtless I have been! I hope you are not very tired. Perhaps," turning to Miss Crawford, "my other companion may do me the honour of taking an arm."

"Thank you, but I am not at all tired." She took it, however, as she spoke, and the gratification of having her do so, of feeling such a connexion for the first time, made him a little forgetful of Fanny. "You scarcely touch me," said he. "You do not make me of any use. Indeed, how *cold* your hand is, in this heat! What a difference in the weight of a woman's arm from that of a man! At Oxford I have been a good deal used to have a man lean on me for the length of a street, and you are only a fly in the comparison."

"I am really not tired, which I almost wonder at; for we must have walked at least a mile in this wood. Do not you think we have?"

"Not half a mile," was his sturdy answer; for he was not yet so much in love as to measure distance, or reckon time, with feminine lawlessness.

Miss Crawford gave him a brilliant look of her suddenly very darkened and intense eyes.

"We have been exactly a quarter of an hour here," said Edmund, taking out his watch.

A few steps farther brought them out at the bottom of the very walk they had been talking of. Here, standing back, well shaded and sheltered, and looking over a ha-ha into the park, was a comfortable-sized bench, on which they all sat down.

"I am afraid you are very tired, Fanny," said Edmund, observing her; "why would not you speak sooner? This will be a bad day's amusement for you if you are worn out. Every sort of exercise fatigues her so soon, Miss Crawford, except riding."

"How abominable in you, then, to let me engross her horse as I did all last week! I am ashamed of you and of myself, but it shall never happen again."

"*Your* attentiveness and consideration makes me more sensible of my own neglect. Fanny's interest seems in safer hands with you than with me."

"I shall soon be rested," said Fanny; "to sit in the shade on a fine day, and look upon verdure, is the most perfect refreshment."

After sitting a little while Miss Crawford was up again. "I must move," said she; "resting fatigues me. I have looked across the ha-ha till I am weary. I must go and look through that iron gate at the same view, without being able to see it so well."

Edmund left the seat likewise. "Now, Miss Crawford, if you will look up the walk, you will convince yourself that it cannot be half a mile long."

"It is an immense distance," said she; "I see *that* with a glance."

He still reasoned with her, but in vain. She would not calculate, she would not compare. She would only smile and assert. At last it was agreed that they should endeavour to determine the dimensions of the wood by walking a little more about it. They would go to one end of it, and be back in a few minutes. Fanny said she was rested, but Edmund urged her to remain where she was with an earnestness she could not resist.

She was left on the bench to think with pleasure of her cousin's care, but with great regret that she was not stronger. She watched them till they had turned the corner, and listened till all sound of them had ceased.

Chapter X

A quarter of an hour, twenty minutes passed, and Fanny was still thinking of Edmund, Miss Crawford, and herself, without interruption from any one. She began to be surprised at being left so long, and to listen with an anxious desire of hearing their steps and their voices again.

For a while there she thought she heard rather unusual sounds in the greenery, distant shufflings and peculiar creature growls, and the sound of things crashing. And just once there was a terrible sound, the thunderous, unnaturally bellowing honk of a monstrous *duck*. . . .

She listened, and at length she heard voices and feet approaching; but she had just satisfied herself that it was not those she wanted, when Miss Bertram, Mr. Rushworth, and Mr. Crawford issued from the same path which she had trod herself, and were before her.

"Miss Price all alone" and "My dear Fanny, how comes this?" were the first salutations. She told her story. "Poor dear Fanny," cried her cousin, "how ill you have been used by them! You had better have staid with us."

Fanny wanted to say she felt as though she had staid with them indeed, considering how much *involvement* Mr. Rushworth had shewn with the countryside, but kindly refrained.

Then seating herself with a gentleman on each side, Maria resumed the conversation which had engaged them before, and discussed the possibility of improvements with much animation. Nothing was fixed on; but Henry Crawford was full of ideas and projects, and, generally speaking, whatever he proposed was immediately approved, first by her, and then by Mr. Rushworth, whose principal business seemed to be to hear the others, the sounds of wildlife in the trees all around, and who scarcely risked an original thought of his own.

After some minutes spent in this way, Miss Bertram, observing the iron gate, expressed a wish of passing through it into the park. It was the very thing of all others to be wished, the best, the only way of proceeding with any advantage, in Henry Crawford's opinion. And he directly saw a knoll not half a mile off, which would give them exactly the requisite command of the house. Go therefore they must to that knoll, and through that gate; but the gate was locked.

Mr. Rushworth growled to himself, wished he had brought the key. He had been very near thinking to bring the key; he was determined he would never come without the key again. But still this did not remove the present evil. They could not get through. And as Miss Bertram's inclination did not lessen, it ended in Mr. Rushworth's declaring outright that he would go and fetch the key. He set off accordingly, with a distinctive amount of wheezing and an occasional howl, followed by "Oh, blimey!"

"It is undoubtedly the best thing we can do now, as we are so far from the house already," said Mr. Crawford, when he was gone. "I dare say, what an *unusual* gentleman our excellent host is. Rather *exuberant,* shall we say."

Fanny coughed.

"Yes, there is nothing else to be done. But now, sincerely, do not you find the place worse than you expected?"

"No, indeed, far otherwise. I find it better, grander, more complete in its style, though that style may not be the best. And to tell you the truth," speaking rather lower, "I do not think that *I* shall ever see Sotherton again with so much pleasure as I do now. Another summer will hardly improve it to me."

After a moment's embarrassment the lady replied, "You are too much a man of the world not to see with the eyes of the world. If other people think Sotherton improved, I have no doubt that you will."

"I am afraid I am not quite so much the man of the world as might be good for me in some points. My feelings are not quite so evanescent, nor my memory of the past under such easy dominion as one finds to be the case with men of the world."

This was followed by a short silence, while Fanny felt the great need to disappear, but of course, could not. Miss Bertram began again. "You seemed to enjoy your drive here very much this morning. I was glad to see you so well entertained. You and Julia were laughing the whole way."

"Were we? Yes, I believe we were; but I have not the least recollection at what. Oh! I believe I was relating to her some ridiculous stories of an old Irish groom of my uncle's. Your sister loves to laugh."

"You think her more light-hearted than I am?"

"More easily amused," he replied; "consequently, you know," smiling, "better company. I could not have hoped to entertain you with Irish anecdotes during a ten miles' drive."

"Naturally, I believe, I am as lively as Julia, but I have more to think of now."

"You have, undoubtedly. And there are situations in which very high spirits would denote insensibility. Your prospects, however, are too fair to justify want of spirits. You have a very smiling scene before you."

"Do you mean literally or figuratively? Literally, I conclude. Yes, certainly, the sun shines, and the park looks very cheerful. But unluckily that iron gate, that ha-ha, give me a feeling of restraint and hardship. 'I cannot get out,' as the starling said." As she spoke, and it was with expression, she walked to the gate: he followed her. "Mr. Rushworth is so long fetching this key!"

"Mayhap, he has been detained by a rabbit." Mr. Crawford's eyes gleamed with delightfully unspoken wickedness.

Fanny coughed again.

"And for the world you would not get out without the key and without Mr. Rushworth's authority and protection, or I think you might with little difficulty pass round the edge of the gate, here, with my assistance. I think it might be done, if you really wished not to be prohibited."

"Prohibited! nonsense! I certainly can get out that way, and I will. Mr. Rushworth will be here in a moment, you know; we shall not be out of sight."

"Or if we are, Miss Price will be so good as to tell him that he will find us near that knoll: the grove of oak on the knoll."

Fanny, feeling all this to be wrong, could not help making an effort to prevent it. "You will hurt yourself, Miss Bertram," she cried; "you will certainly hurt yourself against those spikes; you will tear your gown; you will be in danger of slipping into the ha-ha. You had better not go."

Her cousin was safe on the other side while these words were spoken, and, smiling with all the good-humour of success, she said, "Thank you, my dear Fanny, but I and my gown are alive and well, and so good-bye."

Fanny was again left to her solitude, and with no increase of pleasant feelings, for she was sorry for almost all that she had seen and heard, astonished at Miss Bertram, and angry with Mr. Crawford. By taking a circuitous route, and, as it appeared to her, very unreasonable direction to the knoll, they were soon beyond her eye. For some minutes longer she remained without sight or sound of any companion. She seemed to have the little wood all to herself. She could almost have thought that Edmund and Miss Crawford had left it, but that it was impossible for Edmund to forget her so entirely.

She was again roused from disagreeable musings by sudden footsteps: somebody was coming at a quick pace down the principal walk. She expected Mr. Rushworth, but it was Julia, who, hot and out of breath, and with a look of disappointment, cried out on seeing her, "Heyday! Where are the others? I thought Maria and Mr. Crawford were with you."

Fanny explained.

"A pretty trick, upon my word! I cannot see them anywhere," looking eagerly into the park. "But they cannot be very far off, and I think I am equal to as much as Maria, even without help."

"But, Julia, Mr. Rushworth will be here in a moment with the key. Do wait for Mr. Rushworth."

"Not I, indeed. I have had enough of the family for one morning. Why, child, I have but this moment escaped from his horrible mother. Such a penance as I have been enduring, while you were sitting here so composed and so happy! It might have been as well, perhaps, if you had been in my place, but you always contrive to keep out of these scrapes."

This was a most unjust reflection, but Fanny could allow for it, and let it pass: Julia was vexed, and her temper was hasty. But she felt it would not last, and therefore, taking no notice, only asked her if she had not seen Mr. Rushworth.

"Yes, yes, we saw him. He was posting away as if upon life and death, rough as a wolfhound, and could but just spare time to tell us his errand, and where you all were."

"It is a pity he should have so much trouble for nothing."

"*That* is Miss Maria's concern. I am not obliged to punish myself for *her* sins. The mother I could not avoid, as long as my beastly tiresome aunt was dancing about with the housekeeper, but the son I *can* get away from—fortune has it, *I* am not a *squirrel*."

And Julia immediately scrambled across the fence (rather making Fanny wonder about the squirrel part), and walked away, not attending to Fanny's last question of whether she had seen anything of Miss Crawford and Edmund.

The sort of dread in which Fanny now sat of seeing Mr. Rushworth prevented her thinking so much of their continued absence. She felt that he had been very ill-used, and was quite unhappy in having to communicate what had passed. He joined her within five minutes after Julia's exit. And though she made the best of the story, he was evidently mortified and displeased. At first he scarcely said anything. Only his looks expressed his extreme surprise and vexation, and he walked to the gate and stood there, without seeming to know what to do.

"They desired me to stay—my cousin Maria charged me to say that you would find them at that knoll, or thereabouts."

"I do not believe I shall go any farther," said he sullenly; "I see nothing of them. By the time I get to the knoll they may be gone somewhere else. I have had walking enough. And for a moment or two I thought I had finally caught sight of that infernal duck. But no, it was nothing of the kind."

And he sat down with a most gloomy countenance by Fanny.

"I am very sorry," said she; "it is very unlucky. As for that fowl, I dare say you ought to be careful, for the duck—if it is indeed the same exact creature from Brighton as had menaced Lady Bertram—that one was rather elusive and unpredictable, as you could imagine from seeing it earlier today. I recommend you be on your guard, sir." And she longed to be able to say something more to the purpose, but there was genuinely nothing to add on either subject.

"Oh, with that accursed fowl, never you fear on my behalf, Miss Price," said Mr. Rushworth with a scowl of vengeance, "I can handle it. I dare say, it will be destroyed by tomorrow, I can promise you that. And it will not be pretty."

Fanny really had even less to add to that.

After an interval of silence, "I think they might as well have staid for me," said he.

"Miss Bertram thought you would follow her."

"I should not have had to follow her if she had staid."

This could not be denied, and Fanny was silenced. After another pause, he went on—"Pray, Miss Price, are you such a great admirer of this Mr. Crawford as some people are? For my part, I can see nothing in him."

"I do not think him at all handsome."

"Handsome! Nobody can call such an undersized man handsome. He is not five foot nine. I should not wonder if he is not more than five foot eight. Indeed, he has nothing on that duck; it outweighs him. I think he is an ill-looking fellow. Why, I could probably rip him to shreds in under a minute—*Ahem.* In my opinion, these Crawfords are no addition at all. We did very well without them."

A small sigh escaped Fanny here, and she did not know how to contradict him. Indeed, it might not have been a safe thing to do at all, to contradict him, even if she wanted to—not with the growls that were building in the back of his throat. . . .

"If I had made any difficulty about fetching the key, there might have been some excuse. But I went the very moment she said she wanted it."

"Nothing could be more obliging than your manner, I am sure, and I dare say you walked as fast as you could. But still it is some distance from this spot to the house, and when people are waiting, they are bad judges of time, and every half minute seems like five."

He got up and walked to the gate again, and "wished he had had the key about him at the time." Fanny thought she discerned in his standing there an indication of relenting, which encouraged her to another attempt. She said, "It is a pity you should not join them. They expected to have a better view of the house from that part of the park, and will be thinking how it may be improved; and nothing of that sort, you know, can be settled without you."

She found herself more successful in sending away than in retaining a companion. Mr. Rushworth was convinced. "Well," said he, "if you really think I had better go: it would be foolish to bring the key for nothing. And if I encounter that fowl on the way—" And letting himself out, he walked off without further ceremony.

Fanny's thoughts were now all engrossed by the two who had left her so long ago. Getting quite impatient, she resolved to go in search of them. She followed their steps along the bottom walk, when the voice and the laugh of Miss Crawford once more caught her ear. The sound approached, and a few more windings brought them before her.

They were just returned into the wilderness from the park (to which a sidegate, not fastened, had tempted them), and they had been across a portion of the park into the very avenue which Fanny had been hoping the whole morning to reach at last. Sitting down under one of the trees, it was evident that they had been spending their time pleasantly, unaware of the length of their absence.

Fanny's best consolation was in being assured that Edmund had wished for her very much—he should certainly have come back for her, had she not been tired already. But this was not quite sufficient to do away with the pain of having been left a whole hour, nor to banish the sort of curiosity she felt to know what they had been conversing about all that time. The result of the whole was to her disappointment and depression, as they prepared to return to the house.

On reaching the bottom of the steps to the terrace, Mrs. Rushworth and Mrs. Norris presented themselves at the top, just ready for the wilderness, at the end of an hour and a half from their leaving the house. Mrs. Norris had been too well employed to move faster. Whatever cross-accidents had occurred to intercept the pleasures of her nieces, she had found a morning of complete enjoyment. For the housekeeper, after discussing pheasants, had taken her to the dairy, told her all about their cows, and given her the receipt for a famous cream cheese. Since Julia left them, she had met the gardener, set him right as to his grandson's illness, convinced him that it was an ague, and promised him a charm for it. He, in return, had shewn her all his choicest nursery of plants, and actually presented her with a very curious specimen of heath.

On this *rencontre* they all returned to the house together, there to lounge away the time as they could with sofas, and chit-chat, and *Quarterly Reviews,* till the return of the others, and the arrival of dinner. It was late before the Miss Bertrams and the two gentlemen came in, and their ramble did not appear to have been more than partially agreeable, or at all productive with regard to the object of the day.

By their own accounts they had been all walking after each other, not unlike the fool denizens of *A Midsummer Night's Dream,* and the junction which had taken place at last seemed, to Fanny's observation, to be much too late for re-establishing harmony. She felt, as she looked at Julia and Mr. Rushworth, that hers was not the only dissatisfied bosom amongst them: there was gloom on the face of each. Mr. Crawford and Miss Bertram were much more gay, and she thought that he was taking particular pains, during dinner, to do away any little resentment of the other two, and restore general good-humour.

Dinner was soon followed by tea and coffee—a ten miles' drive home allowed no waste of hours. And from the time of their sitting down to table, it was a quick succession of busy nothings till the carriage came to the door.

Mrs. Norris, having fidgeted about, obtained a few pheasants' eggs and a cream cheese from the housekeeper, and made abundance of civil speeches to Mrs. Rushworth, was ready to lead the way.

At the same moment Mr. Crawford, approaching Julia, said, "I hope I am not to lose my companion, unless she is afraid of the evening air in so exposed a seat. Or perchance the renewed retribution of a flying fowl?" The playful request had not been foreseen, but was very graciously received, and Julia's day was likely to end almost as well as it began. Miss Bertram had made up her mind to something different, and was a little disappointed. But her conviction of being really the one preferred comforted and enabled her to receive Mr. Rushworth's parting attentions as she ought. He was certainly better pleased to hand her into the barouche than to assist her in ascending the box, and his complacency seemed confirmed by the arrangement.

"Well, Fanny, this has been a fine day for you, upon my word," said Mrs. Norris, as they drove through the park. "Nothing but pleasure from beginning to end! I am sure you ought to be obliged to your aunt Bertram and me for contriving to let you go. A pretty good day's amusement you have had!"

Maria was just discontented enough to say directly, "I think *you* have done pretty well yourself, ma'am. Your lap seems full of good things, and here is a basket of something between us which has been knocking my elbow unmercifully—indeed, so much like the dear Egyptian clutter of home."

"My dear, it is only a beautiful little heath, which that nice old gardener made me take. But if it is in your way, I will have it in my lap directly. There, Fanny, you shall carry that parcel for me. Take great care of it: do not let it fall; it is a cream cheese, just like the excellent one we had at dinner. Nothing would satisfy that good old Mrs. Whitaker, but my taking one of the cheeses. I stood out as long as I could, till the tears almost came into her eyes—" and she eventually concluded with—"Take care of the cheese, Fanny. Now I can manage the other parcel and the basket very well."

"What else have you been spunging?" said Maria, half-pleased that Sotherton should be so complimented.

"Spunging, my dear! It is nothing but four of those beautiful pheasants' eggs, which Mrs. Whitaker quite forced upon me. I shall get the dairymaid to set them under the first spare hen, and if they come to good I can have them moved to my own house and borrow a coop—maybe from that wild contraption of dear Tom's where all the hens sit these days—and it will be a great delight to me in my lonely hours. With luck, your mother shall have some eggs."

It was a beautiful evening, mild and still. The drive was as pleasant and serene as nature. But when Mrs. Norris ceased speaking, it was altogether a silent drive to those within. Their spirits were in general exhausted; and whether the day had afforded more pleasure or pain was not easy to surmise.

Chapter XI

The day at Sotherton, with all its imperfections, afforded the Miss Bertrams much more agreeable feelings than were derived from the letters from Antigua, which soon afterwards reached Mansfield. It was much pleasanter to think of Henry Crawford than of their father. And to think of their father in England again within a certain period (which these letters obliged them to do), was a most unwelcome exercise.

In addition, when they had returned home after that outing, it seemed something had *changed*—more so than usual, a peculiar gloom and doom difference was in the air.

Mrs. Grant sat all alone, in a trance, on the sofa in the drawing room. And Lady Bertram greeted them in an especially dazed mood, as she moved down the stairs, holding her pug in one arm and some kind of Egyptian implement in the other, while behind her trailed a maid, looking very disheveled and sickly. Both of them appeared to be distracted, periodically glancing around in a near stupor, as though searching for something—or someone.

"Did you see him, dear?" asked Lady Bertram, staring at Julia so hard that the other had to blink.

"Who, mother?"

"The great Pharaoh, of course, He has returned at last, and walks among us. Must've gone below stairs."

"Beg pardon?"

But Maria opened her eyes wide and poked Julia in the side with her umbrella stick, motioning her to hush. Obviously their mother was having one of those afternoons. Where indeed had been Mrs. Grant, away in the other room instead of watching over her?

"Why, what is it you speak of, Lady Bertram?" said Mrs. Norris, who misheard. "What farrier? Who is the great farrier? Whatever do you speak? Since when do we employ farriers?"

"Hush, please, never mind!" Maria hissed.

But Fanny and Edmund exchanged worried glances.

But there was no sign of *anyone* out of the ordinary, so they soon forgot the incident and retired for the evening. Indeed, it seemed that was the end of it. At least for the moment.

November was the black month fixed for Sir Thomas's return. His business was so nearly concluded as to justify him in proposing to take his passage in the September packet, and he consequently looked forward with the hope of being with his beloved family again soon.

Maria was more to be pitied than Julia. For to her the father brought a husband—his return would unite her to the lover on whom she had chosen her happiness should depend. It was a gloomy prospect, and all she could do was to throw a mist over it, and hope when the mist cleared away she should see something else. Much might happen in thirteen weeks.

Sir Thomas would have been deeply mortified by a suspicion of half that his daughters felt on the subject of his return, and would hardly have found consolation in a knowledge of the interest it excited in the breast of another young lady. Furthermore, Sir Thomas would have been stricken to know that Mansfield Park now had a very tangible, very dangerous, very *undead* new resident.

While the household went about their own business, the Mummy made himself quite at home in the grand attic, and commenced on feeding off the life force of the servants.

They never knew what affliction it was that had come upon them. For when he ventured forth, he could move as silence itself, and come upon them in well-shaded narrow passages and corridors of Mansfield Park. The Mummy merely needed to reach out with a feather-light touch of his hand, and the servant, footman, maid, or butler were immediately mesmerized—their thoughts and mind were carried away into the balmy ancient land of sun and sand and they heard lovers calling, saw tempting feasts, and imagined all other manner of wonder they could only desire in their dreams.

He did as he promised Lady Bertram. With each feeding, the Mummy only took a small portion of the life force, so that the servant would simply grow light-headed and either faint away, only to revive moments later, or merely felt a sudden unpleasant headache, and could easily resume their work.

Lady Bertram checked upon him frequently, running upstairs at every opportunity, and sending up servants throughout the day with minor idiot tasks that were obviously contrived, just to get them into the Mummy's chamber.

"How are we coming along now, your Pharaonic—ahem—royal—Mummyship?" asked Lady Bertram yet again, peeking in at him from the doorway. She looked at the undead creature with a bit of curiosity because each time she saw him, it seemed he looked *better*—more and more alive—by whatever miraculous means.

"You may call me—Lord Rameidas Xethesamen. Or—East Wind. For that is my name." He spoke to her only one time, in a powerful yet hollow-soft voice.

"Lord Eastwind! Ah, how delightful!"

"Delight is not to be found within my name. But—you have done well by me, My Servant," replied the Mummy. "So I will overlook your present ignorance. Very soon, I shall come among you in perfect living flesh."

Lady Bertram blinked. She, somewhat offended to be deemed ignorant, was about to voice it, then prudently thought better of such a *faux pas*. She noted that he was indeed changing before her very eyes, and now looked less a desiccated skeleton draped in skin and rags than a very tanned old sailor with a bad case of scurvy. Indeed, at this rate he would look no worse than Wilcox in a day or two.

The Mummy improved, the more he fed, knew Lady Bertram. What she did not know, however, was that the large crates filled with ancient Egyptians littering her house were undergoing a metamorphosis of their own, by proxy. That is, the contents were.

Mummies were reviving all over Mansfield Park.

They shuffled about, at first rather horrendous in their ragged and desiccated state, and made more than one chambermaid scream at the sight, as she might come upon such in the living room or pantry. But for the moment, they were rather harmless—having been commanded by the Spirit and Mind of their great Pharaoh not to take more life force than he did himself. Indeed, controlled and regulated thus, they were no worse than large horseflies or summer mosquitoes in their minute feedings upon the living.

"What manner of rampant incompetence and dense buffoonery is happening in this house?" the cook bewailed throughout the day, as she would send out one servant after another to do a task and they would not return for hours, or else come back with total amnesia of the event, having to be told again and again. Elsewhere in Mansfield, the lawns would not get watered, linen was not folded, or dusting and cleaning was done three times more than it ought to have been done, by dazed scullery maids.

"Oh, if only Sir Thomas were home!" some of the staff complained amongst themselves. "Her Ladyship is simply not up to overseeing such a large household—" But they did not finish such a disloyal line of thought, and continued about their menial tasks, occasionally stubbing their toes upon a shifted box or crate in the hallway, and crying out in frustration—did it not sit in a different place just moments earlier? Why was this or that crate unlocked, and why was there apparently nothing inside but packing hay and other some such materials, and all that ungodly sand? Who opened these blasted crates anyway, and left them underfoot, in the way of good hardworking folk?

No wonder Sir Thomas was expected by all with a fever pitch. By all the staff, that is—his own family was quite a different matter. . . .

Miss Crawford, on walking up with her brother to spend the evening at Mansfield Park, heard the good news of Sir Thomas's impending arrival. Mrs. Norris gave the particulars of the letters, and the subject was dropt. But after tea, as Miss Crawford was standing at an open window with Edmund and Fanny looking out on a twilight scene, while the Miss Bertrams, Mr. Rushworth, and Henry Crawford were all busy with candles at the pianoforte, she suddenly revived it by turning round towards the group, and saying, "How happy Mr. Rushworth looks! He is hardly growling at all; indeed, he is thinking of November."

Edmund looked round at Mr. Rushworth too, but had nothing to say.

"Your father's return will be a very interesting event."

"It will, indeed, after such an absence; an absence not only long, but including so many dangers."

"It will be the forerunner also of other interesting events: your sister's marriage, and your taking orders."

"Yes."

"Don't be affronted," said she, laughing, "but it does put me in mind of some of the old heathen heroes, who, after performing great exploits in a foreign land, offered sacrifices to the gods on their safe return." And suddenly Miss Crawford looked at him with very dark, very meaningful eyes.

"There is no sacrifice in the case," replied Edmund, with a serious smile, and glancing at the pianoforte again, only to miss her intensity; "it is entirely her own doing."

"Oh yes I know it is. I was merely joking. She has done no more than what every young woman would do; and I have no doubt of her being extremely happy. My other sacrifice, of course, you do not understand."

"My taking orders, I assure you, is quite as voluntary as Maria's marrying."

"It is fortunate that your inclination and your father's convenience should accord so well. There is a very good living kept for you, I understand, hereabouts."

"Which you suppose has biased me?"

"But *that* I am sure it has not," cried Fanny.

"Thank you for your good word, Fanny, but it is more than I would affirm myself. On the contrary, the knowing that there was such a provision for me probably did bias me. Nor can I think it wrong that it should. There was no natural disinclination to be overcome, and I see no reason why a man should make a worse clergyman for knowing that he will have a competence early in life."

"It is the same sort of thing," said Fanny, after a short pause, "as for the son of an admiral to go into the navy, or the son of a general to be in the army, and nobody sees anything wrong in that. Nobody wonders that they should prefer the line where their friends can serve them best, or suspects them to be less in earnest in it than they appear."

"No, my dear Miss Price, and for reasons good. The profession, either navy or army, is its own justification. It has everything in its favour: heroism, danger, bustle, fashion. Soldiers and sailors are always acceptable in society. Nobody can wonder that men are soldiers and sailors."

"But the motives of a man who takes orders with the certainty of preferment may be fairly suspected, you think?" said Edmund. "To be justified in your eyes, he must do it in the most complete uncertainty of any provision."

"What! take orders without a living! No; that is madness indeed; absolute madness."

"Shall I ask you how the church is to be filled, if a man is neither to take orders with a living nor without?"

"And I say, why fill a church in the first place? It has plenty of filling already."

"A man who enters the church cannot be influenced by temptation and reward to the soldier and sailor in their choice of a profession, as heroism, and noise, and fashion, are all against him. Thus, he ought not be suspected of lacking sincerity or good intentions in his choice."

"Oh! no doubt he is very sincere in preferring an income ready made, to the trouble of working for one; and has the best intentions of doing nothing all the rest of his days but eat, drink, and grow fat. It is indolence, Mr. Bertram, and love of ease—a want of all laudable ambition, of taste for good company, or of inclination to take the trouble of being agreeable, which make men clergymen. A clergyman has nothing to do but be slovenly and selfish—read the newspaper, watch the weather, and quarrel with his wife. His curate does all the work, and the business of his own life is to dine." Miss Crawford spoke thus with a truly wicked gleam in her eye. Almost, there was a glimmer of sharp teeth as her lips moved.

"There are such clergymen, no doubt, but I think they are not so common as to justify Miss Crawford in esteeming it their general character. I suspect that you are not judging from yourself, but from prejudiced persons, whose opinions you have been in the habit of hearing. It is impossible that your own observation can have given you much knowledge of the clergy. You can have been personally acquainted with very few. You are speaking what you have been told at your uncle's table."

"I speak what appears to me the general opinion; and where an opinion is general, it is usually correct. Though *I* have not seen much of the domestic lives of clergymen, it is seen by too many to leave any deficiency of information."

"Where any one body of educated men, of whatever denomination, are condemned indiscriminately, there must be a deficiency of information, or (smiling) of something else. Your uncle, and his brother admirals, perhaps knew little of clergymen beyond the chaplains whom they were always wishing away."

"Poor William! He has met with great kindness from the chaplain of the *Antwerp,*" was a tender apostrophe of Fanny's, very much to the purpose of her own feelings if not of the conversation.

"I have been so little addicted to take my opinions from my uncle," said Miss Crawford. "I am not entirely without the means of seeing what clergymen are, being at this present time the guest of my own brother, Dr. Grant. And though Dr. Grant is most kind and obliging to me, a gentleman, a good scholar, clever, respectable, and often preaches good sermons, *I* see him to be an indolent, selfish *bon vivant,* who must have his palate consulted in everything; who will not stir a finger for the convenience of any one; and who, moreover, if the cook makes a blunder, is out of humour with his excellent wife. Henry and I were partly driven out this very evening by a disappointment about a green goose, which he could not get the better of. My poor sister was forced to stay and bear it."

"I do not wonder at your disapprobation, upon my word. It is a great defect of temper, made worse by a very faulty habit of self-indulgence. To see your sister suffering from it must be exceedingly painful. Fanny, it goes against us. We cannot attempt to defend Dr. Grant."

"No," replied Fanny, "but we need not give up on his profession. Whatever profession Dr. Grant had chosen, he would have taken the same temper into it. In the navy or army, he would have had a great many more people under his command than he has now. More would have been made unhappy by him as a sailor or soldier than as a clergyman. Besides, the temper could become worse in a more active, worldly profession, where he would have had less time and obligation. A sensible man like Dr. Grant cannot be in the habit of preaching others their duty every week, without being the better for it himself. It must make him think. I have no doubt he endeavours to restrain himself more often than he would in any other profession."

"We cannot prove to the contrary, to be sure; but I wish you a better fate, Miss Price, than to be the wife of a man whose amiableness depends upon his own sermons."

"I think the man who could often quarrel with Fanny," said Edmund affectionately, "must be beyond the reach of any sermons."

Fanny turned farther into the window; and Miss Crawford had only time to say, in a pleasant manner, "I fancy Miss Price has been more used to deserve praise than to hear it"; when, being earnestly invited by the Miss Bertrams to join in a glee, she tripped off to the instrument, leaving Edmund looking after her in an ecstasy of admiration of all her many virtues, from her obliging manners down to her light and graceful tread.

"There goes good-humour, I am sure," said he presently. "There goes a temper which would never give pain! How well she walks! and how readily she falls in with the inclination of others! joining them the moment she is asked. What a pity," he added, after an instant's reflection, "that she should have been in such hands!"

Fanny agreed to it, and had the pleasure of seeing him continue at the window with her, in spite of the expected glee; and of having his eyes soon turned, like hers, towards the scene without, where all that was solemn, and soothing, and lovely, appeared in the brilliancy of an unclouded night, and the contrast of the deep shade of the woods.

Fanny spoke her feelings. "Here's harmony!" said she; "here's repose! Here's what may leave all painting and all music behind, and what poetry only can attempt to describe! Here's what may calm every care, and lift the heart to rapture! When I look out on such a night as this, I feel as if there could be neither wickedness nor sorrow nor dark Curses in the world."

"I like to hear your enthusiasm, Fanny. It is a lovely night, and they are much to be pitied who have not been taught to feel as you do; who have not been given a taste for Nature in early life."

"*You* taught me to think and feel on the subject, cousin."

"I had a very apt scholar. There's Arcturus looking very bright."

"Yes, and the Bear. I wish I could see Cassiopeia."

"We must go out on the lawn for that. Should you be afraid?"

"Not in the least. It is a great while since we have had any star-gazing. Wait!—Oh, look, cousin! Did you see that? *Someone* is out there, a moving shadow on the lawn—"

"There is no one and nothing outside but stars, Fanny. Yes; I do not know how it has happened that we put off such a joyous pastime as looking at them."

The glee began.

"We will stay till this is finished, Fanny," said he, turning his back on the window. And as the singing advanced, she had the mortification of seeing him advance too, moving forward by gentle degrees towards the instrument. When it ceased, he was close by the singers, among the most urgent in requesting to hear the glee again.

Fanny sighed alone at the window till scolded away by Mrs. Norris's threats of catching cold.

Outside, on the ground below, *someone* stood for a long time, looking up at her silhouette.

The ancient Pharaoh had seen his ancient long-dead bride.

Chapter XII

Sir Thomas was to return in November, and his eldest son had duties to call him earlier home. The approach of September brought tidings of Mr. Bertram—first in a letter to the gamekeeper and then in a letter to Edmund. And by the end of August he arrived himself, to be gay, agreeable, and gallant again as occasion served, or Miss Crawford demanded; to tell of races and Weymouth, unusual schemes and wagers, parties and friends. Six weeks before this might have invoked some interest—had she not currently so much preferred his younger brother, and realized the elder one was a complete idiot.

It was very vexatious, and she was heartily sorry for it. But so it was. And so far from now meaning to marry the elder, she did not even want to attract him beyond what the simplest claims of conscious beauty required. His lengthened absence from Mansfield, made it perfectly clear that he did not care about her; and his indifference was equaled by her own. Were he now to step forth the owner of Mansfield Park, she did not believe she could accept him.

The season and duties which brought Mr. Bertram back to Mansfield took Mr. Crawford into Norfolk. He went for a fortnight to Everingham—a fortnight of such dullness to the Miss Bertrams as ought to have put them both on their guard, and made even Julia admit, in her jealousy of her sister, the absolute necessity of distrusting his attentions, and wishing him not to return.

A fortnight of this sufficient leisure, in the intervals of shooting and sleeping, might have convinced the gentleman that he ought to keep longer away. But thoughtless and selfish, he would not look beyond the present moment. The sisters, handsome, clever, and encouraging, were an amusement to his sated mind. Thus, finding nothing in Norfolk to equal the social pleasures of Mansfield, he gladly returned to it at the time appointed, and was welcomed thither quite as gladly by those whom he came to trifle with further.

Maria, with only Mr. Rushworth to attend to her, was doomed to hear repeated details of his day's sport—his boast of his dogs, his jealousy of his neighbours, his zeal after poachers (and even more so, after vermin), his complaints about "that infernal duck from Brighton" which he still managed not to apprehend—and oh, all that growling! All these subjects did not find their way to female feelings, and so she missed Mr. Crawford grievously.

And Julia, unengaged and unemployed, felt all the right of missing him much more. Each sister believed herself the favourite. Julia might be justified in so doing by the hints of Mrs. Grant, inclined to credit what she wished, and Maria by the hints of Mr. Crawford himself. Everything returned into the same state as before his absence.

Fanny was the only one of the party who found anything to dislike. But since the day at Sotherton, she could never see Mr. Crawford with either sister without suspicion, and seldom without wonder or censure. But her confidence in her own judgment was lacking. Had she been more certain, she would probably have communicated it to her usual confidant. As it was, she only hazarded a hint, and the hint was lost.

"I am rather surprised," said she, "that Mr. Crawford should come back again so soon, after being here so long before, full seven weeks. If he is so very fond of change and moving about, why is he not elsewhere? He is used to much gayer places than Mansfield."

"It is to his credit," was Edmund's answer; "and I dare say it gives his sister pleasure. She does not like his unsettled habits."

"What a favourite he is with my cousins! It is rather uncanny, and one dares say, *unnatural*."

"Yes, his manners to women are such as must please. Mrs. Grant, I believe, suspects him of a preference for Julia; I have never seen a symptom of it, but I wish it may be so. He has no faults but what a serious attachment would remove."

"If Miss Bertram were not engaged," said Fanny cautiously, "I could sometimes almost think that he admired her more than Julia."

"Which is, perhaps, more in favour of his liking Julia best, than you, Fanny, may be aware. A man, before he has quite made up his own mind, will often distinguish the sister or intimate friend of the woman he is really thinking of more than the woman herself. Crawford has too much sense to stay here if he found himself in any danger from Maria. I am not at all afraid for her. She has given proof that her feelings are not strong."

Fanny supposed she must have been mistaken, and meant to think differently in future, but she remained unsure.

The supernatural situation at Mansfield meanwhile continued to develop, and took a rather interesting turn. At one point Lady Bertram made it obvious to all that they now had yet another visitor in the house—a certain young gentleman by the name of Lord Eastwind. Who he was exactly, had never been made clear; a certain distant relation of Sir Thomas, perhaps, or maybe the son of a colleague from Parliament, or possibly even an expert on Egyptology attending from the London Museum upon Lady Bertram's hobbyist pleasure.

Whatever or whoever he was, Lord Eastwind was introduced at dinner one evening, as he came downstairs with Lady Bertram upon his arm, dressed very well in the way of latest London fashion, with a striking face, and cutting a dashing figure, yet somehow, after the initial introductions, going almost unnoticed by everyone in the room. It was almost as if he decreed and intended it to be so.

Fanny observed the very tall and dark young gentleman, raven-haired, soft-spoken, yet somehow seeming filled to overflow with *something;* with leashed energy, a power subdued, hidden, secret. What an odd thing it was, that neither Maria nor Julia paid him a second glance and resumed their enthusiastic conversation with Mr. Crawford! Here before them was a far more handsome, interesting, indeed, far loftier titled gentleman! An infinitely eligible young heir, by Heaven, with likely many a thousand a year! Even Edmund—her dear sensitive one—did not seem to be engaged by or discerned anything unusual in Lord Eastwind, he who had an intense piercing gaze of rather beautiful dark eyes, exotic and utterly fashionable.

What a moment of odd thrill and sudden fright Fanny had when these eyes alighted upon her own during the initial introduction. There was no touch upon her hand, no other intimacy, but the one look. It was almost a moment of *recognition,* a very long instant, before he looked away and conversed politely with the next introduction.

Fanny was not quite bewitched so much as alarmed and confused. And yet, excepting herself, the only other who paid him the least bit of attention from thereon was Lady Bertram—and she merely mumbled in her usual manner about Nile shrubbery and hieroglyphics (to which the exceedingly polite

Lord Eastwind, surprisingly responded with thoughtful and educated facts of an Egyptological nature).

But Fanny was mistaken in at least one more thing. The Crawfords *had* noticed the new visitor, and indeed, a meaningful dark gaze passed between all of them within moments of meeting.

"What brings you here to the country, Eastwind?" said Mr. Crawford somewhat later that same first evening of acquaintance, employing a discreet moment of otherwise enthusiastic conversation between the others. "I venture a guess that you have come from farther than London. Why here?"

"Life," replied the raven-haired gentleman with a very fine smile on his perfect sensuous lips. "I am newly brought to life, if you must know. Country air works wonders, even upon a very antiquated constitution. And the other thing that brings me here is a dear memory. Lady Bertram was kind enough to *accommodate* it."

Across the table, Fanny overheard these cryptic remarks without much comprehension, but with much dread. She could recognize in it a play of double meaning.

"Very well," responded Mr. Crawford. "But if you must enjoy life here in the fresh parklands, be aware that *others* with a similar nature and intentions are here to enjoy and *reap* of it also."

"Don't be selfish, Henry," put in Miss Crawford, with a very dark smile upon her countenance, looking from her brother to the gentleman. "The delightful resources here are in plentiful abundance. Quite enough for all."

And having said that, having had that one pointed conversation, the Crawfords and Lord Eastwind proceeded to ignore each other. Their behavior—unlike the complete lack of notice and almost unnatural disinterest on the part of the Bertram family—held in it a force of conscious intent.

From thereon, Lord Eastwind seemed to have permanently attached himself to the household, and became a discreet favorite of Lady Bertram.

Fanny was privy, one social evening, to the conversation of her aunt Norris on the subject of Maria, as well as to her feelings, and the feelings of Mrs. Rushworth. She would have preferred not to be obliged to listen, for it was while all the other young people were dancing, and she sitting, most unwillingly, among the chaperons at the fire, longing for the re-entrance of her elder cousin, on whom all her own hopes of a partner then depended.

It was Fanny's first ball, though without the preparation or splendour of many a young lady's first ball, being the thought only of the afternoon, built on the late acquisition of a violin player in the servants' hall (the gangly fellow seemed to have arrived out of the blue, with no references, and yet was hired immediately in lieu of his fine playing, alongside a number of other equally unrecommended and equally lumbering fellows, all with rather ghastly parchment skin), and the possibility of raising five couple with the help of Mrs. Grant, Lord Eastwind, and a new intimate friend of Mr. Bertram's just arrived on a visit. It had, however, been a very happy one to Fanny through four dances, and she was quite grieved to be losing even a quarter of an hour. While waiting and wishing, looking now at the dancers and now at the door, this dialogue between the two above-mentioned ladies was forced on her—

"I think, ma'am," said Mrs. Norris, her wolfish eyes directed towards Mr. Rushworth and Maria, who were partners for the second time, "we shall see some happy faces again now."

"Yes, ma'am, indeed," replied the other, with a stately simper, "there will be some satisfaction in looking on *now*, and I think it was rather a pity they should have been obliged to part.

Young folks in their situation should be excused complying with the common forms. I wonder my son did not propose it."

"I dare say he did, ma'am. Mr. Rushworth is never remiss. But dear Maria has such a strict sense of propriety, so much of that true delicacy which one seldom meets with nowadays, Mrs. Rushworth—that wish of avoiding particularity! Dear ma'am, only look at her face at this moment; how different from what it was the two last dances!"

Miss Bertram did indeed look happy, her eyes were sparkling with pleasure, and she was speaking with great animation, for Julia and her partner, Mr. Crawford, were close to her; they were all in a cluster together. How she had looked before, Fanny could not recollect, for she had been dancing with Edmund herself, and had not thought about her.

Mrs. Norris continued, "It is quite delightful, ma'am, to see young people so properly happy, so well suited, and so much the thing! I cannot but think of dear Sir Thomas's delight. And what do you say, ma'am, to the chance of another match? Mr. Rushworth has set a good example, and such things are very catching."

Mrs. Rushworth, who saw nothing but her son, was quite at a loss.

"The couple above, ma'am. Do you see no symptoms there?"

"Oh dear! Miss Julia and Mr. Crawford. Yes, indeed, a very pretty match. What is his property?"

"Four thousand a year."

"Very well. Those who have not more must be satisfied with what they have. Four thousand a year is a pretty estate, and he seems a very genteel, steady young man, so I hope Miss Julia will be very happy."

"It is not a settled thing, ma'am, yet. We only speak of it among friends. But I have very little doubt it *will* be. He is growing extremely particular in his attentions."

Fanny could listen no further. Listening and wondering were all suspended for a time, for Mr. Bertram was in the room again. And though feeling it would be a great honour to be asked by him, she thought it must happen.

However, before Mr. Bertram had moved an iota in her direction, out of nowhere, came forth the dark elegant gentleman with raven hair and a sallow handsome face. Lord Eastwind stood before her, and with a small perfectly executed bow, said:

"May I have this dance, Miss Price?"

Fanny felt a hot distant wind blow, envelop her in a dry merciless ancient embrace—or was it all in her mind? She would have loved nothing better than, in that moment, to refuse him, perchance even to run, but there was no excuse. And thus she rose and complied, giving herself over into his gloved hands.

A butterfly touch of his deft large hand landed over her smaller own. And there was an instant of shock, a tingle along the fingers. They spoke nothing, Fanny waiting for him to utter some platitude so that she could respond in kind, but he remained silent. She never raised her gaze to meet his own, merely observed the lapels of his fine coat. She moved through the steps of the dance, feeling herself grow wooden and stiff with unspeakable tension, with terror, and, for one split instant of breath, a kind of wonder.

It was as if she *knew* him. No, he was no Edmund, never; there was no comparison. But he was *someone* to her.

Someone she knew; had known once, maybe, if only in a fever dream.

The dance ended in blessed relief for Fanny. And yet, as they exchanged the final pleasantries, and his fingers left her trembling own, Fanny felt a kind of loss. He stepped away, was gone in the crowd, like a breath of dark wind. And once again, as always, no one paid the least bit of attention to his coming or going.

Fanny was returned to the vicinity of her aunt, and Mr. Bertram finally approached. He came towards their little circle; but instead of asking her to dance, drew a chair near her, and asked, "Who was that smart fellow you were dancing with, Fanny? I forget his name again, for some infernal reason. Who is he?"

"Lord Eastwind. A favored acquaintance of Aunt Bertram."

"Ah! Egyptology and artifacts. It makes perfect sense now. As such, the fellow interests me no longer."

And then Tom proceeded to give her an account of a newly acquired but ailing horse with the markings, he claimed, of the map of Europe and Asia upon its flanks—verily! (The seller told him it was *not* to be rubbed down for at least a twelvemonth in the flanks area)—and the opinion of the groom, from whom he had just parted. Fanny realized that a dance with him was not to be. And in the modesty of her nature she immediately felt that she had been unreasonable in expecting it.

After he had told of his remarkable horse, he took a newspaper from the table, and looking over it, said in a languid way, "If you want to dance, Fanny, I will stand up with you." With more than equal civility the offer was declined; she did not wish to dance.

"I am glad of it," said he, in a much brisker tone, and throwing down the newspaper again, "for I am tired to death. I only wonder how the good people can keep it up so long. They had need be *all* in love, to find any amusement in such folly; and so they are, I fancy. If you look at them you may see they are so many couple of lovers—all but Yates and East—whatever his name is, and Mrs. Grant—and, between ourselves, she, poor woman, must want a lover as much as any one of them. A desperate dull life hers must be with the doctor," making a sly face as he spoke towards the chair of the latter, who proving, however, to be close at his elbow, made so instantaneous a change of expression and subject necessary, as Fanny, in spite of everything, could hardly help laughing at.

"A strange business this in America, Dr. Grant!" Tom spoke in a quite loud and energetic voice. "What is your opinion? I always come to you to know what I am to think of public matters. Incidentally, what is all this—whoever invited so much inferior rabble to this assembly? Everywhere one turns to look, servant or guest, it appears to be a parade of bad skin! Horrible, sallow faces, whatever is the matter with the neighborhood? Have all the gentlefolk of fine breeding gone to sea, to be replaced by sunburned, scurvy-riddled buccaneers? Behold, for example, that one, strange lumbering fellow, whether dancing or walking in a circle, one cannot tell—why, even his coat is a ragged mess—No, cannot be—indeed, my mistake! Perchance it is simply poorly arranged wrist lace—"

But complain as he did, no one else seemed to remark upon the poor appearance of the general assembly. Even the speaker himself soon blinked a few times and attributed his bizarre first impression to the late hour and to an extra drink.

"My dear Tom," cried his aunt soon afterwards, "as you are not dancing, I dare say you will have no objection to join us in a rubber;[10] shall you?" Then leaving her seat, and coming to him to enforce the proposal, added in a whisper, "We want to make a table for Mrs. Rushworth, you know. Your mother is quite anxious about it, but cannot very well spare time to sit down herself, because of her fringe. Now, you and I and Dr. Grant will just do; and though *we* play but half-crowns, you know, you may bet half-guineas with *him*."

"I should be most happy," replied he aloud, and jumping up with alacrity, "it would give me the greatest pleasure; but that I am this moment going to dance. Come, Fanny," taking her hand, "do not be dawdling any longer, or the dance will be over."

---

[10] Delightful Reader, it is not what you might assume it is.

Fanny was led off very willingly, though it was impossible for her to feel much gratitude towards her cousin, or distinguish, as he certainly did, between the selfishness of another person and his own.

"A pretty modest request upon my word," he indignantly exclaimed as they walked away. "To want to nail me to a card-table for the next two hours with herself and Dr. Grant, who are always quarrelling, and that poking old woman, who knows no more of whist than of algebra. I wish my good aunt would be a little less busy! And to ask me in such a way too! without ceremony, before them all, so as to leave me no possibility of refusing. *That* is what I dislike most. It raises my spleen more than anything, to have the pretence of being asked, of being given a choice, and at the same time addressed in such a way as to obligate! If I had not luckily thought of standing up with you I could not have got out of it. For when my aunt has got a fancy in her head, nothing can stop her."

Chapter XIII

Unlike Lord Eastwind, the Honourable John Yates, the friend of Mr. Bertram, had not much to recommend him beyond habits of fashion and expense. And, being the younger son of a lord with a tolerable independence, Sir Thomas would probably have thought his introduction at Mansfield by no means desirable.

Mr. Bertram's acquaintance with him had begun at Weymouth, where they had spent ten days together in the same society. And the friendship had been sealed by a common interest in idiotic schemes (such as Yates's purchase of "Noah's Rowboat," as Tom so liked to mock it, completely discounting his own stupefying purchases) and perfected by Mr. Yates's being invited to take Mansfield in his way, whenever he could.

Mr. Yates promised to come, and did so, rather earlier than had been expected. It was in consequence of the sudden breaking-up of a large party at the house of another friend. He came on the wings of disappointment, and with his head full of acting, for it had been a *theatrical* party. The play in which he had a part was within two days of performance, when the sudden death of one of the nearest connexions of the family had destroyed the scheme and dispersed the performers. They said it was a tragic wild animal attack, later disguised by the family as a health issue. Other more accurate rumors hinted it was indeed something quite more sinister—a horrendous, unbelievable, monstrous flying fowl, a *duck* of grandiose proportions, was observed in the local countryside, and there was report of horrifying attacks on moonless nights. . . .

Meanwhile, Mr. Yates bewailed the loss of his acting opportunity. To be so near happiness, so near fame, so near the private theatricals at Ecclesford, the seat of the Right Hon. Lord Ravenshaw, in Cornwall, which would of course have immortalised the whole party for at least a twelvemonth! and being so near, to lose it all, was a keen injury. Mr. Yates could talk of nothing else: Ecclesford and its theatre, its arrangements and dresses, rehearsals and jokes.

Happily for him, a love of the theatre and an itch for acting is so strong among young people, that he could hardly out-talk the interest of his hearers. From the first casting of the parts to the epilogue it was all bewitching, and there were few who did not wish to have been involved. The play had been *Lovers' Vows,* and Mr. Yates was to have been Count Cassel.

"A trifling part," said he, "and not at all to my taste, but I was determined to make no difficulties." And he went on at length as to the allocation of the parts. "Our Agatha was inimitable, and the duke was thought very great by many. It would certainly have gone off wonderfully."

The rapt listeners responded with sympathy to his plight.

"It is not worth complaining about; but to be sure the poor old dowager could not have died at a worse time—popped off after getting a fright from that monstrous Brighton Duck, they say, coming out of nowhere and flying in her face—and it is impossible to help wishing that the news could have been suppressed for just the three days we wanted—"

"Wait—did you say, a duck?" Tom was all attention. "Was it by any chance dove-grey with white feather tips? Great marvelous wingspan? Loud thrilling honk?"

"I have no idea," replied Yates indifferently. "The creature killed the dowager, what difference would it make what were its markings?"

"Why, I venture to guess it was indeed my own! the duck I raised and groomed myself, from a tiny duckling! Imported, from Peking by origin, acquired in Brighton, it was my own Quackie! Ah, how I missed her, the dear, destined to live out her days in Mansfield, until she flew into my mother's face—"

Yates shook his head. Ignoring his friend's further tedious ruminations on the subject, he proceeded with his tedious own. "The dowager, being only a grandmother, and all this happening many miles off—regardless if it were the Brighton Duck, or the vapors—I think there would have been no great harm if we had gone on with the play. But Lord Ravenshaw, one of the most correct men in England, would not hear of it."

"An afterpiece instead of a comedy," said Mr. Bertram. "*Lovers' Vows* were at an end, and Lord and Lady Ravenshaw left to act My Grandmother by themselves. Well, to make *you* amends, Yates—especially if it had been my own Quackie at the heart of it, so to speak—I think we must raise a little theatre at Mansfield, and ask you to be our manager. Or, I can do the honors."

The notion took hold of their imagination. Having so much leisure as to make almost any novelty a certain good, and with so much young lively talent and comic taste at their disposal, the novelty of acting was a delight. "Oh for the Ecclesford theatre and scenery to try something with." Each sister could echo the wish; and Henry Crawford was quite alive at the idea.

"I really believe," said he, "I could be fool enough at this moment to undertake any character that ever was written, from Shylock or Richard III down to the singing hero of a farce in his scarlet coat and cocked hat. I feel as if I could be anything or everything; as if I could rant and storm, or sigh or cut capers, in any tragedy or comedy in the English language. What should prevent us? Not these countenances, I am sure," looking towards the Miss Bertrams; "and for a theatre, since we shall be only amusing ourselves, any room in this house might suffice."

"We must have a curtain," said Tom Bertram; "a few yards of green baize, and perhaps that may be enough. Oh! Mayhap we can move aside these infernal crates from Cairo that fill all space, and use them for building blocks, stacking one upon another to form a stage?"

"The horrid boxes are rather heavy, and I doubt mother would approve us going anywhere near them," said Julia, with not a small amount of pique.

"Oh, quite enough," cried Mr. Yates, "with only just a side wing or two run up, doors in flat, and three or four scenes to be let down; nothing more would be necessary on such a plan as this."

"I believe we must be satisfied with *less,*" said Maria. "There would not be time, and other difficulties would arise. We must rather adopt Mr. Crawford's views, and make the *performance,* not the *theatre,* our object. The best plays are independent of scenery. And truly, unless we are putting on a play about Cleopatra and the grand Nile, we would have to close our eyes to imagine anything otherwise in *this* house—"

"Nay," said Edmund, who began to listen with alarm. "Let us do nothing by halves. If we are to act, let it be in a theatre completely fitted up with pit, boxes, and gallery, and let us have a play entire from beginning to end; so as it be a German play, no matter what, with a good tricking, shifting afterpiece, and a figure-dance, and a hornpipe, and a song between the acts. If we do not outdo Ecclesford, we do nothing."

"Why not a fullblown opera, then," sounded the soft, sarcastic voice of Lord Eastwind. "*Aida* has both the grandeur and the scenery. All that is lacking would be dulcet singers. Or perchance not—we have Miss Crawford. But nay, of course, we don't have *Aida* itself, not in another fifty earthly years—"

Once again, it seemed that the only one who heard him speak these decidedly incomprehensible words was Fanny. Lord Eastwind watched her, long moments after he ceased talking.

But Fanny said nothing, and attempted to occupy her gaze elsewhere.

"Now, Edmund, do not be disagreeable," meanwhile said Julia. "Nobody loves a play better than you do."

"True, to see real acting, good hardened real acting; not the raw efforts of gentlemen and ladies, who have all the disadvantages of education and decorum to struggle through."

After a short pause, however, the subject still continued, and was discussed with unabated eagerness. Nothing was settled but that Tom Bertram would prefer a comedy, and his sisters and Henry Crawford a tragedy, and that it was a mere trifle to find a piece which would please them all. The resolution to act seemed so decided as to make Edmund quite uncomfortable. He was determined to prevent it, if possible, though his mother did not evince the least disapprobation.

Lady Bertram merely glanced at Lord Eastwind, and muttered nonsense that sounded like: "Whatever the Lordship His Pharaonic Mummyness commands."

The raven-haired gentleman barely inclined his head. In that moment, a servant walking behind his seat with a tray of tea service, paused momentarily, as though placed in a trance, and went still for a span of three seconds, leaning in sudden weariness against the Lord's chair.

Fanny alone saw the gloved fingers of Lord Eastwind make contact with the servant's coat-sleeves.

It was only for a briefest moment. . . .

And the next, Lord Eastwind's exotic black eyes acquired a new brilliance, and his sallow windblown cheeks appeared to smooth out in a bloom of health.

The same evening afforded Edmund an opportunity of trying his strength. Maria, Julia, Henry Crawford, and Mr. Yates were in the billiard-room. Tom (returning into the drawing-room, where Edmund was standing thoughtfully by the fire, Lady Bertram on the sofa at a little distance, Lord Eastwind reclined in a wingchair moved back in the shadows nearby, and Fanny close beside her ladyship, arranging her work) thus began as he entered—

"Such a horribly vile billiard-table as ours is not to be met with. I can stand it no longer, and nothing shall ever tempt me to use it again. I say, let us pack it up and send it to Egypt! Give them something of ours for a change! Instead, this room can be adapted into a theatre, precisely the shape and length for it; with doors at the farther end. By merely moving the bookcase in my father's room, it will be an excellent greenroom. It seems to join the billiard-room on purpose."

"You are not serious, Tom, in meaning to act?" said Edmund, in a low voice, as his brother approached the fire.

"Not serious! never more so, I assure you. What is there to surprise you in it?"

"I think it would be very wrong.[11] In a *general* light, private theatricals are open to some objections, but as *we* are circumstanced, I must think it would be highly injudicious. It would shew great want of feeling on my father's account, absent as he is, and it would be imprudent with regard to Maria, whose situation is a very delicate one."

"You take up a thing so seriously! as if we were going to act three times a week and invite all the country. But no, we mean nothing but a little amusement among ourselves, no

---

[11] The distasteful pastime of Acting, in particular the enactment of indelicate, suggestive and compromising roles for modern, well-bred young ladies, is a grave sin. Gentle Reader, it is the equal of holding a Mardi Gras in the drawing room, complete with bead tossing, pole dancing, topless floats—in short, nudity and adult situations. It is not to be borne.

audience, no publicity. And as to my father's being absent, the expectation of his return must be a very anxious period to my mother. We can be her means of amusement, keeping up her spirits for the next few weeks. Our mother suffers so!"

As he said this, each looked towards their mother. Lady Bertram, sunk back in one corner of the sofa, the picture of health, wealth, ease, and tranquility, was just falling into a gentle doze over a pile of rolled up papyrus, while Fanny was getting through the few difficulties of her work for her—all the while observed subtly by Lord Eastwind.

Edmund smiled and shook his head.

"By Jove! this won't do," cried Tom, throwing himself into a chair with a hearty laugh. "To be sure, my dear mother, your anxiety—I was unlucky there."

"What is the matter?" asked her ladyship, in the heavy tone of one half-roused; "I was not asleep, merely discussing with the Pharaoh matters of grave import to his esteemed plans for achieving the Divine Living Eternity."

"Oh dear, no, ma'am, nobody suspected you! Well, Edmund," he continued, returning to the former subject, posture, and voice, as soon as Lady Bertram began to nod again, "but *this* I *will* maintain, that we shall be doing no harm."

"I cannot agree with you; I am convinced that my father would totally disapprove it."

"And I am convinced to the contrary. Nobody is fonder of the exercise of talent in young people than my father, and for anything of the acting, reciting kind, he has a decided taste. I am sure he encouraged it in us as boys. How many a time have we mourned over the dead body of Julius Caesar, and *to be'd* and not *to be'd*, in this very room, for his amusement?"

"It was a very different thing. You must see the difference yourself. My father wished us, as schoolboys, to speak well, but he would never wish his grown-up daughters to be acting plays. His sense of decorum is strict."

"I know all that," said Tom, displeased. "I know my father as well as you do; and I'll take care that his daughters do nothing to distress him. Manage your own concerns, Edmund, and I'll take care of the rest of the family."

And he proceeded with arguing his point and ended with, "Everything will be right with Sir Thomas. Don't imagine that nobody in this house can see or judge but yourself. Don't act yourself, if you do not like it, but don't expect to govern everybody else."

"No, as to acting myself," said Edmund, "*that* I absolutely protest against."

Tom walked out of the room as he said it, and Edmund was left to sit down and stir the fire in thoughtful vexation.

Fanny, who had heard it all, and borne Edmund company in every feeling throughout the whole, now ventured to comfort, "Perhaps they may not be able to find any play to suit them. Your brother's taste and your sisters' seem very different."

"I have no hope there, Fanny. If they persist in the scheme, they will find something. I shall speak to my sisters and try to dissuade *them,* and that is all I can do."

"I should think my aunt Norris would be on your side."

"I dare say she would, but she has no influence with either Tom or my sisters that could be of any use; and if I cannot convince them myself, I shall let things take their course, without attempting it through her."

His sisters, to whom he had an opportunity of speaking the next morning, were quite as impatient of his advice, as Tom. Their mother had no objection, occupied with her usual Egypt, and they were not afraid of their father's disapprobation.

Julia *did* seem inclined to admit that Maria's situation might require particular caution and delicacy—but that could not extend to *her*—she was at liberty. And Maria evidently considered her engagement as raising her above restraint. Edmund had little to hope, but he was still urging the subject when Henry Crawford entered the room, fresh from the Parsonage, calling out, "No want of hands in our theatre, Miss Bertram. No want of understrappers: my sister desires her love, and hopes to be admitted into the company, and will be happy to take the part of any old duenna or tame confidante."

Maria gave Edmund a glance, which meant, "What say you now? Can we be wrong if Mary Crawford feels the same?"

Lord Eastwind merely smiled, standing near a window and watching them all.

"What do you think, Miss Price," he said softly, "What will Edmund Bertram do now?"

"Whatever my cousin does I will not question his judgment," replied Fanny.

"A pity," said Lord Eastwind. "For in such intentional blindness you might overlook something of importance."

Meanwhile, Edmund, silenced by the new development, was obliged to acknowledge some modicum of charm in acting.

The scheme advanced. Opposition was vain. And as to Mrs. Norris, he was mistaken in supposing she would wish to make any. She started no difficulties that were not talked down in five minutes by her eldest nephew and niece, who were all-powerful with her. As the play was to bring very little expense to anybody, and none at all to herself, she fancied herself obliged to leave her own house and take up her abode in theirs, that every hour might be spent in their service—all usual yapping and such aside, she was, in fact, exceedingly delighted with the project.

Chapter XIV

Fanny seemed nearer being right than Edmund had supposed. The business of finding a play that would suit everybody proved to be no trifle. The carpenter had was already at work, while a play was still not found. An enormous roll of green baize had arrived from Northampton, and been cut out by Mrs. Norris, and was actually forming into a curtain by the housemaids, and still, no play.

Edmund began almost to hope that none might ever be found—there were much to be attended to, people to be pleased, a need that the play should be at once both tragedy and comedy.

On the tragic side were the Miss Bertrams, Henry Crawford, and Mr. Yates. On the comic, Tom Bertram, not *quite* alone, because it was evident that Mary Crawford's wishes inclined the same way. They wanted a piece containing very few characters, but every character first-rate, and three principal women. All the best plays were run over in vain. Neither *Hamlet,* nor *Macbeth,* nor *Othello,* etc. No piece could be proposed that did not supply somebody with a difficulty. All resulted in complaints: "Oh no, *that* will never do!" or "Nothing but buffoonery from beginning to end."

Fanny looked on and listened, amused to observe the selfishness which, more or less disguised, seemed to govern them all, and wondering how it would end. For her own gratification she could have wished that something might be acted, for she had never seen even half a play, but everything of higher consequence was against it.

Lord Eastwind, ever present and nigh invisible to everyone, seemed to be able to read Fanny's mind upon this occasion also.

"They are amusing in this pursuit of a means to act upon their hidden desires. Each role undertaken has, behind it, a hidden motive."

"It is what I am afraid of," said Fanny. "Especially where it concerns my cousin Maria."

"You cannot stop a butterfly of the night from flinging itself into an open flame," he replied. "I have seen them perish by the hundreds thus, oh so long ago, in the darkest sweetest nights. The more vibrant their wings, the brighter the flames burn, while the pale smoke rises unto heaven."

With her mind alone, Fanny felt a stirring of warm darkness, as though somewhere in the distance a hot wind was rising in an ancient desert. "Poor ancient butterfly . . ." she whispered.

"Is there not a part that you might want to play, Miss Price? Given the ideal role, and unblemished circumstances beyond anyone's reproach, what would you take upon yourself?"

"Nothing," she replied. "I would never act in a play, for it is a vehicle for untruth."

"It does not have to be. Untruth's fairer sister is illusion. And illusion can be radiant. Hence, I don't believe you," he persisted.

Fanny raised her gaze. "Why do you speak to me of such things, Lord Eastwind? Indeed, I am rather surprised you speak to me at all."

And for the first time, she saw the raven-haired gentleman smile. His dark weathered skin creased at the corners of his lips in a surprisingly appealing curvature.

"I speak to *you* only—and always, Miss Price."

And saying this, he was up and gone.

"This will never do," said Tom Bertram at last. "We are wasting time most abominably. Something must be fixed on. No matter what. We must not be so nice. From this moment I take any part you chuse to give me. Let it but be comic, I condition for nothing more."

A pause followed. Taking up one of the many volumes of plays on the table, Tom suddenly exclaimed—"*Lovers' Vows!* And why should not *Lovers' Vows* do for *us* as well as for the Ravenshaws? Here are two capital tragic parts for Yates and Crawford, and here is the rhyming Butler for me. And as for the rest, they may be filled up by anybody. It is only Count Cassel and Anhalt."

The suggestion was generally welcome. Everybody was weary of indecision, and Mr. Yates was particularly pleased—he had been longing to do the Baron at Ecclesford, had grudged every rant of Lord Ravenshaw's, and been forced to re-rant it all in his own room. The role was the height of his theatrical ambition. And he had the advantage of knowing half the scenes by heart already. To do him justice, however, he did not resolve to appropriate it. Remembering that there was some very good ranting-ground in Frederick, he professed an equal willingness for that.

Henry Crawford was ready to take either. Whichever Mr. Yates did not chuse would perfectly satisfy him. Miss Bertram, feeling all the interest of an Agatha in the question, observed to Mr. Yates that height and figure ought to be considered, and that *his* being the tallest, seemed to fit him peculiarly for the Baron. She was acknowledged to be quite right, then she was certain of the proper Frederick. Three of the characters were now cast, besides Mr. Rushworth, who was always answered for by Maria as willing to do anything (foremost, he would make a fine Caliban, Maria had remarked); when Julia, meaning, like her sister, to be Agatha, began to be scrupulous on Miss Crawford's account.

"Here are not women enough. Amelia and Agatha may do for Maria and me, but here is nothing for your sister, Mr. Crawford."

Mr. Crawford desired *that* might not be thought of. His sister had no wish of acting but as she might be useful. But this was immediately opposed by Tom Bertram, who asserted the part of Amelia to be the property of Miss Crawford, if she would accept it. "It falls as naturally, as necessarily to her," said he, "as Agatha does to one or other of my sisters. It can be no sacrifice on their side, for it is highly comic."

A short silence followed. Each sister looked anxious; for each felt the best claim to Agatha, and was hoping to have it. Henry Crawford, who meanwhile had taken up the play, and with seeming carelessness was turning over the first act, soon settled the business.

"I must entreat Miss *Julia* Bertram," said he, "not to engage in the part of Agatha, or it will be the ruin of all my solemnity." (turning to her). "I could not stand your countenance dressed up in woe and paleness. The many laughs we have had together would infallibly come across me, and Frederick and his knapsack would be obliged to run away."

Pleasantly, courteously, it was spoken. But the manner was lost in the matter to Julia's feelings. She saw a glance at Maria which confirmed the injury to herself. It was a scheme, a trick; she was slighted, Maria was preferred.

The smile of triumph which Maria was trying to suppress shewed how well it was understood. And before Julia could command herself enough to speak, her brother spoke also against her: "Oh yes! Maria must and will be the best Agatha. Though Julia fancies she prefers tragedy, there is nothing of tragedy about her. Her features are not tragic features, and she walks too quick, and speaks too quick, and would not keep her countenance. She had better do the Cottager's Wife—a very pretty part. The old lady relieves the high-flown benevolence of her husband with a good deal of spirit."

"Cottager's Wife!" cried Mr. Yates. "What are you talking of? The most trivial, paltry, insignificant part! not a tolerable speech in the whole. An insult to your sister! At Ecclesford the governess was to have done it. Verily, the Brighton Duck could do it! You do not deserve the manager's office, if you cannot appreciate the talents of your company."

"Why, as to *that,* my good friend, till I and my company have really acted there must be some guesswork; but I mean no disparagement to Julia. We cannot have two Agathas, and we must have one Cottager's Wife."

"With all your partiality for Cottager's Wife," said Henry Crawford, "it will be impossible to make it fit your sister. We must not impose on her good-nature. We must not *allow* her to accept the part. Her talents will be wanted in Amelia. That most difficult of parts requires a delicacy of feeling found in a true gentlewoman—a Julia Bertram. You *will* undertake it, I hope?" He turned to her with a look of anxious entreaty, which softened her a little. But while she hesitated, her brother again interposed with Miss Crawford's better claim.

"No, no, Julia must not be Amelia. She would not like it. She would not do well. She is too tall and robust. Amelia should be a small, light, girlish, skipping figure. It is fit for Miss Crawford only. She looks the part, and will do it admirably."

Henry Crawford continued his supplication with Julia. "You must oblige us," said he, "indeed you must. When you have studied the character, I am sure you will feel it suit you. Tragedy may be your choice, but comedy chuses *you.* You will visit me in prison with a basket of provisions; you will not refuse to visit me in prison? Indeed, I see you thus, with your basket."

The influence of his voice was felt. Julia wavered; but was he only trying to soothe and pacify her, and make her overlook the previous affront? She distrusted him. The slight had been real. He was but at treacherous play with her.

She looked suspiciously at her sister. Maria's countenance was to decide it: if she were vexed and alarmed—but Maria looked all serenity and satisfaction. And Julia knew that on this ground Maria could not be happy but at her expense. With hasty indignation, therefore, and a tremulous voice, she said to him, "You do not seem afraid of not keeping your countenance when I come in comical, with a basket of provisions—but it is only as Agatha that I was to be so overpowering!" She stopped—Henry Crawford looked rather foolish, and as if he did not know what to say.

Tom Bertram began again—

"Miss Crawford must be Amelia, an excellent Amelia."

"Do not be afraid of *my* wanting the character," cried Julia, with angry quickness: "I am *not* to be Agatha, and I am sure I will do nothing else. And as to Amelia, it is of all parts in the world the most disgusting to me. I quite detest her. An odious, little, pert, unnatural, impudent girl. I have always protested against comedy, and this is comedy in its worst form."

And speaking thus, she walked hastily out of the room, leaving awkward feelings to more than one, but eliciting compassion only in Fanny—who had been a quiet auditor of the whole, and thought of her cousin's *jealousy* with great pity.

Across the room, Lord Eastwind observed Fanny's reaction, and *knew*.

A short silence succeeded Julia's exit. But her brother soon returned to business, and was eagerly looking over the play, with Mr. Yates's help, to ascertain what scenery would be necessary, and how to remove all bulky items of Egyptian nature out of the way, particularly the life-size golden statuary—while Maria and Henry Crawford conversed together in an under-voice. Her offer to give up the part to Julia, accompanied with: "Though I shall probably do the part very ill, *she* would do it worse," doubtless received all the compliments it called for.

This lasted for some time, then Tom Bertram and Mr. Yates walked off together to consult further in the room now beginning to be called *the Theatre.* Miss Bertram resolved to go down to the Parsonage herself with the offer of Amelia to Miss Crawford, and Fanny remained alone.

The first use she made of her solitude was to take up the volume left on the table, and begin to acquaint herself with the play of which she had heard so much. Her curiosity was awake, and she ran through it with an eagerness, then astonishment, that it could be chosen and performed in a private theatre! Agatha and Amelia appeared to her in their different ways so totally improper—so unfit to be played by any woman of modesty—that she could hardly suppose her cousins were aware of what they were engaging in. Edmund would certainly protest this!

Chapter XV

Miss Crawford accepted her part very readily. And soon after Miss Bertram's return from the Parsonage, Mr. Rushworth arrived, and another character was consequently cast.

Not quite Caliban—he had the offer of Count Cassel and Anhalt, and at first did not know which to chuse, and wanted Miss Bertram to direct him. But upon being made to understand Anhalt a very stupid fellow, he soon decided for the Count.

Miss Bertram approved the decision, for the less he had to learn the better. She very kindly took his part in hand, and shortened every speech possible; besides pointing out the necessity of his being splendidly dressed, and chusing his colours. Mr. Rushworth liked the idea of his finery very well, though affecting to despise it.

Thus much was settled before Edmund, who had been out all the morning, knew anything of the matter. When he entered the drawing-room before dinner, the buzz of discussion was high and Mr. Rushworth stepped forward to tell him the agreeable news.

"We have got a play," said he. "It is to be *Lovers' Vows;* and I am to be Count Cassel, and am to come in first with a blue dress and a pink satin cloak, and afterwards am to have another fine fancy suit, by way of a shooting-dress. Grrrowwr! Ayeee! Ahem! I do not know how I shall like it."

Fanny's eyes followed Edmund, and her heart beat for him as she heard this speech, and saw his look, and felt what his sensations must be.

"Lovers' Vows!" in a tone of the greatest amazement, was his only reply to Mr. Rushworth, and he turned towards his brother and sisters as if hardly doubting a contradiction.

"Yes," cried Mr. Yates. "After all our debatings, *Lovers' Vows* it is! A wonder we did not think of it before. My stupidity was abominable, for here we have all the advantage of what I saw at Ecclesford! We have cast almost every part."

"But what do you do for women?" said Edmund gravely, and looking at Maria.

Maria blushed in spite of herself as she answered, "I take the part which Lady Ravenshaw was to have done, and" (with a bolder eye) "Miss Crawford is to be Amelia."

"I should not have thought it the sort of play to be so easily filled up, with *us*," replied Edmund, turning away to the fire, where sat his mother, aunt, and Fanny, with Lord Eastwind off to the side as usual. Edmund seated himself with a look of great vexation.

"What insurmountable difficulties are placed before you, Mr. Bertram," said Lord Eastwind, surprising Fanny in this, for she had hardly seen him talk to anyone but Lady Bertram and herself.

"What? Oh, indeed," replied Edmund, as though noticing the dark-haired gentleman for the first time.

Mr. Rushworth followed him to say, "I come in three times, and have two-and-forty speeches. That's something, is it not? But I do not much like the idea of being so fine. I shall hardly know myself in a blue dress and a pink satin cloak. Grrraawwrr!"

Edmund could not answer him (though, the image of a portly wolf dressed in pink satin was indelible). In a few minutes Mr. Bertram was called out of the room, accompanied by Mr. Yates, and followed soon by Mr. Rushworth. Edmund almost immediately took the opportunity of saying, "I cannot, before Mr. Yates, speak what I feel as to this play, without reflecting on his friends at Ecclesford. But I must now, my dear Maria, tell *you,* that I think it exceedingly unfit for private representation, and that I hope you will give it up. I cannot but suppose you *will* when you have read it carefully over. Read only the first act[12] aloud to either your mother or aunt, and see how you can approve it!"

"We see things very differently," cried Maria. "I am perfectly acquainted with the play, I assure you. With a very few omissions, I can see nothing objectionable in it; and *I* am not the *only* young woman who thinks it fit for private representation."

"What self-assurance. I marvel at your cousin's ability to persevere in the achievement of her own desire," said Lord Eastwind, turning his face to Fanny only, and heard only by her.

"My Lord," she replied, "yet again I know not what to say. I do not see how desire fits into any of this—only what is dutiful and right."

"And yet," he countered, "here, as everywhere on this mortal plane, desire is what drives the notion of what is dutiful and right."

"Not so!" suddenly exclaimed Fanny, animated and finding herself hot around the cheeks. "At least—forgive me—if such is the sorry end-course of duty, then the very underlying notion of it must be rewritten!"

---

[12] Pure unadulterated debauchery of the lowest fashion; heaving bosoms, and endless lewd opportunities to approach eligible gentlemen one has set one's sights upon, in the guise and manner of a whore of Babylon.

"Duty and Desire are on the opposite parts of the same candle lit at both ends. At some point, burning, they meet in the middle. And, if neither one gives way to the other, the whole candle is consumed. In this case, a candle is a life. Your cousin's life. *Your* life."

"Why is it that whatever you speak of always comes down to flames?" noted Fanny, growing once more calm, and secure in her own thoughts. "A candle need never be lit at both ends. Simply chuse one and let oneself be properly used up by the flames of righteous living. I chuse duty. And if not that, I chuse not to be lit at all."

"A greatest pity ever voiced," replied Eastwind, "for your glorious candle to remain cold and unused, in darkness—*unconsumed.* Is it not better to chuse desire, and shine for all the world to see? Thus, at least, one burns with a bright joyful flame before the final end comes—indeed, an end that need never come. . . ."

"What joy is there, in knowing that one's candle could have been used to light someone's true way instead of selfishly illuminating the world only for oneself? For, Desire ignorant of Duty is a cold joyless thing. I would much rather be unlit and lie in eternal darkness, than to be spent for only my own cause; brief, never-to-be-satiated, inherently alone, ever regretting a better way."

And saying this, Fanny turned away, and attempted to ignore Lord Eastwind and his own—*burning,* as she suddenly came to realize—unrelenting, burning gaze. His was the sun scorching an ancient desert. . . .

Edmund continued to reproach Maria. "I am sorry, but in this matter it is *you* who are to lead. *You* must set the example. If others have blundered, it is your place to put them right, and shew them what true delicacy and decorum are."

This picture of her consequence had some effect, for no one loved better to lead than Maria. And with far more good-humour she answered, "I am much obliged to you, Edmund; you mean very well, but I still think you see things too strongly. And I really cannot undertake to harangue all the rest upon a subject of this kind. *There* would be the greatest indecorum, I think."

"Do you imagine that I could have such an idea in my head? No; let your conduct be the only harangue. Say that, on examining the part, you feel yourself unequal to it. Say this with firmness, and it will be quite enough; the wise will understand your motive. The play will be given up, and your delicacy honoured as it ought."

"Do not act anything improper, here in England, or in the Nile Valley, my dear," said Lady Bertram. "Sir Thomas would not like it.—Indeed, what does the great Pharaoh think? Fanny, ring the bell; His Ancient Lordship and I must have our, that is, my dinner.—To be sure, Julia is dressed by this time."

"I am convinced, madam," said Edmund, preventing Fanny, and ignoring the greater part of his mother's utterances, "that Sir Thomas would not like it."

"There, my dear, do you hear what Edmund says?"

"If I were to decline the part," said Maria, with renewed zeal, "Julia would certainly take it."

"What!" cried Edmund, "if she knew your reasons!"

"Oh! she might think of the difference in our situations—that *she* need not be so scrupulous. No; you must excuse me; I cannot retract my consent. It is too far settled, everybody would be so disappointed, Tom angry; and we shall never act anything."

"I was just going to say the very same thing," said Mrs. Norris. "If every play is to be objected to, you will act nothing, and the preparations will be all so much money thrown away. I do not know the play; but anything a little too warm can be left out. As Mr. Rushworth is to act too, there can be no harm."

And then Mrs. Norris proceeded to talk of carpenters, side-doors, curtains, rings, the poultry-yard, Dick Jackson, bits of board, and other details of the preparations.

Nobody troubled to answer; the others soon returned; and Edmund found that his effort was to be his only satisfaction.

Dinner passed heavily. Mrs. Norris related again her triumph over Dick Jackson, but neither play nor preparation were otherwise much talked of, for Edmund's disapprobation was felt even by his brother, though he would not have owned it. Maria, wanting Henry Crawford's animating support, thought the subject better avoided. Mr. Yates tried to make himself agreeable to Julia. And Mr. Rushworth, having only his own part and his own dress in his head, had soon talked away all that could be said of either, all while fiercely consuming the greater portion of a whole rack of lamb—tearing into the meat with his decidedly oversized canine teeth while muttering growls followed by sudden impassioned lines of dialogue out of *Lovers' Vows.*

Meanwhile, many servants carrying the succession of dishes, stopped for an inexplicable second or two behind the chair occupied by Lord Eastwind. Then, each man blinking and looking dazed, they proceeded on their way, with full use of their faculties. There was neither a single collision or dish dropped, nor a missed footfall.

The Mummy dined as well as the rest of the household.

After dinner, theatrical matters were resumed: there was still a great deal to be settled. Back in the drawing-room, Tom, Maria, and Mr. Yates seated themselves in committee at a separate table, with the play open before them. They were just getting deep in the subject when a most welcome interruption was given by the entrance of Mr. and Miss Crawford. Late and dark and dirty as it was, they could not help coming, and were received with grateful joy.

"Well, how do you go on?" and "What have you settled?" and "Oh! we can do nothing without you," followed the first salutations. Henry Crawford was soon seated with the other three at the table, while his sister made her way to Lady Bertram, and with pleasant attention was complimenting *her*. "I must really congratulate your ladyship," said she, "on the play being chosen; for though you have borne it with exemplary patience, you must be sick of all our noise and difficulties. The actors may be glad, but the bystanders must be infinitely rejoicing in a decision. I do sincerely give you joy, madam, as well as Mrs. Norris, and everybody else who is in the same predicament," glancing half fearfully, half slyly, beyond Fanny to Edmund.

She was very civilly answered by Lady Bertram who then insisted Miss Crawford chuse an amulet or necklet surely belonging to Akhenaten or Nefertiti from her ample collection, to complement her costume, and oh, would she like an urn or a gold scepter to hold while she recited the lines, or perchance a crocodile-headed something or other?

Miss Crawford escaped such offers after several skillful moments, while throwing a single *dark* and reproachful glance in the direction of Lord Eastwind who sat, as usual, in a shadowed location in the room, watching them all.

Fanny noticed the distinct awareness that Miss Crawford showed of Lord Eastwind, and the sharp looks exchanged between them. This served to reinforce in Fanny the frightening notion that Miss Crawford was far *more* than she *seemed*. Fanny was also certain beyond any doubt that Lord Eastwind was *more* than *he* seemed. She was not exactly sure what, but every attempt to discuss his metaphysical peculiarity—indeed, his very presence—with Edmund resulted in strange distractions and almost intentional events coming to interrupt them. Indeed, most of the time, Edmund, as all the rest of them, excepting the Crawfords (and occasionally, the two lupine creatures: Mrs.

Norris and Mr. Rushworth), seemed completely unaware of Lord Eastwind's existence.

Edmund said nothing in response to Miss Crawford. His being only a thespian bystander was not disputed. After continuing in chat with the party round the fire a few minutes, Miss Crawford returned to the party round the table. Standing by them, she seemed to interest herself in their arrangements till, as if struck by a sudden recollection, she exclaimed, "My good friends, you are most composedly at work upon these cottages and alehouses, inside and out; but pray let me know my fate in the meanwhile. Who is to be Anhalt? What gentleman among you am I to have the pleasure of making love to?"

"Ah, at last, we are come to it. What say you now, Miss Price?" whispered Lord Eastwind, so that Fanny started at his soft mesmerizing voice.

For a moment no one spoke. And then many spoke together to tell the same melancholy truth, that they had not yet got any Anhalt. "Mr. Rushworth was to be Count Cassel, but no one had yet undertaken Anhalt."

"Who will he be?" continued Lord Eastwind, whispering intensely. "Who will take the place of her lover?"

"I do not know," responded Fanny in kind, and was heard by no one but Eastwind.

"I had my choice of the parts," said Mr. Rushworth; "but I thought I should like the Count best, though I do not much relish the finery I am to have."

"You chose very wisely, I am sure," replied Miss Crawford, with a brightened look; "Anhalt is a heavy part."

"What does your heart tell you, Miss Price?" persisted Lord Eastwind, "who will it be?"

Fanny felt herself beginning to tremble.

"*The Count* has two-and-forty speeches," returned Mr. Rushworth, "which is no trifle. WROWWR! Ahem, pardon me."

"I am not at all surprised," said Miss Crawford, after a short pause, "at this lack of an Anhalt. Amelia deserves no better. Such a forward young lady may well frighten the men."

"I should be but too happy in taking the part, if it were possible," cried Tom; "but, unluckily, the Butler and Anhalt are in the same scene. I might speak very quickly and run from one side of the stage to the other and attempt both?"

"Your *brother* should take the part," said Mr. Yates, in a low voice. "Do not you think he would?"

"*I* shall not ask him," replied Tom, in a cold, determined manner.

Miss Crawford talked of something else, and soon afterwards rejoined the party at the fire.

"They do not want me at all," said she, seating herself. "I only puzzle them, and oblige them to make civil speeches. Mr. Edmund Bertram, as you do not act yourself, you will be a disinterested adviser; and, therefore, I apply to *you*. What shall we do for an Anhalt? What is your advice?"

"My advice," said he calmly, "is that you change the play."

"*I* should have no objection," she replied; "for though I do not dislike the part of Amelia, I shall be sorry to be an inconvenience. But as they do not chuse to hear your advice at *that table*" (looking round), "it certainly will not be taken."

Edmund said no more.

"What happens next, Miss Price?" said Lord Eastwind.

"I beg you," whispered Fanny to him, "If you have any kindness, you will not speak of this any longer."

"I speak only for *your* sake. Do you not see? Watch now, observe what is said." And Eastwind turned subtly to indicate Miss Crawford.

"If *any* part could tempt *you* to act, I suppose it would be Anhalt," observed the lady archly, after a short pause; "for he is a clergyman, you know."

"*That* circumstance would by no means tempt me," Edmund replied, "for I should be sorry to make the character ridiculous by bad acting."

Miss Crawford was silenced, and with some feelings of resentment and mortification, moved her chair considerably nearer the tea-table, and gave all her attention to Mrs. Norris who was presiding there (and periodically breaking out into yelps of feral agitation).

"Fanny," cried Tom Bertram, from the other table, where the conference was eagerly carrying on, and the conversation incessant, "we want your services."

Fanny was up in a moment, expecting some errand—for the habit of employing her in that way was not yet overcome, in spite of all that Edmund could do.

"Oh! we do not want to disturb you from your seat. We do not want your *present* services. We shall only want you in our play. You must be Cottager's Wife."

"Me!" cried Fanny, sitting down again with a frightened look. "Indeed you must excuse me. I could not act anything if you were to give me the world. No, indeed, I cannot act."

"Indeed, but you must, for we cannot excuse you. It need not frighten you: it is a nothing of a part, a mere nothing, not above half a dozen speeches altogether, and it will not much signify if nobody hears a word you say; so you may be as creep-mouse as you like, but we must have you to look at."

"If you are afraid of half a dozen speeches," cried Mr. Rushworth, "what would you do with such a part as mine? I have forty-two to learn."

"It is not that I am afraid of learning by heart," said Fanny, shocked to find herself at that moment the only speaker in the room, and to feel that almost every eye was upon her; "but I really cannot act."

"Yes, yes, you can act well enough for *us*. Learn your part, and we will teach you all the rest. You have only two scenes, and as I shall be Cottager, I'll put you in and push you about, and you will do it very well, I'll answer for it."

"No, indeed, Mr. Bertram, you must excuse me. You cannot have an idea. It would be absolutely impossible for me. If I were to undertake it, I should only disappoint you."

"Phoo! Phoo! Do not be so shamefaced. You'll do it very well. Every allowance will be made for you. We do not expect perfection. You must get a brown gown, and a white apron, and a mob cap, and we must make you a few wrinkles, and a little of the crowsfoot at the corner of your eyes, and you will be a very proper, little old woman."

"You must excuse me, indeed you must excuse me," cried Fanny, growing more and more red from excessive agitation, and looking distressfully at Edmund. He was kindly observing her. But unwilling to exasperate his brother by interference, he gave her only an encouraging smile.

Lord Eastwind watched them. He then slowly started to raise his hand, palm up, in a peculiar gesture.

Fanny's entreaty had no effect on Tom: he only repeated the same. And it was not merely Tom, for the requisition was now backed by Maria, and Mr. Crawford, and Mr. Yates, with an urgency which differed from his but in being more gentle or more ceremonious, and which altogether was quite overpowering to Fanny. Before she could breathe after it, Mrs. Norris completed the whole by thus addressing her in a whisper at once angry and audible—"What a piece of work here is about nothing: I am quite ashamed of you, Fanny, to make such a difficulty of obliging your cousins in a trifle of this sort—so kind as they are to you! Take the part with a good grace, and let us hear no more of the matter."

Lord Eastwind moved his raised hand palm down and pointed at the doors.

In that moment two servants entered, both in somewhat ill-fitting clothing and with horrendously bad skin. In unison they inquired very politely whether there was anything needed by the ladies and gentlemen—tea service perhaps?

The unhappy tension was broken. Tom shooed the servants out, saying that it was a mistake and nothing was required. But they seemed to ignore him and instead had their faces—dark-skinned and windblown—turned to Lord Eastwind, who nodded silently.

"Do not urge her, madam," said Edmund to Mrs. Norris, finding his voice at last. "It is not fair to urge her in this manner. You see she does not like to act. Let her chuse for herself. Her judgment may be safely trusted. Do not urge her any more."

"I am not going to urge her," replied Mrs. Norris sharply, barely suppressing an angry yelp; "but she is a very obstinate, ungrateful girl, if she does not do what her aunt and cousins wish her—very ungrateful, indeed, considering who and what she is."

Edmund was too angry to speak. But Miss Crawford, looking for a moment with astonished eyes at Mrs. Norris, and then at Fanny, whose tears were beginning to shew themselves, immediately said, with some keenness, "I do not like my situation: this *place* is too hot for me," and moved away her chair to the opposite side of the table, close to Fanny, saying to her, in a seemingly kind, low whisper, as she placed herself, "Never mind, my dear Miss Price, this is a cross evening: everybody is cross and teasing, but do not let us mind them." And with pointed attention Miss Crawford talked to her and endeavoured to raise her spirits, in spite of being out of spirits herself. By a look at her brother she prevented any further entreaty from the theatrical board, and the really good feelings by which she was almost purely governed were rapidly restoring her to all the little she had lost in Edmund's favour.

In his place, Lord Eastwind smiled.

Fanny did not love Miss Crawford. But she felt very obliged for her present kindness. Miss Crawford took notice of Fanny's work, wished *she* could work as well, begged for the pattern, and supposed Fanny was now preparing for her *appearance*—surely she would "come out"[13] when her cousin was married. She asked if Fanny heard lately from her brother at sea, was curious to see the fine young man, advised Fanny to get his picture drawn before he went to sea again. Fanny admitted it to be very agreeable flattery. She listened and answered with more animation than she had intended.

The consultation upon the play still went on, and Miss Crawford's attention was first called from Fanny by Tom Bertram's telling her, with infinite regret, that he found it absolutely impossible for him to undertake the part of Anhalt in addition to the Butler. "But there will not be the smallest difficulty in filling it," he added. "I could name at least six young men within six miles of us, who are wild to be admitted into our company: either of the Olivers or Charles Maddox. I will ride to-morrow morning to Stoke, and ask one of them."

While he spoke, Maria looked in apprehension at Edmund, expecting opposition, but he said nothing. After a moment, Miss Crawford calmly replied, "I have no objection. Have I ever seen either of the gentlemen? Yes, Mr. Charles Maddox, a quiet-looking young man, I remember. Let it be *him:* less unpleasant to me than to have a perfect stranger."

Charles Maddox was to be the man. Tom repeated his resolution of going to him early on the morrow. Julia observed, in a sarcastic manner that "the Mansfield theatricals would enliven the whole neighbourhood exceedingly." Yet Edmund still held his peace, and shewed only a determined gravity.

"I am not very sanguine as to our play," said Miss Crawford, in an undervoice to Fanny, "and I can tell Mr. Maddox that I shall shorten some of our common speeches before we rehearse together. It will be very disagreeable, and by no means what I expected."

---

[13] Not in the "closet" sense. Fie! what Oscar Wildean indelicacy!

Chapter XVI

It was not in Miss Crawford's power to talk Fanny into any real forgetfulness of what had passed. When the evening was over, she went to bed full of it, still agitated by the shock of such an attack from her cousin Tom, and her spirits sinking under her aunt's unkind reproach. To be called into notice in such a manner, coerced to act; and then to have the charge of obstinate ingratitude, with such a hint at her dependent situation! Miss Crawford had protected her only for the time. If they were all to pressure her again, what should she do?

She fell asleep before she could answer the question, dreaming for some reason of dark intense eyes and a searing hot wind in a distant ancient desert, and found it quite as puzzling when she awoke the next morning. The little white attic, which had continued as her sleeping-room ever since her first entering the family, was intolerable—not to mention being situated so near Lady Bertram's favorite forbidden room with its Cursed horrors, which Fanny was beginning to suspect were somehow related not merely to Egypt but to a certain Lord Eastwind and his sudden insinuating presence in the family.

It was fortunate that she had recourse, as soon as she was dressed, to another more spacious and agreeable apartment. It had once been their school-room. Miss Lee had lived there, and there they had read and written, talked and laughed. The room had since become unused and quite deserted, except by Fanny. There she visited her plants and books, kept there due to the deficiency of space in her little chamber above.

Gradually Fanny moved there more of her possessions, and spent more of her time there. With no one to oppose her, she naturally and artlessly worked herself into it. The East room, as it had been called ever since Maria Bertram was sixteen, was now considered Fanny's, almost as decidedly as the white attic. The Miss Bertrams, with their own superior apartments, entirely approved it. And Mrs. Norris, having stipulated for there never being a fire in it on Fanny's account, was tolerably resigned to her having the use of what nobody else wanted—though she would then imply it was the best room in the house.

Even without a fire it was habitable on early spring and late autumn mornings to such a willing soul as Fanny. While there was a gleam of sunshine she hoped not to be driven from it entirely, even when winter came. The comfort of it in her hours of leisure was extreme. She could go there after anything unpleasant below, and find immediate consolation. Her plants, her books—of which she had been a collector from the first hour of her commanding a shilling—her writing-desk, and her works of charity and ingenuity, were all within reach.

As for musing, she could scarcely see an object in that room which had not an interesting remembrance connected with it. Everything was a friend, or bore her thoughts to a friend. And though there had been sometimes much suffering; though her motives had often been misunderstood, her feelings disregarded, and her comprehension undervalued; though she had known tyranny, ridicule, and neglect—yet almost every recurrence of either had led to something consolatory. Her aunt Bertram had spoken for her, or Miss Lee had been encouraging, or (what was yet more frequent or more dear), Edmund had been her champion and her friend. He had supported her, told her not to cry, or had given her some proof of affection which made her tears delightful. The whole was now so blended together, so gentled by time, that every former affliction had its charm.

The room was most dear to her. She would not have changed its furniture for the handsomest in the house, though the original plain furnishings had suffered the ill-usage of children. Its greatest elegancies and ornaments were blessedly not Egyptian—a faded footstool of Julia's work, too ill done for the drawing-room, three transparencies for the three lower panes of one window, a collection of family profiles, thought unworthy of being anywhere else. Over the mantelpiece, a tiny golden figurine of the Goddess Bast as an afterthought from Lady Bertram, and pinned against the wall, a small sketch of a ship sent four years ago from the Mediterranean by William, with *H.M.S. Antwerp* at the bottom, in letters as tall as the mainmast.

To this nest of comforts Fanny now walked—to see if by looking at Edmund's profile she could catch any of his counsel, or by giving air to her geraniums she might inhale a breeze of mental strength herself. But she had more than fears of her own perseverance to remove: she had begun to feel undecided as to what she *ought to do.* And as she walked round the room her doubts were increasing.

Was she *right* in refusing what was so strongly wished for? Was it not ill-nature, selfishness, and a fear of exposing herself? And would Edmund's judgment be enough to justify her denial? Acting seemed so horrible to her that she was inclined to suspect the truth and purity of her own scruples.

The table between the windows was covered with work-boxes and netting-boxes which had been given her at different times, principally by Tom; and she grew bewildered as to the amount of the debt which all these kind memories produced. A tap at the door roused her. Her gentle "Come in" was answered by the appearance of one before whom all her doubts were to be laid. Her eyes brightened at the sight of Edmund.

"Can I speak with you, Fanny, for a few minutes?"

"Yes, certainly."

"I want to consult your opinion."

"My opinion!" she cried, shrinking from such a compliment, highly as it gratified her.

"Yes, your advice and opinion. I do not know what to do. This acting scheme gets worse and worse, you see. They have chosen almost as bad a play as they could. And now, to complete the business, are going to ask the help of a young man very slightly known to any of us. This is the end of all the privacy and propriety. I know no harm of Charles Maddox; but the excessive intimacy which must spring from his being admitted among us in this manner is highly objectionable. It appears to me an evil of such magnitude as must be prevented. Do not you see it in the same light?"

"Yes; but what can be done? Your brother is so determined."

"There is but *one* thing to be done, Fanny. I must take the role of Anhalt myself. Nothing else will quiet Tom."

Fanny could not answer him. But for some reason, in that moment she was reminded of Lord Eastwind's cryptic words earlier, and his steady, exotic, unwavering gaze.

"It is not at all what I like," he continued. "No man can like being driven into the *appearance* of such inconsistency. After opposing the scheme from the beginning, it is absurd of me. But I can think of no other alternative. Can you, Fanny?"

"No," said Fanny slowly, "not immediately, but—"

"But what? I see your judgment is not with me. Think it over. Perhaps you are not so much aware as I am of the mischief that *must* arise from a young man's being received in this manner: placed suddenly on a footing which must do away all restraints. It is all very bad![14] Put yourself in Miss Crawford's place, Fanny. Consider what it would be to act Amelia with a

---

[14] In the Babylonian sense.

stranger. I heard enough of what she said to you last night to understand her unwillingness. She probably had different expectations of the role. Her feelings ought to be respected. Does it not strike you so, Fanny? You hesitate."

"I am sorry for Miss Crawford; but I am sorrier to see you drawn into what you are against, what will be disagreeable to my uncle. It will be such a triumph to the others!"

"They will not have much cause of triumph when they see how infamously I act. But, triumph there will be, and I must brave it. But if I can be the means of restraining them, I shall be well repaid. As I am now, I have no influence. I have offended them, and they will not hear me. But when I have put them in good-humour by this concession, I hope to persuade them to limit the performance to a much smaller circle—to confine it to Mrs. Rushworth and the Grants. Will not this be worth gaining?"

"Yes, it will be a great point."

"But still it has not your approbation. Can you mention any other means of doing equal good?"

"No, I cannot think of anything else."

"Give me your approbation, then, Fanny. I am not comfortable without it."

"Oh, cousin!"

"If you are against me, I ought to distrust myself. And yet—it is absolutely impossible to let Tom go on, riding about the country in quest of anybody who can be persuaded to act. It is dear mindless *Tom* we speak of, you realize—he might return with an ancient "druid" or a piece of the Blarney stone! I thought *you* would have entered more into Miss Crawford's feelings."

"No doubt she will be very glad. It must be a great relief to her," said Fanny, trying for greater warmth of manner.

"She never appeared more amiable than in her kindness to you last night. It gave her a strong claim on my goodwill."

"She *was* very kind, indeed, and I am glad to have her spared . . ."

She could not finish the generous effusion. Her conscience stopt her in the middle, but Edmund was satisfied.

"I shall walk down immediately after breakfast," said he, "and am sure of giving pleasure there. And now, dear Fanny, I will not interrupt you any longer. You want to be reading. But I could not be easy till I had spoken to you, and come to a decision. My head has been full of this matter all night. If Tom is up, I shall go to him directly, before he escapes to plunder Bedlam for our actor! When we meet at breakfast we shall be all in high good-humour at the prospect of acting the fool together with such unanimity. *You,* in the meanwhile, will be taking a reading trip into China, I suppose."—opening a volume on the table and then taking up some others. "I admire your little establishment exceedingly; and as soon as I am gone, empty your head of all this nonsense of acting, and sit comfortably. But do not stay here to be cold."

"Pray, before you are on your way, cousin," said Fanny carefully, "might I ask you what you think of—of Lord Eastwind?"

Edmund creased his brow in thought. "Who? Oh, you mean that—that fellow who is my mother's Egyptian matters confidant? What is his name again? Eastport?"

"Cousin! How odd it is that even *now* you seem barely aware of this man's existence and forget his name a moment after I speak it! Do you not think there is something *strange* about him; how he is here all the while, *watching* us? I—I think he has something to do with the Cursed mystery hidden away in Lady Bertram's favorite chamber near my own little white attic."

"Dearest Fanny, how odd of you to speak of this—this gentleman in such a way, especially when we were just discussing the pressing matter of the play. What has he to do with anything, with the family Curse?"

"But do not you think it even a bit strange? He seems to have *mesmerized* everyone into—ignoring him! And—he talks to Lady Bertram and myself only, it seems. And when he does speak, it is of very strange things. Have you ever spoken more than a word to him?"

"Now that you mention it, I don't recall. I—"

"Exactly so! It's as if he is not here, and yet, he *is,* and he drinks us in, all of us, and Lady Bertram is akin to his mouthpiece, a living servant!"

"What nonsense!"

Fanny paused, then gathered courage and blurted out: "I don't believe he is *human.*"

Edmund stared, his expression slowly growing perturbed from encroaching confusion. "Wait a moment, cousin, of whom are we speaking just now? I don't recall—"

Fanny suddenly felt herself grow very cold.

"Oh, it is of no matter, cousin," she ended quietly, and the fear was all around, coursing though her. "But—indeed, now you must be going."

And thus, Edmund went. But there was no reading, no composure for Fanny. He had told her the most extraordinary, inconceivable, unwelcome news. Yet she could think of nothing else but Lord Eastwind and how Edmund discounted him! And—to be acting! After all his objections, after all she had heard him say, could Edmund be so inconsistent? And, Edmund, so blind! Was he not deceiving himself? Was he not wrong?

Alas! it was all Miss Crawford's doing. Fanny had seen her influence in every speech, and was miserable. The doubts and alarms as to her own conduct, were become of little consequence now. This deeper anxiety swallowed them up. Things should take their course; she cared not how it ended. Her cousins might attack, but she was beyond their reach. And if at last obliged to yield—no matter—it was all misery now.

And—Lord Eastwind was somehow, impossibly, also at the heart of it.

Chapter XVII

It was, indeed, a triumphant day to Mr. Bertram and Maria. Such a victory over Edmund's discretion had been beyond their hopes, and was most delightful. There was no longer anything to disturb them in their darling project. They congratulated each other in private on the jealous weakness to which they attributed the change, with all glee. Edmund might still look grave, and must disapprove the scheme and play; their point was gained. He was to act, and he was driven to it by selfish inclinations. Edmund had descended from that tedious moral elevation which he had maintained before, and they were better and happier for it.

They behaved very well, however, to *him* on the occasion, betraying no exultation beyond the lines about the corners of the mouth, and seemed to think it as great an escape to be quit of the intrusion of Charles Maddox. "To have it quite in their own family circle was what they had particularly wished. A stranger among them would have been the destruction of all their comfort."

When Edmund, pursuing that idea, hinted at a limitation of the audience, they were ready to promise anything. It was all good-humour and encouragement. Mrs. Norris offered to contrive his dress; Mr. Yates assured him that Anhalt's last scene with the Baron admitted a good deal of action, ranting, and emphasis. And with a joyous growl that released a fountain of spittle, Mr. Rushworth undertook to count his speeches.

"Perhaps," said Tom, "Fanny may be more disposed to oblige us now. Perhaps you may persuade *her*."

"No, she is quite determined. She certainly will not act."

"Oh! very well." And not another word was said; but Fanny felt herself again in danger, and her indifference to the danger was beginning to fail her already.

There were not fewer smiles at the Parsonage than at the Park on this change in Edmund. Miss Crawford looked very *dark* and lovely, and entered with such renewed cheerfulness as could have but one effect on him. "He had been right; he was glad." And the morning wore away in sweet satisfactions.

At the request of Miss Crawford, Mrs. Grant had agreed to undertake the part for which Fanny had been wanted, gladdening *her* heart. And yet even this, when imparted by Edmund, brought a pang with it. For it was Miss Crawford to whom she was obliged—whose kind exertions were to excite her gratitude, and who was spoken of with a glow of admiration.

Fanny was saved from the hell of acting; but peace and safety were not to be. Her mind had been never farther from peace. She could not feel that she had done wrong herself, but she was disquieted in every other way. Her heart and judgment were equally against Edmund's decision: she could not acquit his unsteadiness, and his happiness under it made her wretched.

Furthermore, she was full of jealousy and agitation. Miss Crawford came with looks of gaiety which seemed an insult, with friendly expressions towards herself which she could hardly answer calmly. Everybody around her was gay[15] and busy and important; each had their part, their dress, their favourite scene, their friends and confederates. She alone was sad and insignificant, with no share in anything. She might go or stay, be

---

[15] Not in the Lesbos sense—though, there is nothing wrong with that.

in the midst of their noise, or retreat to the solitude of the East room, without being seen or missed. She could almost think anything would have been preferable to this.

In addition, Mrs. Grant, who took the role first offered to Fanny, suddenly gained consequence. She was now popular, wanted and praised. Fanny was in some danger of envying her the character she had accepted; but then thought better of it.

It was at such a moment that Lord Eastwind once again made himself available and stepped away from the shadows, it seemed, to address her.

"What do you dream about, Miss Price? Is there something that you long for, besides being needed by the denizens of this foolish play? Or is there only *one* among them who touches your heart?"

"My poor heart, I beg you, is not a trifle, and I would rather not speak of it altogether."

"Nay, your heart is farther from a trifle than the sun is from the feather of a falcon."

And he stood looking at her closely, so that Fanny felt a tremor run down her spine, as though a hot ancient wind of a faraway land washed over her—but for a moment only."

Mr. Rushworth interrupted the strange reverie by passing between them attired as a pink-and-chartreuse peacock of high fashion, and declaiming the same two lines interspersed with barking, or possibly just hiccoughs, and a phlegmy clearing of his larynx.

As a wind recedes, Lord Eastwind faded back into the shadows.

But, Fanny's heart was not the only saddened one amongst them, as she soon began to acknowledge to herself. Julia was a sufferer too, though not quite so blamelessly.

Henry Crawford had trifled with Julia's feelings. But she had long allowed and even sought his attentions, jealous of her sister. And now that his preference for Maria had been revealed to her, she submitted to it without any alarm for Maria's situation. She either sat in gloomy silence, wrapt in such gravity as nothing could subdue; or, allowing the attentions of Mr. Yates, talked with forced gaiety to him alone, ridiculing the acting of the others and pretending a newfound interest in—of all things—the excavations of Egypt.

Meanwhile, all over Mansfield Park, dazed sleepy servants paraded up and down corridors, entered parlors only to forget their tasks in sudden fits of stupor, then recalling again, and were frequently cornered and gently *touched* by peculiar *others* clad in very shabby torn linen clothing, with terrible skin conditions and a stupefying case of windblown "sailor sunburn"—as Lady Bertram was likely to inform anyone who bothered to ask her "who these strange people were," and who had never previously been seen in the household.

"Sailors! Sailors, all!" she muttered with a beatific expression. "All come forth from the land of Ptolemy and Cleopatra; all quite welcome to stay and attend the Pharaoh, naturally. As long as they only consume vermin, or just take a tad of the *ka,* the breath of life, *downstairs,* it would be just fine, no harm done," at which point the speaker usually hurried to end the conversation with great politeness so as not to offend the poor gently deranged Ladyship.

Fanny herself ran into more than one such strange *unnatural* individual as she went up and down the stairs to her own attic every day. They moved with a strange wooden gait, shuffling about stiffly and very slowly. Once she saw a man miss a doorway and repeatedly attempt to pass through a wall, beating himself against the wallpaper in futility like a horsefly against a windowpane, until the butler came and loudly cleared his throat in arch disapproval. . . .

Another time, just at the lower flight of stairs, she was confronted by a very dried-out looking fellow, with rusty peeling skin, and almost no hair on his scalp. He had such deep eye-sockets that for a moment Fanny thought there were no eyes there at all! After smacking his seemingly toothless gums, he attempted to stop her and slowly raised an arm in her direction.

But just about when his grubby peeling fingers brushed against the muslin of her shoulder, "Fanny stood back in some alarm and said, "I beg pardon, sir, what are you doing? I'd like to pass, please."

"WHA-WA-SHWAH!" said the man softly in a hissing faint rattle of breath, as though his lungs had holes in it and could not properly support the exhalation; and Fanny was certain now he was in his cups.

"Sir, I *am* sorry, but I must pass, please step aside, or I shall be forced to call for assistance—"

But the man ignored her intonation and continued to reach for her, finally placing his fingertips on her arm.

With a small squeak, Fanny slapped his hand away.

"You—you take liberties, sir! Unhand me!"

The strange man—at this point the excellent Reader can safely guess this was none other than a *mummy*—went absolutely still in what appeared to be genuine stunned confusion. And then, as though nothing had been said in protest, he resumed his attempt to feed and reached for Fanny.

Fanny was—as the delicate Reader has come to know—normally a gentle lamb. But there was something decidedly uncanny and, furthermore, decidedly *unholy* about the situation; not to mention, the man creature before her was scandalously bold. And as such, all proprieties must be cast aside in favor of the female protective instinct.

Fanny went directly for his nose.

She suddenly had the reflexes of a London gentleman boxer without ever having been to London or having seen a ringside match. It was as though the good Lord himself imbued her with superhuman strength and speed to serve her in this moment of genuine calamity.

Her small fist connected with the proboscis and there was a moment of *something* giving way. Fanny heard an infernal crunch, felt her fist smashing something clammy, and then stood back to watch the monstrous face caved in, and, in place of the nose, an unholy mess of sanguinity and darkness and—oh horrors!—squirming *maggots*.

The mummy gave a muffled howl, then lurched back against the wall, and fled, flailing its limbs slowly, and nearly crashing downstairs.

Fanny stood trembling, her breath coming fast. "Oh no!—Oh dear! I believe I killed him!" she muttered, looking in disbelieving horror at her one calamity-stained hand.

As soon as she composed herself she slowly made her way below. At the foot of the stairs she was met by the butler, who immediately inquired as to the condition of her sanguined injury.

"My dear Miss Price!" exclaimed Baddeley with alarm, "are you well? What has happened to your hand? Was it a fall? We must have you looked after immediately—"

"Oh no, thank you, sir . . . I have no wish to trouble you or anyone! That is, *this* is not—it is none of my own. I am afraid it is someone else's. A man! A strange man! Indeed, was there a man heading in your direction, by any chance? Just moments earlier? A peculiar looking man, perhaps a servant, someone I have never seen before—"

"Why, no—there has been no one—"

Baddeley was quite in confusion as it is. And then Fanny took him beyond all comprehension, by adding softly, "I am dearly afraid I may have—*killed* him."

But there was no sign of the suspicious subject of Fanny's so-called murder. Indeed, it was as if he had disappeared from the premises, even though Baddeley searched thoroughly and sent a couple of servants to look around the estate.

For a day or two after the affront to Julia's feelings was given—and Fanny demolished her first mummy—Henry Crawford attempted his usual attack of gallantry and compliment. But he had not cared enough to persevere against a few repulses. Soon becoming too busy with his play to have time for more than one flirtation, he grew indifferent to the quarrel.

Mrs. Grant, in lieu of her expectations, was not pleased to see Julia excluded from the play and from his advances. But as Henry must be the best judge of his own behavior, and as he did assure her, with a most persuasive smile, that neither he nor Julia had ever had a serious thought of each other, she could only renew her former cautionary entreaties.

"I rather wonder Julia is not in love with Henry," was her observation to Mary.

"I dare say she is," replied Mary coldly. "I imagine both sisters are."

"Both! no, no, that must not be. Do not give him a hint of it. Think of Mr. Rushworth!"

"You had better tell Miss Bertram to think of Mr. Rushworth. It may do *her* some good. I often think of Mr. Rushworth's property and independence, and wish them in other hands; but I never think of *him* unless I am observing wolfhounds."

"I dare say he *will* be in parliament soon."

"Parliament will benefit from a decrease in at least one kind of vermin."

"When Sir Thomas comes, I dare say he will be in for some borough, but there has been nobody to put him in the way of doing anything yet," observed Mrs. Grant.

"Sir Thomas is to achieve many mighty things when he comes home" said Mary, after a pause. "Perchance he will even have a native Antigua cure for lunacy. Though, likely not the kind that will also grant Mr. Rushworth an additional smidgen of sense."

"Upon Sir Thomas's return you will find he has a fine dignified manner, which suits the head of such a house, and keeps everybody in their place. Lady Bertram seems more of a cipher now than when he is at home—though, no, allow me to retract, she is quite *consumed* by Nile folly even with Sir Thomas at her side—and nobody else can keep Mrs. Norris in order, especially when she has her regular moonlight *affliction*. But, Mary, do not fancy that Maria Bertram cares for Henry. I am sure *Julia* does not, or she would not have flirted as she did last night with Mr. Yates. And though Henry and Maria are very good friends, I think she likes Sotherton too well to be inconstant."

"I would not give much for Mr. Rushworth's chance if Henry stept in before the articles were signed. Of course, matters would stand quite different, if Maria were a rare shank of beef in the moonlight."

"If you have such a suspicion, something must be done."

"One cannot control moonlight—or steaks."

"Now, don't be silly! You know what I mean. As soon as the play is over, we will talk to him seriously, make him know his own mind; and if needed, we will send him away for a time."

Julia *did* suffer, however, though it escaped the notice of many. She had loved, she did love still, and she had all the suffering which a warm temper and a high spirit were likely to endure. Her heart was sore and angry. The sister with whom she was used to be on easy terms was now become her greatest enemy. Julia hoped for some punishment to Maria for conduct so shameful towards herself as well as towards Mr. Rushworth. While triumphant Maria pursued her purpose, Julia could never see Maria distinguished by Henry Crawford without trusting that it would create jealousy, and bring a public disturbance.

Fanny saw and pitied much of this in Julia; but there was no outward fellowship between them. Julia made no communication, and Fanny took no liberties. They were two solitary sufferers, or connected only by Fanny's consciousness. And now that Fanny had had her ghastly dreadful violent encounter with the *undead* in the corridor, there were far greater concerns to weigh her down than mere family decorum.

Something was seriously and metaphysically wrong at Mansfield Park—more so than usual.

Chapter XVIII

Everything was now in a regular train: theatre, actors, actresses, and dresses, were all getting forward. But though no other great impediments arose, Fanny found everyone's initial delight transform into vexations.

Edmund had many. Entirely against *his* judgment, a scene-painter arrived from town, and went to work. Tom began to fret over the scene-painter's slow progress. He had learned his part—*all* his parts—for he took every trifling one that could be united with the Butler, and was impatient to be acting. Every day increased his sense of the insignificance of all his parts together, and regret that some other play had not been chosen—with *more* parts for him.

Fanny, being always a very courteous listener, and often the only listener at hand, came in to hear their complaints and distresses. *She* knew that Mr. Yates was thought to rant dreadfully; that Mr. Yates was disappointed in Henry Crawford; that Tom Bertram spoke so quick he would be unintelligible; that Mrs. Grant spoiled everything by laughing; that Edmund was behindhand with his part, and that it was misery to have anything to do with Mr. Rushworth, who needed a prompter for every speech, stopped to growl during breath pauses, and could seldom get anybody to rehearse with him due to much firing of projectile spittle.

Moreover, her cousin Maria decidedly avoided him, and quite needlessly often rehearsed the first scene between her and Mr. Crawford. . . .

And yet, Fanny derived much innocent audience enjoyment from the play. Henry Crawford acted well, and it was a pleasure to *her* to creep into the theatre, and attend the rehearsal of the first act, in spite of the feelings it excited in some speeches for Maria. Maria, she also thought, acted well, too well. And after the first rehearsal or two, Fanny began to be their only audience—sometimes as prompter, sometimes as spectator—and often very useful.

As far as she could judge, Mr. Crawford was considerably the best actor of all. He had more confidence than Edmund, more judgment than Tom, more talent and taste than Mr. Yates, and less spittle than Mr. Rushworth. She did not like him as a man, but she must admit him to be the best actor, and on this point there were not many who differed from her. Mr. Yates, for one, missed the subtlety and exclaimed against his tameness and insipidity. And the day came at last, when Mr. Rushworth turned to her with a black look, and said, "Do you think there is anything so very fine in all this? For the life and soul of me, I cannot admire him. And, between ourselves, to see such an undersized, little, mean-looking man—I could just *tear* him with my teeth, the pip-squeak that he is—Ahem!—set up for a fine actor, is very ridiculous in my opinion. Arrrggarrh!"

From this moment there was a return of his former jealousy, which Maria was at little pains to remove. And the chances of Mr. Rushworth's ever attaining to the knowledge of his two-and-forty speeches became much less. Fanny, in her pity and kindheartedness, was at great pains to teach him how to memorize, giving him all the help in her power, learning every word of his lines herself, but without any progress on his part.

Many uncomfortable, anxious, apprehensive feelings Fanny certainly had; but the gloom of her first theatrical worries was proved to have been unfounded.

A far more dire concern was instead before her. Every now and then, Fanny considered if she might attempt to speak to Edmund on the secret subject between them, and to divulge to him the violent confrontation on the stairs and her role in possibly killing someone—whether a man or a creature of the Curse, she was unsure. Neither was she sure of Baddeley's effectiveness in his search of the premises, nor whether the danger was still present.

The servants and staff continued behaving strangely, unnoticed by all, and this time Fanny paid more attention to their comings and goings, and also, to the odd manner with which many of them seemed to *react* to Lord Eastwind.

They *obeyed* him—indeed, rather subtly, and almost instinctively. They moved like theatre puppets to each tiny lift of his finger, or his turn of head or an intense look of his exotic eye.

And when Lord Eastwind noted Fanny's discreet glances in his direction, he always acknowledged her—with a tiny nod or a ghost of a smile.

It was as though he was biding his time.

There was a great deal of needlework to be done, in which Fanny's help was wanted; and Mrs. Norris claimed it—"Come, Fanny," she cried, "these are fine times for you, but you must not be always walking from one room to the other, and doing the lookings-on at your ease; I want you here. I have been slaving to contrive Mr. Rushworth's cloak, and now you may give me your help in putting it together. If nobody did more than *you,* we should not get on very fast."

Fanny took the work very quietly, without attempting any defence; but her kinder aunt Bertram observed on her behalf—

"One cannot wonder, sister, that Fanny *should* be delighted: it is all new to her, you know. You and I used to be very fond of a play ourselves, and so am I still. As soon as I am a little more at leisure, what with the clay tablets and the amulet box of Osiris for the Pharaoh, *I* mean to look in at their rehearsals too. What is the play about, Fanny? you have never told me. In what bygone era of Egypt does the scenery lie?"

"Oh! sister, pray do not ask her now; for Fanny is not one of those who can talk and work at the same time. It is about *Lovers' Vows*. Nothing to do with the Nile or crocodiles, dead or living, I assure you." And Mrs. Norris glared in the direction of Lord Eastwind who sat on the other side of Lady Bertram, shadowed and silent.

"I believe," said Fanny to her aunt Bertram, "there will be three acts rehearsed to-morrow evening, and that will give you an opportunity of seeing all the actors at once."

"You had better stay till the curtain is hung," interposed Mrs. Norris; "in a day or two—very little sense in a play without a curtain—and one will find it draw up into handsome festoons."

Lady Bertram seemed quite resigned to waiting, and began to polish the side of a gilded Thoth statuette.

Fanny did not share her aunt's composure. She thought of the morrow a great deal, for if the three acts were rehearsed, Edmund and Miss Crawford would then be acting together for the first time. The third act would bring a scene between them which interested her most particularly, and which she was longing and dreading to see how they would perform. The subject of it was love—a marriage of love was to be described by the gentleman, and a near declaration of love by the lady. Fanny had read the scene with painful, wondering emotions, and looked forward to their performance in trepidation. She did not *believe* they had yet rehearsed it, even in private.

Furthermore, what made it worse for Fanny was an unexpected discovery she made about Miss Crawford. Some time after tea, Miss Crawford had excused herself, and Fanny incidentally happened to follow her into a corridor leading to the way to the kitchen.

Here, Miss Crawford ran into a female servant who carried a small washbasin on her way to perform cleaning chores. Just a few steps behind, unnoticed by the maid, came a strange shambling fellow with a terrible windblown complexion—reminding Fanny so much of the dreadful man she herself boxed on the face, but this one was definitely not the same man, even though he walked with the same telltale stiffness and momentarily bumped into a wall. All three of them—Miss Crawford, maid, fellow—paused.

"Pardon me, Miss," said the maid. And then she noticed the man behind her, and gave a small squeal of alarm, nearly dropping her basin.

The man raised one hand and reached for her. It was the same exact motion, Fanny realized, as the one she had fought off. The same strange peculiarity. And as the maid froze, mesmerized by him, there was the same menace. . . .

But in that instant an even greater oddity took place.

Miss Crawford went as still and lifeless as a wooden thing, and, unlike the maid, she did not freeze. Instead, Miss Crawford *hissed.*

And then—as Fanny could see from her semi-concealed location down the corridor—Miss Crawford bared her teeth in a terrifying grimace, and her face became *different* somehow, dark and menacing, and her teeth, why, they were not dainty but long and sharp and *inhuman,* while her eyes, oh, they suddenly glowed *red*—

The man-creature stopped trying to reach the maid and backed away, slowly—as though conceding defeat to a far more powerful adversary. He then turned away and disappeared back where he came from.

Miss Crawford meanwhile slowly approached the maid (who remained dazed and still petrified in the same stance), and she drew forward, raised her own delicate hand to move away the maid's small muslin collar and expose the throat, and leaned in, and—as Fanny watched in abject disbelief—she opened her mouth wide, unhinged her jaw beyond any imaging, and bit the maid on the neck.

And then, for several long seconds Miss Crawford proceeded to *feed.*

When she was done, the maid swayed in weakness, still dazed, and her neck held a red stain, as fine scarlet rivulets went running down the front of her apron. The wound was tiny, however, and miraculously appeared to close up in seconds.

Miss Crawford's lips were stained deep rose red, and she wiped them delicately with her tongue, her face growing normal again—her normal charming self. And then, straightening her own clothing as though nothing happened, she was on her way to the powder room.

Fanny stood in the corridor, watching the maid, who was now the only one of them remaining, and who suddenly came to, gasped, and held on to her neck, swaying momentarily. She then took better hold of her basin, and with more difficulty and weakness than before, shaking lightly, was on her way.

Fanny remained, mouthing the Lord's Prayer, and suddenly hoping she might never have to face Miss Crawford again.

She had to speak to Edmund, to warn him that he was in the greatest danger of his life.

The morrow came, the plan for the evening continued, and Fanny's agitation did not lessen. She worked very diligently under her aunt's directions, but concealed a very absent, anxious mind. About noon she made her escape with her work to the East room, that she might have no part in another most unnecessary rehearsal of the first act, which Henry Crawford was just proposing, and to avoid the sight and sound and saliva of Mr. Rushworth. A glimpse, as she passed the hall, of the two ladies walking up from the Parsonage made no change in her wish of retreat, and she worked and meditated in the East room, undisturbed, for a quarter of an hour, when a gentle tap at the door was followed by the entrance of . . . Miss Crawford.

Fanny's heart skipped a beat.

"Am I right? Yes; this is the East room. My dear Miss Price, I beg your pardon, but I have made my way to you on purpose to entreat your help." Miss Crawford's face held no trace of her earlier horrific aspect.

Fanny, quite surprised, but with her wits about her, shewed herself mistress of the room by her civilities, and pretended ignorance of any danger. She looked at the bright bars of her empty fireplace grate with a careful display of concern.

"Thank you; I am quite warm, very warm," said Miss Crawford. She indeed appeared peaches and roses, her cheeks blooming with vivacity. Fanny now imagined well the dire cause of that healthy glow. . . .

Miss Crawford continued: "Allow me to stay here a little while, and do have the goodness to hear me my third act. I have brought my book, and if you would but rehearse it with me, I should be *so* obliged! I came here to-day intending to rehearse it with Edmund—by ourselves—against the evening, but he is not in the way; and if he *were,* I do not think I could go through it with *him,* till I have hardened myself a little; for really there is a speech or two. You will be so good, won't you?"

Fanny was most civil in her assurances, though she could not give them in a very steady voice. She also felt a great urge to touch the small hidden cross hanging underneath her gown. Would it be enough to protect her from *this* manner of *evil?*

"Have you ever happened to look at the part I mean?" continued Miss Crawford, opening her book. "Here it is. I did not think much of it at first—but, upon my word. There, look at *that* speech, and *that,* and *that*. How am I ever to look him in the face and say such things? Could you do it? But then he is your cousin, which makes all the difference. You must rehearse it with me, that I may fancy *you* him, and get on by degrees. You *have* a look of *his* sometimes."

"Have I? I will do my best with the greatest readiness; but I must *read* the part, for I can say very little of it." Fanny's reply came in a far steadier voice than she dared to hope for. She also began to wonder about the local availability of holy water—something Edmund himself had taught her as to be effective against evil, when they had last discussed the family Curse. She must obtain a vial the next time they visited the Parsonage chapel.

"You need say *none* of it, I suppose. You are to have the book, of course. Now—We must have two chairs at hand for you to bring forward to the front of the stage. There—very good school-room chairs, not made for a theatre, I dare say; much more fitted for little girls to sit and kick their feet against when they are learning a lesson. What would your governess and your uncle say to see them used for such a purpose? Could Sir Thomas look in upon us just now, he would bless himself, for we are rehearsing all over the house. Yates is storming away in the dining-room, and the theatre is engaged of course by those indefatigable rehearsers, Agatha and Frederick. By the bye, I looked in upon them five minutes ago, and it happened to be exactly at one of the times when they were trying *not* to embrace, and Mr. Rushworth was with me. I thought he began to look a little queer and rather *wolfish,* so I turned it off as well as I could, by whispering to him, 'We shall have an excellent Agatha; there is something so *maternal* in her manner, so completely *maternal* in her voice and countenance.' Was not that well done of me? He brightened up directly. Now for my soliloquy."

She began, and Fanny joined in with modest feeling, wondering meanwhile what she might do if Miss Crawford were to suddenly rise and attack her mid-sentence. They had got through half the scene, when a tap at the door brought a pause, and the entrance of Edmund, the next moment, suspended it all.

Surprise, consciousness, and pleasure appeared in each of the three on this unexpected meeting; as Edmund was come on the very same business that had brought Miss Crawford. He too had his book, and was seeking Fanny, to ask her to rehearse with him, without knowing Miss Crawford to be in the house; and great was the joy and animation of being thus thrown together.

She could not equal them in their warmth. *Her* spirits sank under the glow of theirs, and Fanny felt herself becoming too nearly nothing. And now, she could not even warn Edmund of the danger that Miss Crawford represented. They must now rehearse together.

Edmund insisted it, till the quite willing lady could refuse no longer. Fanny was expected only to prompt and observe them—judge and critic, and, unknown to Edmund, a secret protector. For, more than once, Fanny noted how Miss Crawford subtly used her nuances of gaze and voice to nigh-mesmerize Edmund in the midst of his declamations. And each time it happened, Fanny was there, to make a small noise, a shuffle of pages, a clearing of her throat—which served to return him to awareness. It was so perfectly timed that even Miss Crawford began to notice that she was being obstructed from her mysterious dark intents.

Miss Crawford turned then, at last, and trained the full force of her intense basilisk gaze upon Fanny.

It was unclear as to what results she was expecting, but in response, Fanny merely blinked, and then inquired very politely—and very much in control of her faculties—"Miss Crawford? Is there something you require? Is anything wrong?"

Miss Crawford only continued to stare at her, periodically narrowing and widening her eyes, all without blinking, and Fanny began to sense a great gathering of cold in the room all around them, a buildup of pressing darkness. Poor Edmund, meanwhile, had gone into a definite daze, and was motionless.

"Miss Crawford?" repeated Fanny, not sure what else to do at that point, short of continuing to pretend ignorance. "Miss Crawford, you appear to have a facial tick."

Miss Crawford finally gave up the stare and in arch annoyance lifted one brow. "Miss Price," she said. "My dear Fanny Price, I want you to rise from your seat. Get up, Fanny, and dance a reel for me."

"Beg pardon?" said Fanny, allowing one of her own brows to rise.

Miss Crawford's lips parted in surprise. She then leaned forward in Fanny's direction and redoubled her stare. "*Look into my eyes,* Miss Price!" she uttered in a decidedly commanding tone of voice.

"Miss Crawford, I *am* looking into your eyes, as you say," replied Fanny, in an unexpectedly calm manner. "And indeed, they are quite lovely. But—whatever do you mean that I dance a reel? I am certainly at a loss, and unsure of your meaning, Miss Crawford—is there a reel required in this scene of *Lovers' Vows?*"

The darkness pressed in from all directions, and suddenly Miss Crawford's eyes shone with that same deep coal-red spark.

"LOOK INTO MY EYES!" she exclaimed in a terrible voice.

"Upon my word, there is certainly no need to shout," said Fanny, putting down the book calmly.

This stunned Miss Crawford completely. She sat back in her chair, and then said, "Unbelievable. . . . Could it be that—that you are one of those rare few who are immune to the *gaze* of such as myself?"

"Such as yourself, Miss Crawford?" said Fanny. "And what might that be?"

"I suspect," said Miss Crawford, "that you know quite well already."

"I am afraid your meaning is quite beyond me."

But, for the first time, Fanny smiled.

Immediately, the sensation of pressing encroaching darkness receded. Fanny Price felt an unbelievable confident calm, and an inner sense of power building up deep inside her chest, as normally would joy or utter exultation. She was no longer helpless and terrified of what was before her.

"Yes . . ." said the creature that was Miss Crawford. "You need pretend no longer. I see you *know* me. What am I, dear Fanny?"

"You are a creature of the night, Miss Crawford. Neither dead nor truly living. I have learnt of your kind in Mrs. Radcliffe's novels, if I recall. You find sustenance in the drinking of that which courses in the veins of the living. The ancient Vampyre, or—*vampire*."

"Ah, how clever you are indeed, Miss Price. You have discovered me. What, then, will you do now?"

"That, Miss Crawford, depends entirely on you."

Fanny Price drew forward and stared directly at the vampire. Mary Crawford stared back.

"Look into *my* eyes, Miss Crawford. What do you see?"

"I see a foolish young girl. One who is bursting with newfound confidence and is, in truth, a breath away from death."

"I suggest you look again. What you should see is the one *person* who will not allow you to commit any more evil under this roof. My cousin Edmund, and all of Mansfield Park are not yours for the taking!"

The elegant vampire laughed. "Oh, is that so, foolish Fanny? And how do you intend to stop me? Edmund is mine, you know. I shall have him in the end. It is what I came here to do. You are powerless against me."

Fanny bit her lip, took a deep breath, and said: "Miss Crawford, I must kindly ask you to leave. Get out of my room, before I use that fireplace poker on you!"

But before Miss Crawford could hiss or attack, Fanny pulled out the little cross hidden close to her heart, and she raised it before the vampire. "Out!" repeated Fanny. "And do take your copy of that horrid *Lovers' Vows* with you."

Miss Crawford was gone out the door quicker than Fanny could blink. And immediately Edmund came to himself with a shudder, smack in the middle of declaiming a line.

"Oh, Fanny!" he said then, seeing they were only two in the room. "Where is Miss—"

But Fanny took his copy of the play out of his hands and put it on the desk. And then, with a deep breath, she told him all about Miss Crawford.

"No! It cannot be!" exclaimed Edmund, with desperate eyes, when Fanny was done. "I refuse to believe it! There are enough Curses upon our heads as it is! Not *she!* She is pure and delightful and kind and oh—"

"She is a *vampire,* cousin. She has charmed you. And I am sorry to say this, but she intends to do you, and all of us, a great evil."

Edmund suddenly got up from his seat and pushed back the chair with a terrible scrape against the floor. Never had

Fanny seen him so distraught and furious—her kindest gentlest Edmund!—as he was in that moment.

And then, in absolute silence, he left the room, slamming the door behind him.

The first regular rehearsal of the three first acts was certainly to take place in the evening: Mrs. Grant and the Crawfords were engaged to return for that purpose after dinner; and every one concerned was looking forward with cheerful eagerness. Tom was enjoying such progress towards the end; Edmund was in renewed spirits from the morning's rehearsal (inexplicably so, thought Fanny in dread; he had to have flatly disbelieved all the things told him about Miss Crawford!), and little vexations seemed everywhere smoothed away. All were alert and impatient, and with the exception of Lady Bertram and her ever-attendant Lord Eastwind, Mrs. Norris, and Julia, everybody was in the theatre at an early hour. Having illuminated it as well as its unfinished state admitted, they were waiting only for the arrival of Mrs. Grant and the Crawfords to begin.

They did not wait long for the Crawfords, but there was no Mrs. Grant. She could not come. Dr. Grant, professing an indisposition, could not spare his wife. Fanny had a momentary dark thought that mayhap Miss Crawford had turned on her own sister and *fed* on her. . . .

"Dr. Grant is ill," said Miss Crawford, with mock solemnity. "He has been ill ever since he did not eat any of the pheasant today. He fancied it tough, sent away his plate, and has been suffering ever since."

Here was disappointment! Mrs. Grant's non-attendance was sad indeed. Her pleasant cheerful presence was not only valuable but *now* absolutely necessary. They could not act or rehearse without her. The comfort of the whole evening was destroyed. What was to be done? Tom, as Cottager, was in despair. Mr. Rushworth looked ready to chew his own coatsleeves as though they were lamb chops. After a pause of perplexity, some eyes began to be turned towards Fanny, and a voice or two to say, "If Miss Price would be so good as to *read* the part." She was immediately surrounded by supplications; everybody, even Edmund said, "Do, Fanny, if it is not *very* disagreeable to you." And Miss Crawford joined in, gifting her with a dark wicked smile.

But Fanny still hung back. She could not endure the idea of it. Why not someone else? Indeed, why had she attended the rehearsal at all, when it was her duty to keep away? She was properly punished.

"You have only to *read* the part," said Henry Crawford, with renewed entreaty. His gaze, Fanny noted incidentally, was almost as compelling as his vampire sister's. Could it be that he too was—

Fanny did not want to follow that sudden horrid thought.

"And I do believe she can say every word of it," added Maria, "for she could put Mrs. Grant right the other day in twenty places. Fanny, I am sure you know the part."

Fanny could not say she did *not;* and as they all persevered, as Edmund repeated his wish, she must yield. She would do her best. Everybody was satisfied; and she was left to the tremors of a most palpitating heart, while the others prepared to begin.

Somewhere in the shadows, Lord Eastwind watched them all, and Fanny in particular, in his usual intense silence.

They *did* begin; and were too much engaged in their own noise to be struck by an unusual noise in the other part of the house—a noise quite unlike the normal gentle settling noises of the house or the rustle of the household or the opening crates as the servants and the mummies proceeded on their daily routine—when the door of the room was thrown open.

Julia appeared, and, with a face all aghast, exclaimed, "My father is come! He is in the hall at this moment."

Chapter XIX

How is the consternation of the party to be described? To the greater number it was a moment of absolute horror. Sir Thomas in the house!

Julia's looks made it indisputable. And after the first starts and exclamations, not a word was spoken for half a minute: each with an altered countenance was looking at some other, and almost each was feeling it a stroke the most unwelcome, most ill-timed, most appalling! Mr. Yates might consider it only as a vexatious interruption for the evening, and Mr. Rushworth might imagine it a blessing; but every other heart was sinking under some degree of self-condemnation or undefined alarm. "What will become of us? what is to be done now?" It was a terrible pause; and terrible to every ear were the corroborating sounds of opening doors and passing footsteps.

Julia was the first to move and speak again. Jealousy and bitterness had been suspended: selfishness was lost in the common cause. But at the moment of her appearance, Frederick was listening with looks of devotion to Agatha's narrative, and pressing her hand to his heart. As soon as Julia noticed this, and saw that he still kept his station and retained her sister's hand, her wounded heart swelled again with injury. Looking as red as she had been white before, she turned out of the room, saying, "*I* need not be afraid of appearing before him."

Her going roused the rest; and at the same moment the two brothers stepped forward, feeling the necessity of doing something: they must go to the drawing-room directly. Maria joined them; the very circumstance which had driven Julia away was to her the sweetest support. Henry Crawford's retaining her hand at such a moment, was worth ages of doubt and anxiety. She was equal to encounter her father.

They walked off, utterly heedless of Mr. Rushworth's repeated question of, "Shall I go too? Had not I better go too? Ayiiiie! Argh! Will not it be right for me to go too?" But they were no sooner through the door than Henry Crawford encouraged him to pay his respects to Sir Thomas without delay, and sent him after the others with delighted haste.

Fanny was left with only the Crawfords and Mr. Yates, and Lord Eastwind in the shadows. She had been quite overlooked by her cousins. Since her own opinion of her claims on Sir Thomas's affection was much too humble, she was glad to remain behind and gain a little breathing-time. Her agitation exceeded all that was endured by the rest. She was nearly fainting: all her former habitual dread of her uncle was returning, and with it compassion for him and for almost every one of the party, with solicitude on Edmund's account indescribable, and with terror on account of the new evils in the house in the shape of Miss Crawford and Heaven knows *what else*. . . .

She had found a seat, where, in excessive trembling that no vampire or mummy encounter could elicit in comparison, she endured all these fearful thoughts. The other three, no longer under any restraint, were giving vent to their feelings of vexation, and mercilessly wishing poor Sir Thomas had been twice as long on his passage, or were still in Antigua.

The Crawfords were more warm on the subject than Mr. Yates, from better understanding the family, and judging more clearly of the mischief that must ensue. The ruin of the play was to them a certainty. Mr. Yates considered it only as a temporary interruption, and could even suggest the possibility of the rehearsal being renewed after tea, when the bustle of receiving Sir Thomas were over. The Crawfords laughed at the idea; and having soon agreed on the propriety of their walking quietly home and leaving the family to themselves, proposed Mr. Yates accompany them to spend the evening at the Parsonage. But Mr. Yates could not perceive it necessary. He said "he preferred remaining where he was, that he might pay his respects to the old gentleman handsomely."

Fanny was just beginning to collect herself, when this point was settled, and being commissioned with the brother and sister's apology, quitted the room herself to perform the dreadful duty of appearing before her uncle.

Too soon did she find herself at the drawing-room door. After pausing for courage, she turned the lock in desperation, and the lights of the drawing-room, and all the collected family, were before her. As she entered, her own name caught her ear. Sir Thomas was at that moment looking round him, and saying, "But where is Fanny? Why do not I see my little Fanny?"

On perceiving her, came forward with a kindness which astonished and penetrated her, calling her his dear Fanny, kissing her affectionately, and observing with decided pleasure how much she was grown! Fanny knew not how to feel, nor where to look. He had never been so *very* kind to her in his life. His manner seemed changed, his voice was quick from the agitation of joy and tenderness. He led her nearer the light and looked at her again—observing that he need not inquire about her health, for her appearance spoke sufficiently on that point.

Her fine blush replacing paleness pointed to her equal improvement in health and beauty. He inquired next after her family, William, and his kindness was such as made her reproach herself for loving him so little, and thinking his return a misfortune. She saw that he was grown thinner, and had the burnt, worn look of fatigue and a hot climate, attaining *almost* that dreadful "windblown sailor" complexion that so many servants seemed to wear around the house.

Sir Thomas was indeed the life of the party, who at his suggestion now seated themselves round the fire. The delight of his sensations in being again in his own house, in the centre of his family, after such a separation, made him communicative and chatty in a very unusual degree. He was ready to give every information as to his voyage, and answer every question of his two sons almost before it was put. His business in Antigua had been prosperously rapid, and he came directly from Liverpool in a private vessel; he told them as he sat by Lady Bertram and looked with heartfelt satisfaction on the faces around him—all collected together exactly as he could have wished. Mr. Rushworth was not forgotten: a most friendly reception and warmth of hand-shaking met him, and he was now included as intimately connected with Mansfield. Since Mr. Rushworth made no untoward howl just yet, Sir Thomas liked him already.

Of all present, Sir Thomas was welcomed with most enjoyment by his wife, who was really extremely happy to see him, and whose feelings, despite their absolute metaphysical dominion over by a certain resurrected Pharaoh, were so warmed by his sudden arrival as to place her nearer agitation than she had been at the sight of the grandest shipment from Cairo.

Lady Bertram took no delay but introduced her husband immediately to Lord Eastwind, who was given a once-over and an immediate warm handshake, and—after a long look from the raven haired gentleman—Sir Thomas was absolutely enchanted with their guest. He then promptly forgot his existence, as had everyone else in the household.

Fanny once again noted this disturbing detail as she watched their introductions. How could anyone overlook, indeed, not look for an extended pleasurable time at such a fine figure as that of Lord Eastwind, in his dark handsomeness, his somber elegance and his refined exotic manner? Whatever was going on in the family? Was everyone but herself completely blind?

Lady Bertram, meanwhile, after blissfully presenting Eastwind, continued being *almost* fluttered for a few minutes, and remained so animated as to put away her papyrus work, move pug and several large clay tablets from her side, and give all her attention and all the rest of her sofa to her husband.

She had no anxious guilt to cloud *her* pleasure: her own time had been irreproachably spent during his absence. She had raised and unleashed the grand Mummy, done a great deal of carpet-work, made many yards of fringe; and would have answered as freely for the good conduct of all the young people as for her own. It was so agreeable to her to see him again, to hear him talk, to have her ear amused and filled by his narratives, that she began particularly to feel how dreadfully she must have missed him, and how impossible it would have been for her to bear a lengthened absence, even while surrounded by her dear Egypt and its returned Pharaoh.

Mrs. Norris was by no means to be compared in happiness to her sister. Not that *she* was incommoded by many fears of Sir Thomas's disapprobation, for her judgment had been so blinded that, except by the instinctive caution with which she had whisked away Mr. Rushworth's pink satin cloak as her brother-in-law entered, she could hardly be said to shew any sign of alarm. But she was vexed by the *manner* of his return. Instead of seeing him first, and having to spread the happy news through the house, Sir Thomas had sought no confidant but the butler, and followed him into the drawing-room. Mrs. Norris felt herself defrauded of use—whether his arrival or his death were to be the thing unfolded. Now she was labouring to be important where nothing was wanted but peace and silence. Sir Thomas resolutely declined all dinner: he would rather wait for tea. Still

Mrs. Norris managed, in the most interesting moment of his retelling of his travels, to burst through his recital with the proposal of soup.

Sir Thomas could not be provoked. "Still the same anxiety for everybody's comfort, my dear Mrs. Norris. But indeed I would rather have nothing but tea."

"Well, then, Lady Bertram, suppose you speak for tea directly; suppose you hurry Baddeley a little; he seems behindhand to-night." She carried this point with a yelp, and Sir Thomas's narrative proceeded.

At length there was a pause. His immediate tales were exhausted, and it seemed enough to look joyfully around him at the beloved circle. But the pause was not long. In the elation of her spirits Lady Bertram became talkative, and what were the sensations of her children upon hearing her say, "How do you think the young people have been amusing themselves lately, Sir Thomas? Whilst the Nile flows deep, they have been acting. We have been all alive with acting."

"Indeed! and what have you been acting?"

"Oh! they'll tell you all about it."

"The *all* will soon be told," cried Tom hastily, and with affected unconcern; "but it is not worth while to bore my father with it now. You will hear enough of it to-morrow, sir. We have just been amusing my mother, just within the last week, to get up a few scenes, a mere trifle. Such incessant rains almost since October began, that we have been confined to the house. I have hardly taken out a gun since the 3rd. There has been no attempting anything since. Though, *I* never saw Mansfield Wood so full of pheasants in my life as this year. I hope you will take a day's sport there yourself, sir, soon."

For the present the danger was over, and Fanny's sick feelings subsided. But when tea was brought in, Sir Thomas got up, saying he could no longer be in the house without looking into his own dear room. He was gone before anything had been said to prepare him for the change he must find there; and a pause of alarm followed his disappearance. Edmund was the first to speak—

"Something must be done," said he.

"It is time to think of our visitors," said Maria, still feeling her hand pressed to Henry Crawford's heart, and caring little for anything else. "Where did you leave Miss Crawford, Fanny?"

Fanny told of their departure, and delivered their message.

"Then poor Yates is all alone," cried Tom. "I will go and fetch him."

To the theatre he went, and reached it just in time to witness the first meeting of his father and his friend. Sir Thomas had been a good deal surprised to find candles burning in his room; and on casting his eye round it, to see other symptoms of recent habitation and a general air of confusion in the furniture.

A solitary servant—new to Sir Thomas, and a rather shabby and lumbering fellow—stood bumping into a wall for several long rather stunning moments before apparently finding a proper doorway and making himself scarce without even a proper bow of greeting.

The removal of the bookcase from before the billiard-room door struck Sir Thomas especially, but he had hardly any time to feel astonished at all this, before there were sounds from the billiard-room to astonish him still further. Someone was talking there in a very loud accent; he did not know the voice—more than talking—not quite howling, but almost hallooing.

He stepped to the door, and, opening it, found himself on the stage of a theatre, opposite a ranting young man, who appeared likely to knock him down backwards. At the very moment of Yates perceiving Sir Thomas, and giving perhaps the very best start he had ever given in the whole course of his rehearsals, Tom Bertram entered at the other end of the room.

Never had Tom found greater difficulty in keeping his countenance. His father's looks of solemnity and amazement on this his first appearance on any stage, and the gradual metamorphosis of the impassioned Baron Wildenheim into the well-bred and easy Mr. Yates, making his bow and apology to Sir Thomas Bertram, was such an exhibition, such a piece of true acting, as he would not have lost upon any account. It would be the last—in all probability—the last scene on that stage; but he was sure there could not be a finer. The house would close with the greatest *éclat*.

There was little time, however, for the indulgence of any images of merriment. It was necessary for him to step forward and assist the introduction, and awkwardly he did his best. Sir Thomas received Mr. Yates with all the appearance of cordiality, but was really as far from pleased with the necessity of the acquaintance as with the manner of its commencement. Mr. Yates's family and connexions were sufficiently known to him to render his introduction as the "particular friend"—another of the hundred particular, equally witless friends of his son—exceedingly unwelcome. It needed all the felicity of being home again to save Sir Thomas from anger on finding himself bewildered in his own house, and forced to admit the acquaintance of a young fool whom he felt sure of disapproving.

Tom understood his father's thoughts to the best of his own questionable ability, and began to see that there might be some ground for offence—some reason for the glance his father gave towards the ceiling and stucco of the room and inquired with mild gravity after the fate of the billiard-table. After a few minutes of Sir Thomas exerting himself to speak with Mr. Yates, the three gentlemen returned to the drawing-room together, Sir Thomas with an increase of gravity.

"I come from your theatre," said he composedly, as he sat down; "I found myself in it rather unexpectedly. Its vicinity to my own room—in every respect it took me by surprise, as I had not the smallest suspicion of your acting having assumed so serious a character. It appears a neat job, however, as far as I could judge by candlelight."

And then he would have changed the subject, and sipped his coffee in peace. But Mr. Yates, without discernment of Sir Thomas's meaning, or delicacy, or discretion, continued on the topic of the theatre, even retelling the whole history of his disappointment at Ecclesford. Sir Thomas listened most politely, but found much to offend his ideas of decorum, and confirm his ill-opinion of Mr. Yates.

"This was, in fact, the origin of *our* acting," said Tom, after a moment's thought. "My friend Yates brought the infection from Ecclesford, and it—ahem—*spread.*"

"Yes indeed, like sweet reeds fluttering on the banks of the Nile," intoned Lady Bertram. "Little green scarabs running along the shore into the sand—"

Mr. Yates took the thespian subject and carried on, regardless of Sir Thomas's growing dark looks and everyone's relentless fidgeting.

Not less acutely was it felt by Fanny, who had edged back her chair behind her aunt's end of the sofa—finding herself somehow in the vicinity of Lord Eastwind—and, screened from notice herself, saw all that was passing before her. Such a look of reproach at Edmund from his father she never expected to witness. That it was deserved, was a sorrow indeed. Sir Thomas's look implied, "On *your* judgment, Edmund, I depended; what have you been about?" She knelt in spirit to her uncle, and her bosom swelled to utter, "Oh, not to *him!* Look so to all the others, but not to *him!*"

"You are unhappy, Miss Price?" said a soft voice. And she turned to observe Lord Eastwind addressing her with his enigmatic expression.

"I am—indeed, I am concerned. My uncle is growing more miserable with every word, and the longer this dire situation goes on, the worse—"

"Would it make you relieved, Miss Price, if there is to be some distraction?"

Fanny was perplexed. "What do you mean?"

"This," said Lord Eastwind. And he slowly moved his hand palm up, then brought it down again. . . .

Mr. Yates was still talking. "To own the truth, Sir Thomas, we were in the middle of a rehearsal when you arrived this evening. We were going through the three first acts, and not unsuccessfully upon the whole. Our company is now so dispersed, from the Crawfords being gone home, that nothing more can be done to-night; but if you will give us the honour of your company to-morrow evening—"

Before he could finish the utterance, Mr. Yates choked. He started coughing, and seemed to go into a full-blown fit, his face growing red. And then suddenly he coughed up something in his throat.

It came forth out of his mouth—a bright green beetle the size of a crown piece—and scuttled down his cravat and jacket.

Julia gave a tiny gasp.

But Mr. Yates was not done. In the next breath, he coughed up another beetle. And then another. With each breath he took, they seemed to pop out of him, and went rushing down his clothing and onto the floor. It was one, two, five, twelve—an endless array of green beetles. . . .

Maria began to shriek.

"Ye gads!" cried Tom, rising up from his chair, as one beetle made directly for him and climbed up his pant leg. "What in bl—"

"Oh—oh dear," mumbled Lady Bertram. "What pretty scarabs, Mr. Yates. But, how odd of you."

"Mr. Yates!" said Sir Thomas in a loud command voice. "Pray, what is happening? Someone, get Baddeley! What is this? What strange terrible thing—fetch a physician!"

Mr. Yates had risen from his seat, and was now turning purple with choking, while the beetles were rushing forth in a pearly-green stream and filling the parlor, climbing up chair legs and table legs and curtains and walls and *people,* while everyone else too had gotten up and was backing away in terrible alarm, accompanied by the screams of the two Miss Bertrams.

There was quite an upheaval. "This is not natural!" Edmund exclaimed. "It is, by Heaven, surely the Curse come upon us!" He grabbed a nearby piece of sewing that Mrs. Norris had abandoned, and used the long fabric to swat at the insects and at Mr. Yates, attempting to squelch the flow of the creatures issuing out of Mr. Yates's mouth. "If at all capable, get a hold of yourself, Yates! Fight it!"

Mrs. Norris herself was meanwhile stunned, and had acquired the look of a hungry wolfhound who had just sighted prey. Good thing no one was looking, because Mrs. Norris, moving faster than an Oriental acrobat, grabbed one green squirming thing and popped it in her mouth. The same condition was to be observed in Mr. Rushworth, and he began to make minor yelping noises and move in on the beetles.

"What is going on?" exclaimed Sir Thomas, batting at his chest to throw off the insects, and nearly overturning a chair, as the flow of beetles continued.

Fanny was breathing fast, and she too had jumped out of her seat. But she had a very sinking suspicion, and immediately addressed Lord Eastwind.

"Sir," she said with quiet urgency amid the mayhem, bravely ignoring the three large horrid things crawling up her legs and skirts. "If *you* are in any way responsible for this, I beg you to stop it *immediately!*"

Lord Eastwind was the only one sitting quietly and deeply in his chair, leaning back in relaxation. "But you desired a distraction," he said with faint sarcasm.

"Not like this! What kind of abomination is this? And what kind of powers do you seem to have? I promise you, I have no desire to see any more of it!"

"As you wish."

And with those soft barely heard words, there was an immediate sensation of tremor in the atmosphere of the room, and the green beetles suddenly wavered in the air like a desert mirage, and *disappeared.*

There was no trace of them. Everyone was still batting away at their clothing in horrific alarm, and squashing non-existent things on the floor, and Mr. Rushworth attempted to chew a beetle in his teeth that was no longer there.

Mr. Yates gave a final choke, then cleared his throat. Eyes popping from effort, still red as a beet, he stood up straight and made a short embarrassed bow to the company.

"What in all creation was that?" said Sir Thomas, recovering himself after a long terrible silence. "Those insects! A whole army! I have never seen anything like it, not even in Antigua! They came forth out of you, Mr. Yates! Are you—well?"

"Ahem," replied Yates. "I appear to be fine, and I assure you, Sir Thomas, I am quite perplexed myself as to what had just happened."

"Not as much as I am," muttered Tom under his breath, scratching his head and straightening the corners of his jacket lapels. "Edmund? Have you any notion? Is it—unholy?"

"Indeed, I have no doubt! It's the Curse," whispered back his brother.

"But I thought that was nonsense," Tom retorted.

"Well, and what do you think now?"

Fanny meanwhile sat down once again and turned to Lord Eastwind, "My Lord," she said. "Who *are* you?"

"Miss Price," he replied, "I am your distraction."

All talk of acting and theatre was indeed forgotten. After making certain that Mr. Yates was indeed in the best of health, and then giving instructions to Baddeley to look into the vermin insect infestation on the estate, Sir Thomas changed the subject to a more pleasant one.

"Mr. and Miss Crawford were mentioned in my last letters from Mansfield. Do you find them agreeable acquaintance?"

Tom, still reeling somewhat from the unbelievable scarab attack, was the only one at all ready with an answer, but he being entirely without particular regard for either, jealousy or love, could speak very handsomely of both. "Mr. Crawford was a most pleasant, gentleman-like man; his sister a sweet, pretty, elegant, lively girl."

Who has very sharp teeth, Fanny wanted to say, but kept silent, naturally.

But Mr. Rushworth could be silent no longer. "I do not say he is not gentleman-like, considering; but you should tell your father he is not above five feet eight, or he will be expecting a well-looking man. Grrr!"

Sir Thomas did not quite understand this, nor did he expect the growl (he had also luckily missed the display of voracious scarab chewing during moments of earlier mayhem) and looked with some surprise at the speaker.

"If I must say what I think," continued Mr. Rushworth, "in my opinion it is very disagreeable to be always rehearsing. I am not so fond of acting. We are a great deal better employed, sitting comfortably here among ourselves, and doing nothing."

Sir Thomas looked again, decided to overlook the growling, and then replied with an approving smile, "Our sentiments on this subject are much the same, which gives me sincere satisfaction. That I should be cautious is perfectly natural. But at your time of life to feel all this, is most favourable for yourself, and for everybody connected with you."

Sir Thomas meant to give Mr. Rushworth's opinion a compliment. He was aware that he must not expect a genius in Mr. Rushworth. But as a well-judging, steady young man, he intended to value him very highly.

It was impossible for many of the others not to smile. Mr. Rushworth hardly knew what to do. But by looking most exceedingly pleased with Sir Thomas's good opinion, and saying scarcely anything, he thus did his best towards preserving that good opinion a little longer.

Chapter XX

Edmund's first object the next morning was to see his father alone, and give him a fair statement of the whole acting scheme, defending his own share in it as far only as he could. He was anxious, while vindicating himself, to say nothing unkind of the others: but there was only one amongst them whose good conduct he could mention. "We have all been to blame," said he, "every one of us, excepting Fanny. She is the only one who has judged rightly throughout; who has been consistent. *Her* feelings have been steadily against it. She never ceased to think of what was due to you. You will find Fanny everything you could wish."

Sir Thomas was particularly gratified to hear this said of Fanny. As far as all the rest of them, he saw all the impropriety of such a scheme. He felt it too much. And having shaken hands with Edmund, he meant to forget how much he had been forgotten himself. Soon, the house was cleared of every object enforcing the remembrance, and restored to its proper state. He did not enter into any remonstrance with his other children. The conclusion of everything would be sufficient.

There was one person, however, in the house, whom he could not leave to learn his sentiments merely through his conduct. He could not help giving Mrs. Norris a hint of his disapproval. The young people had been very inconsiderate in forming the plan, but they were young; and, excepting Edmund, of unsteady characters. He had higher hopes, however of Mrs. Norris's judgment.

Mrs. Norris was a little confounded and as nearly being silenced as ever she had been in her life. For she was ashamed to confess having never seen any of the impropriety[16] which was so glaring to Sir Thomas. To make up for it, Mrs. Norris insinuated in her own praise her exertion and many sacrifices on behalf of the family, her many excellent economic hints to Lady Bertram and Edmund, resulting in considerable household savings, and indeed, a minor reduction of Egyptian crates in the main parlor (which of course was merely the result of mummies quitting their resting places).

But her chief strength lay in Sotherton. Her greatest glory was in having formed the connexion with the Rushworths. *There* she was impregnable. She took to herself all the credit of bringing Mr. Rushworth's admiration of Maria to any effect. "If I had not been active," said she, "and made a point of being introduced to his mother, and then prevailed on my sister to pay the first visit, I am certain, nothing would have come of it. Mr. Rushworth is the sort of amiable modest young man who needs a great deal of encouragement, and there were girls enough on the catch for him if we had been idle. But I left no stone unturned. I was ready to move heaven and earth! You know the distance to Sotherton; it was in the middle of winter—"

"I know how justly great your influence is with Lady Bertram and her children, and am the more concerned that it should not have been."

"My dear Sir Thomas, if you had seen the state of the roads *that* day! I thought we should never have got through them!" And Mrs. Norris proceeded to speak at length of her brave ordeal.

---

[16] Of the Babylonian variety.

"I hope we shall always think the acquaintance worth the trouble taken to establish it," said Sir Thomas. "There is nothing very striking in Mr. Rushworth's manners, but I was pleased last night with what appeared to be his sensible opinion on one subject: his decided preference of a quiet family party to the bustle and confusion of acting."

"Yes, indeed, and the more you know of him the better you will like him. He is not a shining character, but he has a thousand good qualities; and is *so* disposed to look up to you—"

Sir Thomas gave up, obliged to admit to himself that her sentiment did sometimes overpower her judgment.

It was a busy morning with him. He had to reinstate himself in all the concerns of his Mansfield life: to see his steward and his bailiff; to enquire about sudden rare insect infestations, and about all the new apparently useless servants with the peeling skin conditions who, in truly brutish fashion, refused to answer when hailed—why had they been taken on?

In the intervals of business, Sir Thomas walked to his stables and his gardens, active and methodical, resuming his seat as master of the house at dinner. He had set the carpenter to work in reverting the billiard-room. The scene-painter was dismissed, having spoilt only the floor of one room, ruined all the coachman's sponges, and made five of the under-servants idle and dissatisfied. Sir Thomas hoped that another day or two would suffice to wipe away every trace of what had been, even to the destruction of every unbound copy of *Lovers' Vows* in the house, for he was burning all that met his eye.

Mr. Yates—having more or less recovered after serving as the grand scarab conduit of the night before—was beginning now to understand Sir Thomas's intentions, though not their source. He and his friend had been out with their guns the chief of the morning, and Tom had taken the opportunity of explaining, with proper apologies for his father's particularity. Mr. Yates felt the acute thespian disappointment for a second time—severe ill-luck! And his indignation was such, that he was ready to resume his arguments with Sir Thomas.

He was bent on it, while in Mansfield Wood, and all the way home. But there was a something in Sir Thomas, when they sat round the same table, which made Mr. Yates think it wiser to let the matter drop. He had known many disagreeable fathers before, but never had he seen one of that class so unintelligibly moral, so infamously tyrannical as Sir Thomas. Verily, he was not a man to be endured but for his children's sake, and he might be thankful to his fair daughter Julia that Mr. Yates did yet mean to stay a few days longer under his roof.

The evening passed with external smoothness, though almost every mind was ruffled. The music which Sir Thomas called for from his daughters, helped to conceal the want of real harmony. Maria was in a good deal of agitation. It was of the utmost consequence to her that Crawford should now lose no time in declaring himself. She had been expecting to see him the whole morning, and all the evening, to no avail. Mr. Rushworth had set off early with the great news for Sotherton; and she dearly hoped he would never trouble to return. But they had seen no one from the Parsonage, beyond a friendly note from Mrs. Grant to Lady Bertram. It was the first day for many weeks, in which the families had been wholly divided, without bringing them together in some way.

The morrow did not vanquish the acute suffering. Henry Crawford was again in the house: he walked up with Dr. Grant, who was anxious to pay his respects to Sir Thomas. At a rather early hour they were ushered into the breakfast-room, where were most of the family. Sir Thomas soon appeared, and Maria saw with delight and agitation the introduction of the man she loved to her father.

Her sensations were indefinable. And so were they a few minutes afterwards upon hearing Henry Crawford, who had a chair between herself and Tom, ask the latter in an undervoice whether there were any plans for resuming the play after the present happy interruption (with a courteous glance at Sir Thomas), because, in that case, he should make a point of returning to Mansfield at any time required by the party. He was going away immediately, to meet his uncle at Bath. But if there were any prospect of a renewal of *Lovers' Vows,* he should hold himself positively engaged here.

It was well at that moment that Tom had to speak, making it clear to Henry that the play was all over and done with. They then proceeded to discuss Bath at this time of the year, and the stables there, where Tom claimed he had seen a remarkable creature, half-horse, half-goat, for only £250. . . .

Soon Henry turned to Maria, repeating much of what he had already said, with only a softened air and stronger expressions of regret. But he was going, and voluntarily. For, except what might be due his uncle, his engagements were all self-imposed. He might talk of necessity, but she knew his independence. The hand which had so pressed hers to his heart! Her spirit supported her, but the agony of her mind was severe.

She had not long to endure listening to words which his actions contradicted. He was gone—he had touched her hand for the last time, he had made his parting bow. Henry Crawford was gone—from the house, and within two hours afterwards from the parish. And so ended all the hopes his selfish vanity had raised in Maria and Julia Bertram.

Julia could rejoice that he was gone. His presence was beginning to be odious to her; and if Maria gained him not, she was now cool enough to dispense with any other revenge. She did not want exposure to be added to desertion. With Henry Crawford gone, she could even pity her sister.

With a purer spirit did Fanny rejoice in the intelligence. She heard it at dinner, and felt it a blessing. The others mentioned it with varied degrees of regret—from the sincerity of Edmund's too partial regard, to the unconcern of his mother speaking entirely by rote as she declaimed something poetic, ancient, and once encoded in hieroglyphics to Lord Eastwind. Mrs. Norris wondered how was it that Mr. Crawford and Julia had come to nothing.

Another day or two, and Mr. Yates was gone likewise. In *his* departure Sir Thomas felt the chief interest. Wanting to be alone with his family, the presence of Mr. Yates, trifling and confident, idle and expensive, was vexatious. In himself he was wearisome, but as the friend of Tom and the admirer of Julia he became offensive. Sir Thomas had been quite indifferent to Mr. Crawford's going or staying: but his good wishes for Mr. Yates's having a pleasant journey, as he walked with him to the hall-door, were given with genuine satisfaction.

Mrs. Norris contrived to remove one last article from Sir Thomas's sight that might have distressed him. The theatre curtain, over which she had presided with such talent and such success, went off with her to her cottage, where she happened to be particularly in want of green baize to cover up a certain window on moonlit nights. . . .

Chapter XXI

Sir Thomas's return made a striking change in the ways of the family, independent of *Lovers' Vows*. Under his government, Mansfield was an altered place. Some members of their society sent away, and the spirits of many others saddened—it was all sameness and gloom compared with the past—a sombre family party rarely enlivened. There was little intercourse[17] with the Parsonage. Sir Thomas was particularly disinclined for any engagements but in one quarter. The Rushworths were the only addition to the domestic circle.

Edmund did not wonder that such should be his father's feelings, but he regretted the exclusion of the Grants. "They," he observed to Fanny, "have a claim. They seem to belong to us; to be part of ourselves. If only my father knew them better, he would value their society as it deserves; for they are exactly the sort of people he would like. Dr. and Mrs. Grant would enliven us, make our evenings pass away with more enjoyment."

"Do you think so?" said Fanny: "in my opinion, my uncle values the very quietness you speak of, and the repose of his own family circle is all he wants. And it does not appear to me that we are more serious than we used to be. There was never much laughing in his presence."

---

[17] Oh, in Heaven's name, how inappropriate, for a House of God!

"I believe you are right, Fanny," was his reply, after a short consideration. "I believe our evenings are rather returned to what they were. The novelty was in their being lively. Yet, how strong the impression that only a few weeks will give! I have been feeling as if we had never lived so before."

"I suppose I am graver than other people," said Fanny. "The evenings do not appear long to me. I love to hear my uncle talk of the West Indies. I could listen to him for an hour together. It entertains *me* more than many other things. But then, I am unlike other people, I dare say."

"Why should you dare say *that?*" (smiling). "Do you want to be told that you are only unlike other people in being more wise and discreet?"

"No," replied Fanny with a sigh, breaching a certain taboo subject. "I am indeed unlike other people—for I seem to observe and *perceive* certain things that others do not, and to be *unaffected* by certain other things that everyone else is affected by."

Edmund became serious. "Of what do you speak, Fanny?"

And Fanny could not hold back any longer. "Oh, cousin!" she exclaimed. "Did you not yourself unveil to me the dark Curse of this household, when we were but children? You would speak innocently and at length of it then. You would make plans for how to confront and Exorcise the evil! But now, it seems, your memory and your vision have both closed up, and you are hardly aware of the compounding unnatural *strangeness* that has been going on at Mansfield Park! Miss Crawford is a vampire! Your own aunt, Mrs. Norris, and I dare say Mr. Rushworth, are both blatant werewolves (and everyone knows about those two and yet you all chuse to overlook the fact, and the relentless growling)! Your mother is possessed by some unspeakable ancient Egyptian force and frequently speaks in tongues! Just yesterday, Mr. Yates had an army of beetles coming out of his mouth! And—and Lord Eastwind? Why is it that no one notices him, when he is surely at the heart of it all?"

"Why, hush, Fanny! Please, be not so loud, when you speak of the Curse," Edmund began to whisper. And then grew silent in consternation. A moment later he added, "Wait—Lord East Who?"

In that very instant, Fanny wanted to take herself upstairs to her little room and repeatedly strike her forehead against the wall or the little writing-desk. . . .

"Lord Eastwind," she repeated in a loud intense whisper, and pointed. "Look, Edmund! Look, in the name of all that is good and right, look over there—*see* him? He is sitting in that chair next to Lady Bertram."

But Edmund blinked, and leaned forward. "Fanny, dearest Fanny, I am sorry, but I do not see who you speak of. Indeed, there is no one there—"

In that moment Lord Eastwind, as though aware he was the subject of discussion, turned his attention from Lady Bertram and gave Fanny his unblinking gaze, and then, a subtle smile.

Unwilling to speak of the Curse, Edmund changed the subject to rather surprising, new, and happier things.

"Ask your uncle what he thinks of you, Fanny, and you will hear compliments."

Such language was so new to Fanny that it quite embarrassed her.

"Your uncle thinks you very pretty, dear Fanny—and that is the long and the short of the matter. Anybody but myself would have made something more of it, and anybody but you would resent that you had not been thought very pretty before. But the truth is, your uncle never did admire you till now—and now he does. Your complexion is so improved!—and you have gained so much countenance!—and your figure—nay, Fanny, do not turn away about it—it is but an uncle. If you cannot bear an uncle's admiration,[18] what is to become of you? You must really begin to harden yourself to the idea of being worth looking at. You must try not to mind growing up into a pretty woman."

"Oh! don't talk so!" cried Fanny, distressed by more feelings than he was aware of. So flustered was she that she did not notice how, in that moment, Lord Eastwind was watching their exchange with an even more steady gaze than ever before.

Edmund saw her distress, and added, more seriously—

"Your uncle is disposed to be pleased with you in every respect; and I only wish you would talk to him more. You are one of those who are too silent in the evening circle."

"But I do talk to him more than I used. I am sure I do. Did not you hear me ask him about the slave-trade last night?"

"I did—and was hoping the question would be followed by others. It would have pleased your uncle to be inquired of farther."

"And I longed to do it—but there was such a dead silence! My cousins were sitting without speaking a word. I did not want to set myself off at their expense by shewing the interest which he must wish his own daughters to feel."

"Miss Crawford was very right in what she said of you the other day: that you seemed almost as fearful of notice and praise as other women were of neglect. She has great discernment. I know nobody who distinguishes characters better."

"Edmund, she is a vam—"

But he would not let her finish, would not hear of it, and continued, "For so young a woman she is remarkable! And, I wonder what she thinks of my father! She must admire him, I feel sure of their liking each other. He would enjoy her liveliness."

"*Liveliness* is not quite the word one might use—"

"Oh Fanny, stop it, I entreat you."

---

[18] Gentle Reader, here we speak not of *that* kind of uncle.

"Indeed. She must know herself too secure of the regard of all the rest of you," said Fanny, with half a sigh, "to have any apprehension of being disliked by Sir Thomas. And, after Sir Thomas settles in and decides once more to open the family circle to outside company, I dare say, we shall be meeting again in the same sort of way."

"This is the first October that she has passed in the country since her infancy. Mrs. Grant is very anxious for her not finding Mansfield dull as winter comes on."

Fanny could have said a great deal, but it was safer to say nothing, and leave untouched all Miss Crawford's resources—her accomplishments, her spirits, her importance, her friends, her dire sanguine habits—lest it should betray her into any observations seemingly unhandsome. And she began to talk of something else.

"To-morrow, I think, my uncle dines at Sotherton, and you and Mr. Bertram too. We shall be quite a small party at home. I hope my uncle may continue to like Mr. Rushworth."

"That is impossible, Fanny. He must like him less after to-morrow's visit, for we shall be five hours in his company. I should dread the stupidity of the day, if there were not a much greater evil to follow—the impression it must leave on Sir Thomas. He cannot much longer deceive himself. I am sorry for them all, and would give anything that Rushworth and Maria had never met."

A misfortune exacerbated even further by the subsequent meeting of Mr. Rushworth and Mrs. Norris under dire moonlit circumstances, thought Fanny.

In this quarter, indeed, disappointment was impending over Sir Thomas. Not all his good-will for Mr. Rushworth, not all Mr. Rushworth's deference for him, could prevent him from soon discerning some part of the truth—that Mr. Rushworth was not only a lycanthrope but an inferior young man, as ignorant in business as in books, with opinions in general unfixed (unlike his spittle), and without seeming much aware of it himself.

"Incidentally, it is quite obvious, but when have Mrs. Norris and Mr. Rushworth been *thrown together* so as to produce the certain unmentionable circumstances?" Sir Thomas discreetly inquired. Edmund responded he was uncertain.

In short, Sir Thomas had expected a very different son-in-law. Beginning to feel grave on Maria's account, he tried to understand *her* feelings. Little observation there was necessary to tell him that there was indifference, at best. Her behaviour to Mr. Rushworth was careless and cold. She did not like him. Sir Thomas resolved to speak seriously to her. Advantageous as would be the alliance, and long standing and public as was the engagement, her happiness must not be sacrificed to it. Mr. Rushworth had, perhaps, been accepted on too short an acquaintance, and, on knowing him better, she was repenting.

With solemn kindness Sir Thomas addressed her: told her his fears, inquired into her wishes, entreated her to be open and sincere, and assured her that every inconvenience should be braved, and the connexion entirely given up, if she felt herself unhappy in the prospect of it. He would act for her and release her. Maria had a moment's struggle as she listened, but then gave her answer immediately. She thanked her father and declared she had no desire of breaking her engagement. She had the highest esteem for Mr. Rushworth and had no doubt of her happiness with him.

Sir Thomas was satisfied. Besides, it was an alliance which he could not have relinquished without pain, and Mr. Rushworth was young enough to improve in good society. And if Maria could speak so securely of her happiness without the blindness of love, she ought to be believed. A well-disposed young woman, who did not marry for love, was in general but the more attached to her own family. The nearness of Sotherton to Mansfield must naturally be a continual supply of the most amiable enjoyments. So reasoned Sir Thomas, happy to escape the embarrassing evils of a broken engagement.

As for Maria, she had pledged herself anew to Sotherton. Safe from the possibility of giving Crawford the triumph of destroying her prospects, she retired in proud resolve, determined to behave more cautiously to Mr. Rushworth in future, that her father might not again suspect her.

Had Sir Thomas applied to his daughter within the first three or four days after Henry Crawford's leaving Mansfield, while her feelings were raw, her answer might have been different. But now, when there was no return, no message, no symptom of a softened heart, her mind became cool enough to seek all the comfort that pride and revenge could give.

Henry Crawford had destroyed her happiness, but he should not know that he had done it. He should not destroy her credit, her appearance, her prosperity, too. He should not have to think of her as pining for *him,* rejecting Sotherton and London, independence and splendour, for *his* sake. She must escape from him and Mansfield as soon as possible, and find consolation in fortune and consequence, bustle and the world.

Thus, Mr. Rushworth could hardly be more impatient for the marriage than Maria. In all the important preparations for matrimony she was ready—her hatred of home and Egypt, restraint, the misery of disappointed affection, and contempt of the man she was to marry. The preparations of new carriages and furniture might wait for London and spring.

The principals being all agreed in this respect, it soon appeared that a very few weeks would be sufficient for such arrangements as must precede the wedding.

Mrs. Rushworth was quite ready to make way for the fortunate young woman whom her dear son had selected; very early in November she removed herself to Bath. And before the middle of the same month, the ceremony took place which gave Sotherton another mistress.

It was a very proper wedding. The bride was elegantly dressed; the two bridesmaids were duly inferior; her father gave her away; her mother stood with salts in one hand and an imported palm-frond fan in the other; her aunt tried to cry but yelped instead; and the service was impressively read by Dr. Grant.

It was done, and they were gone. Sir Thomas felt as an anxious father must feel; Lady Bertram felt very little of anything. Mrs. Norris, happy to assist in the duties of the day, by spending it at the Park to support her sister's spirits, and drinking the health of Mr. and Mrs. Rushworth, was all joyous delight and suppressed howling.

The plan of the young couple was to proceed, after a few days, to Brighton, then on to the wider amusements of London.

Julia was to go with them to Brighton. Since rivalry between the sisters had ceased, they had been gradually recovering much of their former good understanding. Some other companion than Mr. Rushworth was of the first consequence to his lady; and Julia was quite as eager for novelty and pleasure as Maria.

Their departure made another material change at Mansfield, a chasm which required some time to fill up. While over the months the household had picked up a discreet yet inordinate amount of supernatural *residents,* mostly of deceased Egyptian origin, the family circle became greatly contracted. And though the Miss Bertrams had latterly added little to its gaiety, they could not but be missed. Even their generally unaware mother missed them. And how much more their tenderhearted cousin, who wandered about the quiet mummy-infested house, and thought of them, and felt for them, with a degree of affectionate regret which they had never done much to deserve!

Chapter XXII

Fanny's consequence increased on the departure of her cousins. As the only young woman in the drawing-room, it was impossible for her not to be more noticed than she had ever been before; and "Where is Fanny?" became no uncommon question, even without her being wanted for any one's convenience.

Many evenings were spent with Lady Bertram pulling Fanny in as a third in discussions with the ever-present Lord Eastwind who spoke in a quiet voice of remarkable clarity and intensity of faraway lands, ancient times, and golden palaces filled with wonders. Fanny listened reluctantly at first, but then was gradually enchanted, unable to help her own curiosity. And she came to regard those comfortable evenings with an odd pleasure, almost looking forward to the strange extravagant tales and the sound of *his* voice.

There was something dark and terrible about Lord Eastwind, she knew very well. She could not trust him, not ever. And yet, there was also something very intimate and familiar. Sometimes, when the candlelight fell a certain way, and his profile turned from her, she recalled faint glimmers of dear memory, oh so long ago. It was in the way his dark locks of hair curved gently and fell from the back. The hollow almost delicate line of his cheekbones. The manner in which his fine lips curved and the sweet corners formed around his mouth when he smiled that faint ever-subtle smile. The well-defined brows shadowing those startling eyes. . . .

If he ever caught her watching, he did not make it known. Instead, he continued to speak in a voice that was impossible to ignore—like dark profound music, just barely hinting at distant, fierce, unknowable light.

Fanny decided that, whoever he truly *was,* whatever effect he had on her, it made him this much more dangerous.

Not only at home did Fanny's value increase, but at the Parsonage too. In that house, which she had hardly entered twice a year since Mr. Norris's death, she became a welcome invited guest, and in the gloom and dirt of November, most acceptable to Mary Crawford. Her visits there, beginning by chance, were continued by solicitation. Mrs. Grant was genuinely eager to get any change and entertainment for her sister, not realizing of course how much discomfort it would cause Fanny to be in Miss Crawford's supernaturally dangerous company.

Fanny, having been sent into the village on some errand by her aunt Norris, was overtaken by a heavy shower close to the Parsonage. Being descried from one of the windows endeavouring to find shelter under an oak just beyond their premises, she was forced, not without reluctance on her part, to come in. When Dr. Grant himself went out with an umbrella, there was nothing to be done but to get into the house as fast as possible.

To Miss Crawford, who had just been contemplating the tedious dismal rain, and the even more dismal chance of seeing a single creature beyond themselves for the next twenty-four hours, the sight of Miss Price dripping with wet in the vestibule, was delightful. The value of an event on a wet day in the country was most forcibly brought before her. She was all alive—insofar as much as she could ever be *alive* again—directly, and among the most active in being useful to Fanny, and providing her with dry clothes.

Fanny, after being obliged to submit to all this attention, assisted and waited on by mistresses and maids, was also obliged to be fixed downstairs in their drawing-room for an hour while the rain continued.

The two sisters were so pleasant and kind to her, that Fanny might have enjoyed her visit could she have believed herself not in the way, and had it not been for the fact that Miss Crawford was liable to feel a certain sanguine *hunger* any moment.

It was beginning to look brighter, when Fanny, observing a harp in the room, asked some questions about it, in order to put off any possible vampiric intentions, and disclosed her wish to hear it.

"Shall I play to you now?" said Miss Crawford. "What will you have?"

Anything but a reel, thought Fanny, but voiced a more polite response.

Miss Crawford played accordingly; happy to have a new listener who seemed so much obliged, so full of wonder at the performance, and who shewed herself not wanting in taste. She played till Fanny's eyes, straying to the window on the weather's being evidently fair, spoke what she felt must be done.

"Another quarter of an hour," said Miss Crawford, "and we shall see how it will be. Do not run away the first moment of its holding up. Those clouds look alarming. And—" she added with a sarcastic smile in a high whisper, "I promise not to bite."

"I have no doubt. But the clouds are passed over," said Fanny.

"I know a black cloud when I see it; and you must not set forward while it is so threatening."

"I believe the threat lies within as well as without."

Miss Crawford laughed. "Ah, well said. However, I want to play something more to you—a very pretty piece—and your cousin Edmund's prime favourite. You must stay and hear your cousin's favourite."

Fanny felt that she must; and though she had not waited for that sentence to be thinking of Edmund, such a memento made her particularly awake to his idea, and she fancied him sitting in that room again and again, perhaps in the very spot where she sat now, listening with constant delight to the favourite air, played with superior tone and expression. . . . Thus impatient to be gone she was kindly asked to call again.

Such was the origin of the sort of intimacy which took place between them within the first fortnight after the Miss Bertrams' going away—an intimacy resulting principally from Miss Crawford's desire of something new, and which had little reality in Fanny's feelings. Fanny went to her every two or three days: it seemed a kind of dark fascination, a sort of fragile truce. She went, and they sauntered about together many an half-hour in Mrs. Grant's shrubbery, the weather being unusually mild for the time of year, and venturing sometimes even to sit down on one of the benches.

"This is very pretty," said Fanny, looking around her as they were thus sitting together one day; "every time I come into this shrubbery I am more struck with its growth and beauty. Three years ago, this was nothing but a rough hedgerow along the upper side of the field, and now it is converted into a walk." And then she waxed philosophical about time and memory and the passing of seasons, which unfortunately fell on deaf—or better to say, *dead*—ears.

Miss Crawford, untouched and inattentive, had nothing to say; and Fanny, perceiving it, brought back her own mind to what she thought must interest.

"It may seem impertinent in *me* to praise, but I must admire the taste Mrs. Grant has shewn in all this."

"Yes," replied Miss Crawford carelessly, "it does very well for a place of this sort. Till I came to Mansfield, I had not imagined a country parson ever aspired to a shrubbery, or anything of the kind."

"I am so glad to see the evergreens thrive!" said Fanny, in reply. "My uncle's gardener always says the soil here is better than his own, and so it appears from the growth of the laurels and evergreens in general. The evergreen! How beautiful!" And she continued, in the same vein, to praise nature.

"To say the truth," replied Miss Crawford, who was far more interested in what actually flowed in veins, "I am something like the famous Doge at the court of Louis XIV.; and may declare that I see no wonder in this shrubbery equal to seeing myself in it. If anybody had told me a year ago that this place would be my home—"

"*Too* quiet for you, I believe."

"I should have thought so, but," and her eyes brightened with an almost unholy light, "I never spent so happy a summer. But then," with a more thoughtful air and lowered voice, "there is no saying what it may lead to."

Fanny's heart beat quickly.

Miss Crawford went on—

"I am conscious of being far better reconciled to a country residence than I had ever expected to be. An elegant, moderate-sized house in the centre of family connexions, and commanding the first society in the neighbourhood. There is nothing frightful in such a picture, is there, Miss Price? One need not envy the new Mrs. Rushworth with such a home as *that*."

"Envy Mrs. Rushworth!" was all that Fanny attempted to say.

"Come, come, it would be very un-handsome in us to be severe on Mrs. Rushworth, with her new *wolfish* spouse, for I look forward to our owing her a great many happy hours. I expect we shall be all very much at Sotherton. Such a match as Miss Bertram has made is a public blessing; for the first pleasures of Mr. Rushworth's wife must be to fill her house, and give the best balls in the country."

Fanny was silent, and Miss Crawford relapsed into thoughtfulness, till suddenly looking up at the end of a few minutes, she exclaimed, "Ah! here he is." It was not Mr. Rushworth, however, but Edmund, who then appeared walking towards them with Mrs. Grant. "My sister and Mr. Bertram. I am so glad your eldest cousin is gone, that he may be Mr. Bertram again. There is something in the sound of Mr. *Edmund* Bertram so formal, so pitiful, so younger-brother-like, that I detest it."

"How differently we feel!" cried Fanny. "To me, the sound of *Mr.* Bertram is so cold and nothing-meaning, so entirely without warmth or character! It just stands for a gentleman, and that's all. But there is nobleness in the name of Edmund. It is a name of heroism and renown; of kings, princes, and knights; and seems to breathe the spirit of chivalry and warm affections."

"I grant you the name is good in itself, and *Lord* Edmund or *Sir* Edmund sound delightfully. But sink it under the chill, the annihilation of a Mr., and Mr. Edmund is no more than Mr. John or Mr. Thomas. Well, shall we join and disappoint them of half their lecture upon sitting down out of doors at this time of year, by being up before they can begin?"

Edmund met them with particular pleasure. It was the first time of his seeing them together since their newfound better acquaintance. A friendship (merely a truce, in Fanny's secret thoughts) between two so very dear to him was exactly what he could have wished.

"Well," said Miss Crawford tauntingly, "and do you not scold us for our imprudence for sitting down?"

"Perhaps I might have scolded," said Edmund, "if either of you had been sitting down alone; but while you do wrong together, I can overlook a great deal."

Oh dear, yes indeed, thought Fanny sadly.

"They cannot have been sitting long," cried Mrs. Grant, "for when I went up for my shawl I saw them from the staircase window, and then they were walking."

"And really," added Edmund, "the day is so mild, that your sitting down for a few minutes can be hardly thought imprudent."

"Upon my word," cried Miss Crawford, "you are two of the most disappointing and unfeeling kind friends I ever met with! You do not know how much we have been suffering, nor what chills we have felt!"

"Do not flatter yourself, my dearest Mary," said Mrs. Grant. "You have not the smallest chance of moving me. I have my alarms, but they are quite in a different quarter." And she proceeded to bemoan the dangers of leaving plants out overnight during unpredictable turning weather.

"The sweets of housekeeping in a country village!" said Miss Crawford archly. "Commend me to the nurseryman and the poulterer."

"My dear child, commend Dr. Grant to the deanery of Westminster or St. Paul's, and I should be as glad of your nurseryman and poulterer as you could be. But we have no such people in Mansfield. Instead we have an oddly shuffling fellow or two with horrid skin, who bump around all day uselessly underfoot, and seem to do no work at all. What would you have me do?"

"I mean to be too rich to lament anything of the sort. A large income is the best recipe for happiness I ever heard of."

"You intend to be very rich?" said Edmund, with a look which, to Fanny's eye, had a great deal of serious meaning.

"To be sure. Do not you? Do not we all?"

"I cannot intend anything which must be so completely beyond my power to command. Miss Crawford may chuse her degree of wealth. She has only to fix on her number of thousands a year, and there can be no doubt of their coming. My intentions are only not to be poor."

"By moderation and economy, and bringing down your wants to your income, and all that. I understand you—and a very proper plan it is for a person at your time of life, with such limited means and indifferent connexions. What can *you* want but a decent maintenance? You have not much time before you; and your relations are in no situation to do anything for you. Be honest and poor, by all means—but I shall not envy you; I do not much think I shall even respect you. I have a much greater respect for those that are honest and rich."

"Your degree of respect for honesty, rich or poor, is precisely what I have no manner of concern with. I do not mean to be poor but something between."

"But I do look down upon 'between,' if it might have been higher. There is no contentment in obscurity, when it might have risen to distinction."

"But how may it rise? How may my honesty at least rise to any distinction?"

This was not so very easy a question to answer, and occasioned an "Oh!" of some length from the fair lady before she could add, "You ought to be in parliament, or you should have gone into the army ten years ago."

"Ah, parliament. I believe I must wait till there is an especial assembly for the representation of younger sons who have little to live on. No, Miss Crawford," he added, in a more serious tone, "there *are* distinctions which I aspire to, but they are of a different character."

Miss Crawford made some laughing answer, which was sorrowful food for Fanny's observation. Without much more pause, Fanny made her adieus; and Edmund suddenly recalled that his mother had been inquiring for her, and that he had walked down to the Parsonage on purpose to bring her back.

Fanny's hurry increased; she found from Edmund's manner, that he *did* mean to go with her. In the moment of parting, Edmund was invited by Dr. Grant to eat his mutton with him the next day. Fanny had barely time for an unpleasant feeling on the occasion, when Mrs. Grant, with sudden recollection, turned to her and asked for the pleasure of her company too.

This was so new an attention, so perfectly new a circumstance in the events of Fanny's life, that she was all surprise and embarrassment. She stammered that she did not suppose it would be in her power, while looking at Edmund for support.

But Edmund, delighted on her behalf, said he could not imagine his mother would make any difficulty of sparing her, and advised enthusiastically that the invitation be accepted.

"And you know what your dinner will be," said Mrs. Grant, smiling—"the turkey, and I assure you a very fine one; for, my dear," turning to her husband, "cook insists upon the turkey's being dressed to-morrow."

"Very well," cried Dr. Grant, "all the better; I am glad to hear you have anything so good in the house. But Miss Price and Mr. Edmund Bertram, I dare say, would take their chance."

The two cousins walked home together; and, except in the discussion of this engagement, it was a thoughtful, silent walk.

Chapter XXIII

"But why should Mrs. Grant ask Fanny?" said Lady Bertram. "How came she to think of asking Fanny? Fanny never dines there, you know, in this sort of way. I cannot spare her, there are rolls of papyrus to sort, and I am sure she does not want to go. Fanny, you do not want to go, do you?"

"If you put such a question to her," cried Edmund, preventing his cousin's speaking, "Fanny will immediately say No; but I am sure, my dear mother, she would like to go; and I can see no reason why she should not, and your papyrus can certainly wait for another day."

"I cannot imagine why Mrs. Grant should think of asking her. She never did before. She used to ask your sisters now and then, but she never asked Fanny."

"If you cannot do without me, ma'am—" said Fanny, in a self-denying tone.

"But my mother will have my father with her all the evening."

"To be sure, so I shall. And certainly, the Pharaoh is always at my side."

"Suppose you take my father's opinion, ma'am."

"That's well thought of. So I will, Edmund. I will ask Sir Thomas, as soon as he comes in, whether I can do without her."

In that moment Lord Eastwind, seated closely on the other side of Lady Bertram, leaned in to whisper something in her ladyship's ear.

Fanny glanced at him cautiously out of the corner of her eye. One never knew but to expect another scarab army. And yet, she had to admit that Mr. Yates regurgitating beetles had been a rather wickedly gratifying sight. . . .

"As you please, ma'am, but I meant my father's opinion as to the *propriety* of the invitation's being accepted—I think he will consider it a right thing by Mrs. Grant, as well as by Fanny, that being the *first* invitation it should be accepted."

"I do not know. We will ask him. But he will be very much surprised that Mrs. Grant should ask Fanny at all."

There was nothing more to be said, till Sir Thomas were present. Since it involved Lady Bertram's own evening's comfort for the morrow, so much uppermost in her mind, she called him to ask.

Her tone of calm languor, for she never took the trouble of raising her voice, was always heard and attended to; and Sir Thomas attended. Fanny immediately slipped out of the room; for to hear herself the subject of any discussion with her uncle was more than her nerves could bear. She was more anxious perhaps than she ought to be—but if her uncle were to have grave looks directed to her, and at last decide against her, she might not be able to appear properly submissive and indifferent. Her cause, meanwhile, went on well. It began, on Lady Bertram's part, with—"I have something to tell you that will surprise you. Mrs. Grant has asked Fanny to dinner."

"Well," said Sir Thomas, as if waiting more to accomplish the surprise.

"Edmund wants her to go. But how can I spare her?"

"She will be late," said Sir Thomas, taking out his watch; "but what is your difficulty?"

Edmund found himself obliged to speak and fill up the blanks in his mother's story. He told the whole; and she had only to add, "So strange! for Mrs. Grant never used to ask her."

"But is it not very natural," observed Edmund, "that Mrs. Grant should wish to procure so agreeable a visitor for her sister?"

"Nothing can be more natural," said Sir Thomas, after a short deliberation; "I can see no reason why she should be denied the indulgence."

"But can I do without her, Sir Thomas?"

"Indeed I think you may."

"She always makes tea, you know, when my sister is not here."

"Your sister, perhaps, may be prevailed on to spend the day with us, and I shall certainly be at home."

"Very well, then, Fanny may go, Edmund."

The good news soon followed her. Edmund knocked at her door on his way to his own.

"Well, Fanny, it is all happily settled, and without the smallest hesitation on your uncle's side. He had but one opinion. You are to go."

"Thank you, I am *so* glad," was Fanny's instinctive reply. Though when she had turned from him and shut the door, she could not help feeling, "And yet why should I be glad? for am I not certain of seeing or hearing something there to pain me?"

In spite of this conviction, however, she was glad. Simple as such an engagement might appear in other eyes, it had novelty and importance in hers, for, excepting the day at Sotherton, she had scarcely ever dined out before.

But Mrs. Norris, invited by Sir Thomas to keep Lady Bertram company, was in a very ill humour, ready to spoil Fanny's pleasure.

"Upon my word, Fanny, you are in high luck to meet with such attention and indulgence! You ought to be very much obliged to Mrs. Grant for thinking of you, and to your aunt for letting you go, and you ought to look upon it as something extraordinary. For I hope you are aware that the compliment is intended to your uncle and aunt and me. Mrs. Grant thinks it a civility due to *us* to take a little notice of you. If your cousin Julia had been at home, you would not have been asked at all."

Mrs. Norris had now so ingeniously done away all Mrs. Grant's part of the favour, that Fanny, who found herself expected to speak, could only say that she was very much obliged to her aunt Bertram for sparing her.

"Oh! depend upon it, your aunt can do very well without you, or you would not be allowed to go. *I* shall be here. And I hope you will have a very *agreeable* day, and find it all mighty *delightful*. But I must observe that five is the very awkwardest of all possible numbers to sit down to table; and I cannot but be surprised that such an *elegant* lady as Mrs. Grant should not contrive better! Remember that, Fanny. Five—only five to be sitting round that table. However, you will have dinner enough on it for ten, I dare say."

Mrs. Norris fetched breath, and went on again, warning Fanny not to be forward, not to step out of one's proper sphere, not to give opinions, and to stay for only as long as Edmund.

"Yes, ma'am, I should not think of anything else."

"And if it should rain, you must manage as well as you can, and not be expecting the carriage to be sent for you."

Her niece thought it perfectly reasonable. She rated her own claims to comfort as low even as Mrs. Norris could. And when Sir Thomas soon afterwards, just opening the door, said, "Fanny, at what time would you have the carriage come round?" she felt a degree of astonishment which made it impossible for her to speak.

"My dear Sir Thomas!" yelped Mrs. Norris, red with anger and beginning to growl in an undertone of a hound whose bone is suddenly threatened, "Fanny can walk."

"Walk!" repeated Sir Thomas, in a tone of most unanswerable dignity, and coming farther into the room. "My niece walk to a dinner engagement at this time of the year! Will twenty minutes after four suit you?"

"Yes, sir," was Fanny's humble answer, given with the feelings almost of a criminal towards Mrs. Norris. She followed her uncle out of the room, having staid behind him only long enough to hear these words spoken in angry agitation—

"Quite unnecessary! a great deal too kind! But Edmund goes; true, it is upon Edmund's account. I observed he was hoarse on Thursday night."

But this could not impose on Fanny. She felt that the carriage was for herself, and herself alone: and her uncle's consideration of her, coming immediately after such representations from her aunt, cost her some tears of gratitude when she was alone.

The coachman drove round to a minute; Sir Thomas saw them off in punctuality.

"Now I must look at you, Fanny," said Edmund, with the kind smile of an affectionate brother, "and tell you how I like you. As well as I can judge by this light, you look very nicely indeed. What have you got on?"

"The new dress that my uncle was so good as to give me on my cousin's marriage. I thought I ought to wear it as soon as I could, and that I might not have such another opportunity all the winter. I hope you do not think me too fine."

"A woman can never be too fine while she is all in white. No, I see no finery about you; nothing but what is perfectly proper. Your gown seems very pretty. I like these glossy spots. Has not Miss Crawford a gown something the same?"

In approaching the Parsonage they passed close by the stable-yard and coach-house, where the grooms with terrible peeling complexions were shuffling about in strange lumbering slow-motion.

"Heyday!" said Edmund, "here's company, here's a carriage! who have they got to meet us, alongside these buffoonish fellows?" And letting down the side-glass to distinguish, "'Tis Crawford's, Crawford's barouche, I protest! There must be his own two men pushing it back into its old quarters, and not doing too fine a job of it I must say—odd, how they stumble about! He is here, of course. This is quite a surprise, Fanny. I shall be very glad to see him."

There was no occasion, there was no time for Fanny to say how very differently she felt; but the idea of having such another to observe her was a great increase of the trepidation with which she walked into the drawing-room.

In the drawing-room Mr. Crawford certainly was, having been just long enough arrived to be ready for dinner. The smiles and pleased looks of the three others standing round him, shewed how welcome was his sudden coming for a few days on leaving Bath. A very cordial meeting passed between him and Edmund; and with the exception of Fanny, the pleasure was general; and even to *her* there might be some advantage in his presence, since every addition to the party allowed her to be less noticed.

She was soon aware of this herself. A happy flow of conversation prevailed, and she was not required to take any part—brother and sister conversed about Bath, the two young men about hunting, Mr. Crawford and Dr. Grant traded politics, and Mr. Crawford and Mrs. Grant conversed on generalities. Fanny listened quietly, passing a very agreeable day.

She could not compliment the newly arrived gentleman, however, with any appearance of interest in a scheme for extending his stay at Mansfield. Her opinion was sought on the weather, but her answers were as short and indifferent as civility allowed. She could not wish him to stay, and would much rather not have him speak to her.

Her two absent cousins, especially Maria, were much in her thoughts on seeing him. But no embarrassing remembrance affected *his* spirits. Here he was apparently as willing to stay and be happy without the Miss Bertrams, as if he had never known Mansfield in any other state. She heard them spoken of by him only in a general way, till they were all re-assembled in the drawing-room. When Edmund was engrossed apart in some matter of business with Dr. Grant, and Mrs. Grant occupied at the tea-table, Mr. Crawford began talking of them with more particularity to his other sister. With a significant smile, which made Fanny quite hate him, he said, "So! Rushworth and his fair bride are at Brighton, I understand; happy man!"

"Yes, they have been there about a fortnight, Miss Price, have they not? And Julia is with them."

"And Mr. Yates, I presume, is not far off."

"Mr. Yates! Oh! we hear nothing of Mr. Yates. I do not imagine he figures much in the letters to Mansfield Park; do you, Miss Price? I think my friend Julia knows better than to entertain her father with Mr. Yates."

"Poor Rushworth and his two-and-forty speeches!" continued Crawford. "Nobody can ever forget them. Poor fellow! I see him now—his toil and his growling despair. Well, I am much mistaken if his lovely Maria will ever want him to make two-and-forty speeches to her"; adding, with a momentary seriousness, "She is too good for him—much too good." And then changing his tone again to one of gentle gallantry, and addressing Fanny, he said, "You were Mr. Rushworth's best friend. Your kindness and patience can never be forgotten. Your indefatigable patience in trying to make it possible for him to learn his part—to give him a brain which nature had denied—to mix up an understanding for him out of the superfluity of your own! *He* might not have sense enough himself to estimate your kindness, but I may venture to say that it had honour from all the rest of the party."

Fanny coloured, and said nothing.

"It is as a dream, a pleasant dream!" he exclaimed, breaking forth again, after a few minutes' musing. "I shall always look back on our theatricals with exquisite pleasure. We were all alive. There was employment, hope, solicitude, bustle, for every hour of the day. Always some little objection, little doubt, little anxiety to be got over. I never was happier."

With silent indignation Fanny repeated to herself, "Never happier!—never happier than when doing what you must know was not justifiable! when behaving so dishonourably and unfeelingly! Oh! what a corrupted mind!"

"We were unlucky, Miss Price," he continued, in a lower tone, to avoid the possibility of being heard by Edmund, and not at all aware of her feelings, "we certainly were very unlucky. Another week, only one other week, would have been enough for us. I think if we had had the disposal of events—if Mansfield Park had had the government of the winds just for a week or two, about the equinox, there would have been a difference. Not that we would have endangered his safety by any tremendous weather—but only by a steady contrary wind, or a calm. I think, Miss Price, we would have indulged ourselves with a week's calm in the Atlantic at that season."

He seemed determined to be answered. And Fanny, averting her face, said, with a firmer tone than usual, "As far as *I* am concerned, sir, I would not have delayed his return for a day. My uncle disapproved it all so entirely when he did arrive, that in my opinion everything had gone quite far enough."

She had never spoken so much at once to him in her life before, and never so angrily to anyone who was not *supernatural.* And when her speech was over, she trembled and blushed at her own daring.

He was surprised; but after a few moments' silent consideration of her, replied in a calmer, graver tone, and as if the candid result of conviction, "I believe you are right. It was more pleasant than prudent. We were getting too noisy." And then turning the conversation, he would have engaged her on some other subject, but her answers were so shy and reluctant that he could not advance in any.

Miss Crawford, who had been repeatedly eyeing Dr. Grant and Edmund, now observed, "Those gentlemen must have some very interesting point to discuss."

"The most interesting in the world," replied her brother—"how to make money; how to turn a good income into a better. Dr. Grant is giving Bertram instructions about the living he is to step into so soon. I find he takes orders in a few weeks. I am glad to hear Bertram will be so well off—a very pretty income to make ducks and drakes with, and earned without much trouble. He will not have less than seven hundred a year, a fine thing for a younger brother. And as of course he will still live at home, it will be all for his *menus plaisirs*; and a sermon at Christmas and Easter, I suppose, will be the sum total of sacrifice."

His sister tried to laugh off her feelings by saying, "Nothing amuses me more than the easy manner with which everybody settles the abundance of those who have a great deal less than themselves. You would look rather blank, Henry, if your *menus plaisirs* were to be limited to seven hundred a year."

"Perhaps I might; but all *that,* you know, is entirely comparative. Birthright and habit must settle the business. Bertram is certainly well off for a cadet of even a baronet's family. By the time he is four or five and twenty he will have seven hundred a year, and nothing to do for it."

Miss Crawford *could* have said that there would be a something to do and to suffer for it; but she checked herself and let it pass; and tried to look calm and unconcerned when the two gentlemen shortly afterwards joined them.

"Bertram," said Henry Crawford, "I shall make a point of coming to Mansfield to hear you preach your first sermon. I shall come on purpose to encourage a young beginner. When is it to be? Miss Price, will not you join me in encouraging your cousin? Will not you engage to attend with your eyes steadily fixed on him the whole time—as I shall do—not to lose a word; or only looking off just to note down any sentence preeminently beautiful? We will provide ourselves with tablets and a pencil. When will it be? You must preach at Mansfield, you know, that Sir Thomas and Lady Bertram may hear you."

"I shall keep clear of you, Crawford, as long as I can," said Edmund; "for you would be more likely to disconcert me, and I should be more sorry to see you trying at it than almost any other man."

"Will he not feel this?" thought Fanny. "No, he can feel nothing as he ought." *He is a heartless creature, possibly* exactly *like his sister.*

The party being now all united, and the chief talkers attracting each other, she remained silent. A whist-table was formed after tea, for the amusement of Dr. Grant. Miss Crawford took her harp. Fanny had nothing to do but to listen undisturbed the rest of the evening, except when Mr. Crawford now and then addressed to her a question or observation, which she could not avoid answering. Miss Crawford was too much vexed by what had passed to be in a humour for anything but music.

The assurance of Edmund's being so soon to take holy orders, coming upon her like a blow that had been suspended, and still hoped uncertain and at a distance, was felt with resentment and mortification, and *unholy* fear. She was very angry with him. She had thought her dark seductive influence greater, her mesmerizing metaphysical charms of voice and eye having their sublime effects upon him.

Indeed, the vampire *had* begun to think of him; felt that she had, with great regard—as much as her *kind* could feel—with almost decided intentions. But she would now meet him with his own cool feelings. It was plain that he could have no serious views, no true attachment, by fixing himself in a situation which he must know she would never stoop to, nor enter due to her *cursed* state. She would learn to match him in his indifference. She would henceforth admit his attentions without any idea beyond immediate amusement. If *he* could so command his affections despite the mesmerizing dark *power* at her command, *hers* should do her no harm.

The only other alternative was to *turn him* into one such as herself.

Chapter XXIV

Henry Crawford had quite made up his mind by the next morning to give another fortnight to Mansfield. Having sent for his hunters, and written a few lines of explanation to the Admiral, he looked round at his sister as he sealed and threw the letter from him, and seeing the coast clear of the rest of the family, said, with a smile, "And how do you think I mean to amuse myself, Mary, on the days that I do not hunt? I am grown too old to go out more than three times a week; but I have a plan for the intermediate days, and what do you think it is?"

"To walk and ride with me, to be sure."

"Not exactly, though I shall be happy to do both, but *that* would be exercise only to my body, and I must take care of my mind. Besides, *that* would be all recreation and indulgence, without the wholesome alloy of labour, and I do not like to eat the bread of idleness. No, my plan is to make Fanny Price in love with me."

"Fanny Price! Nonsense! No, no. You ought to be satisfied with her two cousins."

"But I cannot be satisfied without Fanny Price, without making a small hole in Fanny Price's heart. You do not seem properly aware of her claims to notice. When we talked of her last night, you none of you seemed sensible of the wonderful improvement that has taken place in her looks within the last six weeks. You see her every day, and therefore do not notice it; but I assure you she is quite a different creature from what she was in the autumn. She was then merely a quiet, modest, not plain-looking girl, but she is now absolutely pretty. I used to think she had neither complexion nor countenance; but in that soft skin of hers, so frequently tinged with a blush as it was yesterday, there is decided beauty. And from what I observed of her eyes and mouth, I do not despair of their being capable of expression enough when she has anything to express. And then, her air, her manner, her *tout ensemble*, is so indescribably improved! She must be grown two inches, at least, since October."

"Phoo! phoo! This is only because there were no tall women to compare her with, and because she has got a new gown, and you never saw her so well dressed before. She is just what she was in October, believe me. The truth is, that she was the only girl in company for you to notice, and you must have a somebody. I have always thought her pretty—not strikingly pretty—but 'pretty enough,' as people say; a sort of beauty that grows on one. Her eyes should be darker, but she has a sweet smile; but as for this wonderful degree of improvement, I am sure it may all be resolved into a better style of dress, and your having nobody else to look at. Therefore, if you do set about a flirtation with her, you never will persuade me that it is in compliment to her beauty, or that it proceeds from anything but your own idleness and folly."

Her brother gave only a smile to this accusation, and soon afterwards said, "I do not quite know what to make of Miss Fanny. I do not understand her. I could not tell what she would be at yesterday. What is her character? Is she solemn? Is she queer?[19] Is she prudish? Why did she draw back and look so grave at me? I could hardly get her to speak. I never was so long in company with a girl in my life, trying to entertain her, and

[19] Once more, we do not set sail to Lesbos at this juncture.

succeed so ill! Never met with a girl who looked so grave on me! I must try to get the better of this. Her looks say, 'I will not like you, I am determined not to like you'; and I say she shall."

"Foolish fellow! And so this is her attraction after all! This it is, her not caring about you, which gives her such a soft skin, and makes her so much taller, and produces all these charms and graces! I do desire that you will not be making her really unhappy. A *little* love, perhaps, may animate and do her good, but I will not have you plunge her deep, for she is as good a little creature as ever lived (which is saying very much, coming from *me*) and has a great deal of feeling. Oh, and another thing—" here Miss Crawford paused meaningfully, throwing off all her playfulness of moments earlier.

"She *knows,* Henry. She knows *what* I am."

Henry raised a brow quizzically. "Is that so?"

"And—she is also impervious to me."

"What?"

"She cannot be controlled in the way of the dark. And—" Mary drew closer and lowered her voice, "she also knows and sees all the rest, too. She knows and senses all that is going on behind the—scenes—at Mansfield Park. She watches the dark ancient lord of Egypt, and the lycantropes. She—I am afraid, my dear, she will constitute a problem for us."

Henry remained silent, plunged in sudden dark thoughts by this revelation. Eventually he said: "I was right to think her unusual, special. This, then was the underlying cause. How strong is she?"

"Remarkably so. And she does not even realize it."

"Well then. I will proceed with what I lightly planned to do—but now, taking this news unto due consideration—thanks to you, sister—it will be serious."

"Serious? I do not think you can charm her, Henry.

"Observe me, my dear."

Miss Crawford signed, half mockery, half darkness.

Henry meanwhile forcefully switched back to his levity. "I shall flirt and charm her like a tiny butterfly. And, it can be but for a fortnight. A fortnight is all that is required. And if a fortnight can kill her, she must have a constitution which nothing could save. No, I will not do her any harm, dear little soul! only want her to look kindly on me, to give me smiles as well as blushes, to keep a chair for me by herself wherever we are, and be all animation when I take it and talk to her; to think as I think, be interested in all my possessions and pleasures, try to keep me longer at Mansfield, and feel when I go away that she shall be never happy again. I want nothing more."

"Moderation itself!" said Mary with a wicked smile. "I can have no scruples now. Well, you will have opportunities enough of endeavouring to recommend yourself, for we are a great deal together."

And without attempting any further remonstrance, she left Fanny to her fate, a fate which, had not Fanny's heart been guarded in a way unsuspected by Miss Crawford, might have been a little harder than she deserved.

For, although there doubtless are such unconquerable young ladies of eighteen as are never to be persuaded into love against their judgment by all that talent, manner, attention, and flattery can do, I have no inclination to believe Fanny one of them. With so much tenderness of disposition, and so much taste, she could not have escaped heart-whole from the courtship (though the courtship only of a fortnight) of such a man as Crawford—in spite of there being previous ill opinion of him to be overcome—had not her affection been engaged elsewhere.

With all the security which love of another could give to the peace of mind he was attacking, his continued unobtrusive attentions, adapting themselves to the gentle delicacy of her character—obliged her very soon to dislike him less than formerly. She had not forgotten the past; she thought as ill of him as ever; but she felt his powers. He was entertaining; and his manners were so improved, so seriously and blamelessly polite, that it was impossible not to be civil to him in return.

A very few days were enough to effect this; and soon circumstances arose which enhanced his chances of pleasing her, and gave her a happiness which disposed her to be pleased with everybody. William, her so long absent and dearly loved brother, was in England again. She had a letter from him, a few hurried happy lines, written as the ship came up Channel, and sent into Portsmouth with the first boat that left the *Antwerp* at anchor in Spithead. When Crawford walked up with the naval newspaper in his hand, which he had hoped would bring the first tidings, he found her trembling with joy over this letter, and listening with a glowing, grateful countenance to the kind invitation which her uncle was dictating in reply.

It was but the day before that Crawford had made himself thoroughly master of the subject, or had in fact become at all aware of her having such a brother, or his being in such a ship, but the interest then excited had been very lively, determining him on his return to town to apply for more information as a method of pleasing her. He was, however, too late. All those fine first feelings, of which he had hoped to be the exciter, were already given. But the kindness of his intention was quite thankfully and warmly acknowledged: for she was elevated beyond common timidity by her love for William.

This dear William would soon be amongst them. There could be no doubt of his obtaining leave of absence immediately, for he was still only a midshipman. And as his parents, from living on the spot, must already have seen him, his direct holidays might with justice be given to the sister, who had been his best correspondent through a period of seven years, and the uncle who had done most for his support and advancement.

Fanny was now in the agitation of a higher nature, watching in the hall, in the lobby, on the stairs, for the first sound of the carriage which was to bring her brother.

It came happily while she was thus waiting; and she was with him as he entered the house. The first minutes of exquisite joy in meeting had no interruption and no witnesses except the servants (some of them going around in circles and bumping into walls). This was exactly what Sir Thomas and Edmund had intended, as they both advised Mrs. Norris to continue where she was, instead of rushing out into the hall as soon as the noises of the arrival reached them.

William and Fanny soon shewed themselves; and Sir Thomas had the pleasure of receiving, in his protégé, a very different person from the one he had equipped seven years ago—a young man of an open, pleasant countenance, and frank, unstudied, but feeling and respectful manners.

It was long before Fanny could recover from the agitating happiness of such an hour. It was some time before she could see in him the same William as before, and talk to him, as her heart had been yearning to do through many a past year. That time, however, did gradually come, with affection on his side as warm as her own, and much less encumbered by refinement or self-distrust. She was the first object of his love, but it was a love which his stronger spirits, and bolder temper, made it as natural for him to express as to feel. On the morrow they were walking about together with true enjoyment, and every succeeding morrow renewed a *tête-à-tête*.

Except for the moments of peculiar delight Edmund's kind consideration of her in the last few months had excited, Fanny had never known so much felicity in her life, as in this communion with the brother and friend who was opening all his heart to her, and telling her all his hopes, fears, and plans—the blessing of a promotion, news of their father, mother, brothers, and sisters, of whom she seldom heard. William was genuinely interested in her life at Mansfield; ready to think of every member of that home as she directed, or differing only by a less scrupulous opinion, and more noisy abuse of their aunt Norris.

With William and Fanny Price, fraternal love was thus still a sentiment in all its prime and freshness.

Their amiable affection advanced each in the opinion of all. Henry Crawford was as much struck with it as any. He honoured the warm-hearted, blunt fondness of the young sailor; and saw, with lively admiration, the glow of Fanny's cheek, the brightness of her eye, the deep interest, the absorbed attention, while her brother was describing the hazards, or terrific scenes, which a period at sea must supply.

It was a picture which Henry Crawford had moral taste enough to value. Fanny's attractions increased—increased twofold; for the sensibility which beautified her complexion and illumined her countenance was an attraction in itself. He was no longer in doubt of the capabilities of her heart. She had feeling, genuine feeling. It would be something to be loved by such a girl, to excite the first ardours of her young unsophisticated mind! She interested him more than he had foreseen. A fortnight was not enough. His stay became indefinite.

Mary Crawford knowingly smiled.

William was often called on by his uncle to be the talker. His stories were amusing in themselves to Sir Thomas, but the chief object in seeking them was to understand the young man by his histories. And he listened to his clear, simple, spirited details with full satisfaction, seeing in them the proof of all things good.

Young as he was, William had already seen a great deal. He had been in the Mediterranean; in the West Indies; had been often taken on shore by the favour of his captain, and in the course of seven years had known every variety of danger which sea and war together could offer. With such means in his power he had a right to be listened to. And though Mrs. Norris could fidget about the room, yapping and growling under her breath, and disturb everybody in the midst of her nephew's account of a shipwreck or an engagement, everybody else was attentive.

Even Lady Bertram could not hear of such horrors unmoved, or without sometimes lifting her eyes from her hieroglyphics to say, "Dear me! how disagreeable! I wonder anybody can ever go to sea. The Nile is so much more pleasant to float upon, I dare say." She then would turn to Lord Eastwind and make some vague remark.

In all of this, it must be said, Lord Eastwind observed Fanny and William together with as much—if not more—avid interest than Mr. Crawford. And apparently he took in just as much, for he addressed William directly once, breaking his unwritten rule of talking to no one but Lady Bertram and Fanny.

"Now that you are here, Mr. Price, joined in happy reunion with your sister, what do you find of greater value in your travels? What one thing would you impart as wisdom?"

William was startled for a moment to hear himself addressed by this *person* whom he had for some reason never previously noticed, nor remembered being introduced to. Honestly flustered by the possibility of such a rudeness on his own part (as he thought), William could only mumble, "I am sorry, sir, you must forgive me if I do not recall your name, but yes, in answer to your interesting question—the one thing in my travels I would put above the rest would be—the moment of coming home. And then again—the moment of embarking on a new journey, when the fresh sea wind calls. Yes, those two moments are of utmost import, it seems, despite all the interim wonder, all the adventures in-between."

"Well said," replied Lord Eastwind. "Such a moment of homecoming and embarkation is also felt when one encounters a person—nay, a dear, most beloved one—of one's lifetime." And speaking thus, he turned to glance at Fanny.

Their gazes met. His eyes—ebony burning intensity, hers, pale gentle skies.

Fanny felt something cut through her, strike her, enter through her breast like needles of hot scalding rain, like wind from a furnace bellows. And she blushed furiously, and looked away. Heaven, where was Edmund?

Lord Eastwind continued looking at her, and this time Henry Crawford noticed. He, like his sister (and indeed like Mrs. Norris and all others of the different flavors of the *unholy* and *cursed* and *dark* persuasion currently residing in Mansfield Park), had no trouble being aware of Lord Eastwind's presence.

William had long since forgotten and looked away in a daze, after answering Eastwind's direct address. But Henry was sharply aware. And suddenly he was intrigued and alarmed by the undercurrent he sensed.

Here before him was a potential serious rival. . . .

While the general conversation continued alongside naval subjects, Henry Crawford slipped into a daydream. Spurred on by the sudden awareness of another possible subject of Fanny's affections (oh, little did he know of the true subject, Edmund!), energized and primed into competition even more than ever, he longed to have been at sea, and seen and done and suffered as much as William. For surely, William was more precious to Fanny that Lord Easwind ever could be!

Henry's heart was warmed, his fancy fired, and he felt the highest respect for a lad who, before he was twenty, had gone through such bodily hardships. The glory of heroism, of usefulness, of exertion, of endurance, made his own habits of selfish indulgence appear in shameful contrast. He wished he had been a William Price, distinguishing himself and working his way to fortune and consequence with so much self-respect and happy ardour, instead of what he was! A William Price—or his heroic equivalent—he thought, alone stood a chance in Fanny's romantic affections.

The wish was rather eager than lasting. He was roused from the reverie of retrospection and regret produced by it, by some inquiry from Edmund as to his plans for the next day's hunting. And he found it was as well to be a man of fortune at once with horses and grooms at his command.

In one respect it was better, as it gave him the means of conferring a kindness where he wished to oblige. William expressed an inclination to hunt. And Crawford could mount him[20] without the slightest inconvenience to himself, and with only some scruples to obviate in Sir Thomas, who knew better than his nephew the value of such a loan, and some alarms to reason away in Fanny. She feared for William; by no means convinced of his own horsemanship in various countries—the rough mounts he had ridden, or his many narrow escapes from dreadful falls—that he was at all equal to the management of a high-fed hunter in an English fox-chase. Not till he returned safe without accident, could she be reconciled to the risk, or feel any of that obligation to Mr. Crawford for lending the horse to William.

Then only could she allow it to be a kindness, and even reward the owner with a smile.

---

[20] Upon my word, not *that* way! That way lies the closet and Lesbos and Oscar Wilde, and—oh, criminy!

Chapter XXV

The intercourse[21] of the two families was at this period more nearly restored to what it had been in the autumn. The return of Henry Crawford, and the arrival of William Price, had much to do with it, but much was still owing to Sir Thomas's better inclinations toward the neighbourly attempts at the Parsonage. His mind, now disengaged from the cares which had pressed on him at first, was at leisure to find the Grants and their young inmates really worth visiting.

Also, Sir Thomas could not avoid perceiving that Mr. Crawford was somewhat distinguishing his niece—and thus could not refrain from giving a more willing assent to invitations on that account.

His readiness, however, in finally agreeing to dine at the Parsonage, proceeded from good-breeding and goodwill alone, and had nothing to do with Mr. Crawford, but as being one in an agreeable group. For, it was in the course of that very visit that he first began to think that Mr. Crawford *possibly was* the admirer of Fanny Price.

The meeting was generally felt to be a pleasant one, and the dinner itself was elegant and plentiful, according to the usual style of the Grants, and too much, according to Mrs. Norris.

---

[21] Gracious now, we must not think such dreadfully Roman things!

She could never behold either the wide table or the number of dishes on it with patience, and always contrived to experience some evil from the passing of the lumbering buffoon servants with bad skin behind her chair (almost *touching* her; but she, with her acute lycanthrope senses, would never let them take such idiot liberties), and to bring away some fresh conviction that, among so many dishes, some must be cold.

In the evening it was found that after making up the whist-table there would remain sufficient for a round game. Lady Bertram soon found herself in the critical situation of being applied to for her own choice between the games, and being required either to draw a card for whist or not. She hesitated. Luckily Sir Thomas was at hand.

"What shall I do, Sir Thomas? Whist and speculation; which will amuse me most? Which of the two is played in the shadow of the great Temple of Karnak?"

Sir Thomas, after a moment's painful thought of temples and shadows, recommended speculation. He was a whist player himself, and perhaps might feel that it would not much amuse him to have her for a partner.

"Very well," was her ladyship's contented answer; "then speculation, if you please, Mrs. Grant. I know nothing about it, but Fanny must teach me."

Here Fanny interposed, however, with anxious protestations of her own equal ignorance; she had never played the game nor seen it played in her life; and Lady Bertram felt a moment's indecision again. But upon everybody's assuring her that nothing could be so easy, that it was the easiest game on the cards, and Henry Crawford's stepping forward with an earnest request to be allowed to sit between her ladyship and Miss Price, and teach them both, it was so settled. Sir Thomas, Mrs. Norris, and Dr. and Mrs. Grant seated themselves at the table of prime intellectual state and dignity. The remaining six, under Miss Crawford's direction, were arranged round the other.

It was a fine arrangement for Henry Crawford, who was close to Fanny, and with his hands full of business, having two persons' cards to manage as well as his own (even though Fanny learned the rules of the game in three minutes), he had yet to inspirit her play, sharpen her avarice, and harden her heart, which, especially in any competition with William, was a work of some difficulty. As for Lady Bertram, he continued in charge of all her fame and fortune through the whole evening, in order to keep her from looking at her cards inappropriately, and to direct her in each move.

He was in high spirits, doing everything with happy ease, in lively turns, quick resources, and playful impudence that could do honour to the game.

That is, until Lord Eastwind silently took a seat on the other side of Fanny.

Henry glared at him mockingly, but Eastwind ignored him after a single unreadable glance, while Fanny, feigning ignorance, felt herself boxed in from all sides.

From the other table Sir Thomas inquired into the enjoyment and success of his lady, but in vain, being unheard; till Mrs. Grant was able to go to her and pay her compliments.

"I hope your ladyship is pleased with the game."

"Oh dear, yes! very entertaining indeed. A very odd game. I do not know what it is all about. I am never to see my cards; and Mr. Crawford does all the rest, like Horus presiding over fate."

Fanny glanced to one side of her where Mr. Crawford was perusing their cards, and then to the other where Lord Eastwind was perusing *her*.

"What is it?" she whispered. "Why do you look at me so?

Lord Eastwind drew his face closer and for a moment would not speak, only gazed at her, like a waking dream.

"I look at you, Miss Price," he replied, "Because, as the sun must rise in the morrow and then sink in the evening, as the wind must sweep the stones smooth with time, it is inevitable. I need to look at you always, because unlike all the rest of them, you are so much *alive*."

"What does that mean, Lord Eastwind?"

"Do you not remember?" His eyes, they were so bright-burning with the darkness now, so vivid in their hidden light, and he drew closer, closer. . . .

For a moment Fanny felt her vision swim and she saw glimmering faint images—memories, indeed—of an ancient sunlit place of brightness, of golden sand and rich verdant greenery among the desert, of blossoms lush and great as they cast their perfume on the wind. Standing upon a marble balcony next to him, she *knew* him, so dear to her—a beautiful young man dressed in linen and gold, with skin deep and dark as dates and warm loving eyes of the color of midnight. She felt his arms around herself in that dream, for they were standing gently entwined as lovers; and she was young and golden-skinned as himself, her hair a fall of night, her slender throat encircled in pearls and cascading glass and lapis, her eyes deep and soft as a doe, and their lips—

"Yes," whispered Lord Eastwind. "You remember . . ."

Fanny slammed the impossible vision away, forcing herself into the present. Her head was swimming with dizziness momentarily, and all around, candlelight, cards, the soft laughter and sounds of merriment returned.

Casting his dark intense gaze down, Lord Eastwind was the one who suddenly looked away.

Fanny glanced down at her own hands and felt her cheeks, her face, indeed, all of herself, burn.

Mr. Crawford had completely missed the pointed exchange between Fanny and Eastwind while explaining something to Lady Bertram. Finally, taking the opportunity of a little languor in the game, he turned to Edmund. "Bertram," he said, "I have never told you what happened to me yesterday in my ride home." And Henry Crawford told him he had seen the small residence, Thornton Lacey.

"It sounds like it," said Edmund; "but which way did you turn after passing Sewell's farm?"

Crawford laughed it off, saying he was unsure.

"You inquired, then?"

"No, I never inquire. But I *told* a man mending a hedge that it was Thornton Lacey, and he agreed to it. At least I *think* he did, or that he was mending anything—he promptly got up and walked directly into the hedge, bumping at the foliage a few times, and I must say he had a dreadful case of parchment skin, shedding rather like a snake after a bout of at least three thousand years worth of desiccation."

"You have a good memory."

"Peeling skin can be indeed quite memorable."

"No, what I mean is, I had forgotten having ever told you half so much of the place."

Thornton Lacey was the name of his impending living, as Miss Crawford well knew; and she discreetly listened in on the conversation.

"Well," continued Edmund, "and how did you like what you saw?"

"Very much indeed. You are a lucky fellow. There will be work for five summers at least before the place is livable."

And then Edmund and Henry argued back and forth about the suitability of the land, and the need to enhance the placement of the farmyard, the front entrance, the blacksmith's shop, the garden, and the views of the meadows presented.

Edmund finally said: "I must be satisfied with rather less ornament and beauty. The house and premises may be made a comfortable gentleman's residence, without any heavy expense, and that must suffice me; and, I hope, may suffice all who care about me."

Miss Crawford, a little suspicious and resentful of a certain tone of voice, made a hasty finish of her card game Another deal proceeded, and Crawford began again about Thornton Lacey, meanwhile telling Lady Bertram with exceeding patience, "Excuse me, your ladyship must not see your cards. There, let them lie just before you. Image them calm as the waters of the Nile, and quite far away in the distance. . . ."

Crawford went on: "The place deserves it, Bertram. You talk of giving it the air of a gentleman's residence. *That* will be done. You may give it a higher character. You may raise it into a *place,* the residence of a man of education, taste, modern manners, good connexions." He paused. Then, turning with a softened voice to Fanny, "*You* think with me, I hope. Have you ever seen the place?"

Fanny gave a quick negative, and tried to hide her interest in the subject by an eager attention to her brother; but Crawford pursued with "No, no, you must not part with the queen. You have bought her too dearly, and your brother does not offer half her value. No, no, sir, hands off, hands off. Your sister does not part with the queen. She is quite determined. The game will be yours," turning to her again; "it will certainly be yours."

"And Fanny had much rather it were William's," said Edmund, smiling at her. "Poor Fanny! not allowed to cheat herself as she wishes!"

Fanny gave him a quick grateful smile of perfect understanding. And then she glanced momentarily to see Lord Eastwind also smile.

"Mr. Bertram," said Miss Crawford, a few minutes afterwards, "you know Henry to be such a capital improver, that you cannot possibly engage in anything of the sort at Thornton

Lacey without accepting his help. Only think how useful he was at Sotherton!"

Fanny's eyes were turned on Crawford for a moment with an expression more than grave—even reproachful; but on catching his, were instantly withdrawn. With something of consciousness he shook his head at his sister, and laughingly replied, "I cannot say there was much done at Sotherton; but it was a hot day, and we were all walking after each other, and bewildered. And one must not forget, Mr. Rushworth was so charmingly *engaged* with the wildlife. Wasn't there some kind of duck? A vicious creature, it flew in your face, Mary—" As soon as a general buzz gave him shelter, he added, in a low voice, directed solely at Fanny, "I should be sorry to have my powers of *planning* judged of by the day at Sotherton. I see things very differently now. Do not think of me as I appeared then."

Sotherton was a word to catch Mrs. Norris, and she called out, in high good-humour, "Sotherton! Yes, that is a place, indeed, and we had a charming day there. William, the next time you come, I hope dear Mr. and Mrs. Rushworth will be at home, and I can answer for your being kindly received by both. Your cousins are not of a sort to forget their relations, and Mr. Rushworth is a most amiable man. They are at Brighton now; in one of the best houses there. When you get back to Portsmouth, you ought to pay your respects to them; and I could send a little parcel by you—"

"I should be very happy, aunt; but Brighton is almost by Beachey Head—"

Mrs. Norris began an eager insistence, when she was stopped by Sir Thomas's saying with authority, "I do not advise your going to Brighton, William, as I trust you may soon have more convenient opportunities of meeting; but my daughters would be happy to see their cousins anywhere."

And the subject dropped.

As yet Sir Thomas had seen nothing to remark in Mr. Crawford's behaviour; but when the whist-table broke up, he found his niece the object of attentions, or rather of professions, of a somewhat pointed character.

Henry Crawford was in the first glow of another scheme about Thornton Lacey, and he told it to Fanny. His plan was to rent the house himself the following winter, that he might have a home of his own in that neighbourhood; and it was not merely for the use of it in the hunting-season. He had set his heart upon having a something there that he could come to at any time, a little homestall at his command, where he might find himself continuing, improving, and *perfecting* that friendship and intimacy with the Mansfield Park family which was increasing in value to him every day.

Sir Thomas heard and was not offended. There was no want of respect in the young man's address; and Fanny's reception of it was so proper and modest, so calm and uninviting, that he had nothing to censure in her. She said little, assented only here and there, and betrayed no inclination either of recognizing any part of the compliment to herself, or of encouraging him. Henry Crawford then addressed himself on the same subject to Sir Thomas, in a more everyday tone, but still with feeling.

"I want to be your neighbour, Sir Thomas, as you have, perhaps, heard me telling Miss Price. May I hope for your acquiescence, and for your not influencing your son against such a tenant?"

Sir Thomas, politely bowing, replied, "It is the only way, sir, in which I could *not* wish you established as a permanent neighbour. I hope, and believe, that Edmund will occupy his own house at Thornton Lacey—Edmund?"

"Certainly, sir," said Edmund, "I intend it. But, Crawford, though I refuse you as a tenant, come to me as a friend. Consider the house as half your own every winter."

"We shall be the losers," continued Sir Thomas at length, and then added, "His going, though only eight miles, will be an unwelcome contraction of our family circle. But it is the natural consequence of his intentions, the duty of a parish priest."

Mr. Crawford bowed his acquiescence.

"I repeat again," added Sir Thomas, "that Thornton Lacey is the only house in the neighbourhood in which I should *not* be happy to wait on Mr. Crawford as occupier."

Mr. Crawford bowed his thanks.

Whatever effect Sir Thomas's little harangue might really produce on Mr. Crawford, it raised some awkward sensations in two of his most attentive listeners—Miss Crawford and Fanny. The former was pondering with downcast eyes on what it would be *not* to see Edmund every day. And the latter imagined with dread the future Thornton as a sadly elegant, modernised, and occasional residence of a man of independent fortune.

It was time to have done with cards. The chief of the party were now collected irregularly round the fire, and waiting the final break-up. William and Fanny were the most detached. They remained together at the deserted card-table, talking very comfortably, and not thinking of the rest. Henry Crawford's chair was the first to be given a direction towards them, and he sat silently observing them for a few minutes; noting the odious vicinity of Lord Eastwind. Sir Thomas meanwhile, conversing with Dr. Grant, observed Crawford.

"This is the assembly night," said William. "If I were at Portsmouth I should be at it, perhaps."

"But you do not wish yourself at Portsmouth, William?"

"No, Fanny, that I do not. I shall have enough of Portsmouth and of dancing too, when I cannot have you. And I do not know that there would be any good in going to the assembly, for I might not get a partner. The Portsmouth girls turn up their noses at anybody who has not a commission. One might as well be *nothing* as a midshipman.

"Oh! shame! But never mind it, William" (her own cheeks in a glow of indignation as she spoke). "It is not worth minding. It is no reflection on *you.* Only think, William, when you are a lieutenant, how little you will care for any nonsense of this kind."

"I begin to think I shall never be a lieutenant, Fanny. Everybody gets made but me."

"Oh! my dear William, do not talk so! My uncle says nothing, but I am sure he will do everything in his power to get you made."

The sight of her uncle nearby induced them to talk of something else.

"Are you fond of dancing, Fanny?"

"Yes, very; only I am soon tired."

"I should like to go to a ball with you and see you dance. Have you never any balls at Northampton? I should like to see you dance, and I'd dance with you if you *would,* for nobody would know who I was here, and I should like to be your partner once more. We used to jump about together many a time, did not we? when the hand-organ was in the street? I am a pretty good dancer in my way, but I dare say you are a better." And turning to his uncle, who was now close to them, "Is not Fanny a very good dancer, sir?"

Mr. Crawford, Lord Eastwind, and Edmund, all had their gazes on her.

Fanny, in dismay at such an unprecedented question, did not know which way to look, or how to answer. Some very grave reproof must be coming to her brother, and sink her to the ground. But, on the contrary, it was no worse than, "I am sorry to say that I am unable to answer your question. I have never seen Fanny dance since she was a little girl; but I trust we shall both think she acquits herself like a gentlewoman when we do see her, which, perhaps, we may have an opportunity of doing ere long."

"I have had the pleasure of seeing your sister dance, Mr. Price," said Henry Crawford, leaning forward, "and will engage to answer every inquiry which you can make on the subject, to your entire satisfaction. But I believe" (seeing Fanny looked distressed) "it must be at some other time. There is *one* person in company who does not like to have Miss Price spoken of."

True enough, he had once seen Fanny dance; and it was equally true that he would now have answered for her gliding about with quiet, light elegance, and in admirable time. But, in fact, he could not for the life of him recall what her dancing had been.

He passed, however, for an admirer of her dancing. Sir Thomas, by no means displeased, prolonged the conversation on dancing in general, and was so engaged in describing the balls of Antigua, that he had not heard his carriage announced, and was first called to it by the yappy bustle of Mrs. Norris.

"Come, Fanny, what are you about? We are going. Do not you see your aunt is going? Quick! I cannot bear to keep good old Wilcox waiting. My dear Sir Thomas, the carriage should come back for you, and Edmund and William."

Sir Thomas could not dissent, as it had been his own arrangement, previously communicated to his wife and sister; but now forgotten by Mrs. Norris.

Fanny's last feeling in the visit was disappointment: for the shawl which Edmund was quietly taking from the servant to put round her shoulders was seized by Mr. Crawford's quicker hand, and she was obliged to be indebted to his more prominent attention.

As she stepped into the carriage, she felt, with another shock, her hand gently held by Lord Eastwind.

Chapter XXVI

William's desire of seeing Fanny dance made more than a momentary impression on his uncle. Sir Thomas remained steadily inclined to gratify so amiable a feeling; to gratify anybody else who might wish to see Fanny dance, and to give pleasure to the young people.

Having thought the matter over, the next morning at breakfast, after recalling what his nephew had said, he added, "I do not like, William, that you should leave Northamptonshire without this indulgence. It would give me pleasure to see you both dance. You spoke of the balls at Northampton. I believe we must not think of a Northampton ball. A dance at home would be more eligible; and if—"

"Ah, my dear Sir Thomas!" interrupted Mrs. Norris, "I knew what you were going to say. If dear Julia were at home, or dearest Mrs. Rushworth at Sotherton, to afford a reason, an occasion for such a thing, you would be tempted to give the young people a dance at Mansfield."

"My daughters," replied Sir Thomas, gravely interposing, "have their pleasures at Brighton, and I hope are very happy; but the dance which I think of giving at Mansfield will be for their cousins."

Mrs. Norris had not another word to say. Her surprise and vexation required some minutes' silence to be settled into composure. A ball at such a time! His daughters absent and herself not consulted!

Edmund, William, and Fanny did, in their different ways, look and speak as much grateful pleasure in the promised ball as Sir Thomas could desire. Edmund's feelings were for the other two. His father had never committed a kindness more to his satisfaction.

Lady Bertram was perfectly quiescent and contented, and had no objections to make, short of mumbling about cat, crocodile, and baboon figurines for background display. Sir Thomas insisted it would give her no trouble (and, by Heaven, no figurines necessary); and she assured him "that she was not at all afraid of the trouble; indeed, she could not imagine there would be any, and that fruits of the Nile as statuary would be lovely."

Mrs. Norris was ready with her suggestions as to the rooms to be used, but found it all prearranged; and the day was settled too. Sir Thomas had been quite amusing himself with organizing the business. He read out-loud his list of the families to be invited, from whom he calculated to collect young people enough to form twelve or fourteen couple: and could detail the considerations which had induced him to fix on the 22nd as the most eligible day. William was required to be at Portsmouth on the 24th; the 22nd would therefore be the last day of his visit. Mrs. Norris was obliged to be satisfied with having been on the point of proposing the 22nd herself.

The ball was now a settled thing. Invitations were sent with despatch, and many a young lady went to bed that night with her head full of happy cares as well as Fanny. To her the cares were sometimes almost beyond the happiness. For, young and inexperienced, with small means of choice and no confidence in her own taste, the "how she should be dressed" was a point of painful solicitude. The solitary ornament in her possession, a very pretty amber cross which William had brought her from Sicily, was the greatest distress of all. She had nothing but a bit of ribbon to fasten it to. Would it be appropriate, considering all the rich ornaments the other young ladies would appear in? And yet not to wear it! William had wanted to buy her a gold chain too, but the purchase had been beyond his means, and therefore not to wear the cross might be mortifying him.

In addition, Fanny felt that the wearing of *any* cross would be a prudent thing, what with so many *unnatural* or *cursed* presences liable to attend the Mansfield Park assembly. These were anxious considerations; enough to sober her spirits even under the prospect of a ball given principally for her gratification.

The preparations meanwhile went on, and Lady Bertram continued to sit on her sofa sorting clay tablets, or attending to Lord Eastwind, without any inconvenience.

Fanny had some extra visits from the housekeeper, and several servants sent up to her arrived either late or in an unnatural daze. At more than one point, Fanny herself interrupted strange goings on in the hallways, once even disengaging a maid from the pawing advances of a slow moving but obviously hungry mummy—ahem—a servant with grossly peeling skin.

"Whoever you are, sir," exclaimed Fanny to the creature, "I insist you take yourself away, for I know very well what you intend to do to this poor girl, and that is just unacceptable. Truly, I insist you withdraw and quit the premises! I beg you not to make me repeat myself."

And when the mummy ignored her polite firmness, and continued reaching for the hypnotized maid, Fanny took the heavy roll of muslin from the maid's limp arms and calmly bashed the mummy in the head.

But—*this* creature fought back!

Making hollow deep rumblings, the mummy raised its arms, and advanced on Fanny! Suddenly Fanny could see the peeling ghastly fingers grew into bony claws before her eyes, and the face—oh! the face was a squirming mass of maggots where she had hit it flatly with the roll of fabric.

Fanny's breath caught in her throat. Head pounding in terror, yet she stood her ground and did not step back.

The mummy opened its already gaping maw wide . . . and it continued opening—wider, wider—and it drew forward, just inches away from Fanny's face.

The cross, the tiny hidden cross at her chest, fell out of her bodice. But it did not seem to make a bit of difference. . . . *Indeed,* her fevered thoughts tumbled, *this creature, surely of Ancient Egypt, predates the coming of the Lord Jesus Christ, ands would likely not even know its holy meaning!*

Desperately, Fanny clutched the roll of muslin in her hands, crumpling the soft fabric intended for her ball dress. Driven by a mad instinct, she bunched together the end into a ball, and—allowing the rest of the roll to unravel to the floor—she used both hands to shove the muslin directly into the mummy's terrifying huge mouth, effectively plugging it.

Whatever had prompted her to wad its mouth, she had no notion! But the mummy made a horrifying stifled noise; and then, as Fanny continued to press and shove the fabric deeper into the unnatural cavity, feeling a *crush* of something horrible giving way, the mummy flailed its horrible desiccated limbs and backed away.

And then it crumbled to the floor.

In a matter of breaths, there was nothing left of it, not even a trace of bones. It became a tiny pile of sand and dust.

Fanny stood breathing harshly, holding the destroyed muslin in her hands, sobbing with fury, sorrow, and a sudden inspiration.

She had prevented the mummy from taking the *breath of life*. And by covering its mouth, the one unnatural vehicle of its resurrection, she had utterly destroyed it.

Fanny's maid was rather hurried in bringing replacement fabric, and making up a new dress for her. Sir Thomas gave orders, and Mrs. Norris ran about.

Edmund was at this time particularly full of cares: his mind being deeply occupied in the consideration of two important events now at hand, which were to fix his fate in life—ordination and matrimony—events of such a serious character as to make the ball, which would be very quickly followed by one of them, appear of little moment in his eyes.

On the 23rd he was going to a friend near Peterborough, in the same situation as himself, and they were to receive ordination in the course of the Christmas week. Half his destiny would then be determined, but the other half might not be so very smoothly wooed.

His duties would be established, but the wife who was to share, animate, and reward those duties, might yet be unattainable.

He knew his own mind, but he was not always perfectly assured of knowing Miss Crawford's. There were points on which they did not quite agree. There were moments in which she did not seem propitious. And though trusting to her affection, and knowing what he had to offer her, he had many anxious feelings, many hours of doubt. His conviction of her regard for him was sometimes very strong. But at other times doubt and alarm intermingled with his hopes.

He thought of her disinclination for privacy and retirement, her decided preference of a London life. What could he expect but a determined rejection?

The issue of all depended on one question. Did she love him well enough to forego what had used to be essential points? And this question he was continually repeating to himself.

Miss Crawford was soon to leave Mansfield. He had seen her eyes sparkle as she spoke of the dear friend's letter, which claimed a long visit from her in London. He had since heard her express herself differently, with other feelings, more chequered feelings: he had heard her tell Mrs. Grant that she should leave her with regret; that neither the friends nor the pleasures she was going to were worth those she left behind, that she was already looking forward to being at Mansfield again. Was that a "yes"?

With such matters to ponder over, Edmund could not think very much of the upcoming ball.

Independent of his two cousins' enjoyment in it, the evening was to Edmund of no higher value than any other meeting of the two families. In every meeting there was a hope of receiving further confirmation of Miss Crawford's attachment; but the whirl of a ballroom, perhaps, was not particularly favourable to the expression of serious feelings. To engage her early for the two first dances was all the preparation for the ball which he could enter into.

Thursday was the day of the ball; and on Wednesday morning Fanny, still unable to satisfy herself as to what she ought to wear, determined to seek the counsel of the more enlightened, and apply to Mrs. Grant and her sister and their acknowledged taste. Edmund and William were gone to Northampton, Mr. Crawford likewise out, so she walked down to the Parsonage with hope of obtaining a private discussion. Indeed, the privacy of such a discussion was a most important part of it to Fanny.

She met Miss Crawford within a few yards of the Parsonage. Still holding to their unspoken *truce,* she explained her business at once, and inquired if she would be so kind as to give her opinion. Miss Crawford appeared gratified by the application, and after a moment's thought, urged Fanny's returning with her in a more cordial manner than usual, and promising with a charming wicked smile, to attempt nothing *untoward.* The vampire proposed their going up into her room, where they might have a comfortable coze, without disturbing Dr. and Mrs. Grant. It suited Fanny; and with honest gratitude on her side for such unexpected amiability, they proceeded indoors, and upstairs, and were soon deep in the interesting subject.

Miss Crawford, pleased with the appeal, forgot the vampiric temptation of *sanguinity* and instead gave her all her best judgment and fashion taste. The dress being settled in all its grander parts—"But what shall you have by way of necklace?" said Miss Crawford with hardly a trace of sarcasm. "Shall not you wear your brother's cross?"

And as she spoke she was undoing a small parcel, which Fanny had observed in her hand when they met. Fanny acknowledged her wishes and doubts on this point: she did not know how either to wear the cross, or to refrain from wearing it.

"Pray, my dear, do not be detained from your holy object by consideration of *my own* kind," said Miss Crawford with a smile.

"I am not," said Fanny. "What concerns me are the feelings of my dear brother, William."

She was answered by having a small trinket-box placed before her, and being requested to chuse from among several gold chains and necklaces.

Such had been the parcel with which Miss Crawford was provided, and such the object of her intended visit. In the kindest oddest manner she now urged Fanny's taking one for the cross and to keep for her sake, saying everything she could think of to obviate the scruples which were making Fanny start back at first with a look of horror at the proposal.

"You see what a collection I have," said Miss Crawford; "more than I ever use or think of. I do not offer them as new. I offer nothing but an old necklace. Naturally, no crosses here. But also nothing one might consider unholy. You must forgive the liberty, and oblige me."

Fanny still resisted, and from her heart. The gift was too valuable, and the intentions too suspect. But Miss Crawford persevered, and argued the case with so much earnestness, as to be finally successful.

Fanny found herself obliged to yield, and proceeded to make the selection. She looked and looked, longing to know which might be least valuable. She fancied there was one necklace more frequently placed before her eyes than the rest. It was of gold, prettily worked. And though Fanny would have preferred a longer, plainer chain, she hoped, in fixing on this, to be chusing what Miss Crawford least wished to keep.

Miss Crawford smiled her perfect wicked approbation; and hastened to complete the gift by putting the necklace round her, and making her see how well it looked. Fanny had not a word to say against its becomingness, and was exceedingly pleased. She would rather be obliged to some other less *undead* person. But Miss Crawford had anticipated her wants.

"When I wear this necklace I shall always think of you," said Fanny with genuine feeling, "and feel how very kind you were—despite the dark nature of *yourself*."

"You must think of somebody else too, when you wear that necklace," replied Miss Crawford. "You must think of Henry, for it was his choice in the first place. He gave it to me, and with the necklace I make over to you all the duty of remembering the original giver."

Fanny, in great astonishment and confusion, would have returned the present instantly. To take what had been the gift of another person, of a brother too—impossible!

With embarrassment quite diverting to her companion, she laid down the necklace again on its cotton, resolved either to take another or none at all.

"My dear child," said Miss Crawford, laughing, "what are you afraid of? Do you think Henry will claim the necklace as mine, and fancy you did not come honestly by it? or are you imagining he would be too much flattered by seeing round your lovely throat an ornament which his money purchased three years ago, before he knew there was such a throat in the world? or perhaps"—looking archly—"you suspect a confederacy between us, that I am now doing this with his knowledge and at his desire?"

"I would not be surprised if it were indeed thus," whispered Fanny.

"Come, prove me wrong," said the vampire. "Show me your courage in taking it."

Fanny blushed.

"Well, then," replied Miss Crawford more seriously, "take the necklace, and say no more about it. It being a gift of my brother's need not make any difference. Rest assured, it makes none for me. He is always giving me something or other. I have innumerable presents from him. I would rather part with it and see it in your possession than any other. Such a trifle."

Fanny decided not to make any further opposition; and accepted the necklace again but without enthusiasm, for there was an inexplicable expression in Miss Crawford's eyes.

It was impossible for Fanny to be insensible of Mr. Crawford's change of manners. She had long seen it. He evidently tried to please her: he was gallant, attentive, as he had been to her cousins. He wanted, she supposed, to cheat her of her heart's peace as he had cheated them. Whether he might have some ulterior motive in this necklace—she could not be convinced that he had not.

Reflecting upon this, she walked home, with new cares to weigh her down.

Chapter XXVII

On reaching home Fanny went immediately upstairs to deposit the unexpectedly acquired necklace in some favourite box in the East room, which held all her smaller treasures. But on opening the door, she was surprised to find her cousin Edmund there, writing at the table! Such a sight, having never occurred before, was wonderful and welcome.

"Fanny," said he directly, leaving his seat and his pen, and meeting her with something in his hand, "I beg your pardon for being here. I came to look for you, and after waiting a little, started to leave a note. My business is merely to beg your acceptance of this little trifle—a chain for William's cross. I have only just now received it at Northampton. I hope you will like the chain itself; it has the simplicity of your taste. Consider it a token of the love of one of your oldest friends."

And so saying, he was hurrying away, before Fanny, overpowered by a thousand feelings of pain and pleasure, could speak. But she then called out, "Oh! cousin, stop a moment, pray stop!"

He turned back.

"I cannot attempt to thank you," she continued, in a very agitated manner; "I feel much more than I can possibly express. Your goodness in thinking of me in such a way is beyond—"

"If that is all you have to say, Fanny . . ." He smiled, turning away again.

"No, no, it is not. I want to consult you."

Almost unconsciously she had now undone the parcel he had just put into her hand, and seeing before her, in all the niceness of jewellers' packing, a plain gold chain, perfectly simple and neat, she could not help bursting forth again, "Oh, this is beautiful indeed! This is the very thing, precisely what I wished for! This is the only ornament I have ever had a desire to possess. It will exactly suit my cross. They must and shall be worn together."

"My dear Fanny, you feel these things a great deal too much. I am most happy that you like the chain, and that it should be here in time for to-morrow; but your thanks are far beyond the occasion. It is my pleasure!"

Upon such expressions of affection Fanny could have lived an hour without saying another word. But Edmund brought her back to the moment by saying, "But what is it that you want to consult me about?"

It was about Miss Crawford's necklace, which she now most earnestly longed to return. She told him of her recent visit. And now her raptures might well be over; for Edmund was so struck with the circumstance, so delighted with what Miss Crawford had done, so gratified by such a coincidence of conduct between them, that Fanny could not but admit the superior power of Miss Crawford over his own mind. It was some time before she could get his attention or any answer: he was in a reverie of fond reflection. But when he did return to himself, he was very decided in opposing what she wished.

"Return the necklace! No, my dear Fanny, upon no account. It would be mortifying her severely."

"I should not have thought of returning it," said Fanny, "but being her brother's present, is it not fair to suppose she would rather not part with it?"

"It ought not to prevent you from keeping it. No doubt it is handsomer than mine, and fitter for a ballroom."

"No, it is not handsomer, not at all, and, for my purpose, not half so fit. The chain will agree with William's cross beyond all comparison better than the necklace."

"For one night, Fanny, for only one night, if it *be* a sacrifice. I am sure you will make that sacrifice rather than give pain to one who has been so studious of your comfort. Miss Crawford's attentions to you have been—impeccable; and to decline them must have something the *air* of ingratitude, even though I know it is farthest from your nature. Wear the necklace, as you are engaged to do, to-morrow evening, and let the chain be kept for commoner occasions. This is my advice. I would not have the shadow of a coolness between the two whose intimacy I have been observing with the greatest pleasure. I would not have the shadow of a coolness arise," he repeated, his voice sinking a little, "between the two dearest objects I have on earth."

He was gone as he spoke. And Fanny remained to calm herself as best she could. She was one of his two dearest—that must support her. But the other: the first! She had never heard him speak so openly before, and though it told her no more than what she had long perceived, it was a stab, for it told of his own convictions and views. They were decided. He would marry Miss Crawford.

But—had she even been untainted by the *dark*—did Miss Crawford deserve him? He was deceived in her: he gave her merits which she had not. Her faults were what they had ever been, but he saw them no longer. And he absolutely refused to see the vampire in her.

Till she had shed many tears, Fanny could not subdue her agitation. The dejection which followed could only be relieved by fervent prayers for his happiness—and his safety.

It was Fanny's intention to try to overcome all that bordered on selfishness, in her affection for Edmund.

To her he could be nothing under any circumstances; nothing dearer than a friend. Why did such a forbidden idea of anything otherwise even occur to her? It ought not to have touched her imagination. She would endeavour to be rational, and to deserve the right of judging of Miss Crawford's character, by a sound intellect and an honest heart.

She had all the heroism of principle, and was determined to do her duty. But, having also many of the feelings of youth and nature, she seized the scrap of paper on which Edmund had begun writing to her, as a treasure beyond all her hopes. And reading with the tenderest emotion these words, "My very dear Fanny, you must do me the favour to accept," she locked it up with the chain, as the dearest part of the gift.

It was the only thing approaching a letter, which she had ever received from him. She might never receive another; it was impossible that she ever should receive another so perfectly gratifying in the occasion and the style. Two blessed lines! The enthusiasm of a woman's love!

Having controlled her thoughts and comforted her feelings, Fanny was able in due time to go down and resume her usual employments near her aunt Bertram.

Upon seeing Lord Easwind there—nothing out of the usual—she was momentarily subject to an unexpected blush.

"Miss Price," spoke he, addressing her with a soft gaze of his impossible deep eyes. "You are likely already engaged for the first several dances. Might I ask for but a single dance, somewhere in the middle of the joyful evening?"

"You may, sir." relied Fanny.

Lord Eastwind's face seemed, in that moment, to be transcendent. "Then you make me the happiest of the *living*."

Thursday, predestined to hope and enjoyment, came; and opened with more kindness to Fanny than expected. Soon after breakfast a very friendly note was brought from Mr. Crawford to William, stating that as he found himself obliged to go to London on the morrow for a few days, he hoped that William could decide to leave Mansfield half a day earlier and accept a companionable place in his carriage.

Mr. Crawford meant to be in town by dinner-hour, and William was invited to dine with him at the Admiral's. The proposal was a very pleasant one to William himself, who enjoyed the idea of travelling post with four horses, and such a good-humoured, agreeable friend.

Fanny, from a different motive, was exceedingly pleased. Though this offer of Mr. Crawford's would rob her of many hours of his company, she was too happy in having William spared from the fatigue of an otherwise long journey. Sir Thomas approved of it for another reason. His nephew's introduction to Admiral Crawford might be of service. Upon the whole, it was a very joyous note. Fanny's spirits lived on it half the morning, deriving some pleasure from its writer being himself to go away.

As for the ball, so near at hand, she had too many agitations and fears to have half the enjoyment in anticipation which she ought to have had. Many young ladies looking forward to the same event in easier situations might be experiencing less novelty, less interest, less gratification. Miss Price, known only by name to half the people invited, was now to make her first appearance, and must be regarded as the queen of the evening.

Who could be happier than Miss Price?

But Miss Price had not been brought up to the trade of *coming out;*[22] and had she known in what light this ball was considered respecting her, it would very much have lessened her

[22] Closets, again? Fie, not the closets!

comfort by increasing the fears she already had of doing wrong and being looked at. To dance without much observation or any extraordinary fatigue, to have strength and partners for about half the evening, to dance a little with Edmund, and not a great deal with Mr. Crawford, to see William enjoy himself, and be able to keep away from her aunt Norris, was the height of her ambition.

As these were the best of her hopes, they could not always prevail. In the course of a long morning, spent principally with her two aunts, she was often under the influence of much less sanguine views. William, determined to make this last day a day of thorough enjoyment, was out snipe-shooting; Edmund was likely at the Parsonage; and Fanny was left alone to bear the worrying and teeth-gnashing of Mrs. Norris, of all things on the eve of the full moon!

Moreover, Mrs. Norris was particularly cross because the housekeeper would have her own way with the ball supper. *Her,* Fanny could not avoid, though the housekeeper might.

Fanny was worn down at last into thinking that everything pertaining to the ball was a horrid evil. When sent off with a parting worry to dress, she moved languidly towards her own room, and felt decidedly incapable of happiness.

As she walked slowly upstairs she thought of yesterday. Her musings were interrupted around the corner by the sight of another shabby-skinned mummified fellow in the process of sipping the *breath of life* from yet another innocent lamb of a maid. The maid hug limp over a banister. And if she moved but one wrong inch, she might tumble and hurt herself! The mummy was leaning over her, his horrible mouth over the maid's ear, using the opening to reach through to her inner *being* and claim her life force.

"Oh, for goodness sake!" exclaimed Fanny, hurrying her step to reach the top landing where the unholy scene was being enacted. "*You*—whoever you are! In the name of Heaven, stop it!"

The mummy naturally ignored her.

Upon my word, Fanny thought, what was it with these things? They grew more insolent by the hour, going about their feeding business in plain sight! The first time or two Fanny had been unsure, but now she was certain. The many coffin-sized crates piled all over the estate, the endless strange parade of loutish servants, their abysmal hanging strips of dead skin, indeed their horrific maggot-crawling visage when disturbed—these were *creatures undead,* exhumed from their many thousand-year-old Egyptian resting place by some zealous doctorate-endowed idiot, and then somehow returned to life, no doubt by some equally idiot action of Lady Bertram. . . .

And what of Lord Eastwind? He had to be involved—

But—now was not the time to lose in contemplation. Since no one else was up to it, Fanny had to do something about *this* particular mummy and *this* particular endangered maid.

Having no roll of muslin at her disposal, Fanny considered what else was closest to her, for a weapon.

It had to be something one could use to stuff in the mouth. . . .

Fortunately, this particular maid was newly come from Sir Thomas's plantation, on the way to the kitchen with a basket full of large apples, to be used for the supper dessert. (What was she doing up here instead of down in the kitchen, Fanny had no notion of, but suspected the mummy had lured the maid up the flight of stairs to such a convenient secluded spot.)

Fanny bent down and gathered apples in both hands. She then stepped up to the mummy, knocked politely on its shoulder, and when the creature turned, started stuffing large apples into its gaping maw.

The mummy's eye-sockets widened and it began to flail and choke. Bits of apple and juice went flying about like spittle (by the bye, how was Mr. Rushworth? one fondly wondered). Fanny grabbed hold of the maid with her left hand before she plummeted over the banister, and with her right she continued to shove apples, until she heard a satisfying—and yes, rather terrifying, but Fanny was getting used to it—crunch.

"There! I dare say, a stuffed suckling pig would envy your condition!" she exclaimed, as the mummy, cut off from its source of the *breath of life,* fell before her, turning, as had the other, to dust.

That is, dust and apples. Suitably battered, they rolled about on the crunchy floor amongst the remains of sand.

The maid came to in a flutter, and started apologizing profusely.

"If you don't mind," said Fanny, "I see those fallen apples are a bit spoiled. If you please, I suggest you do not use them in the pie tonight."

Fanny continued upstairs.

"Fanny," said a voice at that moment near her. Starting and looking up, she saw, across the lobby she had just reached, Edmund himself, standing at the head of a different staircase. He came towards her. "You look tired and fagged, Fanny. You have been walking too far."

I have been liberating serving staff of this household from the clutches of the unholy. 'Tired and fagged' is rather not the term one would use, Fanny wanted to say but wisely held back, saying instead: "No, I have not been out at all."

"Then you have had fatigues within doors, which are worse. You had better have gone out."

I have been crushing skulls, Fanny thought. *Within doors.*

Not liking to complain, she found it easiest to make no answer; and though he looked at her with his usual kindness, she believed he had soon ceased to think of her. He did not appear in spirits. They proceeded upstairs together, their rooms being on the same floor above.

"I come from Dr. Grant's," said Edmund presently. "You may guess my errand there, Fanny." And he looked so conscious, that Fanny could think but of one errand, which turned her too sick for speech. "I wished to engage Miss Crawford for the two first dances," was the explanation that followed, and brought Fanny to life again, enabling her to utter something like an inquiry as to the result.

"Yes," he answered, "she is engaged to me; but" (with a smile that did not sit easy) "she says it is to be the last time that she ever will dance with me. She is not serious. I think, I hope, I am sure she is not serious; but I would rather not hear it. She never has danced with a clergyman, she says, and she never *will*."

"On would think—dancing with a clergyman would not be the most appealing diversion to a vampire," said Fanny musingly. "Indeed, that's a bit of an unnatural notion, one might say."

"What? Oh, Fanny, I pray you, stop with this nonsense already!" Edmund was indeed stunned to be reminded yet again of such a thing.

"What would it take to convince you?"

Edmund shook his head, sadly. "It has to be nerves, dear Fanny, That is it, indeed, you are thus nonsensical, why, with all the excitement of the evening to come, it is but natural—"

Fanny sighed and once again let the matter drop.

Edmund continued on the original topic. "For my own sake, I could wish there had been no ball just at—I mean not this very week, this very day; to-morrow I leave home."

Fanny struggled for speech, and said, "I am very sorry that anything has occurred to distress you. Including my own—*words*. This ought to be a day of pleasure. My uncle meant it so."

"Oh yes, yes! and it will be a day of pleasure. It will all end right. I am only vexed for a moment. In fact, it is not that I consider the ball as ill-timed. But, Fanny," stopping her, by taking her hand, and speaking low and seriously, "you know what all this means. You see how it is; and could tell me, perhaps better than I could tell you, how and why I am vexed."

You are in love with a charming undead *fiend who wears well the latest fashion,* Fanny wanted to say. *Vexation is the least of your calamities.*

"Let me talk to you a little," he continued. "You are a kind listener. I have been pained by her manner this morning, and cannot get the better of it. I know her disposition to be as sweet and faultless as your own—"

Fanny choked.

"—but the influence of her former companions gives to her sometimes a tinge of wrong. She does not *think* evil, but she speaks it—"

Sucks it . . .

"—speaks it in playfulness; and though I know it to be playfulness, it grieves me to the soul."

"The effect of—education," said Fanny gently. And she thought of how a vampire might be first *educated*—

Edmund could not but agree to it. "Yes, that uncle and aunt! They have injured the finest mind. For, sometimes, Fanny, I own to you, it does appear more than manner: it appears as if the mind itself was tainted."

Oh dear sweet Lord! How Fanny wanted to strike her head against a hard surface.

And yet, this had to be an appeal to her judgment, and therefore, after a moment's consideration, said, "If you only want me as a listener, cousin, I will be as useful as I can; but I am not qualified for an adviser. Do not ask advice of *me*. I am not competent."

"You are right, Fanny, to protest against such an office, but you need not be afraid. It is a subject on which I should never ask advice. I only want to talk to you."

"One thing more. Excuse the liberty; but take care *how* you talk to me. Do not tell me anything now, which hereafter you may be sorry for. The time may come—"

The colour rushed into her cheeks as she spoke.

"Dearest Fanny!" cried Edmund, pressing her hand to his lips with almost as much warmth as if it had been Miss Crawford's, "you are all considerate thought! But it is unnecessary here. The time will never come. No such time as you allude to will ever come. I begin to think it most improbable: the chances grow less and less; and even if it should, there will be nothing to be remembered by either you or me that we need be afraid of."

I may be afraid, by that point, on behalf of things far worse, thought Fanny.

"I can never be ashamed of my own scruples," Edmund went on. "If they are removed, it must be by changes that will only raise her character. You are the only being upon earth to whom I should say what I have said. But you have always known my opinion of her; you can bear me witness, Fanny, that I have never been blinded—"

Fanny held her breath with all force known to man.

"—How many a time have we talked over her little errors! You need not fear me; I have almost given up every serious idea of her; but I must be a blockhead indeed, if, whatever befell me, I could think of your kindness and sympathy without the sincerest gratitude."

He had said enough to shake the experience of eighteen. He had said enough to give Fanny some happier feelings than she had lately known (and, in another manner, to drive her somewhat insane). With a brighter look, she answered, "Yes, cousin, I am convinced that *you* would be incapable of anything else, though perhaps some might not. I cannot be afraid of hearing anything you wish to say. Do not check yourself. Tell me whatever you like."

They were now on the second floor, and the appearance of a housemaid—fortunately, this one without a mummy in tow—prevented any further conversation. For Fanny's relief it was concluded: had he been able to talk another five minutes, there is no saying that he might not have talked away all Miss Crawford's faults and his own despondence.

But as it was, they parted with looks on his side of grateful affection, and with some very precious sensations on hers. She had felt nothing like it for hours. Since the first joy from Mr. Crawford's note to William had worn away, she had been in a state absolutely the reverse; no comfort, no hope within her. Now everything was smiling.

William's good fortune returned again upon her mind, and seemed of greater value than at first. The ball, too—such an evening of pleasure before her!

It was now a real animation; and she began to dress for it with much of the happy flutter which belongs to a ball. All went well: she did not dislike her own looks; and when she came to the necklaces again, her good fortune seemed complete, for upon trial the one given her by Miss Crawford would by no means go through the ring of the cross. *Why am I not surprised?* thought Fanny at this minor irony.

She had, to oblige Edmund, resolved to wear it; but it was *too large* for the purpose. His, therefore, must be worn; and having, with delightful feelings, joined the chain and the cross—those memorials of the two most beloved of her heart, those dearest tokens so formed for each other by everything real and imaginary—and put them round her neck, and seen and felt how full of William and Edmund they were, she was able, without an effort, to resolve on wearing Miss Crawford's necklace too.

She acknowledged it to be right. Miss Crawford had a claim; and when it no longer interfered with the stronger claims, the truer kindness of another, she could do her justice even with pleasure to herself. The necklace really looked very well; and Fanny left her room at last, comfortably satisfied with herself and all about her.

Her aunt Bertram had remembered her on this occasion with an unusual degree of wakefulness. As though all Egypt were momentarily knocked out of her by a bit of sense, it had really occurred to her, unprompted, that Fanny, preparing for a ball, might be glad of better help than the upper housemaid's. Thus, when dressed herself, Lady Bertram actually sent her own maid to assist her—too late, of course, to be of any use. Mrs. Chapman had just reached the attic floor, unaccosted by any *undead* hungry things, when Miss Price came out of her room completely dressed, and only civilities were necessary. But Fanny felt her aunt's attention almost as much as Lady Bertram or Mrs. Chapman could do themselves.

Chapter XXVIII

Her uncle and both her aunts were in the drawing-room when Fanny went down. To the former she was an interesting object, and he saw with pleasure the general elegance of her appearance, and her being in remarkably good looks. The neatness and propriety of her dress was all that he would allow himself to commend in her presence, but upon her leaving the room again soon afterwards, he spoke of her beauty with very decided praise.

"Yes," said Lady Bertram, "she looks very well, befitting a Royal Consort of the Nile. I sent Chapman to her."

"Look well! Oh, yes!" cried Mrs. Norris (glancing only once at the large outside windows upon which the curtains were still not drawn and the evening progressed to moonrise), "she has good reason to look well with all her advantages: brought up in this family as she has been, with all the benefit of her cousins' manners before her. Only think, my dear Sir Thomas, what extraordinary advantages you and I have been the means of giving her. The very gown you have been taking notice of is your own generous present to her when dear Mrs. Rushworth married. What would she have been if we had not taken her by the hand?"

Sir Thomas said no more. But when they sat down to table the eyes of the two young men assured him that the subject might be gently touched again, when the ladies withdrew, with more success.

Fanny saw that she was approved; and the awareness of looking well made her look still better. Already happy, she was soon made happier still. . . .

Edmund, holding open the door when she was following her aunts out of the room, said, as she passed him, "You must dance with me, Fanny; you must keep two dances for me; any two that you like, except the first."

Her heart sang!

She had nothing more to wish for. She had hardly ever been in a state so nearly approaching high spirits in her life.

Her cousins' former gaiety on the day of a ball was no longer surprising to her. She felt it to be indeed very charming, and was actually practising her steps about the drawing-room as long as she could be safe from the notice of her aunt Norris, who was entirely taken up in fresh arranging and injuring the noble fire which the butler had prepared, then glancing with caution at the darkening windows.

Half an hour followed that would have been at least languid under any other circumstances, but Fanny's happiness still prevailed. She had but to think of her conversation with Edmund, and the restlessness of Mrs. Norris, the yawns of Lady Bertram, was of no consequence!

The gentlemen joined them; and soon after began the sweet expectation of a carriage. A general spirit of ease and enjoyment prevailed. They all stood about and talked and laughed, and every moment had its pleasure and its hope. Attentive servants circulated discreetly, carrying buffet fare to be set out for later. Fanny felt that there must be a struggle in Edmund's cheerfulness, but it was delightful to see the effort so successfully made.

When the carriages were really heard, when the guests began really to assemble, her own gaiety of heart was much subdued. The sight of so many strangers threw her back into herself. And besides the gravity and formality of the first great circle, demanded by the manners of Sir Thomas and Lady Bertram, she found herself occasionally called on to endure something worse. . . .

She was *introduced* here and there by her uncle. She was forced to be spoken to, and to curtsey, and speak again. This was a hard duty, and she was never summoned to it without looking at William, as he walked about at his ease in the background of the scene, and longing to be with him.

The entrance of the Grants and Crawfords was a favourable epoch. The stiffness of the meeting soon gave way before their popular manners and more diffused intimacies. Little groups were formed, and everybody grew comfortable. A delightful bowl of aromatic punch was visited often, and, right next to it, the negus was even more popular.

Fanny would have been again most happy, could she have kept her eyes from wandering between Edmund and Mary Crawford. *She* looked all loveliness—and what might not be the end of it?

Her own musings were brought to an end on perceiving Mr. Crawford before her. He engaged her almost instantly for the first two dances.

"Will you do me the honor, Miss Price?" he said, treading the edge of charm and yet all serious politeness—exactly as he imagined she would prefer him to be. And Fanny acquiesced, meanwhile noticing with an unexpected glance that Lord Eastwind, dressed in splendid formal darkness, watched her with intense, somehow *familiar* eyes—oh, that indescribable look of his! it truly made something in her chest constrict. Yes, she recalled, she owed him a single dance. . . .

Her happiness on this occasion was very much divided. To be secure of a partner at first was a most essential good—for the moment of beginning was now growing seriously near; and she so little understood her own claims as to think that if Mr. Crawford had not asked her, she must have been the last to be sought after. She feared she should have received a partner only through a series of inquiry, and bustle, and interference, which would have been terrible. . . .

But at the same time there was a pointedness in his manner of asking her which she did not like. She saw his eye glancing for a moment at her necklace, with a smile—she thought there was a smile—which made her blush and feel wretched. And though there was no second glance to disturb her, though he seemed then to be only quietly agreeable, she could not get the better of her embarrassment. It was heightened by the idea of his noticing it. She had no composure till he turned away to some one else. Then she could allow herself to feel the genuine satisfaction of having a partner, a voluntary partner, secured before the dancing began.

When the company were moving into the ballroom, she found herself for the first time near Miss Crawford, whose eyes and smiles were immediately and more unequivocally directed as her brother's had been, upon the necklace. Fanny, anxious to get the story over, hastened to explain the second necklace: the real chain.

Miss Crawford listened; and all her intended compliments and insinuations to Fanny were forgotten. She felt only one thing; and, eyes brightening, she exclaimed with eager pleasure, "Did he? Did Edmund? That was like himself. No other man would have thought of it. I honour him beyond expression." And she looked around as if longing to tell him so.

He was not near; he was attending a party of ladies out of the room. Instead, Mrs. Grant came up to the two girls, and taking an arm of each, they followed with the rest.

Fanny's heart sunk, but there was no time to consider Miss Crawford's feelings. They were in the ballroom, the violins were playing, and her mind was in a flutter that forbade its fixing on anything serious. She must watch the general arrangements, and see how everything was done.

Ah, the brilliant candlelight! The splendid golden glow!

In a few minutes Sir Thomas came to her, and asked if she were engaged; and the "Yes, sir; to Mr. Crawford," was exactly what he had intended to hear.

Mr. Crawford was not far off; Sir Thomas brought him to her, saying something which stunned Fanny—that *she* was to lead the way and open the ball. This was an idea that had never occurred to her before.

Whenever she had thought of the minutiae of the evening, it had been as a matter of course that Edmund would begin with Miss Crawford. The impression was so strong, that though *her uncle* spoke the contrary, she could not help an exclamation of surprise, a hint of her unfitness, an entreaty even to be excused. To be urging her opinion against Sir Thomas's was a proof of the extremity of the case. But such was her horror at the first suggestion, that she could actually look him in the face and say that she hoped it might be settled otherwise.

Her protests were in vain. Sir Thomas smiled, tried to encourage her, and then looked too serious, and said too decidedly, "It must be so, my dear," for her to hazard another word. She found herself the next dizzying moment conducted by Mr. Crawford to the top of the room, and standing there to be joined by the rest of the dancers, couple after couple, as they were formed.

She could hardly believe it. To be placed above so many elegant young women! The distinction was too great. It was treating her like her cousins! And her thoughts flew to those absent cousins with most unfeigned and truly tender regret, that they were not at home to take their own place in the room, and have their share of this pleasure. So often had she heard them wish for a ball at home as the greatest of all felicities! And to have them away when it was given—and for *her* to be opening the ball—and with Mr. Crawford too!

She hoped they would not envy her that distinction *now.* But when she looked back to the state of things in the autumn, to what they had all been to each other when once dancing in that house before, the present arrangement was almost more than she could understand herself.

The ball began. It was rather honour than happiness to Fanny, for the first dance at least. Her partner was in excellent spirits, and tried to impart them to her. But she was a great deal too much frightened to have any enjoyment till she could suppose herself no longer looked at.

Young, pretty, and gentle, however, she had no awkwardnesses that were not as good as graces, and there were few persons present that were not disposed to praise her. She was attractive, she was modest, she was Sir Thomas's niece. And she was soon said to be admired by Mr. Crawford. It was enough to give her general favour.

Sir Thomas himself was watching her progress down the dance with pleasure. He was proud of his niece. And without attributing all her personal beauty, as Mrs. Norris seemed to do, to her transplantation to Mansfield, he was pleased with himself for having supplied everything else: education and manners she owed to him.

Miss Crawford saw much of Sir Thomas's thoughts as he stood. Desiring to recommend herself to him, she took an opportunity of stepping aside to say something agreeable of Fanny. Her praise was warm, and he received it as she could wish, joining in it as far as discretion and politeness would allow. Sir Thomas certainly appeared to greater advantage on the subject than his lady did soon afterwards. Mary, perceiving her on a sofa very near, turned round before she began to dance, to compliment Lady Bertram on Miss Price's looks.

"Yes, the Royal Consort of the Pharaoh does look very well," was Lady Bertram's placid reply (at which Miss Crawford momentarily grew very, very still). "Chapman helped her to dress. I sent Chapman to her." Not that she was really pleased to have Fanny admired; but she was so struck with her own kindness in sending Chapman to her, that she could not get it out of her head.

Miss Crawford knew Mrs. Norris too well to think of gratifying *her* by commendation of Fanny. To her, it was as the occasion offered—"Ah! ma'am, how much we want dear Mrs. Rushworth and Julia to-night!"

And Mrs. Norris paid her with as many smiles and courteous words as she had time for, amid so much occupation as she found for herself in making up card-tables, giving hints to Sir Thomas, trying to move all the chaperons to a better part of the room, and shutting window curtains against the coming moonlight.

Miss Crawford blundered most towards Fanny herself in her intentions to please and thus cement their currently rather amiable truce. She meant to give her little heart a happy flutter, fill her with sensations of delightful self-consequence. Misinterpreting Fanny's blushes, she thought she must be doing so when she went to her after the two first dances, and said, with a significant look, "Perhaps *you* can tell me why my brother goes to town to-morrow? He says he has business there, but will not tell me what. The first time he ever denied me his confidence! But this is what we all come to. All are supplanted sooner or later. Now, I must apply to you for information. Pray, what is Henry going for?"

Fanny protested her ignorance as steadily as her embarrassment allowed. And, as always in her interactions with

Miss Crawford, the feel of a cross—this time, dear William's cross!—around her neck was suddenly a double blessing.

"Well, then," replied Miss Crawford, laughing, "I must suppose it to be purely for the pleasure of conveying your brother, and of talking of you by the way."

Fanny was confused, discontent. Yet Miss Crawford wondered why she did not smile. In that moment she thought Fanny odd, over-anxious; thought her anything rather than insensible of pleasure in Henry's attentions. Fanny had a good deal of enjoyment in the course of the evening; but Henry's attentions had very little to do with it. She would much rather *not* have been asked by him again so very soon. She hoped his inquiries of Mrs. Norris about the supper hour were not for the sake of securing her at that part of the evening.

But it was not to be avoided: he made her feel that she was the object of all. Though, she could not say it was unpleasantly done, or there was indelicacy or ostentation in his manner. And sometimes, when he talked of William, he was really not disagreeable, and shewed even a warmth of heart which did him credit.

But still his attentions made no part of her satisfaction. She was happy whenever she looked at William, and saw how perfectly he was enjoying himself. She was happy in knowing herself admired. And she was happy in having the two dances with Edmund still to look forward to, during the greatest part of the evening, her hand being so eagerly sought after, that her indefinite engagement with *him* was in continual perspective.

She was happy even when the two dances did take place; but not from any flow of spirits on his side, or any such expressions of tender gallantry as had blessed the morning. His mind was fagged, and her happiness sprung from being the friend with whom it could find repose.

"I am worn out with civility," said he. "I have been talking incessantly all night, and with nothing to say. But with *you*, Fanny, there may be peace. You will not want to be talked to. Let us have the luxury of silence."

Fanny would hardly even speak her agreement. His weariness, arising probably from the feelings which he had acknowledged in the morning, was to be respected. Thus, they went down their two dances together with such sober calm as might satisfy any looker-on that Sir Thomas had been bringing up no wife for his younger son.

The evening had afforded Edmund little pleasure. Miss Crawford had been in gay spirits[23] when they first danced together, but her gaiety rather sank than raised his comfort. And afterwards (for he found himself still impelled to seek her again), she had absolutely pained him by her manner of speaking of the profession to which he was now on the point of belonging.

They had talked, and they had been silent. He had reasoned, she had ridiculed. They parted at last with mutual vexation.

And, if Edmund had but paid better attention as he walked away, he might have seen Miss Crawford gift him a terrible *dark* look.

Fanny, not able to refrain entirely from observing them, had seen enough to be tolerably satisfied. It was barbarous to be happy when Edmund was suffering. Yet some happiness must and would arise from the very conviction that he did suffer.

When her two dances with him were over, her inclination and strength for more were pretty well at an end. Sir Thomas, having seen her walk rather than dance down the shortening set, breathless, and with her hand at her side, gave his orders for her sitting down entirely. From that time Mr. Crawford sat down likewise.

"Poor Fanny!" cried William, coming for a moment to visit her, and working away his partner's fan as if for life, "how

---

[23] What ghosts of Oscar Wilde? Upon my word!

soon she is knocked up![24] Why, the sport is but just begun. I hope we shall keep it up these two hours. How can you be tired so soon?"

"So soon! my good friend," said Sir Thomas, producing his watch with all necessary caution; "it is three o'clock, and your sister is not used to these sort of hours."

"Well, then, Fanny, you shall not get up to-morrow before I go. Sleep as long as you can, and never mind me."

"Oh! William."

"What! Did she think of being up before you set off?"

"Oh! yes, sir," cried Fanny, rising eagerly from her seat to be nearer her uncle; "I must get up and breakfast with him. It will be the last time, you know; the last morning."

"You had better not. He is to have breakfasted and be gone by half-past nine. Mr. Crawford, I think you call for him at half-past nine?"

Fanny was too urgent, however, and had too many tears in her eyes for denial; and it ended in a gracious "Well, well!" which was permission.

"Yes, half-past nine," said Crawford to William as the latter was leaving them, "and I shall be punctual, for there will be no kind sister to get up for *me*." And in a lower tone to Fanny, "I shall have only a desolate house to hurry from."

After a short consideration, Sir Thomas asked Crawford to join the early breakfast party in that house instead of eating alone. And the readiness with which his invitation was accepted convinced Sir Thomas that the suspicions that led him to arrange this ball, were well founded. . . .

Mr. Crawford was in love with Fanny.

Sit Thomas had a pleasing anticipation of what would be. His niece, meanwhile, did not thank him for what he had just

---

[24] Why, gentle Reader! I beg you to get your mind out of the filth of the gutter!

done. She had hoped to have William all to herself the last morning—an unspeakable indulgence. But though her wishes were overthrown, she was so unused to have her pleasure consulted, or to have things go her way, that she rejoiced in having carried her point so far.

Shortly afterward, Sir Thomas again interfered a little with her inclination, by advising her to go immediately to bed. "Advise" was his word, but it was the advice of absolute power.

While Sir Thomas retired to an adjoining room to speak with some of the gentlemen guests in attendance, Fanny obediently rose from her seat, and received Mr. Crawford's very cordial adieus.

She had every intention to make her way directly to the entrance-door of the ballroom, when Lord Eastwind appeared seemingly out of nowhere, and stood before her. With a tiny inclination of the head, he was offering his gloved hand.

"Miss Price. You have promised me the honor of a single dance tonight. The night may not end without it."

Fanny felt a quickening in her chest, a shortness of breath, while a blush spread to her cheeks and filled her, like ancient fiery wind of the desert.

"Sir—I am rather tired. And it is late."

And yet, even as she said it, she knew that she must acquiesce, and she felt the warmth of his gaze upon her like a thing tangible.

"You . . . promised."

Fanny looked up and for the first time fully met the gaze of his strange *familiar* eyes.

The world turned. The candlelight flared, seeming to glow more golden, and the dance music gathered around them with a rich swell of the Nile overflowing the boundaries of all.

Fanny took his hand, feeling a jolt of awareness at the touch. All her weariness fled. She was suddenly aflame; she was sun itself, as he led her into the dance.

They spoke not a word. He held her close in moments of coming together as the dance required; and at other times they touched fingertips like reeds moving in the current, gentle, separate yet joined by the flow of waters. . . .

They were invisible to all, and in a world apart. Fanny blinked and thought she saw a thousand years rush by in a whirlwind of clouds racing across the heavens, and mostly a clear bright blue sky, while around her the sand granules whispered, and the grand tons of stone pressed down to conceal her, as she lay, dreaming, desiccating, dreaming again forever, swept into the sweet long eternal memory of the *dead.*

His memory. The dream of an ancient king. The man who knew and *loved* her, oh so long ago.

Fanny came to herself, trembling, as the dance ended. They stood together, close enough to be almost in an embrace, stilled in the last stance, their faces barely apart.

She recognized him, the golden radiant beloved Pharaoh. And she remembered at last—that *she* too, once loved him, before he had died, millennia ago, in her arms.

She knew his name.

Xethesamen. *East Wind.*

And then, unseen by all, the ancient Pharaoh drew his face downward, leaning over her. And he touched his lips upon her own—light as a feather, gentle as the coming of night.

Fanny Price exhaled with a sigh, feeling her very soul, her *ka,* uplift toward him, forgetting for the moment Edmund, Mr. Crawford, the ball—the whole world. Her lips parted in innocence and inevitability to meet his.

In that moment of brief joining, for the first time, *he* truly seemed to come *alive*. His perfect, golden-olive skin glowed with a sheen of health, youth, and vigor; his raven locks shone like silk; his dark eyes were clear as midday.

And immediately, the candles in the ballroom flared impossibly bright. A light warm breeze raced out of nowhere to ruffle the curtains, the tablecloths, the skirts of the dancers and the feathers in their hair. Everything seemed richer; all the senses came roaring into exultation. The colors were more vivid; the scents of ladies' perfume and the late supper banquet were enhanced into an overwhelming fragrance of delight.

People in the ballroom looked around, dancers standing up with renewed zeal and wallflowers coming awake. On her sofa in an alcove near the buffet tables, Lady Bertram woke up with a start, sat up, and said, "Upon my word, a sip of tea would be nice."

"Fanny," meanwhile said her ancient beloved. "You *know* me again, at last. Come! Come with me and be with me again, my one and only love—this time for eternity."

She looked into his haunting familiar eyes.

She thought, for interminably long weighted moments, of desire, duty, need, loneliness, wonder; all the flow of time—all the pasts put together. Time was the great Nile, flowing without end or beginning.

"My East Wind," whispered Fanny. "I was once your West Star. Together we lived and loved and laughed and suffered. You were gone and I waited, through many a lifetime. I remember it all now, all of them, as if it had been yesterday. And now, it is far too late. For, the beacons of our souls have come too far apart."

"But we are together at last!" he exclaimed, agitated as Fanny had never seen him before.

"No, my dear one," she replied sadly. "We are not. I am here. And you are—*dead*."

"No!" His voice was a scalding wind, and everywhere it was rising, mad storm wind, filling the ballroom with billowing desert madness.

"Oh, my beloved soul," said Fanny, "you have been *dreaming* in eternity too long. Poised between the heaven and the earth, you have been locked in neither place. And it is now time for you to move on. *The Book of the Dead* has quickened your mouth with false half-life. You must let it go, and you must sail the boat of Osiris to the place beyond all places into true eternity."

His eyes were agonized, terrible. She saw now, underneath the fashionable trappings of a British gentleman, deeper yet, underneath the gold-braced muscular arms and splendid lapis collar raiment of the Pharaoh, there was desiccated skin hanging over leathery flesh and bone. . . . And beneath his sweet handsome face was a gaping skull, with empty eye sockets and burrowing maggots in the grinning maw of sepulcral darkness.

Fanny stood, her eyes swimming with tears—not of horror, but of agony for her once-beloved; to thus see all the way through, to his ancient, dear bones! It was beyond words, beyond all, into the realm of true silence. . . .

But there was no time to contemplate, because suddenly, the Mummy's skeletal fingers were upon her, squeezing her arms and shoulders painfully; and he held her, and she could see *it,* all of him at last, as his illusion wavered, and his voice cried to her, "*NO!* You are mine, forever!"

There was a shriek somewhere just a few steps away. Turning her head slightly, Fanny saw a young lady, struggling somewhat like herself, in the clutches of a grotesquely peeling desiccated mummy which wore nothing but decaying grave linen and its own bones.

There was another shriek. And another. All the guests regardless of gender, and from all directions in the ballroom were under attack—ladies and gentlemen were being accosted by lumbering creatures who had seemed to be mere servants or dance companions only moments ago, and now were revealed to be walking monsters.

The mummies clawed and grabbed at throats, and clutched at mouths and ears and noses, leaning in with wide unhinged jaws to take the precious *breath of life* from the living.

Suddenly they were everywhere. Glasses and dishes flew, chairs clattered on the floor.

Off in the corner Mrs. Norris suddenly gave a great howl of fury and, like a legion of banshees, went after a mummy who *dared* going after *her*. In truth, dear Reader, the poor mummy never knew what hit it. And thus we leave them for a moment—

Lady Bertram on her sofa was batting away at two creatures with a large oil jar and scepter, muttering all the meantime, "Your Mummyship, please control your minions, they are suddenly out of hand. If you please, as you promised this is quite unacceptable behavior—"

"What is this madness? Heaven help us!" shrieked a dignified matron and used her ostrich fan to pound a mummy on its skull, all uselessly, before it had its way with her.

In contrast, Lady Prescott found herself in the sudden grasp of a similar terrible creature, and the only thing that saved her was her own grand bouquet of feathers that she somehow managed to pluck from her headdress and wave about, eventually forcing all of it in the mouth orifice of the monster—all quite by accident.

Off near the supper table, Colonel Harrison tried to come to the aid of two elderly chaperons who were surrounded by four menacing mummies, and using their fans and handkerchiefs to swat around them helplessly, accompanied by utterances of "Fie! For shame!" But he could only manage to brandish his walking stick and skewer one of the monsters through the gasping chest with it, before realizing that such methods were useless. The mummy continued its attack with Colonel Harrison's cane imbedded like a toothpick in its chest cavity. Luckily, that same stick got caught on a chair back, forcing the mummy to spin around and splatter, head first, into the bowl of negus. Ah, the insult to the negus! It was more than the good colonel could bear. And with an old but never forgotten battle cry of his squadron, he threw himself bodily and crushed the enemy—

On the other end of the ballroom, a certain Miss Maddox was being assailed from two sides. But her sister came to the rescue with an armful of shawls. And like twin Furies denied their London Debut Season, together they grappled with the fiendish creatures, drowning them in heaps of ribboned lace, and being rather vocal about all this being "rather not amiable at all."

Fanny meanwhile struggled in the clutches of her maddened ancient love. All her former sympathy and pity for *him* was now well under control, replaced by frustrated outrage. She struck the Mummy across the hollow spot where would be its cheek, in an approximation of a slap.

"East Wind!" she exclaimed. "I beg you to get a hold of yourself! *And* your unholy servants! I loved you, yes, with all my being, but it is quite decidedly *over!* Time itself has made it so! And this—*display* is not making you, as a choice, any more attractive for me; nor is it making things easier for either one of us!"

In reply he roared, no longer human or coherent.

"You, sir," she cried back, grappling with his claws, "are impossible! You are being a *monster!* Exactly the monster that you now are! I beg you to cease and desist!"

A few feet away, a candlestick in each hand, Edmund was fighting off three mummies simultaneously, each one more horrendously decaying than the other, and one somehow wearing a portion of a footman's livery over the remains of its upper body—its lower body meanwhile, had no pants of any kind.

"Fanny!" cried Edmund. "What is this abomination? It is the Curse, is it not? Oh, Great God of Abraham and the Prophets! I should have listened to you, Fanny, I wanted not to believe in the Curse any more; I was so blind!"

There were quick darting movements underfoot and overhead, the flapping of ancient wings near the chandelier, as more mummies of all *species* were suddenly making an appearance. . . .

Lady Bertram had gotten up completely from her sofa, somehow having beaten off two creatures on her own, completely by accident. And now she raised her voice for the first time in possibly all her married life, and shrilled *terribly* for Baddeley to go and get Sir Thomas, because, surely, they at Mansfield Park were being under attack by all of Egypt!

"And whose fault would *that* be, sister?" growled Mrs. Norris in-between her decidedly useless attempts to gnaw through a mummy's collarbone. "Who started this whole Egyptological disaster of a pastime? Who attended all the foolish lectures in the museums? Who bought crocodile-headed knick-knacks until we are all but drowning in it? Why do we need so much *infernal papyrus?* But, who ever *listens* to me? I work day and night, slaving for the pleasures and comforts of dear Sir Thomas and yourself—"

In the smaller drawing room far down the corridor from the noise and music and bustle of the ballroom, the butler entered and cleared his throat.

"Begging pardon, Sir Thomas—at this late hour, the Lady Bertram sends to inform—there are—baboons in the ballroom."

Sir Thomas, deeply engrossed in a practical and pleasant discussion with Dr. Grant and another gentleman, was somewhat weary of interruptions, and weary of the long evening in general, but duly unperturbed. "Baddeley—be so kind as to remind Her Ladyship, every ballroom has its share of baboons. There is nothing one can do, when those of inferior breeding are allowed to mingle with the better set. One need but revise the regular invitation list to omit the undesirables next time. Do remind me on the morrow—"

"Begging pardon again, but one does not mean to speak in metaphor. There are actual *baboons* in the grand ballroom. Flesh and blood, simian. As early as this noon, perfectly inanimate and on display in this household, together with the other fruits of the Nile, as mummified *objets d'art*. At present, actively consuming the supper buffet spread. And tossing their own excrement at the serving staff."

Sir Thomas became rather still.

"In addition," Baddeley informed his master, "I am told there is a crocodile. A decidedly non-metaphorical one. Also initially hailing from the African Continent. Last seen in the drawing room, gnawing—apparently *something* one would rather not venture to guess. But, I am told, the divan is in shambles."

"What of—the guests?

"Bedlam, sir."

Returning in a run to the ballroom, was none other than William.

He had been just about to exit the house for the evening, when he came upon a terrifying *sight* in the tiny guest parlor near the entrance—a sight that made him turn and dash back, justly concerned on behalf of his dear sister's safety.

"Hey-ho! Men! Anyone? A crocodile!" hallooed William, dashing through the lobby, "What a wonder! There's a live crocodile in that parlor, I just saw it crush a sofa to death! Upon my word, if that sofa had once been alive it is far from being so now—"

William's halfway-sarcastic laughing tone petered out into silence as soon as he looked inside the ballroom and saw what was taking place. His jaw momentarily slackened.

And then, with a brave sailor heave-ho cry, William jumped right in the thick of it, crying, "Fanny! Fear not, dear sister, I am coming!"

But before William took two steps into the room and attempted to engage a pair of mummies in proper midshipman-style combat, Miss Crawford suddenly appeared in his way.

"Stand clear, Miss Crawford!" cried William, drawing a sword. "Two of the enemy right behind you, starboard—"

But the lovely, delightful, charming, *amiable* Miss Crawford (whom William found "not bad at all" in the way of womanhood) suddenly . . . hissed at him. Her pretty dark eyes were glowing with a decidedly unnatural wicked light. And she parted her lovely mouth to display some rather sharp looking fangs.

"What in blazes—" began William. But in that moment, before Miss Crawford could strike, he was rescued by none other than his aunt Norris.

"Back off, you vampiric harridan!" growled and roared Mrs. Norris, showing some rather sharp and even *bigger* teeth herself, and looking, to be honest, not very well, and somewhat hirsute around the forehead. "Hands off my dear nephew William, you shameless hussy! What, you think you can take advantage of the situation and grab a bit of bite to eat? Not in *this* house, thou—whore of Babylon! Mansfield Park may have its share of monthly discomforts and unfortunate circumstances, but at least it is all in the family!"

Miss Crawford—who had indeed decided to take advantage of the present chaos to conveniently quench her own unnatural hunger—now hissed violently. And, though her fingertips had grown amazingly extended sharp claws, they were no match for the grotesquely large, hairy knuckles of Mrs. Norris. And so Miss Crawford moved away with a toss of her head. Really! There was plenty of other "feeding material" walking upright in other more discreetly situated rooms of the estate.

In the center of the ballroom, Fanny had freed herself from the death grip embrace of the Mummy, who had released her more due to his shock and tragic disbelief than any display of sheer force on her part.

Edmund, meanwhile, had discovered, just as Fanny had, days earlier, that the holy cross held no power over mummies. That, of course, made him utterly despondent, until Fanny lifted his spirits with the logical explanation: that these mummies were surely before the Lord's time and simply had no notion of its holy meaning.

"Upon my word! there must be some other holy thing that can be used against them!" Edmund cried.

"Yes, as soon as I find one, I will be sure to inform you!"

"They are relentless, Fanny! They keep coming! Nothing seems to stop them! Mayhap, if I begin to recite the Lord's Prayer—"

"Probably not the best thing to do at the moment; if you do but recall the cross and its *lack of effect,* dear Edmund—" responded Fanny over her shoulder, as she was backing away from the Mummy while also staving off two others with her rather useless fan. "In the meantime," she added, "I can recommend an effective solution! They *can* be stopped, indeed, defeated, by plugging up their mouths! I can vouch for it! Stopper up the orifice with anything at hand—scarf, apple, table napkins—"

"What? Are you sure, Fanny?" William had finally made his way through the ballroom to be at her side. His sword was duly used to hack up countless desiccated limbs. And yet, despite his general courage, efficiency of movement, and prowess, William was ready to admit having had no effect whatsoever upon the general state of the enemy. Sure, the enemy was now *in more pieces* than it had been before, and yet—the pieces themselves—they tended to fall apart and then terrifyingly come together again, and the broken mummies were made whole! Indeed, what a frustrating, blasted, whack-a-mole abomination!

"Yes, I am very certain of it, William, dear! By covering up their mouths we rid them of the *breath of life*—the very thing that animates them and that which they feed upon when they attack the living!"

"However do you know all this, Fanny?" Edmund was in his shirtsleeves, having taken off his evening jacket, and was bunching it up into a large wad.

"You truly do not want to know, cousin," she replied, throwing off a small baboon that had attached itself to the back of her prettily-coiffed head and was about to take a bite of the *breath of life* from her ear. . . .

But where—the observant Reader asks—where in all this was Mr. Crawford? What kind of eager lover did it make him, not to be at his chosen and favored lady's side in a time of such dire danger?

But—for once Mr. Crawford was not to blame. For, he was, in fact, otherwise preoccupied. And his preoccupation had to do with a very real, very *immediate* threat to his life from a very real, very large, very hairy giant *werewolf.*

The werewolf had cornered Mr. Crawford in a small alcove just near the entrance of the ballroom, and was growling like a maddened overgrown boar and a pack of hounds all put together. Looming about eight feet tall, the giant hairy form roared, moving slowly forward and gnashing its monstrous teeth.

Backed to the wall, Henry kept his cool.

"A fine evening, Rushworth," he said. "A full moon tonight, as is obvious by your—ahem—full condition. Incidentally, whatever are you doing here, miles away from Brighton and your delightful spouse?"

The werewolf roared quite ground-shakingly upon hearing "delightful spouse" and took another elephant-heavy step, clawed legs like trunks, crashing against the parquet floor.

"Now, now—there is no need to get all riled up, good fellow. Upon my word, no need for such a display at all," said Mr. Crawford very calmly, taking a small sidestep into the direction of the larger ballroom.

The werewolf gathered itself for a spring and was about to lunge. . . . But Henry Crawford was saved, in the nick of time, and without a nick of intention, once again by none other than Mrs. Norris.

It bears repeating yet again, dear Reader, that the moon was full that night. It shone rather bloated and pallid, mid-heavens, and cast its sickly light upon all those unfortunate enough to be *affected* by it.

Yes, most of the curtains were drawn at Mansfield Park. But the moon heeded no satin, no cotton, no brocade barrier to wield its dire effect upon the mind, spirit, and *body*.

Mrs. Norris was all fired up. She had been made savage by her battle of the *undead* Egyptians, her sensitive and attuned life force churned up into a fighting frenzy. Which each moment she turned more and more beastly and lupine, until her teeth were heavy and sharp enough to gnaw through mummy bones. And eventually the roar and great howl of a fellow creature such as herself (coming from a mere ten feet away in an alcove) set her own nature into it final course of monthly transformation.

When Mrs. Norris heard the cry of the werewolf, she had no thought for who it was—who it could be. She merely rushed headlong toward it.

And as she ran, she *turned*.

When Henry Crawford braced himself for a mortal strike from Mr. Rushworth, he was taken quite aback to find another werewolf coming up on his other side. This one was slightly smaller, more grey and scruffy.

"Well, I'll be d—d," whispered Henry. "But—I am quite glad to see you! Mrs.—ahem—Norris? What a lovely evening."

And without another word, Henry backed away, escaping quietly. He was quite safe indeed now. For, the two wolves had seen each other.

At first, they both froze, Mr. Rushworth's portly brutish wolf stunned into amazement, and Mrs. Norris's lesser creature startled into a yelp. Mr. Rushworth had forgotten Crawford completely, and now his fur stood on its hackles, because here before him was immediate competition.

The two wolves took only several breaths to size each other up while baring teeth and growling like all Hades. And in the next three breaths they were upon each other—a giant ball of fur and claws and hairy limbs, louder than all the cats of London.

Another moment and they had gone rolling and clawing and roaring out of the alcove, out the door of the ballroom, on and on, through the lobby and corridors, past the parlor with the crocodile, down the staircases past the kitchens, and out of the house and continued out into the wilderness of the moonlight-bathed night outside. . . .

"This is decidedly not seemly or amusing! Quite! And it all ought to stop! Right this instant! Sir Thomas! *You must have it stop!*" Lady Bertram was shrieking, batting away with both hands at her finely coiffed head where two flying falcons were taking turns dive-bombing her, while from a mantelpiece, at least four mid-sized baboons were pelting her with their excrement and an occasional dish of Turkish Delight, or plum pudding, or, quite inevitably, a small stuffed game hen. They had armed themselves with whatever remained of the supper buffet, and were now doling it out to everyone in sight.

Sir Thomas had arrived on the scene, and stood at the door rather stunned for the first moment of seeing the events of the ballroom. Then, he was assailed by a mummy, and the self-preservation instinct took over.

Edmund, seeing his father, dutifully imparted urgent advice across the room. "Strike the mouth, sir! The mouth is their vulnerable spot, use anything at hand to stopper it like a bottle and cork mechanism, if you please—"

"Understood!" his father retorted, picking up the Cornish hen and shoving it powerfully into the nearest mummy's gaping maw. With a crunch, the thing collapsed and then fell into dust. "By George! that should do it," said Sir Thomas with grim satisfaction, picking up a bowl of stuffed quail.

A few feet away Baddeley came up in haste, his hands loaded with household firearms. "Sir Thomas! If you please, your fowling piece! Or, if you prefer, the larger musket—"

"I fear those are unnatural fowl." Sir Thomas grimly pointed at the several flying creatures near the chandelier. "I doubt these will have any effect. As I am told—and I have observed just now, in practice—we must aim for their mouth area. Though, I do prefer *not* to have any buckshot damage the crown moulding of the room, nor the imported window glass, which came at a considerable expense of over fifty pounds each during the most recent renovations. That was not last November but, if I recall, the fall before last—"

A number of mummies came up on both sides, preventing any further architectural discussion. Before he went to war with this set, Sir Thomas whispered conspiratorially to Baddeley, with a pointed look in Lady Bertram's direction: "As I said, beware striking the windows . . . but any cat statuary or other such *imported* merchandize is fair game."

"Understood, Sir. Would you prefer me to—ahem—aim at anything in particular?"

"Strike far and wide, Baddeley, strike far and wide!"

And the butler, putting his mind to a rising flock of pheasants, dutifully complied.

Mr. Crawford arrived at the center of the ballroom melee, having escaped unscathed from the two lycanthropes.

"My dear Miss Price!" he exclaimed, making his way between struggling guests and mummies. "A thousand pardons! But I am, at last, at your service!" And he also stripped to his shirtsleeves to use his jacket as an Egyptian mouth-wad.

But Fanny was in that moment far more gravely preoccupied. The Mummy of the ancient Pharaoh had ceased coming at her momentarily and turned his maddened firestorm-being upon Edmund who happened to be nearest Fanny.

A great skeletal arm with suddenly needle-sharp claws reached with impossible force to strike, and Edmund was reeling from the blow upon his chest.

"No!" Fanny exclaimed. And without any thought of consequences, she placed herself between Edmund and the Mummy. "No, you must not hurt him! Please, I beg of you, no! Strike me if you must, but not him, never *him!*"

The world momentarily seemed to stop.

"*This* one. . . ." said East Wind. "Then, indeed, you truly *care* about this one? You—*love* him?"

And tears welling in her eyes, Fanny took a resolute breath, stretched her arms on both sides of her, fingers spread wide, in a gesture of protection. "Yes!" she whispered, barely mouthing the words so that only her *undead* ancient beloved could hear her—and none other.

The light seemed to go out of him.

The storm raging, receded. Lord Eastwind, impeccable and handsome, once more clad in elegant formal evening attire, stood in silence for a moment, looking at her with grief-stricken eyes.

And when next Fanny blinked, he was no longer *there.*

The same could not be said of the other mummies in the room. They still growled and roared and attempted to feed on everyone and everything. But in the moment of Lord Eastwind's *disappearance,* it seemed they had lost most of their enthusiasm.

Breathing in gasps, Edmund straightened, holding his chest in pain, saying, "What? Where? Where did the villain go?"

"Miss Price? You are unharmed, I pray?" Mr. Crawford's perfectly solicitous inquiry at her side came many minutes too late.

But Fanny, stunned and broken, had eyes only for the spot which was now empty. Two instants of pause she allowed herself. And next, she turned away and was coming to assist Edmund, exclaiming in concern over his possible injury.

Within minutes, it seemed, the tide of battle had turned. Those mummies that were not vanquished by means of "oral suppository" decided to take themselves off elsewhere, and started quitting the ballroom in droves. Shrieks and random screams of elegant lady guests were still heard all around the estate, as baboons, flying fowl, even a slithering snake or two, were discovered here and there; but somehow soon they too were gone. There were reports that a number of the lesser creature mummies found their original spots around the house and then became motionless objects, striking the same exact poses in which they were originally placed many thousand years ago. A terrible wonder indeed!

The crocodile in the front parlor was found to have crawled back to his prominent spot upstairs near the mantel and was now still and motionless in mummified ancient splendor.

"Too bad the sofa could not be made to do the same!" bewailed a housemaid, picking up the pieces of wood and batting and brocade.

Edmund was in grim spirits. His hurt was minimal, mostly the wind having knocked out of him. But he said, "Is the *monster* gone, Fanny? Oh, what are we to do?"

"He is gone indeed, dearest cousin, I am sure of it," replied Fanny, fussing with the front of his scratched shirt where there were seeping sanguine spots.

"Oh, Fanny! But—is he *vanquished?*"

Fanny stopped. She thought and wondered, but somehow had no answer even for her own self. "That, I do not know."

"The we must find out! And soon! There is no moment to lose, the Curse must be eradicated!"

"I believe it is safe to surmise that we are out of danger at present," said Mr. Crawford. "Now then—" and he carefully stepped over a puddle of supper buffet and mummy sand remains on the parquet floor—"The night is late even for myself, and I strongly suggest Miss Price indeed heed her uncle's excellent advice from some half hour earlier and retire for the evening. We will take it from here, Miss Price, you need have no worry on anyone's part."

"He is quite right, dear sister!" said William, coming up to them in the meanwhile. He was breathing fast but in raging high spirits, and his already hale complexion was definitely the better for it after having done the vigorous exercise, the happy battle-exertion. "Go rest, Fanny! Oh, want a splendid ball you've had for your coming out! Upon my word, Fanny, this has been the *best* assembly *ever!* Never have I had such a grand old time at a silly dance!" And William sheathed his sword merrily. Kissing his sister on the cheek lightly, and promising to see her in a very few hours (for it was near dawn), he headed out, this time without any other complications to interrupt him.

"Go, Fanny. Fear not, I am perfectly uninjured. And he is quite right," repeated Edmund.

Her mind still in a whirlwind, Fanny nodded quietly, and made her real adieus this time.

Thus, indeed, it was time—to pass quietly away; stopping at the entrance-door, like the Lady of Branxholm Hall, "one moment and no more," to view the happy and ultimately terrible scene of Bedlam, and take a last look at the five or six determined guests who were still reeling and putting themselves together after the battle before fleeing the premises, and the genuine unmummified servants hard at work picking up and sweeping away the damages.

And then, time to be creeping slowly up the principal staircase, pursued by the memory of the ceaseless country-dance music—*his* dark anguished *beloved* familiar eyes—no, stop!—feverish with hopes and fears, soup and negus, sore-footed and fatigued, restless and agitated, yet feeling, in spite of everything, that a ball was indeed a thing both delightful and horrifying; and *this* one, indeed, her *own ball,* will likely be remembered in all the neighborhood for many years to come. . . .

Chapter XXIX

In the morning, the ball was over, the mummies nowhere in sight, and much of the cleanup was still to come. And the breakfast was soon over too. All throughout, everyone ate in subdued solemnity, Sir Thomas decidedly troubled and deep in thought, Mr. Crawford impeccable, Edmund grim and absentminded, and only William darting quick happy looks at Fanny and whispering repeatedly, *"Best . . . ball . . . ever!"*

It did not help Sir Thomas's sense of decorum or his mood to have learned earlier that Mrs. Norris *and* Mr. Rushworth—of all people!—were found at dawn, *tête-à-tête* in the front parlor, both in some unspeakable state of dishabille, sound asleep on either ends of the room, one (Mrs. Norris) oblivious to the world, in a deep wing chair, the other (Mr. Rushworth) stretched out in bulk along the sofa, snoring loud enough to bring down the ceiling.

Not that they needed any more methods of bringing down the ceiling or any other portion of the building, thank you, thought Sir Thomas unhappily.

In addition to all this, to the decidedly unnatural couple occupying the parlor, there was also a terrifying third. Perched on top of the mantelpiece, regal and vicious, sat none other than the Brighton Duck.

As the housekeeper entered the room, it woke, squawked and honked and screeched like a squadron of banshees, and then, flapping its mighty wingspan, flew into Mrs. Norris's sleeping face in final triumph and then lifted, circled the room, and flew past the stunned housekeeper out into the hallway and lord knows where outside. . . .

And if that wasn't bad enough—

Upon being woken up by what she thought was a squawking housekeeper, Mrs. Norris pulled a shawl around her and started in amazement at the nearby sight of her dear niece's spouse. She then said, "Oh gracious, I must've nodded off . . ." And then, coming fully awake: "Dearest Mr. Rushworth! What a wonder! Why, whatever are you doing here? A delight, indeed, a heavenly delight! But—is our dear Maria here too? Or, is something the matter? Oh dear, is everything as it ought to be at Brighton? Is she in good health? What—"

Mr. Rushworth came to himself. He cleared his throat, looked about him in stunned amazement for a moment, adjusted his tattered coat and loosely torn, decidedly *uncivil* breeches, and then said, "Argh! Blimey! That is—Ahem! pardon me, Mrs. Norris, what am I doing here? What happened? I do not remember having arrived here, indeed, last night seems to be all a blur—there was a blimey-bright moon, and that infernal flying fowl—"

"Oh, it must be the drink—that horrid negus was too strong! I told Lady Bertram, I did, it was just too potent, I said, but no—" muttered Mrs. Norris, beginning to fuss and get up. Then she saw her own somewhat *uncivil* condition of dress, and yelped in alarm. Hurriedly she excused herself and, covered in the roomy shawl, backed out of the parlor, to the accompaniment of some rather amazed and scandalized glares of the housekeeper.

Of all of this Sir Thomas was informed. And as he sat later at breakfast, his mind going over the various incurred monetary damages in the ballroom and elsewhere—for any thought of mummies was somewhat beyond him right this moment—he thought that a scandalous *incident* between Mrs. Norris and Mr. Rushworth was the last thing the family needed. And, for shame! Mrs. Norris, who would have thought something like that of her—a widow, too! and at her age! And with his daughter's husband! Surely it was all a misunderstanding (he had no doubt whatsoever); but oh! how much it held the *appearance* of impropriety! Furthermore, there was once again that *duck,* somewhere on the premises. . . . Sir Thomas never thought he would have himself think such murderous thoughts, but something had to be done—

And Mr. Rushworth—supposedly too chagrined to present himself before his father-in-law that day, he got himself out of Mansfield Park in a hurry, borrowing a horse from the stables.

Unable to think any farther, Sir Thomas concentrated upon easier concerns.

At last, breakfast was over, the last kiss was given, and William was gone. Mr. Crawford had, as he foretold, been very punctual, thought Fanny, and short and pleasant had been the meal, with hardly a mention of anything *disastrous* from last night.

After seeing William to the last moment, Fanny walked back to the breakfast-room with a very saddened heart to grieve over the melancholy change. And there, her uncle kindly left her to cry in peace, conceiving, perhaps, that the deserted chair of each young man might exercise her tender enthusiasm, and that the remaining cold pork bones and mustard in William's plate might but divide her feelings with the broken egg-shells in Mr. Crawford's. She sat and cried *con amore* as her uncle intended, but it was *con amore* fraternal and no other. William was gone, and she now felt as if she had wasted half his visit in idle cares and selfish solicitudes unconnected with him.

And yet, it was far better to cry over William's leaving than to think of the other, the night before—no, do not think—*his* anguished eyes. . . .

It was a heavy, melancholy day. Soon after the second breakfast, Edmund bade them good-bye for a week, and mounted his horse for Peterborough, and then was gone. He did not even pause long enough to talk with Fanny privately about the consequences of the Curse, as she surely expected him to do—oh, how could he continue to remain so closed about it, even after the *events* of last night? Nothing remained of last night but remembrances, stunning terrors and wonders, which she had nobody to share in.

Sir Thomas sent Baddeley and a cadre of servants to investigate the estate and the grounds, but not a single mummy was found, not even a peeling bit of grave linen. They turned Mansfield Park upside down, to no avail. All the crates stacked around the household were empty, and were immediately ordered to be disposed of, in great haste. A similar fate awaited a great deal of other archeological items—though, to be honest, so many of them were now in blessed shards (Baddeley proved a fine marksman).

"Send any valuables off to the London Museum, post haste. As for the rest—*burn it,* all if you must. Use it for kindling. Or have it delivered back to Egypt, for all I care!" exclaimed Sir Thomas. "As long as I never need lay an eye upon a blasted crocodile-cat-ibis-falcon-baboon-dragoon-*whatever*-headed atrocity, or one of those mummified monsters again!"

Lady Bertram, too, was in a daze from the night before, stunned and halfway freed from her mesmerized condition.

There was no longer a mysterious Lord Eastwind ever-present at her side. He was gone without a trace. And Lady Bertram did not seem to particularly remember.

In fact, she was utterly *confused,* in most ways in denial of what has happened, and refusing to remember any of it—for the moment. When Fanny attempted to talk to her—she must talk to *somebody* of the ball at least, if not its *aftermath*—her aunt had seen so little of what had passed. Lady Bertram was not certain of anybody's dress or anybody's place at supper but her own. "She could not recollect what it was that she had heard about one of the Miss Maddoxes, or what it was that Lady Prescott had noticed in Fanny: she was not sure whether Colonel Harrison had been talking of Mr. Crawford or of William when he said he was the finest young man in the room—somebody had whispered something to her; she had forgot to ask Sir Thomas what it could be." And these were her longest speeches and clearest communications, not a word of Egypt or the *mayhem* that occurred toward the latter part of the night. The rest was only a languid "Yes, yes; very well; did you? did he? I did not see *that;* I should not know one from the other." This was very bad. It was only better than Mrs. Norris's sharp answers would have been—but she was home, suffering the aftereffects of a certain monthly *affliction.*

The evening was heavy like the day. "I cannot think what is the matter with me," said Lady Bertram, when the tea-things were removed. "I feel quite stupid. It must be sitting up so late last night. Fanny, you must do something to keep me awake. I cannot work. Fetch the cards; I feel so very stupid. Fetch the *papyrus*—no!"

The cards were brought, and Fanny played at cribbage with her aunt till bedtime; the servants quietly cleaning up, and Sir Thomas reading to himself.

Fanny thought and thought again of the difference which twenty-four hours had made in that room, and all that part of the house. Last night it had been hope and smiles, bustle and motion, noise and brilliancy, terror and *revelation,* in the drawing-room, and out of the drawing-room, and everywhere. Now it was languor, and heartbreak, and broken shards of ancient clay pottery, traces of sand, and all but solitude.

A good night's rest improved her spirits. She could think of William the next day more cheerfully; and as the morning afforded her an opportunity of talking with Mrs. Grant and Miss Crawford, raising the shade of a departed ball, she could afterwards bring her mind to a sort of calm.

They were indeed a smaller party than she had ever known, and *he* was gone on whom the comfort and cheerfulness of every family meeting and every meal chiefly depended. But this was to be endured.

Edmund.

He would soon be always gone.

"We miss our two young men," was Sir Thomas's observation on both the first and second day, as they formed their very reduced circle after dinner. And in consideration of Fanny's swimming eyes, nothing more was said on the first day than to drink their good health; but on the second it led to something farther. William was kindly commended and his promotion hoped for. "And there is no reason to suppose," added Sir Thomas, "but that his visits to us may now be tolerably frequent. As to Edmund, we must learn to do without him. This will be the last winter of his belonging to us, as he has done."

"Yes," said Lady Bertram, "but I wish he was not going away. *They* are all going away, I think. I wish they would stay at home."

This wish was levelled in part at the sudden loss of Egypt, and at Julia, who had just applied for permission to go to town with Maria. As Sir Thomas thought it best that the permission should be granted, Lady Bertram was lamenting the change it made in the prospect of Julia's return. A great deal of good sense followed on Sir Thomas's side, reconciling his wife to the arrangement. Lady Bertram agreed to it all with a dazed "Yes"; and at the end of a quarter of an hour's silent consideration spontaneously observed, "Sir Thomas, I have been thinking—and I am very glad we took Fanny as we did, for now the others are away we feel the good of it."

Sir Thomas immediately improved this compliment by adding, "Very true. We shew Fanny what a good girl we think her by praising her to her face. She is now a very valuable companion. If we have been kind to *her,* she is now quite as necessary to *us*."

"Yes," said Lady Bertram presently; "and it is a comfort to think that we shall always have *her*."

Sir Thomas paused, half smiled, glanced at his niece, and then gravely replied, "She will never leave us, I hope, till invited to some other home that may reasonably promise her greater happiness than she knows here."

"And *that* is not very likely to be, Sir Thomas. Who should invite her? Maria might be very glad to see her at Sotherton now and then, but she would not think of asking her to live there. I am sure Fanny is better off here. Besides, I cannot do without her."

The week which passed so quietly and peaceably at the great house in Mansfield had a very different character at the Parsonage. To the young lady in each family, it brought very different feelings. What was peace and comfort to Fanny was tediousness and vexation to Mary. In most points of interest they were exactly opposed to each other—even without a consideration of vampirism. To Fanny's mind, Edmund's absence was really a relief. To Mary it was painful. She felt the want of his society every hour, and derived irritation from considering the object for which he went. He could not have devised anything more likely to raise his consequence than this week's absence, occurring as it did at the very time of her brother's going away, of William Price's going too, and completing the general break-up of their animated party.

They were now a miserable trio, confined within doors by a series of rain and snow. Miss Crawford was angry with

Edmund for adhering to his own notions in defiance of her (indeed, they had hardly parted friends at the ball), but she could not help thinking of him continually, dwelling on him, longing again for the almost daily meetings they lately had. He should not have left home for a week, when her own departure from Mansfield was so near.

Then she began to blame herself. She wished she had not spoken so warmly in their last conversation. She had used some strong, contemptuous expressions in speaking of the clergy—which could not be helped, naturally, because of her own dark *nature*. Regardless, it was ill-bred; it was wrong. She wished such words unsaid with all her dark *undead* heart.

Her vexation did not end with the week. She learned that he had actually written home to defer his return, having promised to remain some days longer with his friend.

If she had felt impatience and regret before—if she had been sorry for what she said—she now felt it all tenfold more. And she had to contend with one disagreeable emotion entirely new to her—jealousy. His friend Mr. Owen had sisters; he might find them attractive. But, at any rate, his staying away at a time when she was to remove to London, meant something unbearable. Had Henry returned, she should now have been leaving Mansfield. It became absolutely necessary to try to learn something more from Fanny.

Thus, Mary made her way to the Park, for the chance of hearing anything—for the sake of hearing his name.

When at last Lady Bertram left the room, leaving her alone with Fanny, Miss Crawford began, with a voice as well regulated as she could—"And how do *you* like your cousin Edmund's staying away so long? Being the only young person at home, I consider *you* as the greatest sufferer. You must miss him. Does his staying longer surprise you?"

"I do not know," said Fanny hesitatingly. "Yes; I had not particularly expected it."

"Perhaps he will always stay longer than he talks of. It is the general way all young men do."

"He did not, the last time he went to see Mr. Owen."

"He finds that house more agreeable *now*. He is a—very pleasing young man himself, and I cannot help being concerned at not seeing him again before I go to London. I expect Henry every day, and there will be nothing to detain me at Mansfield. I should like to have seen him once more, I confess. But you must give my compliments to him. Though, is not there a something between compliments and—and love—to suit the sort of friendly acquaintance we have? But compliments must suffice. Was his letter a long one?"

"I only heard a part of the letter. It was to my uncle, very short, but a few lines. His friend had pressed him to stay longer, and he had agreed."

"Oh! if he wrote to his father; no wonder he was concise. If he had written to you, there would have been more particulars. How many Miss Owens are there?"

"Three grown up."

"Are they musical?"

"I do not at all know. I never heard."

"That is the first question, you know," said Miss Crawford, trying to appear gay[25] and unconcerned, "which every woman who is musical herself asks about another. But it is very foolish to ask questions about any young ladies—for one knows, without being told: they are all very accomplished and pleasing, and one very pretty. There is a beauty in every family. Two play on the pianoforte, and one on the harp; and all sing."

"I know nothing of the Miss Owens," said Fanny calmly.

"Well, when your cousin comes back, he will find Mansfield very quiet; all the noisy ones gone, your brother and mine and myself."

---

[25] Oh dear, not again. Banish the thought!

Fanny felt obliged to speak. "You cannot doubt," said she. "You will be very much missed by many."

"Even by *you,* knowing in full what I *am?*"

Fanny smiled sadly.

Miss Crawford turned her eye on her, as if wanting to hear or see more, and then laughingly said, "Oh yes! missed as every noisy *evil* is missed when it is taken away—a difference felt. But I am not fishing; don't compliment me. If I *am* missed, I may be found—by those who want to see me."

Now Fanny could not bring herself to speak, and Miss Crawford was disappointed. For in her perverse, conflicted depths of *darkness* she had hoped to hear some pleasant assurance of her power from one who she thought must know, and her spirits were clouded again.

"The Miss Owens," said she, soon afterwards; "suppose one of them settled at Thornton Lacey. How should you like it? Sir Thomas Bertram's son is somebody; and now he is in their own line. Their father, brother, they are all clergymen together. He is their lawful property; he fairly belongs to them."

"No," said Fanny stoutly, "I do not expect it at all."

"Not at all!" cried Miss Crawford with alacrity. "I wonder at that. But I dare say you know exactly—perhaps you do not think him likely to marry at all—or not at present."

"No, I do not," said Fanny softly, hoping she did not err either in the belief or the acknowledgment of it.

Her wickedly charming companion looked at her keenly; and, gratified by Fanny's blush, said, "He is best off as he is."

Chapter XXX

Miss Crawford's uneasiness was much lightened by this conversation. She walked home again in high spirits—if such may be attributed to a spiritless vampire—and she even felt a sudden sympathetic zest for the living, a *hunger* unlike the usual.

That very evening brought her brother down from London, in quite more than his usual cheerfulness. Still refusing to tell her what he had gone for might have irritated, but now it was a pleasant joke. And the next day *did* bring a surprise to her. Henry had said he should just go and ask the Bertrams how they did, and be back in ten minutes, but he was gone above an hour. When his sister met him at last impatiently in the garden, and cried out, "My dear Henry, where can you have been all this time?" he said he had been sitting with Lady Bertram and Fanny.

"Sitting with them an hour and a half!" exclaimed Mary.

But this was only the beginning of her surprise.

"Yes, Mary," said he, drawing her arm within his, and walking along the sweep as if not knowing where he was: "I could not get away sooner; Fanny looked so lovely! I am quite determined, Mary. My mind is entirely made up. Will it astonish you? No: you must be aware that I am quite determined to marry Fanny Price."

The surprise was now complete. For, in spite of whatever behavior, a suspicion of his having any such views had never entered his sister's imagination. She looked so astonished, that he was obliged to repeat, more solemnly.

The conviction of his determination, once admitted, was not unwelcome. There was even pleasure with the surprise. Mary was in a state of mind to rejoice in a connexion with the Bertram family, and to be not displeased with her brother's marrying a little beneath him.

"Yes, Mary," was Henry's concluding assurance. "I am fairly caught. You know with what idle designs I began; but this is the end of them. I have, I flatter myself, made no inconsiderable progress in her affections; but my own are entirely fixed."

"Lucky, lucky girl!" cried Mary, as soon as she could speak; "what a match for her! My dearest Henry, this must be my *first* feeling; but my *second* is, I approve your choice from my soul, and foresee your happiness as heartily as I desire it. You will have a sweet little wife; all gratitude and devotion. Exactly what you deserve. What an amazing match for her! Our wolfish Mrs. Norris often talks of her luck; what will she say now? The delight of all the family, indeed! And she has some *true* friends in it! How *they* will rejoice! But tell me all about it! When did you begin to think seriously about her?"

Nothing could be more impossible than to answer such a question. "How the pleasing plague had stolen on him" he could not say. His sister eagerly interrupted him with, "Ah, my dear Henry, and this is what took you to London! This was your business! You chose to consult the Admiral before you made up your mind."

But this he stoutly denied. He knew his uncle too well to consult him on any matrimonial scheme. The Admiral hated marriage, and thought it never pardonable in a young man of independent fortune.

"When Fanny is known to him," continued Henry, "he will doat on her. She is exactly the woman to do away every prejudice of such a man as the Admiral. But till it is absolutely settled, he shall know nothing of the matter. No, Mary, you are quite mistaken. You have not discovered my business yet."

"Well, well, I am satisfied. I know now to whom it must relate, and am in no hurry for the rest. Fanny Price! quite wonderful! That Mansfield should have done so much for—that *you* should have found your fate in Mansfield! But you are quite right; you could not have chosen better. There is not a better girl in the world, and you do not want for fortune. And as to her connexions, they are more than good. She is niece to Sir Thomas Bertram; that will be enough for the world. But—tell me more. What are your plans? Does she know her own happiness?"

"No."

"What are you waiting for?"

"For—for very little more than opportunity. Mary, she is not like her cousins; but I think I shall not ask in vain."

"Oh no! you cannot. Were you even less pleasing—supposing her not to love you already (of which, however, I can have little doubt)—you would be safe. The gentleness and gratitude of her disposition would secure her all your own immediately. I do not think she would marry you *without* love—that is, if there is a girl in the world capable of being uninfluenced by ambition, I can suppose it her—but ask her to love you, and she will never have the heart to refuse."

Henry was happy to talk at length, to dwell on his own sensations, on Fanny's charms. Fanny's beauty of face and figure, Fanny's graces of manner and goodness of heart, were the exhaustless theme. The gentleness, modesty, and sweetness of her character! Her temper he had good reason to depend on and to praise. He had often seen it tried. Was there any one of the family, excepting Edmund, who had *not* in some way or other continually exercised her patience and forbearance?

Her affections were evidently strong. To see her with her brother! What could more delightfully prove that the warmth of her heart was equal to its gentleness, than with her love in view? Then, her *understanding* was beyond every suspicion—quick and clear, perceptive to the core. And her manners were the mirror of her own modest and elegant mind. Nor was this all. Henry Crawford had too much sense not to feel the worth of good principles in a wife. He talked of her having a steadiness and regularity of conduct, such a high notion of honour, observance of decorum, faith and integrity, her being well principled and religious.

"I could so wholly and absolutely confide in her," said he; "and *that* is what I want."

"The more I think of it," Mary Crawford cried, "the more am I convinced that you are doing quite right. And though I should never have selected Fanny Price as the girl most likely to attach you, I am now persuaded she is the very one to make you happy. Your wicked project upon her peace turns out a clever thought indeed, with the best results."

"It was bad, very bad of me. But I did not know her then; and she shall have no reason to lament the hour that first put it into my head. I will make her very happy, Mary; happier than she has ever yet been herself, or ever seen anybody else. I will not take her from Northamptonshire. I shall let Everingham, and rent a place in this neighbourhood; perhaps Stanwix Lodge."

"Ha!" cried Mary; "settle in Northamptonshire! That is pleasant! Then we shall be all together."

When she had spoken it, she recollected herself, and wished it unsaid. But there was no need; for her brother saw her only as the supposed inmate[26] of Mansfield parsonage.

"You must give us more than half your time," said he. "I cannot admit Mrs. Grant to have an equal claim with Fanny and

[26] Neither Bedlam nor the Tower of London are suggested here.

myself, for we shall both have a right in you. Fanny will be so truly your sister!"

Mary made grateful assurances. But she had no intention of being the guest of either brother or sister many months longer.

"You will divide your year between London and Northamptonshire?"

"Yes," he said.

"That's right; and in London, of course, a house of your own: no longer with the Admiral. My dearest Henry, the advantage to you of getting away from the Admiral before your manners are hurt by the contagion of his, before you have contracted any of his foolish opinions, or learned to sit over your dinner as if it were the best blessing of life! *You* are not sensible of the gain, for your regard for him has blinded you. But your marrying early may save you. To have you grow like the Admiral, would have broken my *unbeating* heart."

"Well, well, we do not think quite alike here. The Admiral has his faults, but he is a very good man, and has been more than a father to me. Few fathers would have let me have my own way half so much. You must not prejudice Fanny against him. I must have them love one another."

Mary refrained from saying what she felt, and how the Admiral's certain female *companion* has so changed her life to its present state of *non-life*. Henry had never suspected whence his sister's vampirism came from. Meanwhile, there could not be two persons in existence whose characters and manners were less accordant that Fanny and the Admiral: time would discover it to him.

"Henry, I think so highly of Fanny Price, that if I thought the next Mrs. Crawford would have half the reason which my poor ill-used aunt had to abhor the name, I would prevent the marriage. But I know that a wife you *loved* would be the happiest of women. Even when you ceased to love, she would yet find in you the liberality and good-breeding of a gentleman."

The impossibility of not doing everything in the world to make Fanny Price happy, or of *ceasing to love* Fanny Price, was in his eloquent answer.

"Had you seen her this morning, Mary," he continued, "attending with such ineffable sweetness and patience to all the demands of her aunt's stupidity, her colour beautifully heightened as she leant over the work, then returning to her seat to finish a note which she was previously engaged in writing for that stupid woman's service. And all this with such unpretending gentleness—as if it were a matter of course that she was not to have a moment at her own command—her hair arranged as neatly as always, and one little curl falling forward as she wrote, which she now and then shook back. And in the midst of all this, she was still speaking at intervals to *me,* or listening, and as if she liked to listen, to what I said. Had you seen her so, Mary, you would not have implied the possibility of her power over my heart ever ceasing."

"My dearest Henry," cried Mary, stopping short, and smiling in his face, "how glad I am to see you so much in love! It quite delights me. But what will Mrs. Rushworth and Julia say?"

"I care neither what they say nor what they feel. They will now see what sort of woman it is that can attach me, that can attach a man of sense. I wish the discovery may do them good. And they will now see their cousin treated as she ought to be, and I wish they may be heartily ashamed of their own abominable neglect and unkindness. They will be angry," he added, after a moment's silence, and in a cooler tone; "Mrs. Rushworth will be very angry. It will be a bitter pill to her; it will have two moments' ill flavour, and then be swallowed and forgotten. For I am not such a coxcomb as to suppose her feelings for me more lasting than other women's. Yes, Mary, my Fanny will feel a difference indeed: a daily, hourly difference, in the behaviour of every being who approaches her. It will be the completion of my happiness to know that I am the doer of it, that I am the person to give the consequence so justly her due. Now she is dependent, helpless, friendless, neglected, forgotten."

"Nay, Henry, not by all; not friendless or forgotten. Her cousin Edmund never forgets her."

"Edmund! True, I believe he is, generally speaking, kind to her, and so is Sir Thomas in his way; but it is the way of a rich, superior uncle. What can Sir Thomas and Edmund together *do* for her happiness, comfort, honour, and dignity in the world, to what I *shall* do?"

Chapter XXXI

Henry Crawford was at Mansfield Park again the next morning, and at an earlier hour than common visiting warrants. The two ladies were together in the breakfast-room. Fortunately for him, Lady Bertram was on the very point of leaving, and directed a servant to "Let Sir Thomas know."

After her exit, Henry turned instantly to Fanny, and, taking out some letters, said, with a most animated look, "I am gratified by an opportunity of seeing you alone, wishing it more than you can have any idea. Knowing as I do what your feelings as a sister are, what joyous news I now bring! He is made. Your brother is a lieutenant. I have the infinite satisfaction of congratulating you on your brother's promotion. Here are the letters which announce it. You will, perhaps, like to see them."

Fanny could not speak, but he did not want her to speak.

Outside the window, in the shrubbery, came the thrashing sounds of what could only possibly be Mrs. Norris, in pursuit of some field creature, as had become her morning habit, as of late—but Fanny could not think of that, not now—

To see the expression of Fanny's eyes, the change of her complexion, the progress of her feelings, their doubt, confusion, and felicity, was enough.

She took the letters as he gave them. The first was from the Admiral to inform his nephew of his having succeeded in the object he had undertaken, the promotion of young Price. And enclosing two more, one from the Secretary of the First Lord to a friend, whom the Admiral had set to work in the business, the other from that friend to himself, of the circumstance of Mr. William Price's commission as Second Lieutenant of H.M. Sloop *Thrush*.

While her hand was trembling under these letters, her eye running from one to the other, and her heart swelling with emotion, Crawford continued, with unfeigned eagerness—

"I will not talk of my own happiness," said he, "great as it is, for I think only of yours. Compared with you, who has a right to be happy? I have almost grudged myself my own prior knowledge of what you ought to have known before all the world. I have not lost a moment, however." And then Mr. Crawford went on at great passionate length to describe how he had involved himself and his uncle on William's behalf.

"My uncle, who is the very best man in the world, has exerted himself, as I knew he would, after seeing your brother. He was delighted with him. No warmer wishes and higher commendation possible, than those bestowed by my uncle after the evening they had passed together."

"Has this been all *your* doing, then?" cried Fanny. "Good heaven! how very, very kind! Have you really—was it by *your* desire? I beg your pardon, but I am bewildered. How was it? I am stupefied."

From outside the window came a tremendous crash. It almost sounded as though Mrs. Norris had managed to get herself up a tree and then either jumped or *plummeted*—but no, that decidedly could not be—

Henry was most happy to elaborate, by explaining very particularly what he had done on behalf of William.

Fanny's heart was so full, her senses still so astonished, that she overlooked the overt hints in Henry's use of such terms as the *deepest interest; twofold motives; views and wishes more than could be told.* She could listen but imperfectly even to what he told her of William, saying only, "How kind! Oh, Mr. Crawford, we are infinitely obliged to you! Dearest, dearest William!"

She jumped up and moved in haste towards the door, crying out, "I will go to my uncle. My uncle ought to know it as soon as possible."

But this could not be suffered. The opportunity was too fair, and his feelings too impatient. Henry was after her immediately. "She must not go, she must allow him five minutes longer."

He took her hand and led her back to her seat, and was in the middle of his further explanation, before she had suspected for what she was detained. When she did understand it, however, and found herself expected to believe that she had created "sensations which his heart had never known before," and that everything he had done for William was because of his excessive and unequalled attachment to her, she was exceedingly distressed, and for some moments unable to speak.

She considered it all nonsense—mere trifling and gallantry, meant only to deceive. It was treating her improperly and unworthily, in a way she had not deserved. Indeed, it was very like him, entirely consistent with what she had seen before.

But she could not reveal her displeasure, because he had been conferring an obligation, which no indelicacy on his part could diminish. While her heart was still bounding with gratitude on William's behalf, she could not be resentful.

Fanny drew her hand away, and repeatedly attempted in vain to turn away from him. Finally she got up in agitation: "Don't, Mr. Crawford, pray don't! I beg you would not. This is a sort of talking which is very unpleasant to me. I must go away. I cannot bear it."

And her thoughts raced to an image of Edmund's dear kind countenance, which then was replaced, inexplicably, with another, that of dark ancient beauty and intense, beloved, stricken eyes. . . .

But Henry was still talking on, describing his affection, soliciting a return, and, finally, in plain words, offering himself, hand, fortune, everything, to her acceptance.

It was so; he had said it. Her astonishment and confusion increased; and though still did not suppose him serious, she could hardly stand. He pressed for an answer.

"No, no, no!" she cried, hiding her face. "This is all nonsense. Do not distress me. I can hear no more of this. Your kindness to William makes me more obliged to you than words can express. But I do not want, I cannot bear, I must not listen to such—No, no, don't think of me. But you are *not* thinking of me. I know it is all nothing."

She had burst away from him. And at that moment Sir Thomas was heard speaking to a servant in his way towards the room they were in, asking him to go and please attend to Mrs. Norris who must be so volubly *taking her exercise* in full view of all.

It was no time for further assurances or entreaty. Fanny rushed out the opposite door from the one her uncle was approaching, and was walking up and down the East room in the utmost confusion of contrary feeling, before Sir Thomas's politeness or apologies were over, or he had reached the beginning of the joyful intelligence which his visitor came to communicate.

Fanny was feeling, thinking, trembling about everything; agitated, happy, miserable, infinitely obliged, absolutely angry. It was all beyond belief! He was inexcusable, incomprehensible! But such were his habits that he could do nothing without a mixture of evil. In that, he was exactly like his *undead* sister, but without the excuse of vampirism to justify his empty heart!

He had previously made her the happiest of human beings, and now he had insulted—she knew not what to say, how to class, or how to regard it. She would not have him be serious, and yet what else could it be?

But William was a lieutenant. *That* was a fact beyond a doubt. She would think of it and forget all the rest. Mr. Crawford would certainly never address her so again—he must have seen how unwelcome it was to her—and in that case, she could gratefully esteem him for his friendship to William!

She would not stir from the East room, until satisfied that Mr. Crawford had left the house. Then, she was eager to go down and be with her uncle, and have all the happiness of his joy as well as her own on behalf of William.

Sir Thomas was as joyful as she could desire, and very kind and communicative. She had so comfortable a talk with him about William as to make her feel as if nothing had occurred to vex her, till she found that Mr. Crawford was to return and dine with them that day. It was most unwelcome and distressing to see him again so soon.

She tried very hard, as the dinner hour approached, to feel and appear as usual. But it was quite impossible for her not to look most shy and uncomfortable when their visitor entered the room.

Mr. Crawford was not only in the room—he was soon close to her. He had a note to deliver from his sister.

Fanny could not look at him. But there was no consciousness of past folly in his voice. She opened her note immediately, glad to have anything to do, and happy, as she read it, to feel that the fidgetings and rather violent wolfish yelps of her aunt Norris, who was also to dine there, screened her a little from view.

"My dear Fanny,—for so I may now always call you, to the infinite relief of a tongue that has been stumbling at *Miss Price* for at least the last six weeks—I cannot let my brother go without sending you a few lines of general congratulation, and giving my most joyful consent and approval. Go on, my dear Fanny, and without *fear*—either of *myself* and my *nature* or any other thing. If the assurance of my consent will be something; you may smile upon him with your sweetest smiles this afternoon, and send him back to me even happier than he goes.

—Yours affectionately, M. C."

These expressions did Fanny little good; for it was evident that Miss Crawford meant to compliment her on her brother's attachment, even to *appear* to believe it serious.

She did not know what to do, or what to think. She was distressed whenever Mr. Crawford spoke to her (which was much too often). There was something in his voice and manner in addressing her very different from how he talked to the others. Her comfort in that day's dinner was quite destroyed. She could hardly eat anything; and when Sir Thomas good-humouredly observed that joy had taken away her appetite, she was ready to sink with shame, from the dread of Mr. Crawford's interpretation; for though nothing could have tempted her to turn her eyes to the right hand, where he sat, she felt that *his* were immediately directed towards her.

And suddenly, Fanny felt another *familiar* pair of burning eyes, trained upon her from the opposite direction.

Unseen by everyone this time but herself, Lord Eastwind stood a few steps away, in the shadows, watching her.

He has returned. . . .

She was more silent than ever. Her heart had skipped a beat but she forced herself to calm. She would hardly speak even when William was the subject, for his commission came all from the right hand too.

She thought Lady Bertram sat longer than ever, not having the usual Egypt artifacts to mesmerize her, and was in despair of ever getting away. At last they were in the drawing-room, and she was able to *think,* while her aunts discussed William's promotion.

Mrs. Norris seemed probably most delighted with the monetary savings this meant for Sir Thomas. "*Now* William would be able to keep himself, which would make a vast difference to his uncle! It was unknown how much he had cost his uncle; indeed, it would make some difference in *her* presents too. She was very glad that she had given William what she did at parting, something quite considerable, very glad, indeed, with her limited means—"

"I am glad you gave him something considerable," said Lady Bertram, with most unsuspicious calmness, "for *I* gave him only £10."

"Indeed!" cried Mrs. Norris, reddening. "Upon my word, he must have gone off with his pockets well lined, and at no expense for his journey to London either!"

"Sir Thomas told me £10 would be enough."

Mrs. Norris, being not at all inclined to question its sufficiency, began to take the matter in another point.

"It is amazing," said she, "how much young people cost their friends, what with bringing them up and putting them out in the world! Now, take my sister Price's children, I dare say nobody would believe what a sum they cost Sir Thomas every year, to say nothing of what *I* do for them."

"Very true, sister, as you say. But, poor things! they cannot help it; and it makes very little difference to Sir Thomas."

Fanny, meanwhile, speaking only when she could not help it, was earnestly trying to understand what Mr. and Miss Crawford were at. There was everything in the world *against* their being serious. How could *she* have excited serious attachment in such a worldly man? And how could his sister, with all her cynical notions of matrimony, encourage him?

She had quite convinced herself of this before Sir Thomas and Mr. Crawford joined them. The difficulty was in maintaining the conviction after Mr. Crawford was in the room. For he looked at her in a way she did not know how to interpret. In any other man it would have meant something very earnest. But this he might express towards her cousins and fifty other women.

She thought he was wishing to speak to her unheard by the rest—trying for it the whole evening at intervals, whenever Sir Thomas was out of the room, or at all engaged with Mrs. Norris. And she carefully refused him every opportunity.

Indeed, in her conflicted mind, the spectre of a raven-haired gentleman stood up in the corner every time she dared to consider otherwise. . . .

At last Mr. Crawford began to talk of going away. But Fanny's relief was tarnished by his turning to her the next moment, and saying, "Have you nothing to send to Mary? No answer to her note? She will be disappointed if she receives nothing from you. Pray write to her, if it be only a line."

"Oh yes! certainly," cried Fanny, rising in a haste of embarrassment, of wanting to get away. "I will write directly."

She went to the writing table, and prepared her materials without knowing what in the world to say. She had read Miss Crawford's note only once. How to reply to anything so imperfectly understood was most distressing. But, something must be written. And wishing only to give an impression of misunderstanding their intent, she wrote thus, trembling—

> "I am very much obliged to you, my dear Miss Crawford, for your kind congratulations, as far as they relate to my dearest William. The rest of your note I know means nothing; I hope you will excuse my begging you to take no further notice. I have seen too much of Mr. Crawford not to understand his manners; if he understood

> me as well, he would behave differently. I do not know what I write, but it would be a great favour of you never to mention the subject again. With thanks for the honour of your note, I remain, dear Miss Crawford, etc., etc."

The conclusion was scarcely intelligible from increasing fright, for she found that Mr. Crawford, under pretence of receiving the note, was coming towards her.

"You cannot think I mean to hurry you," said he, in an undervoice, perceiving the amazing trepidation with which she made up the note. "Do not hurry yourself, I entreat."

"Oh! I thank you; I have quite done; it will be ready in a moment; I am very much obliged to you; if you will be so good as to give *that* to Miss Crawford."

The note was held out, and must be taken; and as she instantly and with averted eyes walked towards the fireplace, where sat the others, he had nothing to do but to go in earnest.

Fanny thought she had never known a day of greater agitation, both of pain and pleasure. Her note must appear excessively ill-written; the language would disgrace a child. But at least it would assure them both of her being neither imposed on nor gratified by Mr. Crawford's attentions.

Chapter XXXII

Fanny had by no means forgotten Mr. Crawford when she awoke the next morning; but she remembered her note, and was uncertain as to its effect.

If Mr. Crawford would but go away! That was what she most earnestly desired: go and take his *wicked* sister with him, as he had returned to Mansfield in order to do. Why it was not done already she could not devise, for Miss Crawford certainly wanted no delay. Fanny had hoped to hear the day named.

Having so satisfactorily settled the sentiment her note would convey, she was astonished to see Mr. Crawford coming up to the house again, and at an hour as early as the day before—the moment once more coinciding with Mrs. Norris's regular and, these days, rather insolent *martial engagement* with the wildlife in the local shrubbery.

His coming might have nothing to do with her, but she must avoid seeing him if possible. She resolved to remain upstairs during the whole of his visit, unless actually sent for. And as Mrs. Norris was still rampaging near and around the house (observed now by at least two regular servants, upon Sir Thomas's express orders to maintain *general control* and have no repeat of any *untoward incident* even remotely resembling the circumstances of *that ball*), there seemed little danger of her being wanted.

She sat some time in agitation, listening, trembling, and fearing to be sent for every moment. But no footsteps approached the East room. She grew gradually composed, able to hope that Mr. Crawford would go without involving her.

Nearly half an hour had passed, and she was growing very comfortable. Suddenly the sound of a heavy approaching step was heard; unusual in that part of the house: it was her uncle's. She knew it as well as his voice. She had trembled at it as often, and began to tremble again, at the idea of his coming up to speak to her, whatever might be the subject.

It was indeed Sir Thomas who opened the door and asked if he might come in. The terror of his former occasional visits to that room returned, and she felt as if he were going to examine her again in French and English, and—as Lady Bertram once insisted—in elementary hieroglyphics.

She was all attention: placed a chair for him, tried to appear honoured. In agitation, she overlooked the deficiencies of her apartment, till he said, with much surprise, "Why have you no fire to-day?"

There was snow on the ground, and she was sitting in a shawl. She hesitated.

"I am not cold, sir: I never sit here long at this time of year."

"But you have a fire in general?"

"No, sir."

"How comes this about? Here must be some mistake. I understood that you had the use of this room by way of making you perfectly comfortable. Here is some great misapprehension which must be rectified. It is highly unfit for you to sit without a fire. You are not strong. You are chilly. Your aunt cannot be aware of this."

Fanny would rather have been silent; but being obliged to speak, she could not forbear, in justice to the aunt she loved best, from saying something in which the words "my aunt Norris" were distinguishable.

"Ah, I understand," cried her uncle, recollecting himself, and not wanting to hear more: "Your aunt Norris has always been an advocate, and very judiciously, for young people's being brought up without unnecessary indulgences; but there should be moderation in everything. She is also very *hardy*—to say the least—herself, which of course will influence her opinion of the wants of others. But this good principle has been carried too far in your case. Now, I think too well of you, Fanny, to suppose you will ever harbour resentment on account of your aunt Norris—But enough of this. Sit down, my dear. I must speak to you for a few minutes, but I will not detain you long."

Fanny obeyed, with eyes cast down and colour rising. After a moment's pause, Sir Thomas, trying to suppress a smile, went on.

"You are not aware, perhaps, that I have had a visitor this morning—Mr. Crawford. His errand you may probably conjecture."

Fanny's colour grew deeper and deeper. Her uncle, perceiving that she was embarrassed to a degree that made either speaking or looking up impossible, turned away his own eyes gently, and proceeded in his account of Mr. Crawford's visit.

Mr. Crawford's business had been to declare himself the lover of Fanny, make decided proposals for her, and entreat the sanction of the uncle, who seemed to stand in the place of her parents. He had done it all so well, so properly, that Sir Thomas was exceedingly happy to give the particulars of their conversation. Sir Thomas was little aware of what was passing in his niece's mind. He talked, therefore, for several minutes without Fanny's daring to interrupt him.

She had hardly wanted to. Her mind was in too much confusion. She had changed her position; and, with her eyes fixed intently on one of the windows (Mrs. Norris was either swinging from tree to tree, or Fanny was hallucinating in broad daylight), was listening to her uncle in dismay.

For a moment he ceased. But rising from his chair, he said, "And now, Fanny, having performed one part of my commission, and shewn you everything being most assured and satisfactory, I may execute the remainder by prevailing on you to accompany me downstairs. Mr. Crawford, as you have perhaps foreseen, is yet in the house. He is in my room, and hoping to see you there."

There was a look, a start, an exclamation on hearing this, which astonished Sir Thomas. But his astonishment increased on hearing her exclaim—"Oh! no, sir, I cannot, indeed I cannot go down to him. Mr. Crawford must know that: I told him enough yesterday to convince him; he spoke to me on this subject yesterday, and I told him without disguise that it was very disagreeable to me, and quite out of my power to return his good opinion."

"I do not catch your meaning," said Sir Thomas, sitting down again. "Out of your power to return his good opinion? What is all this? I know he spoke to you yesterday, and (as far as I understand) received as much encouragement to proceed as a well-judging young woman could permit herself to give. I was very much pleased with what I collected to have been your behaviour on the occasion. It shewed commendable discretion. But now, when he has made his overtures so properly, and honourably—what are your scruples *now?*"

My heart! thought she, *my heart. . . .*

"You are mistaken, sir," cried Fanny, forced by the anxiety of the moment even to tell her uncle that he was wrong; "you are quite mistaken. How could Mr. Crawford say such a thing? I gave him no encouragement yesterday. On the contrary,

I told him that I would not listen to him, that it was very unpleasant to me in every respect! I begged him never to talk to me in that manner again. I am sure I would have said still more, if I had been quite certain of him being serious! I thought it might all pass for nothing with *him*."

She could say no more; her breath was almost gone.

In her mind's eye she saw Edmund, and *another,* ancient, dark, beloved. . . .

"Am I to understand," said Sir Thomas, after a few moments' silence, "that you mean to *refuse* Mr. Crawford?"

"Yes, sir."

"Refuse him?"

"Yes, sir."

"Refuse Mr. Crawford! Upon what plea? For what reason?"

"I—I cannot like him, sir, well enough to marry him."

"This is very strange!" said Sir Thomas, in a voice of calm displeasure. "There is something here which my comprehension does not reach. Here is a young man wishing to pay his addresses to you, with everything to recommend him: situation, fortune, agreeable character. And he is an acquaintance you have now known for some time. His sister, moreover, is your intimate friend, and he has done *that* for your brother, which should have been sufficient recommendation to you, had there been no other."

"Yes," said Fanny, in a faint voice, and looking down with fresh shame. She did feel almost ashamed of herself, after such a picture as her uncle had drawn, for not liking Mr. Crawford.

"You must have been aware," continued Sir Thomas, "of a particularity in Mr. Crawford's manners to you. This cannot have taken you by surprise. You must have observed his attentions. And though you always received them very properly, I never perceived them to be unpleasant to you. I am half inclined to think, Fanny, that you do not quite know your own feelings."

"Oh yes, sir! indeed I do. His attentions were always—what I did not like."

Sir Thomas looked at her with deeper surprise. "This is beyond me," said he. "This requires explanation. Young as you are, and having seen scarcely any one, it is hardly possible that your affections—"

He paused and eyed her fixedly. He tried to think in vain of any minutiae of *that ball,* if anything untoward had occurred between her and some other gentleman there present. (He could recall nothing now, of course, but the mayhem). He saw her lips formed into a *no*, though the sound was inarticulate, but her face was like scarlet. That, however, in so modest a girl, might be only innocence. And chusing at least to appear satisfied, he quickly added, "No, no, I know *that* is quite out of the question; quite impossible. Well, there is nothing more to be said."

And for a few minutes he did say nothing. He was deep in thought. His niece was deep in thought likewise, trying to harden and prepare herself against further questioning. She would rather die than own the truth (and what *was* truth, indeed? Which dear beloved pair of eyes?); and she hoped, by a little reflection, to fortify herself beyond betraying it.

"Mr. Crawford recommends himself to me by wishing to marry so early," said Sir Thomas, beginning again, with composure, "I am an advocate for early marriages, where every young man with a sufficient income should settle as soon after four-and-twenty as he can. Indeed, I am sorry to think how little likely my own eldest son is to marry early." Here was a glance at Fanny. "Now, Edmund, I consider as much more likely to marry early than his brother. *He,* indeed, I have lately thought, has seen the woman he could love. Am I right? Do you agree with me, my dear?"

"Yes, sir."

It was gently said, and Sir Thomas was easy on the score of the cousins. But Fanny's continued unexplained reaction fueled his displeasure. He got up and walked about the room with a frown, while Fanny dared not lift up her eyes. Shortly afterwards, he said in a voice of authority, "Have you any reason, child, to think ill of Mr. Crawford's temper?"

"No, sir."

She longed to add, "But of his principles I have." But her heart sunk under the appalling prospect of explaining it all. Her ill opinion of him was founded chiefly on observations, which, for her cousins' sake, she could scarcely dare mention to their father. Maria and Julia, and especially Maria, were so closely implicated in Mr. Crawford's misconduct, that she could not give his character, such as she believed it, without betraying them. She had hoped that, to a man like her uncle—so discerning, honourable, good—the simple acknowledgment of settled *dislike* on her side would have been sufficient. To her infinite grief she found it was not.

Sir Thomas came towards the table where she sat in trembling wretchedness, and with cold sternness, said, "It is of no use, I perceive, to talk to you. We had better put an end to this most mortifying conference. Mr. Crawford must not be kept waiting. I will, therefore, only add that you have disappointed every expectation I had formed. For I *had,* Fanny, formed a very favourable opinion of you from the period of my return to England. I had thought you free from willfulness of temper, self-conceit, and every tendency to that independence of spirit which prevails so much in modern days, and which in young women[27] is offensive and disgusting beyond all common offence. But you have now shewn me that you can be willful and perverse; that you can and will decide for yourself, without any consideration or deference for those who have surely some right to guide you. You have shewn yourself very different from anything I had

[27] Harlots, all! Ahem—pray, forgive such an outburst, gentle Reader.

imagined. The advantage or disadvantage of your family never had a moment's share in your thoughts on this occasion. How *they* might be benefited, is nothing to *you*. You think only of yourself, and because you do not feel for Mr. Crawford the *tendre* imagined to be necessary for happiness, you resolve to refuse him at once, without any time for cool consideration. In a wild fit of folly you throw away such an opportunity of being settled in life, as will, probably, never occur to you again. Fanny, you may live eighteen years longer in the world without being addressed by a man of half Mr. Crawford's estate, or a tenth part of his merits! Gladly would I have bestowed either of my own daughters on him. Maria is nobly married; but had Mr. Crawford sought Julia's hand, I should have given it to him more gladly than I gave Maria's to Mr. Rushworth."

After half a moment's pause: "And I should have been very much surprised had either of my daughters, on receiving even *half* as eligible a proposal of marriage, immediately and peremptorily, and without any consultation, put a decided negative on it. I should have been surprised and hurt by such a gross violation of duty and respect. *You* are not to be judged by the same rule. You do not owe me the duty of a child. But, Fanny, if your heart can acquit you of *ingratitude*—"

He ceased. Fanny was by this time crying so bitterly that, angry as he was, he would not press farther. Her heart was almost broken by such a picture of what she appeared to him; by such heavy, rising accusations! Self-willed, obstinate, selfish, and ungrateful. He thought her all this. She had deceived his expectations; she had lost his good opinion. What was to become of her?

"I am very sorry," said she inarticulately, through her tears, "I am very sorry indeed."

"Sorry! yes, I hope you are sorry; and you will probably have reason to be long sorry for this day's transactions."

"I am so perfectly convinced that I could never make him happy," she said, "that I should be miserable myself."

Another burst of tears—but in spite of that burst, and that great black word *miserable,* Sir Thomas began to think a little relenting, a little change of inclination, might have something to do with it; and to augur favourably from the personal entreaty of the young man himself.

He knew her to be very timid, exceedingly nervous; and thought it possible that her refusal might be overturned, with a little time and patience on the lover's side. If the gentleman had but love enough to persevere, Sir Thomas began to have hopes. And these passing reflections cheered him.

"Well," said he, in a tone of becoming gravity, but of less anger, "well, child, dry up your tears. They are no use, and can do no good. You must now come downstairs with me. Mr. Crawford has been kept waiting too long already. You must give him your own answer, and you only can explain to him the grounds for it."

But Fanny shewed such reluctance, such misery, at the idea of going down to him, that Sir Thomas judged it better to indulge her. Indeed, when he looked at his niece, and saw the sorry state of feature and complexion, which her crying had brought her into, he thought there might be as much lost as gained by an immediate interview. Thus, he left by himself, leaving his poor niece to sit and cry over what had passed.

Her mind was all disorder. The past, present, future, everything was terrible. But her uncle's anger gave her the severest pain of all.

She had no one to take her part, to speak for her. Her only friend was absent. He might have softened his father; but perhaps he too would think her selfish and ungrateful. She might have to endure the reproach again and again.

She could not but feel some resentment against Mr. Crawford. Yet—what if he really loved her, and was unhappy too! It was all wretchedness together.

In about a quarter of an hour her uncle returned. She was almost ready to faint at the sight of him. He spoke calmly, however, without austerity, without reproach, and she revived a little. He began with, "Mr. Crawford is gone: he has just left me. I do not want to add to anything you may now be feeling, by an account of what he has felt. Suffice it, that he has behaved in the most gentlemanlike, generous manner, and has confirmed my favourable opinion of him. Upon my representation of what you were suffering, he immediately, and with the greatest delicacy, ceased to urge to see you for the present."

Here Fanny, who had looked up, looked down again.

"Of course," continued her uncle, "if he should request to speak with you alone, be it only for five minutes; such a request ought not to be denied. But there is no time fixed; perhaps whenever your spirits are composed enough. For the present you have only to calm yourself. Check these tears; they do but exhaust you. I advise you to go out: the air will do you good; go out for an hour on the gravel; you will have the shrubbery to yourself. And, Fanny" (turning back again for a moment), "I shall make no mention below of what has passed; I shall not even tell your aunt Bertram. There is no occasion for spreading the disappointment. Say nothing about it yourself."

This was an order to be most joyfully obeyed, a true act of kindness. To be spared from her aunt Norris's interminable reproaches! he left her in a glow of gratitude. Anything might be bearable rather than reproaches. Even to see Mr. Crawford would be less overpowering.

She walked out directly, as her uncle recommended. She quelled her tears and calmed her face, to keep the whole affair from the knowledge of her aunts—anything that might save her from her aunt Norris.

She was struck, when, on returning from her walk and going into the East room again, the first thing which caught her eye was a fire lighted and burning. A fire! Such an indulgence, at this time! She wondered that Sir Thomas had remembered. The housemaid who came in to attend it, mentioned it was to be so every day. Sir Thomas had given orders for it.

"I must be a brute, indeed, if I can be really ungrateful!" said Fanny, to herself.

At dinner, her uncle's behaviour to her was unchanged. But her aunt Norris was soon quarrelling with her when she found that Fanny went on a walk without her knowledge.

"If I had known you were going out, I should have got you to go as far as my house with some orders for Nanny," said Mrs. Norris, and continued to rant about *some people* taking walks in the shrubbery.

Speak not to me *about shrubbery!* Fanny thought bitterly, visualizing Mrs. Norris rampaging there earlier that morning.

"I recommended the shrubbery to Fanny as the driest place," said Sir Thomas. He, too, thought: *The driest place, and for once* you *were not there.*

"Oh!" said Mrs. Norris, with a moment's check, "that was very kind of you, Sir Thomas; but you do not know how dry the path is to my house."

"Dry, and now surely barren of vermin, I suppose," he mumbled under his nose and into his soup, so that no one could hear. "It must be the shrubbery now bears the brunt of invasion."

"Fanny would have had quite as good a walk there, I assure you," continued Mrs. Norris, not hearing Sir Thomas mumble, "with the advantage of being of some use, and obliging her aunt: it is all her fault."

Sir Thomas thought it was unjust toward Fanny, and tried to turn the conversation. But Mrs. Norris had not discernment enough to perceive, not ever, to what degree he thought well of his niece. She continued talking *at* Fanny through the dinner, until Sir Thomas was ready to go outside and take an axe to the shrubbery himself so as not to hear another word.

At last dinner was over, and the evening set in, giving Fanny more time for reflection—to ponder in depth how wrong it was to marry without affection.

When the meeting with Mr. Crawford would take place, he would no doubt be gone from Mansfield. London would soon bring its cure. There he would soon learn to wonder at his infatuation, and be thankful for her refusal.

Soon after tea, her uncle was called out of the room. Fanny thought nothing of it till the butler reappeared ten minutes afterwards, and advancing decidedly towards herself, said, "Sir Thomas wishes to speak with you, ma'am, in his own room."

A suspicion rushed over her, which drove the colour from her cheeks. Instantly rising, she prepared to obey, when Mrs. Norris called out, "Stay, stay, Fanny! where are you going? don't be in such a hurry. Depend upon it, it is not you who are wanted, it is me" (looking at the butler); "but you are so very eager to put yourself forward. What should Sir Thomas want you for? It is me, Baddeley, you mean; I am coming this moment. Sir Thomas wants me, not Miss Price."

But Baddeley—who still had a sore spot for Mrs. Norris, on behalf of her so-called scandalous *tête-à-tête* with Mr. Rushworth the morning after *that ball,* and the daily shrubbery, among other things—was stout in his retort. "No, ma'am, it is Miss Price; I am certain of its being Miss Price." And there was an arch half-smile with the words, which meant, "I do not think you would answer the purpose at all, for there is no young Mr. Rushworth to be concerned with, you shameless—"

Mrs. Norris, much discontented, was obliged to stay.

And Fanny, going as directed, found herself, as she anticipated, in another minute alone with Mr. Crawford.

Chapter XXXIII

The conference was neither so short nor so conclusive as the lady hoped. The gentleman was not so easily satisfied. He had vanity, which inclined him in the first place to think she did love him, though she might not know it herself. The same vanity convinced him that in time he could convince *her*.

"I am very sorry," said Fanny wearily, her eyes sweeping the corner of the room for a memory of other eyes, belonging to a far dearer *one* whom she had refused at a greater price to her soul and heart.

But Mr. Crawford was in love, very much in love. And it was a love which made her affection appear of greater consequence because it was withheld. He was determined to force her to love him.

He would not despair: he would not desist. He had every well-grounded reason for solid attachment. And yet—he knew not that he had a pre-engaged heart to attack. Of *that* he had no suspicion. Indeed, he was the *third* in line to it!

He considered her rather as one who had never thought on the subject of love, guarded by a youth of mind as lovely as of person; whose modesty had prevented her from understanding his attentions. She was but overpowered by the suddenness.

Must it not follow of course, that, when he was understood, he should succeed? He believed it fully. Love such as his, in a man like himself, must with perseverance secure a return. He had so much delight in the idea of obliging her to love him in a very short time, that her not loving him now was scarcely regretted.

A little difficulty to be overcome was no evil to Henry Crawford. He rather derived spirits from it. He had been apt to gain hearts too easily. His situation was new and animating.

To Fanny, however, all this was unintelligible. She found that he meant to persevere, and now, frustration was setting in! Fanny almost imagined a tedious mummy into whose mouth she might stuff some large wad to make it *go away.*

So she told him that she did not love him, could not love him, was sure she never should love him; that such a change was quite impossible; that the subject was most painful to her. She must entreat him never to mention it again, to allow her to leave him at once, and let it be considered as concluded for ever. Their dispositions were so totally dissimilar as to make mutual affection incompatible. They were unfitted for each other by nature, education, and habit.

"Mr. Crawford," whispered Fanny, in conclusion. "You are being beyond unreasonable. After all I have said, is this, in any way, your sister's wicked idea, to torment me so?"

"Ah, you know so little of true wickedness, Miss Price," he continued, in dazzled admiration of her innocence.

But Fanny shattered this illusion entirely. "Miss Crawford is a *vampire,*" she announced, to remind him of what Mary herself had told him some time ago about Fanny's remarkable ability. "I know wickedness when I see it. Believe me, sir, I know far more than you can imagine."

For the first time Henry was genuinely intrigued past his courtship platitudes. Though he had known Fanny had some idea of Mary's *dark* nature, he did not realize to what extent, or that she had put an authentic name to it. And it raised Fanny in his opinion even more—if such a thing were possible. "My dear—Miss Price!" he uttered. "How did you—"

"Of no consequence, how. But let me repeat—I see *everything.*"

For long moments there was silence between them. Mr. Crawford looked on with new respect and absolute renewed fascination.

And then he resumed!

Fanny wanted—as she seemed to be wanting so often recently—to smash her forehead repeatedly against a hard object, to gain at least some measure of oblivion from the idiocy.

Mr. Crawford steadily denied incompatibility between them and declared that he would still love, and still hope!

Fanny's manner was once more gentle, but it concealed the sternness of purpose.

Mr. Crawford was no longer the Mr. Crawford who, as the clandestine, insidious, treacherous admirer of Maria Bertram, had been her abhorrence, whom she had hated to see or to speak to, in whom she could believe no good quality to exist, and whose power, even of being agreeable, she had barely acknowledged. He was now the Mr. Crawford who was addressing herself with ardent, disinterested love; whose feelings were apparently become all that was honourable and upright, whose views of happiness were all fixed on a marriage of attachment; who was describing again his affection, proving as far as words could prove it, and in the language, tone, and spirit of a man of talent too, that he sought her for her gentleness and her goodness. And above all, he was now the Mr. Crawford who had procured William's promotion!

Here was a change, and here were claims which could not but operate! She might have disdained him in all the dignity of angry virtue, in the grounds of Sotherton, or the theatre at

Mansfield Park. But now she must be courteous, and she must be compassionate. She must have a strong feeling of gratitude.

But all things come to a close eventually, and so did their interview.

It was with reluctance that he suffered her to go, and with all hopes intact.

Now she was angry. Here again was a want of regard for others which had formerly so disgusted her. Here again was the same Mr. Crawford.

Had her own affections been free, he *never* could have engaged them! So thought Fanny, in good truth and sober sadness, as she sat near the new luxury of a fire upstairs.

Sir Thomas obliged himself to wait till the morrow for details of what had passed between the young people. He then saw Mr. Crawford, and received his account. The first feeling was disappointment. But there was speedy comfort in the determined views and sanguine perseverance of the lover, and confidence of ultimate success.

At Mansfield Park Mr. Crawford would always be welcome. He had only to consult his own judgment and feelings as to the frequency of his visits. The gentlemen parted the best of friends.

Sir Thomas resolved to abstain from all further interference with his niece. He said to her, with a mild gravity, "Well, Fanny, I have seen Mr. Crawford again, and learnt from him exactly how matters stand between you. He is a most extraordinary young man, and whatever happens, you must feel that you have created an attachment of no common character."

"Indeed, sir," said Fanny, "I am very sorry that Mr. Crawford should continue—I feel most undeservedly honoured; but I am so perfectly convinced, and I have told him so, that it never will be in my power—"

"My dear," interrupted Sir Thomas, "there is no occasion for this. Your feelings are as well known to me as my wishes and regrets must be to you. Nothing more to be said or done. From this hour, you will have nothing to fear. You cannot suppose me capable of trying to persuade you to marry against your inclinations. Your happiness and advantage are all that I have in view. Mr. Crawford proceeds at his own risk. You will see him with the rest of us, in the same manner. He leaves Northamptonshire soon. The future must be very uncertain. And now, my dear Fanny, this subject is closed between us."

The promised departure was all that Fanny could think of with much satisfaction. Her uncle's kindness, however, was sensibly felt. Considering that he had married a daughter to Mr. Rushworth, romantic delicacy was certainly not to be expected from him. She must do her duty, and trust the passing of time . . .

Surely, Mr. Crawford's attachment would not hold out for ever, not with her steady discouragement.

In spite of his intended silence, Sir Thomas found himself once more obliged to mention the subject to his niece, to prepare her for her aunts' discovery. Mr. Crawford's feelings were all known at the Parsonage, where he loved to talk over the future with both his sisters. When Sir Thomas understood this, he almost dreaded the effect of the communication to Mrs. Norris as much as Fanny herself.

Sir Thomas, indeed, was, by this time, classing Mrs. Norris as one of those well-meaning people who are always doing mistaken and very disagreeable things—regardless of any unique *afflictions*.

Mrs. Norris, however, relieved him. She observed forbearance and silence towards their niece, only looked increasingly full of ill-will, and made additional frequent snarls and yaps at inopportune moments. She was more bitterly angry with Fanny for having received such an offer than for refusing it. It was an injury and affront to Julia, who ought to have been Mr. Crawford's choice. Independently of that, Mrs. Norris disliked Fanny, because she had neglected her.

Fanny could have blessed her for allowing her only to see her displeasure, and not to hear it. Rather—she *did* hear it, but as undifferentiated grisly sound effects and not actual words that required acknowledgement.

Lady Bertram took it differently. She had been a prosperous beauty all her life; and beauty and wealth—and until recently, Egyptology—were all that excited her respect. To know Fanny to be sought in marriage by a man of fortune, *raised* her, therefore, very much in her opinion. Fanny *was* very pretty, and she *would* be advantageously married, realized Lady Bertram. And it made her peculiarly proud of her niece.

"Well, Fanny," said she, with extraordinary animation; "I have had a very agreeable surprise this morning. I must just speak of it *once,* I told Sir Thomas, and then I shall have done. I give you joy, my dear niece." And looking at her complacently, she added, "Humph, we certainly are a handsome family!"

Fanny coloured. "My dear aunt, *you* cannot wish me to marry; for you would miss me, should not you?"

"No, my dear, I should not think of missing you, when such an offer comes your way. I could do very well without you, if you were married to a man of such good estate as Mr. Crawford. It is every young woman's duty to accept such a very unexceptionable offer as this."

This was probably the only piece of advice which Fanny had ever received from her aunt. It silenced her.

But Lady Bertram was quite talkative.

"I will tell you what, Fanny," said she, "I am sure he fell in love with you at *that ball;* I am sure the mischief was done that evening—No, not *that mischief!* Well, you know what I mean. You did look remarkably well. Everybody said so. Sir Thomas said so. And you know you had Chapman to help you to dress. I am very glad I sent Chapman to you. I shall tell Sir Thomas that I am sure it was done that evening. Or—no, maybe I ought not to mention *that evening*—" And still pursuing the same cheerful muddled thoughts, she soon afterwards added, “And I will tell you what, Fanny, which is more than I did for Maria: the next time pug has a litter you shall have a puppy. Unless—might you prefer a mummified baboon? We do have plenty left over, but thankfully Sir Thomas does not know—”

Chapter XXXIV

At this point it is likely the observant Reader wonders—whatever happened to the hordes of terrifying mummies that had seemingly disappeared without a trace, at the end of Fanny's debut ball? Their crates were violently disposed of; their various implements swept away. What remains of the *unholy* menace?

In truth, it is with sincere regret we inform that the mummies are far from being gone; farther yet from being dispatched completely. And, it must be admitted, some of the worst is yet to come. But—once again, we are getting ahead of ourselves—

Edmund had great things to hear on his return. Many surprises awaited him. The first was the sight of Henry Crawford and Mary Crawford walking together through the village as he rode into it. He had concluded they were long gone. His absence had been extended purposely to avoid Miss Crawford.

He was returning to Mansfield ready to dwell on melancholy remembrances and tender associations, when her own fair self was before him, leaning on her brother's arm. Edmund found himself receiving a friendly welcome.

Her reception of him was startling. He would have expected anything rather than a look of satisfaction, and words of simple, pleasant meaning. It was enough to set his heart in a glow.

Next, the news of William's promotion was imparted. He found in it a source of most gratifying joy and cheerfulness all dinner-time.

After dinner, when he and his father were alone, he was told Fanny's circumstances, and thus was caught up with all the great events at Mansfield.

Fanny suspected what was going on. They sat so much longer than usual in the dining-parlour, that she was sure they must be talking of her. When tea at last brought them away, and she was to be seen by Edmund again, she felt dreadfully guilty.

He came to her, sat down by her, took her hand, and pressed it kindly. And at that moment she thought that she must have betrayed her emotion in some unpardonable excess.

And in the moment of experiencing Edmund's *familiar* comforting kindness, for some reason she remembered another—Lord Eastwind's elegant *familiar* silhouette, his eyes. . . .

Edmund did not intend, however, by such affectionate action, to be conveying to her he approved. He was, in fact, entirely on his father's side of the question. Though, his surprise was not so great as his father's at her refusing Crawford.

While honouring Fanny's present feelings, he earnestly hoped that it would be a match at last. United by mutual affection, their dispositions were exactly fitted to make them blessed in each other. Crawford had simply not given her time to attach herself. He had begun at the wrong end. With such powers as his, however, and such a disposition as hers, Edmund trusted that everything would work out a happy conclusion. Meanwhile, he saw enough of Fanny's embarrassment to make him scrupulously guard against increasing it.

"But Edmund, how can you think this way?" said Fanny to him in secret. "A connexion to the vampire's brother! He, as indifferent of heart as she is, if still breathing. Even now his declarations of love ring hollow—for how can he know of love? The *true love* that a *true man* alone might feel? Henry is not true, but false as sun's last glimmer at twilight. How, then, can you think him changed or be in earnest after the way he had behaved, falsely encouraging your cousins?"

Edmund's brow darkened once more. "Again, Fanny! You speak of unholy vampires, and I refuse this, utterly, with all my heart. It is not so, *she* is not—"

"Oh, cousin."

And Fanny looked away in sadness.

Crawford called the next day. With Edmund's return, Sir Thomas felt himself at better liberty to ask him to stay for dinner.

Edmund had then ample opportunity to observe how Mr. Crawford was with Fanny. He noted that any encouragement from Fanny rested upon her embarrassment only. He was almost ready to wonder at his friend's perseverance.

Fanny was worth it all—worth every effort of patience, every exertion of mind—but he did not think he could have gone on himself with any woman breathing, without something more to warm his courage than his eyes could discern in hers. But then, Edmund fundamentally did *not* look upon courtship as a competitive sport.

In the evening a few circumstances occurred which he thought more promising. When he and Crawford walked into the drawing-room, his mother and Fanny were sitting intently and silently at work.

"We have not been so silent all the time," said his mother. "Fanny has been reading to me, and only put the book down upon hearing you coming." And sure enough there was a book on the table: a volume of Shakespeare. "She often reads to me; and she was in the middle of a very fine speech of that man's—what's his name, Fanny?—when we heard your footsteps."

Crawford took the volume. "Let me have the pleasure of finishing that speech to your ladyship," said he. "I shall find it immediately." And by artifice he did find it, within a page or two, near enough to satisfy Lady Bertram, who assured him, as soon as he mentioned the name of Cardinal Wolsey, that was it.

Not a look or an offer of help had Fanny given. All attention to her work, she was determined to be disinterested.

But taste was too strong in her. Five minutes into his reading, she was forced to listen—his reading was capital, and her pleasure in good reading extreme. To *good* reading, she had been long used: her uncle, her cousins, all read well, Edmund very well. But in Mr. Crawford's reading there was a variety of excellence beyond what she had ever met with.

The King, the Queen, Buckingham, Wolsey, Cromwell, all were given in turn; for with the happiest knack, the finest verbal nuance, he could always select the best scenes and speeches. And whether it was dignity, pride, tenderness, or remorse, he could express it with equal beauty. It was truly dramatic.

His acting had first taught Fanny what pleasure a play might give, and his reading brought all his acting before her again—perhaps with greater enjoyment, for it came unexpectedly, and with no discomfort of seeing him with Miss Bertram.

Edmund watched the progress of her attention. He was amused and gratified by seeing how she gradually slackened in the needlework, how it fell from her hand while she sat motionless over it. And at last, Edmund saw how the eyes which had appeared so studiously to avoid Henry throughout the day were turned and fixed on Crawford—fixed on him for minutes, fixed on him, in short, till the attraction drew Crawford's upon her, and the book was closed, and the charm was broken.

Then she was shrinking again into herself, and blushing and working as hard as ever; but it had been enough to give Edmund encouragement for his friend. As he cordially thanked him, he hoped to be expressing Fanny's secret feelings too.

"That play must be a favourite with you," said Edmund; "you read as if you knew it well."

"It will be a favourite, I believe, from this hour," replied Crawford; "but I do not think I have had a volume of Shakespeare in my hand before since I was fifteen. But Shakespeare one gets acquainted with without knowing how. It is a part of an Englishman's constitution."

"No doubt one is familiar with Shakespeare in a degree," said Edmund, "from one's earliest years. His celebrated passages are quoted by everybody; they are in half the books we open, and we all talk Shakespeare. But to read him well aloud is no everyday talent."

"Sir, you do me honour," was Crawford's answer, with a bow of mock gravity.

Both gentlemen had a glance at Fanny, to see if a word of accordant praise could be extorted from her; yet both feeling that it could not be. Her praise had been given in her attention; *that* must content them.

Lady Bertram's admiration was expressed, and strongly too. "It was really like being at a play," said she. "I wish Sir Thomas had been here."

Crawford was excessively pleased. If Lady Bertram, with all her languor, could feel this, imagine what her niece, alive and enlightened, must feel!

"You have a great turn for acting, I am sure, Mr. Crawford," said her ladyship soon afterwards.

A great actor indeed, thought Fanny. *He acts even now, a fine subtle role. If he but knew what might touch my heart—being* genuine. *But it is the one role he has not mastered.*

"I expect" Lady Bertram continued, "you will have a theatre at your house in Norfolk, when you are settled there."

"Do you, ma'am?" cried he, with quickness. "No, no, that will never be. Your ladyship is quite mistaken. No theatre at Everingham!" And he looked at Fanny with an expressive smile, which evidently meant, "That lady will never allow a theatre at Everingham."

Edmund saw it all, and saw Fanny so determined *not* to see it.

The subject of reading aloud was further discussed. The two young men were the only talkers, and held a discourse on a number of engaging subjects. Fanny was listening again with great entertainment. But now and then her eyes glanced in the corners, at the shadows, prompted by something—a sensation of being watched by familiar, *beloved,* ancient eyes. . . . She even glanced at Lady Bertram to see if that *someone* whom she had grown to expect as a regular fixture for some months now, was sitting at her ladyship's side. But, no—

"Even in my profession," Edmund was saying, with a smile, "how little the art of reading has been studied!" And he mentioned the importance of fine oratorical delivery.

Edmund had already gone through the service once since his ordination; and upon this being understood, he had a variety of questions from Crawford—genuine questions without any banter or levity which Edmund knew to be most offensive to Fanny. Edmund was more and more pleased. This would be the way to Fanny's heart.

"Our liturgy," observed Crawford, "has beauties, which not even a careless, slovenly style of reading can destroy; but it has also redundancies and repetitions which require good reading not to be felt. For myself, at least, I must confess being not always so attentive as I ought to be" (here was a glance at Fanny); "that nineteen times out of twenty I am thinking how such a prayer ought to be read, and longing to have it to read myself. Did you speak?" stepping eagerly to Fanny, and addressing her in a softened voice; and upon her saying "No," he added, "Are you sure you did not speak? I saw your lips move. I fancied you might be going to tell me I ought to be more attentive, and not *allow* my thoughts to wander. Are not you going to tell me so?"

"No, indeed, you know your duty too well for me to—even supposing—"

She stopt, felt herself getting into a puzzle, and could not be prevailed on to add another word. He returned to his former station, and went on.

"A sermon, well delivered, is more uncommon than prayers well read. The preacher who can touch and affect such an heterogeneous mass of hearers—I should like to be such a man."

Edmund laughed.

"I should indeed," continued Crawford. "I never listened to a distinguished preacher in my life without a sort of envy. But then, I must have a London audience. I could not preach but to the educated; to those capable of estimating my composition. And I do not know that I should be fond of preaching often; now and then, perhaps, but not for a constancy."

Here Fanny, who could not but listen, involuntarily shook her head. And Crawford was instantly by her side again, entreating to know her meaning. He drew up a chair, sat down close by her. Dear little Fanny might be persuaded into explaining away that shake of the head to the satisfaction of her ardent lover.

Fanny, meanwhile, vexed with herself for displaying a reaction, tried to repulse Mr. Crawford. But he was undaunted.

"What did that shake of the head mean?" said he. "What was it meant to express? Disapprobation, I fear. But of what? What had I been saying to displease you? I want to be set right! What did that shake of the head mean?"

In vain was her "Pray, sir, don't; pray, Mr. Crawford," repeated twice over; and in vain did she try to move away. In the same low, eager voice, and the same proximity, he went on. She grew more agitated and displeased.

"How can you, sir? You quite astonish me; I wonder how you can—"

"Do I astonish you?" said he. "Do you wonder? Is there anything in my present entreaty that you do not understand?"

In spite of herself, she could not help half a smile, but she said nothing, thinking, *I am afraid I understand too much.*

"You shook your head at my acknowledging that I should not like to engage in the duties of a clergyman always for a constancy. Yes, that was the word. *Constancy:* I am not afraid of the word!"

"Perhaps, sir," said Fanny, wearied at last into speaking—"perhaps, sir, I thought it was a pity you did not always know yourself as well as you seemed to do at that moment."

Crawford, delighted to get her to speak at any rate, was determined to keep it up. Poor Fanny, who had hoped to silence him by such extreme reproof, found herself sadly mistaken. He was more intent than ever on gaining an explanation, considering that no such opportunity might occur again before his leaving Mansfield. Lady Bertram's being just on the other side of the table was a trifle, for she might always be considered as only half-awake, and Edmund's determined perusal of the paper's advertisements was opportune.

"Well," said Crawford, "I am happier than I was, because I now understand more clearly your opinion of me. You think me unsteady: easily swayed by the whim of the moment, easily tempted, easily put aside. But we shall see. I shall endeavour to convince. My conduct shall speak for me; absence, distance, time shall speak for me. *They* shall prove that I do deserve you. You are infinitely my superior in merit; all *that* I know. You have qualities which I had not before supposed to exist in such a degree in any human creature. You have some touches of the angel in you beyond what one fancies might be. But still I am not frightened. It is not by equality of merit that you can be won. It is he who sees and worships your merit the strongest, who loves you most devotedly, that has the best right to a return. Yes, dearest, sweetest Fanny. Nay—" (seeing her draw back displeased), "forgive me. Perhaps I have as yet no right; but by what other name can I call you? Do you suppose you are ever present to my imagination under any other? No, it is 'Fanny' that I think of all day, and dream of all night. You have given the name such reality of sweetness, that nothing else can now be descriptive of you."

Fanny could hardly have kept her seat any longer, or refrained from trying to get away, had it not been for the sound of approaching relief.

The solemn procession, headed by Baddeley, of tea-board, urn, and cake-bearers, made its appearance, and delivered her. Mr. Crawford was obliged to move. She was at liberty.

Edmund, subtly observing their interaction, was yet inclined to hope that something good had come of it.

Chapter XXXV

Edmund had determined that Crawford should not be mentioned between them unless Fanny wanted it. But after a day or two, he was induced by his father to try to influence his friend.

A day was actually fixed for the Crawfords' departure. Sir Thomas thought it might be as well to make one more effort for the young man before he left Mansfield.

Edmund was not unwilling to get involved. Indeed, he was curious to know Fanny's feelings. She had been used to consult him in every difficulty, and he loved her too well to bear to be denied her confidence now. He hoped to be of service to her—whom else had she to open her heart to? Fanny estranged from him, silent and reserved, was an unnatural state of things; a state which he must break through. Surely, she would *want* him to try.

"I will speak to her, sir: I will take the first opportunity of speaking to her alone."

And upon Sir Thomas's information of her being at that very time walking alone in the shrubbery, Edmund instantly joined her.

"I am come to walk with you, Fanny," said he. "Shall I?" Drawing her arm within his. "It is a long while since we have had a comfortable walk together."

She assented to it all rather by look than word. Her spirits were low. It was quiet all about, with Mrs. Norris decidedly not out foraging the wilderness at the moment. Fanny was glad of the additional privacy (though one could never be certain if, in her *heightened* state, Mrs. Norris was cognizant of anything but the vermin).

"But, Fanny," he presently added, "in order to have a comfortable walk, something more is necessary than merely pacing this gravel together. You must talk to me. I know you have something on your mind. Am I to hear of it from everybody but Fanny herself?"

Fanny, at once agitated and dejected, replied, "If you hear of it from everybody, cousin, there can be nothing for me to tell."

"Not of facts, perhaps; but of feelings, Fanny. I do not mean to press you, however. I had thought it might be a relief."

"I am afraid we think too differently for me to find any relief in talking of what I feel."

"Do you suppose that we think differently? Our opinions are as much alike as ever. But—I consider Crawford's proposals as most advantageous and desirable, if you could return his affection. If you cannot, you have done exactly as you ought in refusing him. Can there be any disagreement between us here?"

"Oh no! But I thought you blamed me. I thought you were against me. This is such a comfort!"

"This comfort you might have had sooner, Fanny, had you sought it. But how could you possibly suppose me against you? How could you imagine me an advocate for marriage without *love?*"

"My uncle thought me wrong—"

"Fanny, I think you perfectly right. I may be sorry, I may be surprised—but I think you perfectly right. You did not love him; nothing could have justified your accepting him."

Fanny had not felt so comfortable for days and days.

"So far your conduct has been faultless, and they were quite mistaken who wished you to do otherwise. But the matter does not end here. Crawford may still hope and persevere."

"Oh! never, never, never! he never will succeed with me." And she spoke with a warmth which quite astonished Edmund. She blushed when she saw his look.

"Never, Fanny? So very determined and positive! This is unlike your rational self."

"I mean," she cried, sorrowfully correcting herself, "that I *think* I never shall—"

"I must hope better things. I wish he had not been obliged to tell you what he was trying for. I wish he had known you as well as I do, Fanny. Between us, I think we should have won you. My theoretical and his practical knowledge together could not have failed. I cannot suppose that you have not the *wish* to love him—the natural wish of gratitude. You must be sorry for your own indifference."

"We are so totally unlike," said Fanny, avoiding a direct answer, "in all our inclinations and ways, that I consider it as quite impossible we should ever be tolerably happy together, even if I *could* like him. Completely dissimilar, we have not one taste in common. We should be miserable."

"You are mistaken, Fanny. The dissimilarity is not so strong. You are quite enough alike. You *have* tastes in common: moral and literary tastes, warm hearts and benevolent feelings. And, Fanny—after hearing him read, and seeing you listen to Shakespeare the other night—who will think you unfitted as companions? There is a decided difference in your tempers, I allow. He is lively, you are serious; but so much the better: his spirits will support yours. It is your disposition to be easily dejected and to fancy difficulties greater than they are. His cheerfulness will counteract this. He sees difficulties nowhere: and his pleasantness and gaiety will be a constant support to you. I am convinced, you have a strong probability of happiness together."

Full well could Fanny guess where his thoughts were now: Miss Crawford's power was all returning. Ah, the wretched vampire with control over his heart! His avoiding her was quite at an end. He had dined at the Parsonage only the preceding day.

After leaving him to his happier thoughts for some minutes, Fanny returned to the discussion of Mr. Crawford. "It is not merely in *temper* and spirits that I consider him totally unsuited to myself. But there is something in him to which I object still more. I cannot approve his character. I have not thought well of him from the time of the play. I then saw him behaving so very improperly and *unfeelingly* by poor *afflicted* Mr. Rushworth, not caring how he exposed or hurt him, and paying attentions to my cousin Maria. In short, at the time of the play, I received an impression which will never be got over."

"My dear Fanny," replied Edmund, scarcely hearing her, "let us not, any of us, be judged by what we appeared at that period of general folly. That is a time which I hate to recollect. Maria was wrong, Crawford was wrong, we were all wrong together; but none so wrong as myself. Compared with me, all the rest were blameless. I was playing the fool with my eyes open."

You still are, she thought sadly.

"As a bystander," Fanny said, "perhaps I saw more than you did; and I do think that Mr. Rushworth, while sometimes very—wolfish, was at other times very jealous."

"Very possibly. No wonder. Nothing could be more improper than the whole business. I am shocked whenever I think that Maria could be capable of it."

"Before the play, I am much mistaken if *Julia* did not think he was paying her attentions."

"Julia! I have heard before from some one of his being in love with Julia; but I could never see anything of it. I think both my sisters were more desirous of being admired by Crawford, than was perfectly prudent. He enjoyed their availability. But his ultimate choice of yourself does him the highest honour. It proves him unspoilt by his uncle."

"I am persuaded that he does not think, as he ought, on serious subjects."

"Say, rather, that he has not *thought* at all upon serious subjects. How could it be otherwise, with such an education and adviser? Crawford's *feelings* have hitherto been too much his guides. You will supply the rest—a woman firm as a rock in her own principles, with a gentleness of character. He has chosen his partner well. Fanny, I know he will make you happy; but you will make him everything."

"I would not engage in such a charge," cried Fanny; "in such an office of high responsibility!"

"As usual, believing yourself unequal to anything! Next to your happiness, Fanny, his has the first claim on me. You are aware of my having an uncommon interest in Crawford."

Fanny was too well aware of it to have anything to say; and they walked on together some fifty yards in mutual silence and abstraction. Edmund first began again—

"I was very much pleased by *her* manner of speaking of it yesterday. I had not depended upon her seeing everything in so just a light. I knew she was very fond of you. Yet I was afraid of her not estimating your worth to her brother quite as it deserved, regretting that he had not fixed on some woman of distinction or fortune. But she spoke of you, Fanny, just as she ought. She desires the connexion as warmly as your uncle or myself. I should not have mentioned the subject, but she immediately introduced it with all that openness of heart, and sweet peculiarity of manner. Mrs. Grant even laughed at her rapidity."

"Was Mrs. Grant in the room, then?"

"Yes, when I reached the house I found the two sisters together by themselves; and when once we had begun, we had not done with you, Fanny, till Crawford and Dr. Grant came in."

"It is above a week since I saw Miss Crawford."

"Yes, she laments it; yet owns it may have been best. You will see her, however, before she goes. She is very angry with you, Fanny; you must be prepared for that. She calls herself very angry, but you can imagine her anger. It is the regret and disappointment of a sister, who thinks her brother has a right to everything he may wish for. She is hurt, as you would be for William; but she loves and esteems you with all her heart."

"I knew she would be very angry with me."

"My dearest Fanny," cried Edmund, pressing her arm closer to him, "do not let the idea distress you. Her heart is made for love and kindness, not for resentment. You should have seen her countenance when she said that you *should* be Henry's wife. And now she speaks of you as 'Fanny,' in sisterly cordiality."

"And Mrs. Grant, did she say—did she speak; was she there all the time?"

"Yes, she was agreeing exactly with her sister. Refusing such a man as Henry Crawford seems more than they can understand. You must prove yourself to be in your senses; nothing else will satisfy them. But this is teasing you. I have done. Do not turn away from me."

"I *should* have thought," said Fanny after a pause, "that every woman must accept the possibility of a man's not being approved. Furthermore, Mr. Crawford took me wholly by surprise. I had no idea that his behaviour to me before had any meaning."

"My dear, dear Fanny, now I have the truth. I told them that you were someone over whom habit had most power and novelty least; and that the very circumstance of the novelty of Crawford's addresses was against him. Miss Crawford made us laugh. She talked of having his addresses most kindly received by you at the end of about ten years' happy marriage."

Fanny could smile with difficulty. Her feelings were all in revolt. She feared she had been doing wrong: saying too much. To have Miss Crawford's liveliness repeated to her at such a moment was a bitter aggravation.

Edmund saw weariness and distress in her face, and immediately resolved to forbear all further discussion; not even to mention the name of Crawford again. He observed—"They go on Monday. I was within a trifle of being persuaded to stay at Lessingby till that very day! What a difference it might have made! Those five or six days more at Lessingby might have been felt all my life."

"You were near staying there?"

"Very. I was most kindly pressed, and had nearly consented. But I knew nothing that had happened here, and felt that I had been away long enough."

"You spent your time pleasantly there?"

"Yes; that is, it was the fault of my own mind if I did not. They were all very pleasant. But I doubt their finding me so."

"The Miss Owens—you liked them, did not you?"

"Yes, very well. But I am spoilt, Fanny, for common female society. Good-humoured, unaffected girls will not do for a man who has been used to sensible women. You and Miss Crawford have made me too particular."

Still, however, Fanny was oppressed and wearied. He saw it in her looks; it could not be talked away. With kindness, he returned her into the house.

Chapter XXXVI

Edmund now believed himself perfectly acquainted with all that Fanny could tell, and he was satisfied. Crawford had been too hasty. Time must be given to make the idea first familiar, and then agreeable to her. Once used to his being in love with her, a return of affection might follow.

He recommended to his father that nothing more be said to her, to influence or persuade. That everything should be left to Crawford, and the natural workings of her own mind.

Sir Thomas agreed it should be so. His only concern was that she might take too long, and the young man's inclination for her would be over.

The promised visit from Miss Crawford was a formidable threat to Fanny, and she lived in continual terror of it. Miss Crawford was an object of painful alarm—both as a sister, partial and angry, so little scrupulous of what she said, and as a *vampire* who might decide to extract unholy revenge. Her displeasure and her happiness were all fearful to encounter. Fanny's only hope was to have others present when they met. She absented herself as little as possible from Lady Bertram, kept away from the East room, and took no solitary walk in the shrubbery, in her caution to avoid any sudden *attack* (and here one does not imply Mrs. Norris). And now she always wore William's cross. . . .

She succeeded. She was safe in the breakfast-room, with her aunt, when Miss Crawford did come. The first misery over, and Miss Crawford looking and speaking with much less particularity than she had anticipated, Fanny began to hope there would be nothing worse to be endured than a half-hour of moderate agitation.

But here she hoped too much. Miss Crawford was determined to see Fanny alone, and said to her in a low voice, "I must speak to you for a few minutes somewhere;" *dark* words that Fanny felt all over her, in all her pulses and all her nerves. Denial was impossible. Her habits of ready submission, made her almost instantly rise and lead the way out of the room. She did it with wretched feelings, but it was inevitable.

It was as if the vampire was controlling her not by *unnatural* means but by force of a guilty conscience. *Evil has no power over me,* thought Fanny ruefully, *but duty does.*

They were no sooner in the hall than all restraint of countenance was over on Miss Crawford's side. She immediately shook her head at Fanny with arch, yet affectionate reproach, and took her hand. She said nothing, however, but, "Sad, sad girl! No, I shall not *bite!* How uncivil of me that would be, how many times must I reassure? But I do not know when I shall have done scolding you."

Miss Crawford had discretion enough to reserve the rest of the discussion till they might be alone. Fanny naturally turned upstairs, and took her guest to the apartment which was now always fit for comfortable use. Opening the door, she had a feeling that she was in for a very distressing scene. But the evil ready to burst on her was at least delayed by the sudden change in Miss Crawford's ideas; by the strong effect on her mind which the finding herself in the East room again produced.

"Ha!" she cried, with instant animation, "am I here again? The East room! Once only was I in this room before!"

She stopped to look about her, and seemingly to recollect, then added, "Once only before. Do you remember it? I came to rehearse. Your cousin came too; and we had a rehearsal. You were our audience and prompter. A delightful rehearsal. I shall never forget it."

Nether will I, thought Fanny. *You told me to dance a reel and I threatened you with a fireplace implement.* Out loud she said, "I remember we had an interesting exchange at the end."

Miss Crawford laughed, and chose to ignore the meaning.

"Here we were, just in this part of the room: here was your cousin, here was I, here were the chairs. Oh! why will such things ever pass away?"

Because I told you to get out?

Happily for her companion, she wanted no answer. Her mind was entirely self-engrossed. She was in a reverie of sweet *selective* remembrances.

"The scene we were rehearsing was so very remarkable! The subject of it so very—very—what shall I say? He was to be describing and recommending matrimony to me. It was very curious, that we should have such a scene to play! I never knew such exquisite happiness in any other than that acting week. His sturdy spirit to bend as it did! Oh! it was sweet beyond expression."

"If I recall," said Fanny, "his spirit was not bent but rather snared."

"Ah, silly Fanny! if I had wanted to snare him I had but to blink. I wanted much *more*. But alas, that very evening destroyed it all and brought your most unwelcome uncle. Poor Sir Thomas, who was glad to see you? Yet, do not imagine I would now speak disrespectfully of Sir Thomas, though I certainly did hate him for many a week."

"Hate comes easiest to such as yourself," said Fanny.

"Indeed," said the vampire. "That is why love and its more complex pursuit is so much more gratifying. But—no, I do Sir Thomas justice now. He is just what the head of such a family should be. Nay, in sober sadness, I believe I now love you all."

And having said so, with a degree of tenderness and consciousness which Fanny had never seen in her before, she turned away for a moment, as though to compose herself.

Presently she said, with a playful smile, "I am now recovered. Let us, dear Fanny, sit down and be comfortable. As to scolding you, which I came fully intending to do, I have not the heart for it."

And then, Miss Crawford smiled a brilliant, genuine, unusual smile and said, "Good, gentle Fanny! when I think of this being the last time of seeing you for I do not know how long, I feel it quite impossible to do anything but love you. Come, let us embrace! I feel very affectionately toward you!"

Fanny was affected despite herself. She had not foreseen anything of this, and her feelings could seldom withstand the melancholy influence of the word "last." She cried as if she had loved Miss Crawford, knowing full well *what* she was, and even so she could not help the moisture welling in her eyes.

Another moment and she would have moved forward with open arms, to embrace the *dark* creature without fear, and merely from a fullness of pity. But suddenly there was a movement in the air, as though a hot wind blew in, out of nowhere, filling the East room with dryness of the desert and a distant ancient perfume of lotus. . . .

Lord Easwind stood before them, in his somber raiment of an elegant gentleman of the ton. He raised his hand in a gesture of caution, and said, "No, Fanny, stop!"

Fanny was frozen in shock.

"No," he continued, looking at her with absolute earnestness. "You must not trust her now—not now, not ever. Do not embrace her darkness. For she means to deceive."

"East Wind!" said Fanny, her mind in a whirlwind. "You have come back! Oh, I had been certain you were gone, I was so sure, that you had quit this sphere—"

He looked at her sadly. "It had been my intent. At the ball, when madness took me as a result of your rejection, I raged, losing the last of my human self. . . . And then I recollected what it was I had loved in you. Unlike so many of the rest of us, you are a thing *unbroken*. And I could not bear to hurt you a moment longer. I left then, Fanny—Miss Price, as I must now once more call you, for I have no recourse to your dear name any more. I left, but I was *not* gone completely, for I could also not bear to be parted from you—not just yet. And thus, unknown to you, I watched you from a distance and from the shadows, and learned that your heart is truly *changed*—"

Miss Crawford interrupted him in that moment, with a furious "Ahem!" and a hiss. Her face was no longer radiant but terrifying. Fanny noted, with yet another measure of shock, that it had darkened and lost all of its rosy complexion, and Miss Crawford truly looked like an animated corpse. "Enough, long-dead, long-winded ancient!" the vampire exclaimed. "Your pretty attempt at rescue is foolish, and you have come to interfere yet again, something I will not tolerate!"

But Fanny was looking at him with a marveling expression. "You have delivered me," she whispered. "It is true, she almost had me! A moment and I would have been in her dark embrace—"

"Upon my word! I intended no such thing!" protested Miss Crawford, but her lengthened fangs certainly belied her words.

"Forgive me, Miss Price," he said, looking at Fanny only. "I had no intention of frightening you, or even letting you see me again—not after that evening when you saw me in all my horror and recoiled—as you justly ought. But I had to interfere. And now, I am once more to leave you, into the Shadow. For it is the one place I may now reside—a half-existence, while my spirit again malingers. Now, Miss Price, are you strong enough to remain with her? To be left alone?"

"I am," said Fanny in a whisper. "I—"

He inclined his head in the lightest gentlemanly bow.

And then he was *gone*.

Fanny watched the empty place where he had been, and took several deep breaths. She then turned to Miss Crawford and said, calmly: "I beg you to retract your teeth, Miss Crawford. There shall be no embracing and no *feeding* tonight. You deceived me with the most horrid method imaginable—kindness. But not ever again."

As though nothing had happened, Miss Crawford tried to speak as before, with an air of fondness. "Truly, I meant no harm! Indeed, I say this again; I hate to leave you. I shall see no one half so amiable where I am going. Who says we shall not be sisters? I feel that we are born to be connected; and those tears you shed, convince me that you felt it too, dear Fanny."

Fanny took another deep breath and resigned herself to hear out the platitudes yet again, but this time safely on her guard. Eventually she said, "But you are only going from one set of friends to another. You are going to a very particular friend."

"Yes, very true. Mrs. Fraser has been my intimate friend for years. But I have not the least inclination to go near her. You have all so much more *heart* among you than one finds in the world at large."

"Then, in Heaven's name, why call her a friend?"

"Ah, innocent Fanny! Friends are of an altogether different species in London."

Fanny shook her head, and firmly kept her hands on William's cross.

After this they sat silent: Fanny meditating on the different sorts of friendship in the world, Mary on something of less philosophic tendency. *She* first spoke again.

"How perfectly I remember my resolving to look for you upstairs, and setting off to find my way to the East room, without having an idea whereabouts it was! How well I remember—"

Sweet Lord in Heaven! Again! At this rate, she intends to kill me with her reminiscences! thought Fanny. And she listened in pained silence, for many long moments, to a very long discourse.

Finally Miss Crawford noted her companion's abstraction. "Why, Fanny, you are absolutely in a reverie."

Fanny opened her eyes with difficulty, wondering the other had not taken the soporific opportunity to feed on her—had she but known.

Miss Crawford switched to a topic of even more immediate *pain*. "Ah! You were thinking, I hope, of one who is always thinking of you. Oh! that I could transport you for a short time into our circle in town, that you might understand how your power over Henry is thought of there! Oh! the envyings and heartburnings of dozens and dozens; the wonder, the incredulity that will be felt at hearing what you have done! For as to secrecy, Henry is quite the hero of an old romance, and glories in his chains. You should come to London to know how to estimate your conquest. If you were to see how he is courted, and how I am courted for his sake!"

And Mary added, "Now, I am well aware that I shall not be half so welcome to Mrs. Fraser in consequence of his situation with you. When she comes to know the truth she will wish me in Northamptonshire again; for she has a stepdaughter whom she is wild to get married, and wants Henry to take. Oh! she has been trying for him to such a degree. Innocent and quiet as you sit here, you cannot have an idea of the *sensation* that you will be occasioning—"

"Pray, do not speak of that."

But Mary was relentless. "In their house, with their spirit of irritation, I shall call to mind the conjugal manners of Mansfield Parsonage with respect. In my heart, I shall be at Mansfield for ever, Fanny. My own sister as a wife, Sir Thomas Bertram as a husband, are my standards of perfection. Poor Janet has been sadly taken in, her match is not ideal—By the bye, another friend, Flora Ross was dying for Henry the first winter she came out. But were I to attempt to tell you of all the women whom I have known to be in love with him, I should never have done. It is you, only *you,* insensible Fanny, who can think of him with anything like indifference! But are you so insensible as you profess yourself? No, no, I see you are not."

There was, indeed, so deep a blush over Fanny's face at that moment as might warrant strong suspicion in a predisposed mind. In fact, it was utter frustration.

"Excellent creature! I will not tease you. Everything shall take its course. But, dear Fanny, you must allow that you were not so absolutely unprepared to have the question asked. You *must* have had some thoughts on the subject. You must have seen that Henry was trying to please you by every attention in his power. Was not he devoted to you at the ball—before all that delightful *mayhem,* of course? And then before the ball, the necklace! Oh! you received it just as it was meant, as conscious as heart could desire. I remember it perfectly."

"Do you mean, then, that your brother knew of the necklace beforehand? Oh! Miss Crawford, *that* was not fair."

"Knew of it! It was his own doing entirely, his own thought. I am ashamed to say that it had never entered my head, but I was delighted to act on his proposal for both your sakes."

"I will not say," replied Fanny, "that I was not half afraid at the time of its being so, for there was something in your look that frightened me for *another* reason than usual—but not at first. And had I any idea of it, nothing should have induced me to accept the necklace. As to your brother's behaviour, certainly I was sensible of a particularity. But then I considered it as meaning nothing, simply being his flippant way. I had not, Miss Crawford, been an inattentive observer of what was passing between him and some part of this family in the summer and autumn. I was quiet, but I was not blind. I saw what Mr. Crawford allowed himself in meaningless gallantries."

"Ah! I cannot deny it. And yes, Fanny, we all know how well you *see* things—it is part of your charm to those of us who can see also. He has been a sad flirt. I have often scolded him for it, but it is his only fault; and there is this to be said—very few young ladies have any affections worth caring for."

Fanny shook her head. "I cannot think well of a man who sports with any woman's feelings. There is often a great deal more suffered than a bystander can guess."

"I do not defend him. I leave him entirely to your mercy, and when he has got you at Everingham, you may lecture him. But his fault, the liking to make girls a little in love with him, is not half so dangerous to a wife's happiness as a tendency to fall in love himself, which he has never been addicted to. And I do seriously and truly believe that he is attached to you in a way that he never was to any woman before; that he loves you with all his heart, and will love you as nearly for ever as possible. If any man ever loved a woman for ever, I think Henry will do as much for you."

Another truly loves me for ever. . . .

Fanny could not avoid a faint smile, but had nothing to say.

For once Mary noticed. "Ah Fanny, I see! You are thinking now of your ancient pharaoh, your haunting lover out of the mists of time. Oh yes, I know all that, I have seen it over these many fortnights. Those of us who are *dark* can recognize and know one another—as you may well imagine. But Fanny, he is laughable—for he is *the past*. Forsake Egypt once and for all. He is but a ghost inhabiting a desiccated body. Not half as potent as a vampire, nor half as *alive*. Your life is yours now, and you may chuse again, safely. Henry is thus at your disposal. In *this* life."

But Fanny held herself back and again said nothing.

"I cannot imagine Henry ever to have been happier," continued Mary presently, "than when he had succeeded in getting your brother's commission."

She had made a sure push at Fanny's feelings here.

"Oh! Yes, I dare say, a rare and unusual kindness."

"I know he must have exerted himself very much. What a happy creature William must be! I wish we could see him."

Poor Fanny's mind was thrown into the most distressing of all its varieties. The recollection of what had been done for William was always the most powerful disturber of every decision against Mr. Crawford.

But Mary suddenly straightened. "Well! I should like to sit talking with you here all day, but we must not forget the ladies below, and so good-bye, my dear, my amiable, my excellent Fanny, I must take leave of you here—longing for a happy reunion under better circumstances. Again—forget the *past!* Think, only—Henry!"

Mary attempted an embrace, but Fanny threw a sidelong glance at the fireplace poker—at which Mary laughed genuinely.

"I shall see your cousin in town: he talks of being there tolerably soon; and Sir Thomas, in the course of the spring; and your eldest cousin, and the Rushworths, and Julia—all but you. Fanny, you must write to me. And you must often call on Mrs. Grant, and make up for my being gone."

Fanny would rather not have been asked, but it was impossible for her to refuse the correspondence. Besides, there was gratitude for their *tête-à-tête* being so much less painful than it could have been.

And whom had she to thank? Lord Eastwind! Fanny was amazed, and, despite herself, gratified that he was still *among* them, somehow; might appear again at a moment's notice. . . .

And yet—I am mad to consider this! To want *him here?*

She forcibly made herself change the direction of her thoughts. It was over, and she had escaped without reproaches and without detection. Her deepest *secret* was still her own. And while that was the case, she thought she could resign herself to almost everything. Let Miss Crawford continue to think that Henry had Lord Eastwind rather than Edmund for his competition (though on account of Lord Eastwind, again, Fanny's heart skipped a beat momentarily).

In the evening there was another parting. Henry Crawford came and sat some time with them. Her heart was softened for a while towards him, because he really seemed to *feel*. Quite unlike his usual self, he scarcely said anything. He was evidently oppressed, and Fanny must grieve for him—oh, poor Fanny! How *many* must she now grieve for?—though hoping she might never see him again till he were the husband of some other woman.

When it came to the moment of parting, he would take her hand, he would not be denied it. He said nothing, however, or nothing that she heard. And when he had left the room, she was better pleased that such a token of friendship had passed.

On the morrow the Crawfords were gone.

And yet—something altogether *different* was in the air.

Chapter XXXVII

Mr. Crawford gone, Sir Thomas's next object was that he should be missed by Fanny. Sir Thomas entertained great hope, watched her closely, but he could hardly tell if there was any change. She was always so gentle and retiring that her emotions were beyond his discrimination. He did not understand her, and therefore applied to Edmund to tell him how she was.

Edmund did not discern any symptoms of regret, and thought his father a little unreasonable in supposing the first three or four days could produce any.

What chiefly surprised Edmund was, that Crawford's sister, the friend and companion who had been so much to her (he thought), should not be more visibly regretted. He wondered that Fanny spoke so seldom of *her*.

Alas! it was this sister, this friend and companion, who was now the chief bane of Fanny's comfort. If she could have believed Mary's future fate as unconnected with Mansfield as she was determined the brother's should be, she would have been light of heart indeed.

But the more Fanny thought, the more deeply was she convinced that everything was now in a fairer train for Miss Crawford's marrying Edmund than it had ever been before. His inclination was stronger, hers less equivocal. His objections, the scruples of his integrity, seemed all done away; doubts and hesitations were equally got over—and equally without apparent reason. It had to be increasing attachment.

His good and her bad—indeed, *dark*—feelings yielded to love, and such love must unite them.

Edmund was to go to town soon; he talked of going, he loved to talk of it. And once he was with Miss Crawford again, Fanny could not doubt the rest. Her acceptance must be as certain as his offer. The prospect of it all was most grievous and harrowing to Fanny.

In their very last conversation, Miss Crawford, in spite of some amiable sensations, and attempts at bizarre personal kindness, had still been the same *undead* Miss Crawford; still led astray and bewildered, and (on so many levels) *darkened,* yet fancying herself growing toward light.

She might "love," in her own perverse, unnatural way, but she did not deserve Edmund by any other sentiment—even had she been fully human.

Fanny believed there was scarcely a second feeling in common between them, and chances of future improvement near impossible. For—if Edmund's influence in this season of love had already done so little in transforming her, his consequent effort would be fully wasted in the years of matrimony.

Such were Fanny's persuasions. She suffered very much, and could never speak of Miss Crawford without pain.

Sir Thomas, meanwhile, went on with his own hopes and observations. But another item gave him a sort of hope: William had obtained a ten days' leave of absence, and was coming to Northamptonshire, the happiest of lieutenants, to share his joy and describe his uniform.

He came; and he would have been delighted to bring his uniform, had not cruel custom prohibited its appearance except on duty. So the uniform remained at Portsmouth, and Edmund conjectured that before Fanny had any chance of seeing it, all its own freshness and all the freshness of its wearer's feelings must be worn away. So reasoned Edmund, till his father made him the confidant of a scheme which placed Fanny's chance of seeing the second lieutenant of H.M.S. *Thrush* in all his glory in another light.

This scheme was that Fanny should accompany her brother back to Portsmouth, and spend a little time with her own family.

It had occurred to Sir Thomas as a right and desirable measure, and he consulted his son. Edmund agreed it was an excellent notion. Furthermore, it was timely, and would be highly agreeable to Fanny. This was enough for Sir Thomas, and he pronounced a decisive "then so it shall be."

In fact, Sir Thomas had a different primary motive in sending her away—not to see her parents again, and not to make her happy. Rather, Sir Thomas had in mind a life lesson. He certainly wished her to go willingly, but he also wished her to be heartily sick of home before her visit ended. Sir Thomas conceived that a little abstinence from the elegancies and luxuries of Mansfield Park would bring her to better appreciate the value of that home of greater permanence, and equal comfort, of which she had the offer from Crawford.

A residence of eight or nine years in the abode of wealth and plenty had somewhat disordered Fanny's powers of comparing and judging. Her father's paltry house would teach her the value of a good income; and Sir Thomas trusted that she would benefit, in her future, for the experiment he had devised.

Fanny was in a quiet rapture when she first understood what was intended: when her uncle made her the offer of visiting the parents, brothers, and sisters, from whom she had been divided almost half her life; of returning for a couple of months to the scenes of her infancy, with William as the protector and companion of her journey.

She was delighted, but her happiness was of a subdued, deep, heart-swelling sort. She could only thank and accept. Afterwards, she could speak more largely to William and Edmund of what she felt. Tenderness and the remembrance of all her earliest pleasures, and her early suffering at parting, came over her with renewed strength. To be in the centre of a circle of family, loved by so many, and more loved by all than she had ever been before; to feel herself the *equal* of those who surrounded her; to be at peace from all mention of the Crawfords, safe from every reproachful look on their account. This was a prospect to be dwelt on!

Edmund, too—to be two months away from *him,* must do her good. At a distance, unassailed by his looks or his kindness, safe from the perpetual irritation of knowing his heart, and striving to avoid his confidence, she should be able to reason herself into a properer state. She should be able to think of him with *that creature* in London, without wretchedness—far easier to endure all this at Portsmouth.

The only drawback was the doubt of her aunt Bertram's being comfortable without her. She was of use to no one else; but *there* she might be missed to a degree that she did not like to think of. And, that part of the arrangement was, indeed, the hardest for Sir Thomas to accomplish.

But he was master at Mansfield Park. He did induce his wife to let her go; obtaining it rather from submission than conviction, for Lady Bertram was convinced of very little more than that Sir Thomas thought Fanny ought to go, and therefore that she must.

In the calmness of her own dressing-room, in the impartial flow of her own meditations (currently harboring a sorry *void* where used to repose all of Ancient Egypt), Lady Bertram could not acknowledge any necessity for Fanny's ever going near a father and mother who had done without her so long, while the girl was so useful to herself. And as to the not missing Fanny (which Mrs. Norris insisted), she refused to admit any such thing.

Sir Thomas had appealed to her reason, conscience, and dignity. He called it a sacrifice, and demanded it of her as such. But Mrs. Norris wanted to persuade her that Fanny could be very well spared.

"That may be, sister," was Lady Bertram's reply. "But I am sure I shall miss her very much."

The next step was to communicate with Portsmouth. Fanny wrote to offer herself. And her mother's answer, though short, was very kind—confirming all the daughter's views of finding happiness in being with her warm and affectionate "mama" (who had certainly shewn no remarkable fondness for her formerly). Now that Fanny knew better how to be useful (she thought) they should soon be what mother and daughter ought to be to each other.

William was almost as happy in the plan as his sister. It would be the greatest pleasure to him to have her there to the last moment before he sailed. And besides, he wanted her so very much to see the *Thrush* before she went out of harbour—the *Thrush* was certainly the finest sloop in the service—and there were several improvements in the dockyard, too, which he quite longed to show off.

"I do not know how it is," said he; "but we seem to want some of your nice ways and orderliness at my father's. The house is always in confusion. You will set things going in a better way. You will tell my mother how it all ought to be, and you will be so useful to Susan, and you will teach Betsey, and make the boys love and mind you!"

There remained but a very few days more to be spent at Mansfield. The young travellers had a minor alarm when Mrs. Norris found out that they were to travel post and was struck with the idea of there being room for a third in the carriage. She was suddenly seized with a strong inclination to go with them, to go and see her poor dear sister Price—and Mrs. Norris went on at great yapping length about it.

William and Fanny were horror-struck at the idea.

All the comfort of their comfortable journey would be destroyed at once. With woeful countenances they looked at each other. Their suspense lasted an hour or two.

Finally, it occurred to Mrs. Norris that, though taken to Portsmouth for nothing, she would not avoid having to pay with her own expenses for the trip back again. Suddenly she recalled that she could not possibly be spared from Mansfield Park at present, and must endure the sacrifice. Thus, her poor dear sister Price was left to all the disappointment of her missing such an opportunity, and another twenty years' absence, perhaps, begun.

Edmund's plans were also affected by this Portsmouth journey, this absence of Fanny's. He too had a sacrifice to make. He had intended, about this time, to be going to London. But now he could not leave his father and mother just when everybody else of most importance to their comfort was leaving them. And thus, with much secret regret, he delayed for a few weeks longer a journey which he hoped would fix his happiness for ever.

He told Fanny of it. She knew so much already, that she must know everything. They had another confidential discourse about Miss Crawford; and Fanny expected it to be the last time in which Miss Crawford's name would ever be mentioned so freely.

Lady Bertram told her niece in the evening to write to her soon and often. And Edmund, at a convenient moment, added in a whisper, "And *I* shall write to you, Fanny, when I have anything worth writing about, anything to say that I think you will like to hear, and that you will not hear so soon from any other quarter." Had she doubted his meaning while she listened, the glow in his face, when she looked up at him, would have been decisive.

Once more it struck her directly in the heart.

For this letter she must try to arm herself. That a letter from Edmund should be a subject of terror!

Poor Fanny! Though she was going willingly and eagerly, the last evening at Mansfield Park was still wretchedness. She was completely sad at parting, had tears for every room in the house, and more for every beloved inhabitant. She clung to her aunt, because she would miss her; she kissed the hand of her uncle with struggling sobs, because she had displeased him. And as for Edmund, she could neither speak, look, nor think, when the last moment came with *him.*

And it was not till it was over that she knew he was giving her the affectionate farewell of a *brother*.

All this passed overnight, for the journey was to begin very early in the morning. When the small, diminished party met at breakfast, William and Fanny were talked of as already gone.

Chapter XXXVIII

The novelty of travelling, and the happiness of being with William, soon produced their natural effect on Fanny's spirits. When Mansfield Park was far behind and they were to quit Sir Thomas's carriage, she was able to take leave of the old coachman, and send back proper messages, with cheerful looks.

There was no end of pleasant talk between the brother and sister. Everything supplied an amusement to the high glee of William's mind. He was full of frolic and joke in the intervals of their higher-toned subjects, all of which ended in praise of the *Thrush,* conjectures how she would be employed, schemes for military action which was to give himself the next promotion, and speculations upon prize-money: to be generously distributed at home (with only enough set aside for a little comfortable cottage, in which he and Fanny were to pass all the rest of their life together).

William also remembered with extreme delight Fanny's debut and *that ball.* "Say, whatever happened to those strange mummified things, Fanny?" he exclaimed. "Did we vanquish them or what? My hand had gotten sore from hacking with the sword and yet they would come! Upon my word, it was a marvel—Sir Thomas, with his wig askew! Lady Bertram all a soggy mess! Those stuffy lords and ladies in their finery, slipping in heaps on the dance floor! And oh! the monkeys, crazy monkeys! Ah! And Baddeley with his musket—"

"Dear William, I do not know. And, pray, let us please not talk about it."

And so William changed the subject with a laugh. But Fanny was momentarily made grave again by the memory, and the knowledge that she was now being watched by a certain ancient *someone,* always.

But—what indeed of all those mummies?

And now it must be told. Dear Reader, the mummies, no longer directed by the single powerful mind of their grand pharaoh—for, in that tragic moment of realization that he was no longer loved, he had released his hold of control over *himself* and over *all*, which unleashed them full force (while at the same time liberating Lady Bertram from her absurd servitude)—the mummies were now scattered at large!

Indeed, some of them had followed Mr. Rushworth's wolfish scent the next day to Brighton, where they began a minor unofficial rampage (not generally discussed in the local ton, though a number of young ladies had been accosted at a promenade and a couple of minor assemblies were infested). Others had naturally gone, in the wake of William, among other reasons, to Portsmouth, where they had lumbered about feeding comfortably on the seaside residents and being taken easily for "windblown sailors." The rest had moved on farther yet, to London! There, of course, the astute Reader can imagine, they simply blended in with the heterogeneous multitude and were hardly noticed at all.

Such was this dire state of matters, of which Fanny had no idea, as she neared Portsmouth with her dear brother.

Fanny's immediate concerns, as far as they involved Mr. Crawford, made no part of their conversation. William knew what had passed, and lamented that his sister's feelings should be so cold towards his kindest benefactor. But he was of an age to be all for love, and therefore unable to blame her, nor distress her by the slightest allusion.

She had reason to suppose herself not yet forgotten by Mr. Crawford. She had heard repeatedly from his sister within the three weeks which had passed since their leaving Mansfield. In each letter there had been a few lines from himself, warm and determined like his speeches.

It was a correspondence which Fanny found quite as unpleasant as she had feared. Miss Crawford's style of writing, lively and affectionate, was itself a flippant *evil,* independent of the portions written by her brother. And then, Edmund would never rest till she had read the whole thing to him. Therefore, Fanny had to listen to his admiration of Mary's language, and the warmth of her attachments.

There was such richness of *allusion* in every letter, that Fanny could not doubt it was always meant for him to hear. Being forced into this odious "intermediary" correspondence was cruelly mortifying. Fanny could only hope that, when she was no longer under the same roof with Edmund, Miss Crawford would have no motive for writing—at Portsmouth their correspondence would dwindle into nothing.

With such thoughts as these, Fanny proceeded in her journey safely and cheerfully, in this dirty month of February. They entered Oxford, but she could take only a hasty glimpse of Edmund's college as they passed along. Here Fanny noticed with vague familiarity a few odd lumbering fellows with scabby skin walking about stiffly, and one man bumping into a wall repeatedly, but did not pay them much heed.

They reached Newbury, where a comfortable meal, uniting dinner and supper, wound up the enjoyments and fatigues of the day.

The next morning saw them off again at an early hour. And uneventfully they at last were in the environs of Portsmouth while there was yet daylight for Fanny to look around and wonder at the new buildings. They passed the drawbridge, and entered the town. And the light was only beginning to fail as, guided by William's powerful voice, they were rattled into a narrow street, leading from the High Street, and drawn up before the door of a small house now inhabited by Mr. Price.

Fanny was all agitation and flutter; all hope and apprehension. The moment they stopped, a trollopy-looking maidservant, waiting for them at the door, stepped forward, and more intent on telling the news than giving them any help, immediately began with, "The *Thrush* is gone out of harbour, please sir, and one of the officers has been here to—"

She was interrupted by a fine tall boy of eleven. Rushing out of the house, he pushed the maid aside, and while William was opening the chaise-door himself, called out, "You are just in time! We have been looking for you this half-hour. The *Thrush* went out of harbour this morning. I saw her! It was a beautiful sight. And they think she will have her orders in a day or two. And Mr. Campbell was here at four o'clock to ask for you: he has got one of the *Thrush's* boats, and is going off to her at six, and hoped you would be here in time to go with him."

A stare or two at Fanny, as William helped her out of the carriage, was all the voluntary notice which this brother bestowed. But he made no objection to her kissing him, though still entirely engaged in detailing further particulars of the *Thrush's* going out of harbour.

Another moment and Fanny was in the narrow entrance-passage of the house, and in her mother's arms. Mrs. Price met her with looks of true kindness, and with features which Fanny loved the more, because they brought her aunt Bertram's before her. And there were her two sisters: Susan, a well-grown fine girl of fourteen, and Betsey, the youngest of the family, about five—both glad to see her in their way, though with no advantage of manner in receiving her. But manner Fanny did not want. Would they but love her, she should be satisfied.

She was then taken into a parlour, so small that her first conviction was of its being only a passage-room to something better. She stood for a moment expecting to be invited on. But when she saw there was no other door, and there were signs of habitation before her, she called back her thoughts, reproved herself, and grieved lest they should have been suspected.

Her mother, however, could not stay long enough to suspect anything. She was gone again to the street-door, to welcome William.

"Oh! my dear William, how glad I am to see you. But have you heard about the *Thrush?* She is gone out of harbour already; three days before we had any thought of it; and I do not know what I am to do about Sam's things, they will never be ready in time; for she may have her orders to-morrow, perhaps. It takes me quite unawares. And now you must be off for Spithead too. Campbell has been here, quite in a worry about you; and now what shall we do? I thought to have had such a comfortable evening with you, and here everything comes upon me at once."

Her son answered cheerfully, telling her that everything was always for the best; and making light of his own inconvenience in being obliged to hurry away so soon.

"To be sure, I had much rather she had stayed in harbour, that I might have sat a few hours with you in comfort; but as there is a boat ashore, I had better go off at once. Whereabouts does the *Thrush* lay at Spithead? But no matter; here's Fanny in the parlour! Come, mother, you have hardly looked at your own dear Fanny yet."

In they both came, and Mrs. Price kindly kissed her daughter again, and commented a little on her growth. She then began to fuss about them being fatigued.

"Poor dears! how tired you must both be! I began to think you would never come. Betsey and I have been watching for you this half-hour. And when did you get anything to eat?

And what would you like to have now? Some meat, or only a dish of tea? And now I am afraid Campbell will be here before there is time to dress a steak, and we have no butcher at hand. It is very inconvenient to have no butcher in the street. The neighborhood these days seems to have no decent folk, only a lot of odd-looking fellows, with atrocious skin, I dare say, all windblown—you could almost call it peeling like a bad onion! We were better off in our last house. Perhaps you would like some tea as soon as it can be got."

They both declared they should prefer it to anything. "Then, Betsey, my dear, run into the kitchen and see if Rebecca has put the water on; and tell her to bring in the tea-things as soon as she can. I wish we could get the bell mended; but Betsey is a very handy little messenger. And Rebecca needs be told twice; lately, she has got a wind-blown sailor fellow who follows her around, so her mind's off work—"

Betsey went with alacrity, proud to shew her abilities before her fine new sister.

"Dear me!" continued the anxious mother, "what a sad fire we have got, and I dare say you are both starved with cold. Draw your chair nearer, my dear. I cannot think what Rebecca has been about. I am sure I told her to bring some coals half an hour ago. Susan, you should have taken care of the fire."

"I was upstairs, mama, moving my things," said Susan, in a fearless, self-defending tone, which startled Fanny. "You know you had but just settled that my sister Fanny and I should have the other room; and I could not get Rebecca to give me any help."

Further discussion was prevented by various bustles: first, the driver came to be paid; then there was a squabble between Sam and Rebecca about the manner of carrying up his sister's trunk. And lastly, in walked Mr. Price himself, his own loud voice preceding him, as with something of the oath kind he kicked away his son's port-manteau and his daughter's bandbox in the passage, and called out for a candle. No candle was brought, however, and he walked into the room.

Uncertain, Fanny had risen to meet him, but sank down again on finding herself undistinguished in the dusk, and unthought of. With a friendly shake of his son's hand, and an eager voice, he instantly began—"Ha! welcome back, my boy. Glad to see you. Have you heard the news? The *Thrush* went out of harbour this morning." And then he went on at great length with loud inebriated animation, concluding with: "If ever there was a perfect beauty afloat, she is one; and there she lays at Spithead, and anybody in England would take her for an eight-and-twenty. I was upon the platform two hours this afternoon looking at her. She lays close to the *Endymion,* between her and the *Cleopatra,* just to the eastward of the sheer hulk."

"Ha!" cried William, "*that's* just where I should have put her myself. It's the best berth at Spithead. But here is my sister, sir; here is Fanny," turning and leading her forward; "it is so dark you do not see her."

With an acknowledgment that he had quite forgot her, Mr. Price now received his daughter. Having given her a cordial hug, and observed that she was grown into a woman, and he supposed would be wanting a husband soon, he seemed very much inclined to forget her again.

Fanny shrunk back to her seat, sadly pained by his language and his smell of spirits. He talked only to his son, and only of the *Thrush,* though William, warmly interested as he was in that subject, more than once tried to make his father think of Fanny, and her long absence and long journey.

After sitting some time longer, a candle was obtained. But there was still no appearance of tea, nor, from Betsey's reports from the kitchen, much hope of any. William determined to go and change his dress, and make the necessary preparations for his removal on board directly, that he might have his tea in comfort afterwards.

As he left the room, two rosy-faced boys, ragged and dirty, about eight and nine years old, rushed in. They were Tom and Charles, just released from school, and coming eagerly to see their sister, and tell that the *Thrush* was gone out of harbour.

"And then, did you see that?" Tom was yelling, "I saw him! The sailor leaned over old Mrs. Potts and he sucked her breath away! He looked all like a scarecrow, and his face was brown like a dry apple, and his skin was peeling worse than the deck of an old sloop! And Mrs. Potts, she just keeled over and fell, and the old dog just walked away! I bet *his* like won't be found on the *Thrush,* he sails some dirty old dingy—"

Charles had been born since Fanny's going away. But Tom she had often helped to nurse, and now felt a particular pleasure in seeing again—though Fanny had to admit his words about a sailor with peeling skin gave her some alarm and pause.

Both were kissed very tenderly. But Tom she wanted to keep by her, to try to trace the features of the baby she had loved, and talked to, of his infant preference of herself. Tom, however, had no mind for such treatment. He came home not to stand and be talked to, but to run about and make a noise. Both boys had soon burst from her, and slammed the parlour-door till her temples ached.

She had now seen all that were at home. There remained only two brothers between herself and Susan, one of whom was a clerk in a public office in London, and the other midshipman on board an Indiaman. But though she had *seen* all the members of the family, she had not yet *heard* all the noise they could make.

William was soon calling out from the landing-place of the second story for his mother and for Rebecca. He was in distress for something he could not find. A key was mislaid. Betsey was accused of having got at his new hat. And some slight, but essential alteration of his uniform waistcoat was entirely neglected.

Mrs. Price, Rebecca, and Betsey all went up to defend themselves, all talking together, but Rebecca loudest. And all was to be done in a great hurry. William tried in vain to send Betsey downstairs, to keep her from being troublesome. Since almost every door in the house was open, all this clamor was plainly distinguished in the parlour, except when drowned at intervals by the superior noise of Sam, Tom, and Charles chasing each other up and down stairs, and tumbling about and hallooing. All that was missing was one loose baboon. . . .

Fanny was almost stunned. The smallness of the house and thinness of the walls brought everything so close to her, that, added to the fatigue of her journey, and all her recent agitation, she hardly knew how to bear it.

Within the room all was tranquil enough. Susan had disappeared with the others. There were only her father and herself remaining. And he, taking out a newspaper (borrowed from a neighbour), applied himself to studying it, without seeming to recall Fanny's existence.

The solitary candle was held between himself and the paper, without any thought of her convenience. But she had nothing to do, and was glad to have the light screened from her aching head, as she sat in bewildered, broken, sorrowful contemplation.

She was at home. But, alas! it was not such a home, she had not such a welcome, as—she checked herself; she was unreasonable. What right had she to be of importance to her family? She could have none, so long lost sight of! William's concerns must be dearest, they always had been, and he had every right.

Yet to have so little said or asked about herself, to have scarcely an inquiry made after Mansfield! It pained her to have Mansfield forgotten; the dear friends who had done so much! But here, one subject swallowed up all the rest. The destination of the *Thrush*—it alone was preeminently interesting.

A day or two might shew the difference. *She* only was to blame. Yet she thought it would not have been so at Mansfield. No, in her uncle's house there would have been consideration, propriety, an attention towards everybody, which was not here.

The only interruption to her thoughts was from a sudden burst of her father's. At a more than ordinary pitch of thumping and hallooing in the passage, he exclaimed, "Devil take those young dogs! How they are singing out! Ay, Sam's voice louder than all the rest! That boy is fit for a boatswain. Holla, you there! Sam, stop your confounded pipe, or I shall be after you."

This threat was palpably disregarded. Though within five minutes afterwards the three boys all burst into the room together and sat down, Fanny could not consider it as a proof of anything more than their being thoroughly fagged. Their hot faces and panting breaths were evidence enough, especially as they were still kicking each other's shins, and hallooing out at sudden starts immediately under their father's eye.

The next opening of the door brought something more welcome: it was for the tea-things, which she had begun almost to despair of seeing that evening. Susan and an attendant girl, whose inferior appearance informed Fanny, to her great surprise, that she had previously seen the upper servant, brought in everything necessary for the meal.

As she put the kettle on the fire and glanced at her sister, Susan appeared torn between shewing her industriousness, and the dread of being thought to demean herself by such. "She had been into the kitchen," she said, "to hurry Sally and help make the toast, and spread the bread and butter, or she did not know when they should have got tea, and she was sure her sister must want something after her journey."

Fanny was very thankful. She admitted she was very glad of a little tea, and Susan immediately set about making it, as if pleased to have the employment all to herself, and acquitted herself very well. Fanny's spirit was as much refreshed as her body, as a result of such well-timed kindness.

Susan had an open, sensible countenance. She was like William, and Fanny hoped to find her like him in disposition and goodwill towards herself.

In this more placid state of things William reentered, followed by his mother and Betsey. He, complete in his lieutenant's uniform, looking and moving all the taller, firmer, and more graceful for it, and with the happiest smile over his face, walked up directly to Fanny. She, rising from her seat, looked at him for a moment in speechless admiration, and then threw her arms round his neck to sob out her various emotions of pain and pleasure.

Anxious not to appear unhappy, she soon recovered herself. Wiping away her tears, she noticed and admired all the striking parts of his dress; listening with reviving spirits to his cheerful hopes of being on shore some part of every day before they sailed, and even of getting her to Spithead to see the sloop.

The next bustle brought in Mr. Campbell, the surgeon of the *Thrush,* a very well-behaved young man, who came to call for his friend. "Upon my word," Mr. Campbell said immediately, "I just had to beat off some rotting fellow with a stick! Three doors down, he leaned in and looked like he was about to kiss me—!"

A chair was found for him, and with some hasty washing, a cup and saucer. And after another quarter of an hour of earnest talk between the gentlemen, noise and bustle, men and boys at last all in motion together, the moment came for setting off. Everything was ready, William took leave, and all of them were gone—the three boys, in spite of their mother's entreaty, determined to see their brother and Mr. Campbell to the sally-port. And Mr. Price walked off at the same time to carry back his neighbour's newspaper.

Something like tranquility might now be hoped for. Rebecca had finally been prevailed on to carry away the tea-things (and for the first time in her life Fanny longingly thought of committing violence upon an actual *non-cursed* being with her fireplace poker). Mrs. Price walked about the room some time looking for a shirt-sleeve, which Betsey at last found in a kitchen drawer. At last, the small party of females was pretty well composed. The mother, having lamented again over the impossibility of getting Sam ready in time, was now at leisure to think of her eldest daughter and the friends she had come from.

A few inquiries began: but one of the earliest—"How did sister Bertram manage about her servants?" "Was she as much plagued as herself to get tolerable servants?"—soon led Mrs. Price's mind away from Northamptonshire, and fixed it on her own domestic grievances. The shocking character, not to mention the peeling skin and poor attitude of all the Portsmouth servants, of whom she believed her own two were the very worst, engrossed her completely. There were just too many louts out and about, according to Mrs. Price. Strange, oddly lumbering stiff fellows, so stiff, one could almost say *deceased*—she could have sworn she saw a dog lift its leg and pee on one!

Fanny listened, with dawning suspicion and alarm.

The Bertrams were thus all forgotten in detailing the faults of the neighborhood in general—and Rebecca in particular, against whom Susan had also much to depose, and little Betsey a great deal more, and who did seem so thoroughly without a single recommendation, that Fanny could not help modestly presuming that her mother meant to part with her when her year was up.

"Her year!" cried Mrs. Price; "I am sure I hope I shall be rid of her before she has staid a year, for that will not be up till November. And now, I dare say, she has a sailor following her around! Grim silent foreign fellow, stiff as a board, shedding bits of rag—not someone I want entering *my* kitchen! Servants are come to such a pass, my dear, in Portsmouth, that it is quite a miracle if one keeps them more than half a year. Whence do they all come, anyway, such horrid unkempt things? I have no hope of ever being settled; and if I was to part with Rebecca, I should only get something worse. Mrs. Garvey from next door got a pair of fool servants who, between the two of them, broke down her back wall completely by bumping into it so much! Have you ever heard of such a thing? And yet I do not think I am a very difficult mistress to please; and with Rebecca, I am sure the place is easy enough, for there is always a girl under her, and I often do half the work myself."

Fanny was silent; but not from being convinced that there might not be a remedy found for some of these evils.

She was thinking of *mummies*. Could they be here? All the way down here, at Portsmouth? And what of their ancient lord?

Fanny's heart began to ache again with a profusion of mixed emotions.

As she now sat looking at Betsey, she could not but think particularly of another sister, a very pretty little girl, whom she had left there not much younger when she went into Northamptonshire, who had died a few years afterwards. There had been something remarkably amiable about her. Is it not so with all the *dead?* But no, do not think—

Fanny in those early days had preferred her to Susan. And when the news of her death had at last reached Mansfield, she had been quite afflicted. The sight of Betsey brought the image of little Mary back again. But she would not have pained her mother by alluding to her for the world. While considering her thus, Fanny noticed that Betsey was holding out something to catch her eyes, meaning to screen it at the same time from Susan's.

"What have you got there, my love?" said Fanny; "come and shew it to me."

It was a silver knife.

Silver is a pure holy metal, used as a defense against the dark—werewolves can die from it, vampires will be marked and harmed—Fanny remembered Edmund telling all this to her once; oh so long ago it seemed, when they still regularly discussed the Mansfield Curse.

Up jumped Susan, claiming the knife as her own, and trying to get it away. But the child ran to her mother's protection, and Susan could only reproach, which she did very warmly, and evidently hoping to interest Fanny on her side. "It was very hard that she was not to have her *own* knife; it was her own knife; little sister Mary had left it to her upon her deathbed, and she ought to have had it to keep herself long ago. But mama kept it from her, and was always letting Betsey get hold of it; Betsey would spoil it, and get it for her own, though mama had *promised* her that Betsey should not have it."

Fanny was quite shocked. Every feeling of duty, honour, and tenderness was wounded by her sister's speech and her mother's reply.

"Now, Susan," cried Mrs. Price, in a complaining voice, "now, how can you be so cross? You are always quarrelling about that knife. Poor little Betsey; how cross Susan is to you! But you should not have taken it out, my dear, when I sent you to the drawer. You know I told you not to touch it, because Susan is so cross about it. I must hide it again, Betsey. Poor Mary little thought it would be such a bone of contention when she gave it me to keep, only two hours before she died. Poor little soul! she could barely speak, and she said so prettily, 'Let sister Susan have my knife, mama, when I am dead and buried.' Poor little dear! she was so fond of it, Fanny, that she would have it lay by her in bed, all through her illness. It was the gift of her good godmother, old Mrs. Admiral Maxwell, only six weeks before she was taken for death. Poor little sweet creature! Well, she was taken away from evil to come. My own Betsey" (fondling her), "*you* have not the luck of such a good godmother. Aunt Norris lives too far off to think of such little people as you."

The last thing aunt Norris, a werewolf, would be gifting is a thing of silver, Fanny thought. *For that matter, a non-lupine aunt Norris were equally unlikely to give away silver, due to an even more dire condition called frugality.*

Fanny had indeed nothing to convey from aunt Norris, but a message to say she hoped that her god-daughter was a good girl, and learnt her book. There had been at one moment a slight murmur in the drawing-room at Mansfield Park about sending her a prayer-book, but nothing came of it. Mrs. Norris had gone home and taken down two old prayer-books of her husband with that idea. But, upon examination, the ardour of generosity went off. One was found to have too small a print for a child's eyes, and the other to be too cumbersome for her to carry about.

Fatigued and unable to sit much longer, Fanny was thankful to accept the invitation of going to bed. Before Betsey had finished crying at being allowed to sit up only *one* extra hour in honour of sister, she was off, leaving all below in confusion and noise again—the boys begging for toasted cheese, her father calling out for his rum and water, and Rebecca never where she ought to be, and very likely consorting with a mummy. . . .

There was nothing to raise Fanny's spirits in the confined and scantily furnished chamber that she was to share with Susan. The smallness of the rooms above and below, the narrowness of the passage and staircase, all struck her beyond her imagination. She soon learned to think with respect of her own little attic at Mansfield Park, in *that* house reckoned too small for anybody's comfort.

Chapter XXXIX

Could Sir Thomas have seen all his niece's feelings, when she wrote her first letter to her aunt, he would not have despaired. Though a good night's rest, a pleasant morning, the hope of soon seeing William again, and the comparatively quiet state of the house (Tom and Charles being gone to school, Sam on some project of his own, and her father on his usual lounges), enabled Fanny to express herself cheerfully on the subject of home, there were still many drawbacks withheld. Could he have seen only half that she felt before the end of a week, he would have thought Mr. Crawford sure of her, and been delighted with his own sagacity.

Before the week ended, it was all disappointment. In the first place, William was gone. The *Thrush* had had her orders, the wind had changed, and he was sailed within four days from their reaching Portsmouth. During those days she had seen him only twice, in a short and hurried way, when he had come ashore on duty.

There had been no free conversation, no walk on the ramparts, no visit to the dockyard, no acquaintance with the *Thrush*—nothing of their plans. Everything in that quarter failed her, except William's affection. His last thought on leaving home was for her. He stepped back again to the door to say,

"Take care of Fanny, mother. She is tender, and not used to roughing it like the rest of us. I charge you, take care of Fanny."

William was gone: and the home he had left her in was the very reverse of what she could have wished. It was the abode of noise, disorder, and impropriety. Nobody was in their right place, nothing was done as it ought to be.

She could not respect her parents as she had hoped. Of her father, her expectations had not been high. But he was more negligent of his family, his habits were worse, and his manners coarser, than she had been prepared for. He did not lack abilities but he had no curiosity, and no learning beyond his profession. He read only the newspaper and the navy-list; he talked only of the dockyard, the harbour, Spithead, and the Motherbank. He swore and he drank, he was dirty and gross. About the only thing he *did not* have was desiccated peeling skin. . . .

Fanny had never been able to recall anything approaching to tenderness in his former treatment of herself. There had remained only a general impression of roughness and loudness; and now he scarcely ever noticed her, but to make her the object of a coarse joke.

Her disappointment in her mother was greater: *there* she had hoped much, and found almost nothing. Every flattering scheme of being of consequence to her soon fell to the ground. Mrs. Price was not unkind; but, instead of gaining on her affection and confidence, and becoming more and more dear, her daughter never met with greater kindness from her than on the first day of her arrival.

The instinct of nature was soon satisfied, and Mrs. Price's attachment had no other source. Her heart and her time were already quite full; she had neither leisure nor affection to bestow on Fanny. Her daughters never had been much to her. She was fond of her sons, especially of William, but Betsey was the first of her girls whom she had ever much regarded. To her she was most injudiciously indulgent. William was her pride;

Betsey her darling; and John, Richard, Sam, Tom, and Charles occupied all the rest of her maternal solicitude, her worries and her comforts. These shared her heart: her time was given chiefly to her house and her servants. Her days were spent in a kind of slow bustle; all was busy without getting on, always behindhand and lamenting it, without altering her ways; wishing to be an economist, without contrivance or regularity; dissatisfied with her servants, without skill to make them better, and whether helping, or reprimanding, or indulging them, without any power of engaging their respect.

Of her two sisters, Mrs. Price very much more resembled Lady Bertram than Mrs. Norris. She was a manager by necessity, without any of Mrs. Norris's inclination for it, or any of her activity. Her disposition was naturally easy and indolent, like Lady Bertram's; and a situation of similar affluence and do-nothingness would have been much more suited to her capacity than the exertions and self-denials of the one which her imprudent marriage had placed her in. She might have made just as good a woman of consequence as Lady Bertram, but Mrs. Norris would have been a more respectable mother of nine children on a small income—that is, if, of course, had she not been *ruled* by the dire regime of the full moon.

Much of all this Fanny realized. She might not dare utter it, but she felt that her mother was a partial, ill-judging parent, a dawdle, a slattern, who neither taught nor restrained her children, whose house was the scene of mismanagement and discomfort from beginning to end, and who had no talent, no conversation, no affection towards herself; no curiosity to know her better, no desire of her friendship, and no inclination for her company.

Fanny was very anxious to be useful, and not to appear above her home, or in any way disqualified or disinclined, by her foreign education, from contributing her help, and therefore set about working for Sam immediately. By working early and late, with perseverance, she did so much that the boy was shipped off at last, with more than half his linen ready. She could not conceive how they would have managed without her.

Sam, loud and overbearing as he was, she rather missed, for he was clever and intelligent, and glad to be employed in any errand in the town. And though spurning the weak remonstrances of Susan, he was beginning to be influenced by Fanny's services and gentle persuasions. She found him the best of the three younger boys after he had gone. Tom and Charles were his juniors, still distant from that age of feeling and reason, and uninterested in making friends or being less disagreeable. Their sister soon despaired of making the smallest impression on *them.* They were untameable. Every afternoon brought a return of their riotous games all over the house; and she very early learned to sigh at the approach of Saturday's constant half-holiday.

Betsey, too, was a spoiled child, the alphabet her greatest enemy, left with the servants at her pleasure, and then encouraged to report any evil of them—Fanny found it hard to love or help her. And of Susan's temper she had many doubts. Her continual disagreements with her mother, her rash squabbles with Tom and Charles, and petulance with Betsey, were very distressing to Fanny. She feared Susan might turn out far from amiable.

Such was the home which was to put Mansfield out of her head, and teach her to think of her cousin Edmund with moderated feelings.

On the contrary, she could think of nothing but Mansfield, its beloved inmates, its happy ways. The elegance, propriety, regularity, harmony, and perhaps, above all, the peace and tranquility of Mansfield, despite its deeply concealed unnatural Curse, were brought to her remembrance every hour of the day.

To the delicate and nervous Fanny, living in incessant noise was a harrowing evil that nothing could ameliorate. It was the greatest misery of all.

At Mansfield, no sounds of contention, no raised voice, no abrupt bursts, no tread of violence, was ever heard; everybody had their due importance; everybody's feelings were consulted. If tenderness was wanting, good sense and good breeding supplied its place. And as to the little irritations sometimes introduced by aunt Norris (such as the most recent regular wartime in the shrubbery), they were short, trifling, as a drop of water to the ocean, compared with the ceaseless tumult of her present abode.

Here everybody was noisy, every voice was loud (excepting, perhaps, her mother's, which resembled the soft monotony of Lady Bertram's, only worn into fretfulness). Whatever was wanted was hallooed for, and the servants hallooed out their excuses from the kitchen. The doors were in constant banging, the stairs were never at rest, nothing was done without a clatter, nobody sat still, and nobody could command attention when they spoke.

In a review of the two houses, as they appeared to her before the end of a week, Fanny was tempted to apply to them Dr. Johnson's celebrated judgment as to matrimony and celibacy, and say, that though Mansfield Park might have some pains, Portsmouth could have no pleasures.

Chapter XL

Fanny was right, not to expect to hear from Miss Crawford at the rapid rate in which their correspondence had begun. Mary's next letter came after a longer interval, but at no great relief to herself.

Here was another strange revolution of mind! Fanny was *glad* to receive the letter when it did come. In her present exile from good society, a letter from one belonging to the set where her heart lived, written with affection and elegance, was thoroughly acceptable. The usual plea of increasing engagements was made in excuse for not having written to her earlier.

> "And now that I have begun," Mary continued, "my letter will not be worth your reading, for there will be no little offering of love at the end from the most devoted H. C. in the world, for Henry is in Norfolk. Business called him to Everingham ten days ago. But there he is, and his absence accounts for any remissness of his sister's in writing. There has been no 'Well, Mary, is not it time for you to write to Fanny?' to spur me on. At last, I have seen your cousins, 'dear Julia and dearest Mrs. Rushworth'; they found me at home yesterday. We *seemed very* glad to see each other, and I do really think we were a little. We had a vast deal to say. Shall I tell you how Mrs. Rushworth looked when your name was mentioned? I did not use to think her wanting in self-possession, but she had not quite

> enough for the demands of yesterday. Upon the whole, Julia was in the best looks of the two, at least after you were spoken of. There was no recovering the complexion from the moment that I spoke of 'Fanny'—spoke of her as a sister should. But Mrs. Rushworth's day of good looks will come; we have cards for her first party on the 28th. Then she will be in beauty, for she will open one of the best houses in Wimpole Street. I was in it two years ago, when it was Lady Lascelle's, and prefer it to almost any I know in London. Henry could not have afforded her such a house. I hope she will recollect it, and be satisfied. As I have no desire to tease her, I shall never *force* your name upon her again. Meanwhile, Baron Wildenheim's attentions to Julia continue, but I do not know if he has serious encouragement. She ought to do better. A poor honourable is no catch; take away his rants, and the poor baron has nothing. If his rents were but equal to his rants! Your cousin Edmund moves slowly; detained, perchance, by parish duties. There may be some old woman at Thornton Lacey to be converted. I am unwilling to fancy myself neglected for a *young* one. Adieu! my dear sweet Fanny, this is a long letter from London: write me a pretty one in reply to gladden Henry's eyes, when he comes back, and send me an account of all the dashing young captains whom you disdain for his sake."

There was great food for chiefly unpleasant meditation in this letter. And yet, it connected her, told her of people and things about whom she had never felt so much curiosity as now. Fanny would have been glad of such a letter every week. Her correspondence with her aunt Bertram was her only concern of higher interest.

As for any society in Portsmouth, that could at all make amends for deficiencies at home, there were none within the circle of her father's and mother's acquaintance to afford her the smallest satisfaction. Fanny saw nobody in whose favour she could wish to overcome her own shyness and reserve. The men appeared to her all coarse (and some indeed has terrifying skin, though, not to the degree of mummification, merely nautical and windblown), the women all pert, everybody underbred (and some appearing rather *inbred*); and she gave as little contentment as she received from introductions either to old or new acquaintance. The young ladies who approached her at first with some respect, in consideration of her coming from a baronet's family, were soon offended by what they termed "airs." Since she neither played on the pianoforte nor wore fine pelisses, they could hand her no right of superiority.

The first solid consolation which Fanny received, was in a better acquaintance with Susan. Susan had always behaved pleasantly to herself, but the determined character of her general manners had astonished and alarmed Fanny. It was at least a fortnight before she began to understand a disposition so totally different from her own.

Susan saw that much was wrong at home, and wanted to set it right. That a girl of fourteen, acting only on her own unassisted reason, should err in the method of reform, was not surprising. Fanny soon became more disposed to admire the natural inclination, than to censure the faults of conduct to which it led. Susan was only acting on the same truths that her own judgment acknowledged. Susan tried to be useful, where *Fanny* might only have gone away and cried. Indeed, things at home would have been worse but for such interposition. Both her mother and Betsey needed to be restrained from offensive indulgence and vulgarity.

In every argument with her mother, Susan had the advantage of reason, and never was there any maternal tenderness to buy her off. She had never known the blind fondness which was for ever producing household evil.

All this became gradually evident, and placed Susan before her sister as an object of mingled compassion and respect. Her manner was wrong, her measures often ill-chosen and ill-timed, her looks and language often indefensible. Yet Fanny felt they might be rectified. Susan looked up to her and wished for her good opinion. And while an office of authority was new to

Fanny—*new* to imagine herself capable of guiding or informing any one—she resolved to give occasional hints to Susan, and share some of her own more favoured education.

Fanny's influence originated in an act of kindness to Susan. It had very early occurred to her that a small sum of money might, perhaps, restore peace for ever on the sore subject of the silver knife, canvassed as it now was continually. Her uncle had given her £10 at parting, and she was willing to be generous. But she was so unused to conferring favours, so unpractised in removing ordinary evils of the non-supernatural kind, or bestowing kindnesses among her equals, and so fearful of appearing to elevate herself as a great lady at home, that it took some time to dare make such a present.

It was made, however, at last. A silver knife was bought for Betsey (and Fanny had in mind *protection* from the *dark* as well as pleasure), and accepted with great delight, its newness giving it every advantage over the other.

Susan was established in the full possession of her own knife. Betsey declared that now she had got one so much prettier herself, she should never want *that* again. And no reproach came from the equally satisfied mother. In one fell swoop, a source of domestic altercation was entirely done away, and it was the means of opening Susan's heart to Fanny.

Susan shewed that she had delicacy: pleased as she was to be mistress of an item for which she had been struggling for at least two years, she yet feared that her sister's act was a gentle reproof designed to establish tranquility in the house.

Her temper was open. She acknowledged her fears, blamed herself for having contended so warmly; and from that hour Fanny understood the worth of her disposition and began to feel again the blessing of affection. She gave advice, too sound to be resisted by a good understanding, and given so mildly and considerately as not to irritate an imperfect temper. And she had the happiness of observing its good effects. More was not expected—Fanny saw with sympathy all that was hourly grating to a girl like Susan. Her greatest wonder soon became that so many good notions should have been hers at all, under the circumstances. Brought up in the midst of negligence and error, Susan had managed to form a solid proper foundation all on her own—she, who had had no cousin Edmund to direct her thoughts or fix her principles.

The intimacy thus begun between them was an advantage to each. By sitting together upstairs, they avoided a great deal of the disturbance of the house; Fanny had peace, and Susan learned to be quietly employed. They sat without a fire; but that was a privation familiar even to Fanny, and she suffered the less because reminded by it of the East room.

It was the only point of resemblance. There was nothing alike in the two apartments. Fanny often heaved a sigh at the remembrance of all her books and boxes, and various comforts at Mansfield. By degrees the girls came to spend the mornings upstairs, at first only in working and talking, but after a few days, the remembrance of the said books grew so potent that Fanny found it impossible not to try for books again.

There were none in her father's house. But wealth is luxurious and daring, and some of hers found its way to a circulating library. She became a subscriber; amazed at her own doings in every way, to be a renter, a chuser of books! And to chuse with another's improvement in mind! But so it was. Susan had read nothing, and Fanny longed to share her own first pleasures, and inspire a taste for the biography and poetry which she delighted in.

In this occupation she hoped to bury some of the recollections of Mansfield. Reading might divert her thoughts from pursuing Edmund to London. She had no doubt of what would ensue there. The promised notification was hanging over her head. The postman's knock brought its daily terrors, and reading could at least temporarily banish them.

Chapter XLI

A week was gone since Edmund might be supposed in town, and Fanny had heard nothing. There were three different conclusions to be drawn from his silence. Either his going had been again delayed, or he had yet procured no opportunity of seeing Miss Crawford alone, or he was too happy for letter-writing!

One morning, having now been nearly four weeks from Mansfield, Fanny and Susan were preparing to remove, as usual, upstairs. They were stopped by the knock of a visitor, whom they felt they could not avoid, judging from Rebecca's alertness in going to the door, a duty which always interested her beyond any other.

It was a gentleman's voice—a voice that Fanny was just turning pale about, when Mr. Crawford walked into the room.

Good sense will always act when really called upon. Fanny found that she had been able to name him to her mother, and recall her remembrance of the name, as that of "William's friend," though she could not previously have believed herself capable of uttering a syllable at such a moment.

Mr. Crawford, here at Portsmouth! Fanny wanted nothing more than to disappear like a little mouse into the floor (where either Mr. Rushworth or Mrs. Norris were more than welcome to do away with her—a fate less disastrous than what awaited her in the present moment).

The consciousness of his being known there only as William's friend was some support. Having introduced him, and being all reseated, Fanny did not know how to proceed next. The terrors of what this visit might lead to were overpowering, and she fancied herself on the point of fainting away.

While Fanny was trying to keep herself alive, their visitor, who had at first approached her with as animated a countenance as ever, was wisely and kindly keeping his eyes away, and giving her time to recover. Indeed, he devoted himself entirely to her mother, addressing her, and attending to her with the utmost politeness and propriety, at the same time with a degree of friendliness, of interest at least, which was making his manner perfect.

Mrs. Price's manners were also at their best. Warmed by the sight of such a friend to her son, and wishing to appear to advantage before him, she was overflowing with gratitude—artless, maternal gratitude—which could not be unpleasing. Mr. Price was out, which she regretted very much.

Fanny was just recovered enough to feel that *she* could not regret it. For, as mentioned before, short of having that telltale peeling skin and the movements of a walking stiff, her father was decidedly *unpresentable*. Furthermore, to her many other sources of uneasiness was now added the severe one of shame for the home in which Mr. Crawford found her. She might scold herself for the weakness, but there was no scolding it away. She was ashamed, and she would have been yet more ashamed of her father than of all the rest.

They talked of William, a subject on which Mrs. Price could never tire. Here, Mr. Crawford was as warm in his commendation as even her heart could wish. Mrs. Price felt that she had never seen so agreeable a man in her life. She was only astonished to find that, so great and so agreeable as he was, he should be come down to Portsmouth neither on a visit to the port-admiral, nor the commissioner, nor yet with the intention of going over to the island, nor of seeing the dockyard.

Nothing of all that she had been used to think of as the proof of importance, or the employment of wealth, had brought him to Portsmouth. He had reached it late the night before, was come for a day or two, was staying at the Crown, had accidentally met with a navy officer or two of his acquaintance since his arrival, but had no object of that kind in coming.

By the time he had given all this information, it was not unreasonable to suppose that Fanny might be looked at and spoken to. At that point, she was tolerably able to bear his eye.

He mentioned that he had spent half an hour with his sister the evening before his leaving London; that she had sent her best and kindest love, but had had no time for writing. He thought himself lucky in seeing Mary for even half an hour, having spent scarcely twenty-four hours in London, after his return from Norfolk, before he set off again. Also, her cousin Edmund was in town, had been in town a few days. Mr. Crawford had not seen him himself, but Edmund was well, had left them all well at Mansfield, and was to dine with the Frasers.

Fanny listened collectedly, even to the last-mentioned circumstance. Nay, it seemed a relief to her worn mind to be at any certainty. The words, "then by this time it is all settled," passed through her thoughts, without more evidence of emotion than a faint blush.

After talking a little more about Mansfield, a subject in which her interest was most apparent, Crawford began to hint at the expediency of an early walk.

"It was a lovely morning, and at that season of the year a fine morning so often turned off, that it was wisest for everybody not to delay their exercise;"—such hints produced nothing. He soon proceeded to a positive recommendation to

Mrs. Price and her daughters to take their walk without loss of time.

Now, Mrs. Price scarcely ever stirred out of doors, except of a Sunday. She owned she could seldom, with her large family, find time for a walk.

"Would you, then, persuade your daughters to take advantage of such weather, and allow me the pleasure of attending them?" Mr. Crawford's charm was potent here as well.

Mrs. Price was greatly obliged and very complying. "Her daughters were very much confined; Portsmouth was a sad place with a shabby lumbering populace, with the worst of skin conditions; they did not often get out; and she knew they had some errands in the town, which they would be very glad to do."

And the consequence was, that Fanny, strange as it was—strange, awkward, and distressing—found herself and Susan, within ten minutes, walking towards the High Street with Mr. Crawford.

It was soon pain upon pain, confusion upon confusion; for they were hardly in the High Street before they met her father, whose appearance was not the better from its being Saturday. He stopt; and, ungentlemanlike as he looked, Fanny was obliged to introduce him to Mr. Crawford.

"Sir!"

"Fanny!"

"Mr. Price."

"Mr. Crawford."

"Father!"

"Susan!"

"Mr. Price."

"Mr. Crawford."

That went on for quite some while. . . . The harrowing introductions over with eventually, Fanny had now to deal with the potentially even more harrowing consequences.

She could not have a doubt of the manner in which Mr. Crawford must be struck. He must be ashamed and disgusted altogether. He must soon give her up, and cease to have the smallest inclination for the match. And yet—though she had been so much wanting his affection to be cured, *this* was a sort of cure that would be almost as bad as the complaint. . . .

For, surely, there is scarcely a young lady in the United Kingdoms who would not rather put up with the misfortune of being sought by a clever, agreeable man, than have him driven away by the vulgarity of her nearest relations. Indeed, Fanny could recall talk of exactly such a situation—a proverbially vulgar family, spoken of everywhereabouts—with a quite desperate *mama,* a dreadful overabundance of unattached daughters, and the surname of Bennet. . . .

Mr. Crawford probably could not regard his future father-in-law with any idea of taking him for a model in dress; but (as Fanny instantly, and to her great relief, discerned) her father was a very different man, a very different Mr. Price, in his behaviour to this most highly respected stranger, from what he was in his own family at home. His manners now, though not polished, were more than passable—they were grateful, animated, manly. His expressions were those of an attached father, and a sensible man. His loud tones did very well in the open air (though still not dulcet, and somewhat tending to scatter pigeons, seagulls, and all other flying fowl from the vicinity), and there was not a single oath to be heard.

Such was his instinctive compliment to the good manners of Mr. Crawford. And, be the consequence what it might, Fanny's immediate feelings were infinitely soothed.

The conclusion of the two gentlemen's civilities was an offer of Mr. Price's to take Mr. Crawford into the dockyard. Mr. Crawford, desirous of accepting as a favour what was intended as such, though he had seen the dockyard again and again, and hoping to be so much the longer with Fanny, was very gratefully disposed to avail himself of the invitation—if the Miss Prices were not afraid of the fatigue. And as it was ascertained that they were not, to the dockyard they were all to go.

Mr. Price would have turned thither directly, without the smallest consideration for his daughters' errands in the High Street. Mr. Crawford took care, however, that they should be allowed to go to the shops they came out expressly to visit. It did not delay them long, for Fanny would not inconvenience anyone. Before the gentlemen, as they stood at the door, could do more than begin upon the last naval regulations, or settle the number of three-deckers now in commission, their companions were ready to proceed.

They were then to set forward for the dockyard at once, and the walk would have been conducted—according to Mr. Crawford's opinion—in a singular manner, had Mr. Price been allowed the entire regulation of it. The two girls would have been left to follow, and keep up with them or not, as they could, while the two gentlemen walked on together at their own hasty pace. Instead, Mr. Crawford was able to introduce some improvement occasionally, though by no means to the extent he wished—he absolutely would not walk away from them; and at any crossing or any crowd, when Mr. Price was only calling out, "Come, girls; come, Fan; come, Sue, take care of yourselves; keep a sharp lookout!" he would give them his particular attendance.

At one point they passed a goods warehouse loading facility, and there was a remarkable number of boxes and wooden crates stacked along the row, many of them marked with big red crosses which, according to Mr. Price, indicated non-delivery, or a sort of "return to sender" status. "We have been getting a remarkable amount of these around town most recently. Crates everywhere! Rumor has it, they were returned by some lordship because his good spouse had overextended herself in the purchasing department. Upon my word! Look at 'em! Most hailing from Cairo! Hah! Well then, back they go, all the way to Africa!"

While her father continued speaking, Fanny had an extremely sinking feeling right then, a feeling of impending dread and a terrible suspicion.

Mr. Crawford momentarily threw her one very knowing glance.

It was also the moment in which Fanny happened to glance closer at one of the crates, and noticed that its nailed lid had apparently come loose somehow, and now was *moving,* all of its own accord. . . .

"Oh dear . . ." said Fanny. She just could not help herself, it came out.

Crawford glanced in the direction of her stare and lifted one brow quizzically. "Could it be, dear Fanny," he whispered, leaning in, "that we are about to be re-acquainted with one of Lady Bertram's exotic *purchases?* Ah, but you *do* know what I mean; please, I beg you do not attempt to disguise it."

And as Fanny looked at him with desperate eyes, he nodded once then spoke much louder on behalf of Mr. Price: "I believe we should take a right turn here instead, sir. I think I see an interesting dock structure in the distance. Let us make some haste!"

Thus, cleverly redirecting her father's attention, and quickening his pace as though particularly interested in sightseeing, Mr. Crawford had them all away from the imminent danger within the crates.

Once fairly in the dockyard, he began to reckon upon some happy intercourse with Fanny (no, not of *that* kind, you—bad, naughty-minded Reader!), as they were very soon joined by a brother lounger of Mr. Price's, who was come to take his daily survey of how things went on, and who must prove a far more worthy companion than Mr. Crawford. Indeed, after a time the two officers seemed very well satisfied going about together, and discussing matters of equal and never-failing interest.

Meanwhile, the young people sat down upon some timbers in the yard, or found a seat on board a vessel in the stocks which they all went to look at. Despite throwing occasional wary glances in all directions, Fanny was most conveniently in want of rest. Crawford could not have wished her more fatigued or more ready to sit down; but he could have wished her sister away.

A quick-looking girl of Susan's age was the very worst third in the world: totally different from Lady Bertram, all eyes and ears; and there was no introducing the main point before her. He must content himself with being only generally agreeable, and letting Susan have her share of entertainment, with the indulgence, now and then, of a look or hint for the better-informed and conscious Fanny. Especially now that they knew there was a certain familiar *unnatural* danger to be dealt with.

He mostly talked of Norfolk: he had been there some time, and there reposed his present important schemes. Such a man could come from no place, no society, without importing something to amuse. His journeys and his acquaintance were all of use, and Susan was entertained in a way quite new to her.

For Fanny, somewhat more was related than the accidental agreeableness of the parties he had been in. For her approbation, the particular reason of his going into Norfolk was given. It had been real business, relative to the renewal of a lease in which the welfare of a large and industrious family was at stake. Suspecting his agent of some underhand dealing, Mr. Crawford had determined to go himself, and thoroughly investigate the merits of the case. He had gone, had done even more good than he had foreseen. In performing a duty, he had been gratified.

In short, he had introduced himself to some good people and worthy causes on his own estate. This was aimed, and well aimed, at Fanny. It was pleasing to hear him speak so properly. In this; he had been acting as he ought. To be the friend of the poor and the oppressed! Nothing could be more grateful to her; and she was on the point of giving him an approving look, when it was all frightened off by his adding something of his hoping soon to have an assistant, a friend, a guide in every plan of utility or charity for Everingham—a *somebody* that would make Everingham a dearer object than it had ever been yet.

She turned away, and wished he would not say such things. She was willing to allow he might have more good qualities than she had been wont to suppose. Indeed, Fanny began to feel the possibility of his turning out well at last. . . . But he was and must ever be completely unsuited to her, and ought not to think of her. . . .

It was at that point that at least several dozen lumbering and oh-so-terribly familiar figures of Fanny's most inconvenient nightmares, suddenly appeared. They were moving slowly and stiffly from the direction of the stockyard, the entrance to the docks, the loading areas, the berths, and indeed, from every other alley and direction, it seemed. Their arms were frequently extended or raised before them, reaching out for anything and everything in their path (and often catching on things in their way, which spun them around like weather vanes and made them walk in the opposite direction—hence the familiar "circle spinning," which was the term that Mr. Rushworth had once used to refer to local "louts" at Sotherton).

Mummies!

From some distance came Mr. Price's loud exclamation, followed by an oath. "What's this, blasted lunatics! Where did they all come from?" hollered Mr. Price, and his officer companion echoed him with reasonably potent oaths of his own.

"Oh, father!" exclaimed Fanny. "Run, I beg you, run!"

"What? What's this, Fan? The Price men do not run from anything!"

"In that case, sir, I suggest you walk very fast and, if necessary, aim for their mouth!"

There was a sound of struggle, many particularly dire oaths, and suddenly Mr. Price and his fellow officer came into view, moving in a half-canter that was attempting to be a dignified walk, in their direction. They were followed by a sea of swaying, lumbering mummies.

"What in blazes is that?" Mr. Price was yelling. "Who are these ruffians? I say, run, Fan and Sue, make haste! They do appear to mean business!"

Poor Susan! Amid of all this, she was the only one absolutely confounded and therefore doubly terrified.

"Here, take my hand, Susan," said Fanny, at the same time as Mr. Crawford bravely said, "Miss Price, I beg you to take my hand—"

"I dare say, we cannot all be holding hands!" exclaimed Fanny in frustration. "For I need at least one hand free for pummeling!"

Susan's eyes widened and her jaw dropped in amazement. Her timid, gentle-mannered older sister was looking and acting like she had never seen her before! A true wonder!

Mr. Crawford gallantly stood in a manner so as to block the oncoming. He then started to take off his fine jacket and roll it up into a very large wad.

Fanny, meanwhile, drew Susan to her with both hands, and spoke very quickly and with a great deal of excitement and fortitude. "To quickly explain: these are mummies, Susan," she said.

"Mommies? What—whose mommies? What is that?"

"In a nutshell, three-thousand year old, dead, embalmed and dried out Egyptians, Susan. The process is called *mummification,* but there is no time to go into descriptive detail, nor to properly inform you of the techniques used, such as organ removal, brain pulling and hinged hooks—"

"Who? What? Dead? But—then why are they *moving?*"

"They are brought back to life, to walk among the living. Or had been—by a very dear but very foolish person we both know. They subsist on the *breath of life* that is in all of us, and the only way to stop them from feeding on the life force is to stop up their mouth."

"Why, that is surely nonsensical! And—*who* in their right mind bought them to life?"

Fanny sighed. "I am truly ashamed to admit; it is none other than our own, dear aunt Bertram. Remember that little cat-headed Egyptian statuette you had received last Christmas? It is but one of the symptoms of her malady!"

"Oh dear, gracious me!"

"Yes, Susan, my love. I realize it is a bit too much to take in all at once—"

But Susan's open mouth widened into a grin. "Oh, no, not at all, I understand!" she exclaimed.

"Less talk, my dears, and more mouth-crushing action, if you please," quipped Mr. Crawford, glancing at Fanny once with a meaningful tiny smile, as he used his fine jacket to stifle the vanguard mummy that had reached him first.

Fanny went to work. A package of High Street purchases was in her hands, of just the right size to be of use as a blunt projectile. "Watch this, Susan, dear! I endeavored to better your mind with reading and education, but at present juncture, this will do just as well!" And, before a mummy could lean in and assail her with its rotting skin, she firmly shoved the package in its gaping maw and pushed, very *very* hard. Moments later came a satisfying crunch, a collapse, and the mummy disintegrated into dust.

Susan gave a loud exclamation of delight.

"This is all very charming, of course," said Mr. Crawford, as he simultaneously crushed two mummies at once, one with his elegant gloved fist in its mouth, and the other with the elbow adroitly shoved in a nice move of gentlemanly combat. "But we really ought to be heading back out of this area. Too much infestation here. I suggest some haste—"

"Well, how do you like that, eh? *Yah bloody whoreson!*" Mr. Price was roaring a few steps away, as he had figured out the proper method and shoved his hat into the maw of a mummy, followed by his hand, up to the elbow.

"Ahem—we are moving out, Mr. Price!" said Crawford loudly, but with much steady composure, realizing that the inebriated battle enthusiasm of the older gentleman could land him in a bit of a jam. "Let us continue this, but closer to your residence, now—"

"Indeed, indeed, by all means!" said Mr. Price, while his officer friend was putting the blunt end of a gin bottle into a mummy's orifice.

And so they made their way backwards, out of the stocks and dockyard area.

But here, a grim discovery awaited them. The way out was blocked by a veritable sea of the *undead.* Most of the mummies had come forth out of the same marked crates that they had passed earlier on their way into the dockyard.

"This is highly regretful, but we appear to be surrounded," said Mr. Crawford through his teeth. Then he added, "I suggest we make a breach—plow through them in a direct line. Single-file is best. Now, allow me, I will go first—"

In that moment, as Fanny was gathering herself for the ramming assault, the air about them seemed to waver, and a hot dry wind blew in a sudden great gust.

Lord Eastwind stood directly before them, dressed in a fine gentleman's walking attire, high polished Hessians and elegant topcoat and hat, a slim walking stick in one gloved hand.

Fanny gave a small shriek, and her heart started to beat faster than already it was, while her breath was aflutter.

This time, everyone present could *see* him.

"Eastwind."

"Crawford."

"Sir!"

"Fanny . . ."

"Mr. Price."

"Susan."

"Mr.—"

"Mummy!"

This went on for quite some time—or would have done so, had not the mummy horde neared, close enough to bump noses with all of them.

Like a wall of approaching sand, the *undead* came, ready to besiege them from all sides. Eyeless faces wrapped in rags, with only a hint of the skulls underneath, and dark gaping mouths. . . . Desiccated skeletal arms wrapped in bits of ancient linen waved about, and there was a hum of ever-present wind.

"A fine day, Miss Price," said Lord Eastwind with a small tip of the hat to her, and his back brazenly turned to the approaching army. His eyes—oh, his dear *familiar* understanding eyes!

"Sir . . ." whispered Fanny.

Mr. Price was non-plussed. "And who is this gentleman, Fan? Do we know him?"

"Indeed, sir." Fanny could hardly gather words. "This is—this is Lord Eastwind, a—dear friend of the Bertram family."

"Oh, is he, then? Well, then sir, it is a pleasure to make your acquaintance. How'd you do? All the way to Portsmouth are you come, is it?"

"Oh! Father! Oh! Fanny!" Susan was meanwhile pointing at the approaching mummies. "Oh! Oh! Oh!"

"The pleasure is all mine," replied Eastwind with an equally polite bow to Mr. Price.

"Taking a walk, Eastwind?" said Mr. Crawford in a subtly sarcastic tone which only Fanny discerned.

"Oh! Mr. Crawford! Oh! *OH!*" Susan was going into minor conniptions. One nearest mummy had literally pulled off her bonnet and was trying to chew it while Susan was beating back at it with her packages; two others were reaching for Crawford and Fanny.

"A walk that lead me here. To see if I can be of assistance," said the raven-haired gentleman. "And it appears I am just in time."

He raised his walking stick. With a single sweep that cleared about five feet nearest him, he turned around, and started walking before them out of the dockyard, while mummies scattered like old fallen leaves before a storm.

"Upon my word!" said Mr. Price, "how jolly fine of you! And look, the ruffians are falling back! Hah! That oughta teach yah to mess with the likes of us! Hah!"

Without a word they walked between the parted ranks of the mummies, and emerged in a clearing that led to the rest of town.

Behind them, the mummies seemed to have stilled, all to a creature, and stood in odd frozen ranks, somehow even more menacing in perfect motionless silence than when they were moving.

In one manner or another, Lord Eastwind placed himself at Fanny's side, and whispered: "My dear Miss Price—forgive me, but I could not come to your aid any earlier. It takes great will and *life force* for me to materialize and put on proper flesh, and now it is only by your will alone that I may do so. And you had not *willed* me to come until that last moment."

"What do you mean?" Fanny whispered back.

"If you must know, I no longer *rule* them . . . I have given up my will over them, and now there is no turning back. They obey me only as their former lord and Pharaoh. And as such, it will not last. But—for the moment it had sufficed." And then, leaning in closer, so that she could almost feel his warm gentle gust of breath upon her cheek, he added: "I ask that you stay clear of places such as this, and that you take good care for your safety. I—might not always be there to protect you."

Fanny parted her lips to reply, but he turned away. And with another elegant tip of the hat to everyone, he was on his way, walking at a fast pace.

"But—wait!" cried Mr. Price in his wake. "Good sir, won't you have a bite of mutton at my place? Surely you must be thanked properly!"

But in the next blink, Eastwind had turned the corner and was gone.

"Well, blimey! Well, shiver me timbers!" said both Mr. Price and his officer friend simultaneously.

After a pause where they all milled about, glaring behind them at the frozen lot of dead Egyptians, and around them for more mummies, Mr. Crawford cleared his throat politely. "I suggest we move along," he said. "Now then—" And as though nothing had happened, he offered his arms to Fanny on one side, and Susan on the other.

Fanny's mind and spirit were reeling—least of all because of the mummies.

The conversation took several long minutes to settle, what with Susan asking many pointed questions, and her father muttering, "All right, who exactly were those villains? Would someone care to explain? Were they asylum inmates? Or, maybe prison escapees? Although, where does it take for a man to be incarcerated, to have his skin rot to such a measure? Now *those* were some ugly bast—"

Mr. Crawford skillfully avoided making any definitive answers, and instead turned the talk to Mansfield. He could not have chosen better. That was a topic to bring back Fanny's attention and her looks almost instantly.

Now in particular, it was a real indulgence to her to hear or to speak of Mansfield. So long divided from everybody who knew the place, and now with Lord Eastwind's brief appearance to serve as a bittersweet reminder, she felt it quite the voice of a friend when Crawford mentioned it. It led the way to her fond exclamations in praise of its beauties and comforts, speaking of her uncle as all that was clever and good, and her aunt as having the sweetest of all sweet tempers.

"But aunt Bertram awakened those mummies!" Susan pointed out in all reasonableness.

"Hush, dear," replied Fanny gently. "We shall talk of that later—"

Mr. Crawford admitted to having a great attachment to Mansfield himself. He looked forward to spending very much of his time there, or in the neighbourhood. He particularly expected a very happy summer and autumn there this year; infinitely superior to the last, and under much better circumstances.

"Mansfield, Sotherton, Thornton Lacey," he continued; "What a society will be comprised in those houses! And at Michaelmas, perhaps, a fourth may be added: some small hunting-box in the vicinity of everything so dear; for as to any partnership in Thornton Lacey, as Edmund Bertram once good-humouredly proposed, I hope I foresee two excellent, irresistible objections to that plan."

Fanny was doubly silenced here. Though when the moment had passed, she regretted not asking him to say something more of his sister and Edmund. It was a subject which she must learn to speak of. Her weakness in that regard would soon be quite unpardonable.

When Mr. Price and his friend had seen all that they wished, and talked all they would of the "insolent dockyard villains"—as they came to refer to the mummies—the others were ready to return.

In the course of their walk back, Mr. Crawford contrived a minute's privacy for telling Fanny that his only business in Portsmouth was to see her; that he was come down for a couple of days on her account, and hers only, and because he could not endure a longer total separation.

"To be honest, I had no idea to see Eastwind here," he added, looking meaningfully into her eyes. "Could it be, sweet, kind Fanny, that he is the reason for your denial of me? All this time, could it have been *he,* indeed who has taken your heart?"

"No. He is but a family friend," tried Fanny. But, proper deception was never in her nature. However, to keep her *true secret,* waylay the truth she must.

Crawford's countenance shewed a light smile.

"You must be aware," he spoke, "that I understand very well who and what he is. He is an ancient lord of Egypt, an echo of the past. I knew him for what he was from the beginning. You think me insensible to his presence all last autumn and summer, during our Mansfield thespian delights?"

"No, sir, I do not," replied Fanny, thinking that someone who has a vampire for a sister surely learnt a long time ago to recognize and perceive all flavors of the *unnatural*.

"He was a shadow eternal. He attached himself to Lady Bertram, of course, but his real object was always *you*."

"I—know."

"Why yes, you do indeed, Fanny! Amazing all-seeing you!"

"Sir, please. I beg you not to speak in this manner."

"Why? Is it because—possibly—you *love* him, this ancient ghost?"

"Your jealousy in this regard is stunning and gives me sorrow. And no, I do not."

Mr. Crawford seemed to take this as she wanted him to, and did not pursue the questioning of her heart's true desire.

"Then, dearest Fanny, I dare continue to hope on my own behalf," he said gallantly, adding then hastily: "But of course I might never presume to impose on you with these feelings again, unless you find them interesting. Indeed, the matter of Eastwind is settled and I now put him out of our minds. *He* might continue to languish for love of you (and who could blame him?), while it is but his minions that might as yet be of continued concern to us."

Fanny truly did not want to hear any more—of his feelings, of his suspicions, all spoken in platitudes.

She was sorry, really sorry he continued to feel this way. And yet in spite of this and other things which she wished he had not said, she thought him altogether improved since she had seen him. He was much more gentle, obliging, and attentive to other people's feelings than he had ever been at Mansfield.

She had never seen him so agreeable—so *near* being agreeable. His behaviour to her father could not offend, and there was something particularly kind and proper in the notice he took of Susan—not to mention the chivalry with which he placed himself in the path of mummified danger to protect them. He was decidedly improved. She wished the next day over, she wished he had come only for one day; but it was not so very bad as she would have expected: the pleasure of talking of Mansfield was so very great!

Before they parted, she had to thank him for another pleasure, and one of no trivial kind. Her father asked him to do them the honour of taking his mutton with them (since "that most excellent Lord Eastwind" as a mutton companion was not to be), and Fanny had time for only one thrill of horror, before Mr. Crawford declared himself prevented by a prior engagement. He was engaged to dinner already both for that day and the next; he had met with some acquaintance at the Crown who would not be denied. He should have the honour, however, of waiting on them again on the morrow.

And so they parted—Fanny in a state of actual felicity from escaping so horrible an evil!

To have had him join their family dinner-party, and see all their deficiencies, would have been dreadful! Mr. Price would probably be carrying on at length about mummies in the dockyards, and how they all battled the villains. Then there was the dire matter of Rebecca's cookery and Rebecca's waiting. And one could not forget little Betsey's eating at table without restraint, and pulling everything about as she chose—quite like having a baboon in the family. Fanny herself was not yet enough inured to Betsey's habits, for her often to make a tolerable meal. *She* was nice only from natural delicacy, but *he* had been brought up in a school of luxury and epicurism.

Chapter XLII

The Prices were just setting off for church the next day when Mr. Crawford appeared again. He came, not to stop, but to join them. He was asked to go with them to the Garrison chapel, which was exactly what he had intended, and they all walked thither together.

Luckily, the streets were clear of any suspicious peeling louts, observed Mr. Price loudly, and Fanny allowed herself a minor shudder.

The family were now seen to advantage. Nature had given them no inconsiderable share of beauty, and every Sunday dressed them in their cleanest skins and best attire. Sunday always brought this comfort to Fanny, and on this Sunday she felt it more than ever.

Her poor mother now did not look so very unworthy of being Lady Bertram's sister as she was but too apt to look. It often grieved Fanny to think of the contrast between them; to think that where nature had made so little difference, circumstances should have made so much. That her mother—as handsome as Lady Bertram, and some years her junior—should have an appearance so much more worn and faded, so slatternly, so shabby! But Sunday made her a very creditable and tolerably cheerful-looking Mrs. Price, coming abroad with a fine family of children, feeling a little respite of her weekly cares, and only discomposed if she saw her boys run into danger, or Rebecca pass by with a flower in her hat, followed closely by an odd lumbering fellow.

In chapel they were obliged to divide, but Mr. Crawford took care not to be divided from the female branch. After chapel he still continued with them, and made one in the family party on the ramparts.

Mrs. Price took her weekly walk on the ramparts every fine Sunday throughout the year, always going directly after morning service and staying till dinner-time. It was her public place: there she met her acquaintance, heard a little news, talked over the badness of the Portsmouth servants, the rabble with foul skin conditions, and wound up her spirits for the six days ensuing.

Thither they now went, Mr. Crawford most happy to consider the Miss Prices as his peculiar charge. And before they had been there long, somehow or other, Fanny could not have believed it, but he was walking between them with an arm of each under his—with no impending danger of mummies present—and she did not know how to prevent or put an end to it. It made her uncomfortable for a time, but yet there were enjoyments in the day and in the view which would be felt.

The day was uncommonly lovely. It was really March; but it was April in its mild air, brisk soft wind, and bright sun, occasionally clouded for a minute. Everything looked so beautiful under the influence of such a sky, the effects of the shadows pursuing each other on the ships at Spithead and the island beyond, with the ever-varying hues of the sea, now at high water, dancing in its glee and dashing against the ramparts with so fine a sound.

All this produced altogether such a combination of charms for Fanny, as made her gradually almost careless of the circumstances. Nay, had she been without his arm, she would soon have known that she *needed* it, for she wanted strength for a two hours' saunter of this kind, coming upon a week's previous inactivity. Fanny was beginning to feel the effect of being debarred from her usual regular exercise; she had lost ground as to health since her being in Portsmouth. And but for Mr. Crawford and the beauty of the weather, Fanny would soon have been knocked up now. (Why—you insufferable Reader! This is quite beyond the disciplinary power of a mere footnote! I shall not endeavour to call you "gentle" any longer for you are indeed being shameless, now! *Knocked up* is not what you think it means!)

The loveliness of the day, and of the view, Mr. Crawford felt like herself. They often stopt with the same sentiment and taste, leaning against the wall, some minutes, to look and admire. And, considering he was not Edmund, Fanny could not but allow that he was sufficiently open to the charms of nature, and very well able to express his admiration.

She had a few tender reveries now and then, which he could sometimes take advantage of to look in her face without detection; and the result of these looks was, that though as bewitching as ever, her face was less blooming than it ought to be. She *said* she was very well, and did not like to be supposed otherwise. But take it all in all, he was convinced that her present residence could not be comfortable, and therefore could not be salutary for her. He was growing anxious for her being again at Mansfield, where her own happiness (and his in seeing her) must be so much greater.

"You have been here a month, I think?" said he.

"No; not quite a month. It is only four weeks to-morrow since I left Mansfield."

"You are a most accurate and honest reckoner. I should call that a month."

"I did not arrive here till Tuesday evening."

"And it is to be a two months' visit, is it not?"

"Yes. My uncle talked of two months. I suppose it will not be less."

"And how are you to be conveyed back again? Who comes for you?"

"I do not know. I have heard nothing about it yet from my aunt. Perhaps I may be to stay longer. It may not be convenient for me to be fetched exactly at the two months' end."

After a moment's reflection, Mr. Crawford replied, "I know Mansfield, I know its way. I know its faults towards *you.* I know the danger of your being so far forgotten, as to have your comforts give way to the imaginary convenience of any single being in the family. I am aware that you may be left here week after week, if Sir Thomas cannot settle everything for coming himself, or sending your aunt's maid for you, without involving the slightest alteration of the arrangements which he may have laid down for the next quarter of a year. This will not do. Two months is an ample allowance; I should think six weeks quite enough. I am considering your sister's health," said he, addressing himself to Susan, "which I think the confinement of Portsmouth unfavourable to. She requires constant air and exercise. When you know her as well as I do, I am sure you will agree that she ought never to be long banished from the free air and liberty of the country. If, therefore" (turning again to Fanny), "you find yourself growing unwell, and any *difficulties* arise about your returning to Mansfield—natural or *otherwise*—without waiting for the two months to be ended, *that* must not be regarded of consequence. If you feel yourself at all less strong or comfortable than usual, simply let my sister know! Give her only the slightest hint, she and I will immediately come down, and take you back to Mansfield. You know the ease and the pleasure and *feeling* with which this would be done."

Fanny thanked him, but tried to laugh it off by saying that she was perfectly capable of taking military action against mummified Egyptians on her own, if things came to such.

"That you are indeed, bravest Fanny. And yet, I am perfectly serious," he replied, "as you perfectly know. And I hope you will not be cruelly concealing any tendency to indisposition. Indeed, you shall *not.* It shall not be in your power—for so long only as you positively say, in every letter to Mary, 'I am well,' and I know you cannot speak or write a falsehood—so long only shall you be considered as well."

Fanny thanked him again, but was affected and distressed to a degree that made it impossible for her to say much, or even to be certain of what she ought to say. This was towards the close of their walk. He attended them to the last, and left them only at the door of their own house, when he knew them to be going to dinner, and therefore pretended to be waited for elsewhere.

"I wish you were not so tired," said he, still detaining Fanny after all the others were in the house—"I wish I left you in stronger health. I wish—Is there anything I can do for you in town? I have half an idea of going into Norfolk again soon." And Mr. Crawford proceeded to give the details of his estate business and property issues with an agent in his employ, concluding with: "Shall I go? Do you advise it?"

"I advise! You know very well what is right," said Fanny gently.

"Yes. When you give me your opinion, I always know what is right. Your judgment is my rule of right."

"Oh, no! do not say so. We have all a better guide in ourselves, if we would attend to it, than any other person can be. Good-bye; I wish you a pleasant journey to-morrow."

"Is there nothing I can do for you in town?"

"Nothing; I am much obliged to you."

"Have you no message for anybody?"

"My love to your sister, if you please. And when you see my cousin, my cousin Edmund, I wish you would be so good as to say that I suppose I shall soon hear from him."

"Certainly; and if he is lazy or negligent, I will write his excuses myself."

Mr. Crawford could say no more, for Fanny would be no longer detained.

He pressed her hand, looked at her, and was gone.

He went to while away the next three hours as he could, with his other acquaintance, till the best dinner that a capital inn afforded was ready for their enjoyment, and *she* turned in to her more simple one immediately.

Their general fare bore a very different character; and could Mr. Crawford have suspected how many privations, besides that of exercise, she endured in her father's house, he would have wondered that her looks were not much more affected than he found them.

She was so little equal to Rebecca's puddings and Rebecca's hashes, brought to table with half-cleaned plates, and not half-cleaned knives and forks, that she was very often constrained to defer her heartiest meal till she could send her brothers in the evening for biscuits and buns. After being nursed up at Mansfield, it was too late in the day to be hardened at Portsmouth. And though Sir Thomas, had he known all, might have thought his niece in the most promising way of being starved, both mind and body, into a much juster value for Mr. Crawford's good company and good fortune, he would probably have feared to push his experiment farther, lest she might *die* under the cure.

Fanny was out of spirits all the rest of the day. It did not help that Susan constantly cornered her in private and asked giddy, giggling, pointed questions about the two exciting gentlemen of their acquaintance—Mr. Crawford and the terribly handsome and mysterious Lord Eastwind—until Fanny wanted to hide.

Though tolerably secure of not seeing Mr. Crawford again, she could not help being low. It was parting with somebody of the nature of a friend. And though, in one light, Fanny was glad to have him gone, it seemed she was now deserted by everybody. It was a sort of renewed separation from Mansfield. And she could not think of his returning to town, and being frequently with Mary and Edmund, without feelings so near akin to envy as made her hate herself for having them.

Her dejection had no abatement from anything passing around her. A friend or two of her father's spent the long, long evening there; and from six o'clock till half-past nine, there was little intermission of noise or grog, or talk of the "pockmarked villainous rabble" out on the streets these days (the mummies were now seen more frequently in all parts of town).

She was very low. The wonderful improvement which she still fancied in Mr. Crawford was the nearest to administering comfort of anything within the current of her thoughts. Not considering in how different a circle she had been just seeing him, nor how much might be owing to contrast, she was quite persuaded of his being astonishingly more gentle and regardful of others than formerly.

And, if in little things, must it not be so in great? So anxious for her health and comfort, so very feeling as he now expressed himself, and really seemed—might not it be fairly supposed that he would not much longer persevere in a suit so distressing to her?

Fanny dared thus to hope—at the same time as she dared not to think of a pair of *intimate,* sorrowful, ancient eyes. . . .

Chapter XLIII

It was presumed that Mr. Crawford was travelling back to London on the morrow, for nothing more was seen of him at Mr. Price's. And two days afterwards, it was a fact ascertained to Fanny by a letter from his sister, opened and read by her, on another account, with the most anxious curiosity:—

> "I have to inform you, my dearest Fanny, that Henry has been down to Portsmouth to see you; that he had a delightful walk with you to the dockyard last Saturday (though, with those tedious mummified *things* there, as he says, I dare imagine, it might have been little time for a lover's exchange), and one still more to be dwelt on the next day, on the ramparts; when the balmy air, the sparkling sea, and your sweet looks and conversation were altogether in the most delicious harmony, and afforded sensations which are to raise ecstasy even in retrospect. This, as well as I understand, is to be the substance of my information. He makes me write, but I do not know what else is to be communicated, except this said visit to Portsmouth, and these two said walks, and his introduction to your family, especially to a fair sister of yours, a fine girl of fifteen, who was of the party on the ramparts, taking her first lesson, I presume, in love.
>
> "I have not time for writing much, but this could not be delayed. My dear, dear Fanny, if I had you here, how I would talk to you! You should listen to me till you were tired, and advise me; but it is impossible to put a hundredth

part of my mind on paper, so I will abstain altogether, and leave you to guess what you like. I have no news for you. I ought to have sent you an account of your cousin's first party, but I was lazy, and now it is too long ago. Suffice it, that everything was just as it ought to be, in grand impeccable style, and that her own dress and manners did her the greatest credit—though at some point our poor Mr. Rushworth was *seen* to growl and howl outright, in a particularly unseemly manner, and it was *talked of.* My friend, Mrs. Fraser, is mad for such a house, and it would not make *me* miserable. I go to Lady Stornaway after Easter. Lord S. is not half as ill-looking as I used to think—at least, one sees many worse. He will not do by the side of your cousin Edmund.

"Of the last-mentioned hero, what shall I say? If I avoided his name entirely, it would look suspicious. We have seen him two or three times, and my friends here are very much struck with his gentlemanlike appearance. Mrs. Fraser declares she knows but three men in town who have so good a person, height, and air. And I must confess, when he dined here the other day, there were *none* to compare with him, and we were a party of sixteen. Luckily there is no distinction of dress nowadays to tell tales, but—but—but Yours affectionately."

"I had almost forgot (it was Edmund's fault: he gets into my head more than does me good) one very material thing I had to say from Henry and myself—I mean about our taking you back into Northamptonshire. My dear little creature, do not stay at Portsmouth to lose your pretty looks and to be overrun by tedious ancient mummies. Those vile sea-breezes are the ruin of beauty and health. My poor aunt always felt affected if within ten miles of the sea, which the Admiral of course never believed, but I know it was so—or at least I did, while I was still *alive*. I am at your service and Henry's, at an hour's notice. I should like the scheme, and we would make a little circuit, and shew you Everingham in our way (again, fear not, sweet! no *biting* shall ever be endeavoured in your vicinity), and perhaps you would not mind passing through London, and seeing the inside of St. George's, Hanover Square. Only keep your cousin Edmund from me at such a time: I should not like to be tempted. What a long letter! one word more. Henry, I find, has some idea of going into Norfolk again upon some business that *you* approve; but this cannot possibly be permitted before the middle of next week; he cannot be

> spared till after the 14th, for *we* have a party that evening. The value of a man like Henry, on such an occasion, is priceless, truly inestimable. He will see the Rushworths, which I am not sorry for—having a little curiosity, and so I think has he—though he will not acknowledge it."

Fanny read the letter eagerly and deliberately. It supplied matter for much reflection, and greater suspense than ever. The only certainty to be drawn from it was, that nothing decisive had yet taken place. Edmund had not yet spoken.

How Miss Crawford really felt, or how she meant to act, whether his importance to her had changed, were subjects for endless and fruitless conjecture, for days on end. The most persistent idea was that Miss Crawford, after proving herself cooled by a return to London habits, would yet prove herself in the end too much attached to him to give him up. She would try to be more ambitious than her heart would allow. She would hesitate, she would tease, she would condition, she would require a great deal, but she would finally accept.

This was Fanny's most frequent expectation. A house in town—that, she thought, must be impossible. Yet there was no saying what Miss Crawford might not ask. The prospect for her cousin grew worse and worse.

The woman who could speak of him, and speak only of his appearance! What an unworthy attachment! To be deriving support from the commendations of Mrs. Fraser! *She* who had known him intimately half a year! Fanny was ashamed of her, and constantly had to remind herself of the vampire nature which could neither properly love nor suffer.

Those parts of the letter which related only to Mr. Crawford and herself, touched her, in comparison, slightly. Whether or when Mr. Crawford went into Norfolk was certainly no concern of hers. Though, everything considered, she thought he *would* go without delay.

That Miss Crawford should endeavour to secure a meeting between him and Mrs. Rushworth, was all in her worst line of conduct, and grossly unkind and ill-judged. Fanny hoped *he* would not be moved by any such degrading curiosity. At least he acknowledged no such inducement. Indeed, his sister ought to have given him credit for better feelings than her own.

Fanny was even more impatient for another letter from town after receiving this. For a few days she was so unsettled, that her usual readings and conversation with Susan were much suspended. She could not command her attention as she wished, and replied with absentminded vagueness to Susan's usual carryings on (and on, and on, and on, and on, and—) about the elegant Mr. Crawford and the dark and beautiful Lord Eastwind.

If Mr. Crawford remembered to pass on her message to her cousin Edmund, she thought it very likely that Edmund would write to her at all events—it would be most consistent with his usual kindness. But since no letters appeared, she was in a most anxious state.

At length, she achieved composure. Suspense must be submitted to, and not allowed to wear her out or make her useless. Time, and her own exertions, helped. She resumed her attentions to Susan, and again awakened the same interest in them.

Susan was growing very fond of her, and there was an increasingly complex sense of admiration building within her—an appreciation of her sister not only as a mentor and arbiter of worldly good taste, but as someone brave and mysterious in more ways than Susan could imagine. It was an awareness of Fanny's true *goodness*.

Susan did not have an equal early delight in books, which had been so strong in Fanny (having a disposition much less inclined to sedentary pursuits, or to information for information's sake). But she had so strong a desire of not *appearing* ignorant, that, with a good clear understanding, she made a most attentive, profitable, thankful pupil.

Fanny was her oracle. Fanny's explanations and remarks were a most important addition to every essay, or every chapter of history. From social mores to mummies—what Fanny told her of former times dwelt more on her mind than the pages of Goldsmith; and she paid her sister the compliment of preferring her style to that of any printed author. The early habit of reading was wanting.

Their conversations, however, were not always on subjects so high as history or morals. Mansfield Park as a topic was prominent. A description of people, manners, amusements—all the ways of Mansfield Park—was a favorite.

Susan, who had an innate taste for the genteel and well-appointed, was eager to hear, and Fanny could not but indulge herself in dwelling on so beloved a theme. She hoped it was not wrong. Though, after a time, Susan's very great admiration of everything said or done in her uncle's house, and earnest longing to go into Northamptonshire, seemed almost to blame her for exciting feelings which could not be gratified.

Poor Susan was very little better fitted for her father's home than her elder sister. Fanny grew thoroughly to understand this, and began to feel that when her own release from Portsmouth came, her happiness would be reduced in leaving Susan behind.

That a girl so capable of being made everything good should be left in such hands, distressed Fanny more and more. Were *she* to have her own home to invite Susan to, what a blessing it would be! And had it been possible for her to return Mr. Crawford's regard, the likelihood of his being very open to such a measure would have increased all her own comforts. She thought he was really good-tempered, and could fancy his most amiable approval of such a plan.

Chapter XLIV

Seven weeks of the two months were very nearly gone, when the one letter so long expected—the letter from Edmund—was put into Fanny's hands.

As she opened, and saw its length, she prepared herself for a minute detail of happiness and a profusion of love and praise towards the fortunate creature who was now mistress of his fate. These were the contents—

> "MY DEAR FANNY,—
>
> Excuse me that I have not written before. Crawford told me that you were wishing to hear from me, but I found it impossible to write from London, and persuaded myself that you would understand my silence. Could I have sent a few happy lines, they should not have been wanting, but nothing of that nature was ever in my power. I am returned to Mansfield in a less assured state than when I left it. My hopes are much weaker. You are probably aware of this already. So very fond of you as Miss Crawford is, it is most natural that she should tell you enough of her own feelings to furnish a tolerable guess at mine. I will not be prevented, however, from making my own communication. Our confidences in you need not clash. I ask no questions. There is something soothing in the idea that we have the same friend—that whatever unhappy differences of opinion may exist between us, we are united in our love of you.

"It will be a comfort to me to tell you how things are, and my present plans—if they might be called such. I was three weeks in London, and saw her (for London) very often. I had every attention from the Frasers that could be reasonably expected. I dare say I was not reasonable in carrying with me hopes of an intercourse[28] at all like that of Mansfield. It was her manner, however, rather than any unfrequency of meeting. Had she been *different* when I did see her, I should have made no complaint, but from the very first she was altered: my first reception was so unlike what I had hoped, that I had almost resolved on leaving London again directly.

"I need not particularise. You know the weak side of her character, and may imagine the sentiments which were torturing me. She was in high spirits, and surrounded by those who gave all the support of their own bad sense to her too lively mind. I do not like Mrs. Fraser, a cold-hearted, vain woman, who has married entirely from convenience. Though evidently unhappy in marriage, she faults not her judgment, temper, or disproportion of age, but that she is less affluent than many of her acquaintance (especially her sister, Lady Stornaway), and is the determined supporter of everything sufficiently mercenary and ambitious.

"I look upon Miss Crawford's intimacy with those two sisters as the greatest misfortune. They have been leading her astray for years. Could she be detached from them!—and sometimes I do not despair of it, for the affection appears to me principally on their side. They are very fond of her; but I am sure she does not love them as she loves you. When I think of her great attachment to you, her judicious, upright conduct as a sister, she appears a very different creature, capable of everything noble, and I am ready to blame myself for being too harsh of her playfulness.

"I cannot give her up, Fanny. She is the only woman in the world whom I could ever think of as a wife. If I did not believe that she had some regard for me, of

[28] O ye most shameless Reader! Such thoughts as these, why, this is not to be borne! I beg you now, in all righteousness to think of something pure and unsullied to cleanse the filthy recesses of your mind, else there will be no recourse but to notify the appropriate moral authorities!

course I should not say this, but I do believe it. I am convinced that she is not indifferent. I have no jealousy of any individual. It is the influence of the fashionable world altogether that I am jealous of. It is the habits of wealth that I fear. Her ideas are not higher than her own fortune may warrant, but they are beyond what our incomes united could authorise. There is comfort, however, even here. I could better bear to lose her because not rich enough, than because of my profession. That would only prove her affection not equal to sacrifices, which I am scarcely justified in asking. Her prejudices, I trust, are not so strong as they were.

"You have my thoughts exactly as they arise, my dear Fanny—contradictory, but a faithful picture of my mind. Having once begun, it is a pleasure to tell you all I feel. I cannot give her up. Connected as we already are, to give up Mary Crawford would be to give up the society of some of those most dear to me; to banish myself from the very houses and friends whom I should turn to for consolation. The loss of Mary is the loss of *Crawford and of Fanny*.

"Were it a decided thing, an actual refusal, I should know how to bear it, and in the course of a few years—but I am writing nonsense. Until I am refused, I will not cease to try for her. The only question is *how?* I thought of going to London again after Easter. Then I resolved on doing nothing till she returns to Mansfield in June. But June is at a great distance, and I believe I shall write to her. I have nearly determined on explaining myself by letter. Considering my present miserable state, a letter will be decidedly the best method of explanation.

"I shall be able to write much that I could not say, giving her time for reflection. I am less afraid of the result of reflection than of an immediate hasty impulse answer. My greatest danger would lie in her consulting Mrs. Fraser. A letter exposes to all the evil of consultation, and where the mind is undecided, an adviser may lead it unwisely. But—I must think this matter over a little. This long letter, full of my own concerns alone, will be enough to tire even the friendship of a Fanny.

"The last time I saw Crawford was at Mrs. Fraser's party. I am more and more satisfied with all that I see and hear of him. There is not a shadow of wavering. He

> thoroughly knows his own mind, and acts up to his resolutions: an inestimable quality. I could not see him and my eldest sister in the same room without recollecting what you once told me, and I acknowledge that they did not meet as friends. There was marked coolness on her side. They scarcely spoke. I saw him draw back surprised, and I was sorry that Mrs. Rushworth should resent any former supposed slight to Miss Bertram.
>
> "You will wish to hear my opinion of Maria's degree of comfort as a wife. There is no appearance of unhappiness. I hope they get on pretty well together. I dined twice in Wimpole Street, and might have been there oftener, but it is mortifying to be with Rushworth as a brother, even without all the wolfish things that come with him. Julia seems to enjoy London exceedingly. I had little enjoyment there, but have less here. We are not a lively party. You are very much wanted. I miss you more than I can express. My mother desires her best love, and hopes to hear from you soon. She talks of you almost every hour, and I am sorry to find how many weeks more she is likely to be without you. My father means to fetch you himself, but it will not be till after Easter, when he has business in town. You are happy at Portsmouth, I hope, but this must not be a yearly visit. I want you at home, that I may have your opinion about Thornton Lacey. I have little heart for improvements till I know that it will ever have a mistress. I think I shall certainly write. It is quite settled that the Grants go to Bath; I am glad of it.—Yours ever, my dearest Fanny."

"Never! I will certainly never wish for a letter again!" was Fanny's secret declaration as she finished this. "What do they bring but disappointment and sorrow? Not till after Easter! How shall I bear it? And my poor aunt talking of me every hour!"

Fanny checked her thoughts as well as she could, but she was near to thinking that Sir Thomas was quite unkind, both to her aunt and to herself.

As for the main subject of the letter, there was nothing in that to soothe irritation. She was almost vexed into displeasure and *anger* against Edmund.

"There is no good in this delay," said she. "Why is not it settled? He is blinded, and nothing will open his eyes; nothing can, after having had truths before him so long in vain. He will marry the charming vampire—though I have no notion how *that* perversion against all Laws of God and nature shall be managed, a clergyman conjoined[29] with a demon—and be poor and miserable, and possibly bitten and eventually *undead* himself! God grant that her influence does not destroy him, or make him cease to be respectable!"

She looked over the letter again. "'So very fond of me!' Hah! 'tis nonsense all. She loves nobody but herself and her brother. 'Her friends leading her astray for years!' She is quite as likely to have led *them* astray, and made a nice meal of it, too.

"They have all, perhaps, been corrupting one another. But if they are so much *fonder of her* than she is of them, she is the less likely to have been hurt, except by their flattery. 'The only woman in the world whom he could ever think of as a wife.' I firmly believe it—and despair. It is an attachment to govern his whole life. Accepted or refused, his heart is wedded to her eternally. 'The loss of Mary is the loss of Crawford and Fanny.' Edmund, you do not know me. The families would never be connected if *you* did not connect them! Oh! write, write. Finish it already, this torture. Let there be an end! Fix, commit, condemn yourself."

But such sensations were too much like resentment to linger in Fanny. She was soon more softened and sorrowful. His warm regard, his kind expressions, his confidential treatment, touched her strongly. He was only too good to everybody. It was a letter, in short, which she hated, yet needed as a precious thing.

Anyone addicted to letter-writing without having much to say (this includes a large proportion of the female world), must feel that Lady Bertram was cheated of being the one to relate such a capital piece of Mansfield news as the certainty of

---

[29] Not in the Siamese sense.

the Grants going to Bath—cheated by her thankless son who used only a sentence where she would have spread it over a whole page. For though Lady Bertram rather shone in the epistolary line (having early in her marriage, from the want of other employment, and the circumstance of Sir Thomas's being in Parliament, got into the way of making and keeping correspondents, and thus embroiled herself in the archeological quagmire of Ancient Egypt), and formed a fine writing style, in which little substance was enough for a long missive: she could not do entirely without *any*. She must have something to write about, even to her niece; and being so soon to lose all the benefit of Dr. Grant's gouty symptoms and Mrs. Grant's morning calls, it was very hard upon her to be deprived of one of the last epistolary uses she could put them to.

There was a rich amends, however, preparing for her. Lady Bertram's hour of good luck came. Within a few days from the receipt of Edmund's letter, Fanny had one from her aunt, beginning thus—

> "MY DEAR FANNY,—
>
> I take up my pen to communicate some very alarming intelligence, which I make no doubt will give you much concern".

This was a great deal better than mere particulars of the Grants' intended journey. Indeed, the present intelligence was of a nature to promise occupation for the pen for many days to come, being no less than the dangerous illness of her eldest son, of which they had received notice by express a few hours before.

Tom had gone from London with a party of young men to Newmarket, where a neglected fall after foolishly attempting to scale a wall without a rope, and a good deal of drinking had brought on a fever. When the party broke up, he was unable to move, and had been left by himself at the house of one of these young men, in sickness, solitude, and the attendance only of servants. Instead of a speedy recovery and the rejoining of his friends, his illness increased considerably. It was not long before he was so ill that his physician sent a letter to Mansfield.

> "This distressing intelligence, as you may suppose," observed her ladyship, after giving the substance of it, "has agitated us exceedingly. We are greatly alarmed and apprehensive for the poor invalid, whose state Sir Thomas fears may be very critical. Edmund kindly proposes attending his brother immediately, but I am happy to add that Sir Thomas will not leave me on this distressing occasion, as it would be too trying for me. We shall greatly miss Edmund in our small circle, but I trust he will find the poor invalid in a less alarming state than might be apprehended, and that he will be able to bring him to Mansfield shortly. Sir Thomas thinks it best, and the poor sufferer will soon be able to bear the removal without inconvenience or injury. As I have little doubt of your feeling for us, my dear Fanny, under these distressing circumstances, I will write again very soon."

Fanny's feelings on the occasion were indeed considerably more warm and genuine than her aunt's style of writing. She felt truly for them all. Tom dangerously ill, Edmund gone to attend him, the sadly small party remaining at Mansfield—these were cares to shut out almost every other care.

She could just find selfishness enough to wonder whether Edmund *had* written to Miss Crawford before this summons came. But this was soon replaced with purely affectionate altruistic anxiety.

Her aunt did not neglect her: she wrote again and again. They were receiving frequent accounts from Edmund, and these were as regularly transmitted to Fanny, in the same diffuse style, and the same medley of trusts, hopes, and fears, all following and producing each other at haphazard. It was a sort of playing at being frightened.

The sufferings which Lady Bertram did not see had little power over her fancy; and she wrote very comfortably about agitation, and anxiety, and poor invalids—till Tom was actually conveyed to Mansfield, and her own eyes had beheld his altered appearance. Then, her letter to Fanny was finished in a different style, in the language of real feeling and alarm—she wrote as she might have spoken.

> "He is just come, my dear Fanny, and is taken upstairs; and I am so shocked to see him, that I do not know what to do. I am sure he has been very ill. Poor Tom! I am quite grieved for him, and very much frightened, and so is Sir Thomas; and how glad I should be if you were here to comfort me. But Sir Thomas hopes he will be better to-morrow, and says we must consider his journey."

The real solicitude now awakened in the maternal bosom was not soon over. Tom's extreme impatience to be removed to Mansfield, and the comforts of home and family, had probably induced his being conveyed thither too early. A return of fever came on, and for a week he was in a more alarming state than ever.

They were all very seriously frightened. Lady Bertram wrote her daily terrors to her niece, who might now be said to live upon letters, and pass all her time between suffering from that of to-day and looking forward to to-morrow's. Without any particular affection for her eldest cousin, Fanny's tenderness of heart made her feel that she could not spare him, and the purity of her principles added yet a keener solicitude. She considered how little useful, how little self-denying his life had been.

Susan was her only companion and listener in this—always ready to hear and sympathise. Nobody else could be interested in so remote an evil as illness in relations many miles away. Seeing her daughter with a letter, Mrs. Price might ask a brief question, followed by the quiet observation of, "My poor sister Bertram must be in a great deal of trouble."

So long divided and so differently situated, the ties of blood were little more than nothing. An attachment, originally as tranquil as their tempers, was now become a mere name. Mrs. Price did quite as much for Lady Bertram as Lady Bertram would have done for Mrs. Price.

Three or four Prices might have been swept away in the oceans, consumed by mummies, or by the likes of a Mr. Rushworth at the height of a full moon—any or all except Fanny and William, that is—and Lady Bertram would have thought little about it.

Or, perhaps she might have caught from Mrs. Norris's lips the cant of its being a very happy thing—a great blessing to their poor dear sister Price to have them so well *provided for*.

Chapter XLV

About a week after his return to Mansfield, Tom's immediate danger was over, and he was so far pronounced safe as to make his mother perfectly easy. Being now used to the sight of him in his suffering, helpless state, and hearing only the best, and never thinking beyond what she heard, with no disposition for alarm and no aptitude at a hint, Lady Bertram was the happiest subject in the world for a little medical imposition.

The fever was subdued; the fever had been his complaint; of course he would soon be well again. Lady Bertram could think nothing less, and Fanny shared her aunt's security, till she received a few frightening lines from Edmund, written purposely to give her a clearer idea of his brother's situation, and acquaint her with the apprehensions which he and his father had imbibed from the physician with respect to some strong hectic symptoms, which seemed to seize the frame on the departure of the fever. They judged it best that Lady Bertram should not be alarmed; worries would hopefully prove unfounded. But there was no reason why Fanny should not know the truth. They were apprehensive for his lungs.

A very few lines from Edmund shewed her the patient and the sickroom in a clearer light than all Lady Bertram's sheets of paper could do. They also filled her with trepidation.

> "It is the Curse, dearest Fanny, I have no doubt of it, I *see* it before me! Tom's malady has a supernatural underlying cause. Thus, as it is my duty as a man of the cloth, I must perform the holy ritual of Exorcism to rid this house of evil—once and for all. And now, I pray you speak to no one of this just yet."

Oh, Edmund, thought Fanny. *If only you could recognize and see evil so clearly at other times. . . .*

In the meantime, Lady Bertram was dreadfully useless. There was hardly any one in the house who might not have described his condition, from personal observation, better than herself; or who was not more useful to her son.

She could do nothing but glide in quietly and look at him. But when able to talk or be talked to, or read to, Edmund was the companion Tom preferred. Aunt Norris worried him by her cares, and Sir Thomas knew not how to bring down his conversation or his voice to the gentle level needed by the irritated and feeble. Edmund was the only one. Fanny found her estimation of him higher than ever when he appeared as the attendant, supporter, cheerer of a suffering brother.

There was not only the debility of recent illness to assist: there was also, as she now learnt, nerves much affected, spirits much depressed to calm and raise, and finally, the various secret holy rituals to enact in exactness, purity, and haste, when no one else was present. Her own imagination added that there must be a mind to be properly guided and a soul rescued from *dark* torment.

The family were not consumptive, though definitely Cursed, and Fanny was more inclined to hope than fear for her cousin, except when she thought of Miss Crawford. But heartless Miss Crawford gave her the idea of it all being a sort of good luck—it would indeed be good luck to Mary's selfishness and vanity to have Tom pass on, and Edmund become the only son!

Even in the sick chamber the fortunate Mary was not forgotten. Edmund's letter had this postscript:

> "On the subject of my last, I had actually begun a letter when called away by Tom's illness, but I have now changed my mind, and fear to trust the influence of friends. When Tom is better, I shall go. Meanwhile, back to the Exorcism."

Fanny bit her lips and thought, *Oh, if only he would Exorcise Miss Crawford!*

Such was the state of Mansfield, and so it continued, with scarcely any change, till Easter. A line occasionally added by Edmund to his mother's letter was enough for Fanny's information. Tom's amendment was alarmingly slow. Edmund had used up many basins of holy water, had gone slightly hoarse from reciting ritual prayers, and all in all, the evil was taking some time to remove itself—though he had all hopes of succeeding at last, and Tom had quit all talk of horseracing wagers and for once did not seem to be swayed by the offer to purchase a "double-headed lamb" that Baddeley was made to tell him about as a kind of test of his faculties.

Easter came particularly late this year, as Fanny sorrowfully considered, on first learning that she had no chance of leaving Portsmouth till after it.

It came, and she had yet heard nothing of her return—nothing even of the going to London, which was to precede her return. Her aunt often expressed a wish for her, but there was no notice, no message from the uncle on whom all depended.

She supposed he could not yet leave his son, but it was a cruel, terrible delay to her. At the end of April it would be almost three months, instead of two, that she had been away. Her days were passing in a state of penance which they would never understand. And who could yet say when there might be leisure to think of or fetch her?

When she had been coming to Portsmouth, she had loved to call it her home, had been fond of saying that she was going *home;* the word had been very dear to her. And so it still was, but it must be applied to Mansfield. *That* was now the home.

Portsmouth was Portsmouth; Mansfield was home. They had been long so arranged in her secret meditations, and nothing was more consolatory to her than to find her aunt using the same language: "I much regret your being from *home* at this distressing time, so very trying to my spirits. I trust and hope, and sincerely wish you may never be absent from home so long again," were most delightful sentences to her.

Still, however, it was her private regale. Delicacy to her parents made her careful not to betray such a preference of her uncle's house. It was always: "When I go back into Northamptonshire," or: "When I return to Mansfield—"

But at last the longing grew stronger and overthrew caution. Fanny found herself talking of what she should do when she went home before she was aware. She reproached herself, coloured, and looked fearfully towards her father and mother. She need not have been uneasy. There was no sign of displeasure, or even of hearing her. They were perfectly free from any jealousy of Mansfield. She was as welcome to wish herself there as to be there.

It was sad to Fanny to lose all the pleasures of spring. She had not known before what pleasures she *had* to lose in passing March and April in a town. What animation, both of body and mind, she had derived from watching the advance of that season which cannot be unlovely, and seeing its increasing beauties from the earliest flowers in the warmest divisions of her aunt's garden, to the opening of leaves of her uncle's plantations, and the glory of his woods.

To be losing such pleasures because she was in the midst of closeness, noise, confinement, bad air, bad smells, substituted for liberty, freshness, fragrance, and verdure, was infinitely worse. But even this regret was feeble, compared with being missed by her best friends, and the longing to be useful to those who actually wanted her!

Could she have been at Mansfield, she might have been of service to every creature in the house. Were it only in supporting the spirits of her aunt Bertram, keeping her from the evil of solitude, or the still greater evil of a restless, officious lupine companion, too apt to be heightening danger in order to enhance her own importance—Fanny's being there would have been a general good. She loved to fancy how she could read to her aunt, talk to her. She imagined the many walks up and down stairs she might have saved her, and how many messages she might have carried. Even the old familiar, oddly *dear* clutter of Egyptian artifacts—much reduced since Sir Thomas's Grand Purge after *that ball,* but still present in some cases, in a cat-headed gold figurine here, a crocodile-headed knick-knack there. . . .

Fanny made herself stop that particular course of thought, for that way lay folly and the remembrance of a certain intense pair of *familiar* eyes—

It astonished her that Tom's sisters could be satisfied with remaining in London at such a time, through an illness which had, under different degrees of danger, lasted several weeks. *They* could have returned to Mansfield whenever they chose! Travelling could be no difficulty to *them!*

She could not comprehend how both could still keep away. If Mrs. Rushworth could imagine any interfering obligations, Julia was certainly able to quit London whenever she chose. It appeared from one of her aunt's letters that Julia had offered to return if wanted, but this was all. It was evident that she would rather remain where she was.

Fanny was disposed to think the influence of London very much at war with all respectable attachments. She saw the proof of it in Miss Crawford, as well as in her cousins. *Her* attachment to Edmund had been the most respectable part of her character; her friendship for Fanny had been blameless. Where was either sentiment now?

It was so long since Fanny had had any letter from her, that she had reason to think lightly of that "friendship." It was weeks since she had heard anything of Miss Crawford or anyone else in town, except through Mansfield. Indeed, she might never know whether Mr. Crawford had gone into Norfolk again or not till they met, and might never hear from his sister any more this spring. However, the following letter was received to revive old and create some *new* sensations—

> "Forgive me, my dear Fanny, as soon as you can, for my long silence, and behave as if you could forgive me directly. This is my modest request and expectation, for you are so good, that I depend upon being treated better than I deserve, and I write now to beg an immediate answer. I want to know the state of things at Mansfield Park, and you, no doubt, are perfectly able to give it.
>
> "One should be a brute not to feel for the distress they are in; and from what I hear, poor Mr. Bertram has a bad chance of ultimate recovery. I thought little of his illness at first. I looked upon him as the foolish sort to be made a fuss with, and to make a fuss himself in any trifling disorder, and was chiefly concerned for those who had to nurse him. But now it is confidently asserted that he is really in a decline, the symptoms are alarming, and that part of the family are aware of it. If it is so, you must be in that informed part, and therefore I entreat you to let me know if I have been rightly informed. How rejoiced I shall be if this were a mistake, but the report is so prevalent that I confess I cannot help trembling.
>
> "To have such a fine young man cut off in the flower of his days is most melancholy. Poor Sir Thomas will feel it dreadfully. I really am quite agitated on the subject. Fanny, Fanny, I see you smile and look cunning, but, upon my honour, I never bribed a physician in my

life—nor had I gone near enough to have a delightful sanguine sip. . . .

"Poor young man! If he is to die, there will be *two* poor young men less in the world. And with a fearless face and bold voice would I say to any one, that wealth and consequence could not fall into more deserving hands. It was a foolish precipitation last Christmas, but the evil of a few days may be blotted out in part. Varnish and gilding hide many stains. It will be but the loss of the Esquire after *his* name. With real affection, Fanny, like mine, more might be overlooked.

Write to me by return of post, judge of my anxiety, and do not trifle with it. Tell me the real truth, as you have it from the fountainhead. And now, do not trouble yourself to be ashamed of either my feelings or your own. Believe me, for *such* one as myself, they are not only natural, they are philanthropic and virtuous. I put it to your conscience, whether 'Sir Edmund' would not do more good with all the Bertram property than any other possible 'Sir.' Had the Grants been at home I would not have troubled you, but you are now the only one I can apply to for the truth, his sisters not being within my reach. Mrs. R. has been spending the Easter with the Aylmers at Twickenham, and is not yet returned; and Julia is with the cousins who live near Bedford Square. Could I immediately apply to either, however, I should still prefer you, because they have all along been so unwilling to have their own amusements cut up, as to shut their eyes to the truth. I suppose Mrs. R.'s Easter holidays will not last much longer. The Aylmers are pleasant people; and her husband away, she can have nothing but enjoyment. I give her credit for promoting Mr. R.'s going dutifully down to Bath, to fetch his mother or howl at the moon there; but how will she and the dowager agree in one house? Henry is not at hand, so I have nothing to say from him. Do not you think Edmund would have been in town again long ago, but for this illness?

—Yours ever,

MARY."

"I had actually begun folding my letter when Henry walked in. . . . But he brings no intelligence to prevent my sending it. Mrs. R. knows a decline is apprehended; he saw her this morning: she returns to Wimpole Street to-day; the old lady is come.

> "Now do not make yourself uneasy with any queer fancies because he has been spending a few days at Richmond. He does it every spring. Be assured he cares for nobody but you. At this very moment he is wild to see you, and occupied only in contriving the means for doing so. In proof, he repeats, and more eagerly, what he said at Portsmouth about our conveying you home, and I join him in it with all my *dark* but insightful soul. Dear Fanny, write directly, and tell us to come. It will do us all good. He and I can go to the Parsonage, and be no trouble to our friends at Mansfield Park. It would really be gratifying to see them all again, and a little addition of society might be of infinite use to them. As to yourself, you must feel yourself to be so wanted there, that you cannot in *conscience* keep away, when you have the means of returning. I have not time or patience to give half Henry's messages; be satisfied that the spirit of each and every one is unalterable *affection.*"

Fanny's disgust at the greater part of this letter, and her extreme reluctance to bring Mary and her cousin Edmund together, would have made her incapable of responding either to accept or decline the concluding offer.

To herself, individually, it was most tempting. To be finding herself, perhaps within three days, transported to Mansfield, was an image of the greatest felicity. But it would have been a drawback to owe such felicity to persons whose feelings and conduct she condemned—the sister's feelings, the brother's conduct, *her* cold-hearted ambition, *his* thoughtless vanity. To have him still the acquaintance, the flirt perhaps, of Mrs. Rushworth!

She was mortified. She had thought better of him. Happily, however, she was not left to weigh and decide between opposite inclinations. There was no occasion to determine whether to keep Edmund and Mary asunder. Her awe of her uncle, and her dread of taking a liberty with him, made it instantly plain to her what she had to do.

She must absolutely decline the proposal. If he wanted, Sir Thomas would send for her. Even to suggest an early return was a presumption.

She thanked Miss Crawford, but gave a decided negative. "Her uncle, she understood, meant to fetch her; and as her cousin's illness had continued so many weeks without her being thought at all necessary, she must suppose her return would be unwelcome at present, and that she might be an encumbrance."

Fanny's representation of her cousin's state was exactly according to her own belief of it, and would convey to the sanguine mind of her vampiric correspondent the hope of everything she was wishing for. Edmund would be forgiven for being a clergyman, it seemed, under certain conditions of wealth. And this, she suspected, was the full extent of any "conquest of prejudice" with which he was so ready to congratulate himself.

Mary had only learnt to think nothing of consequence but money.

Chapter XLVI

As Fanny could not doubt that her answer was a disappointment to Mary, she was rather in expectation, from her knowledge of Miss Crawford's temper, of being urged again. Though no second letter arrived for the space of a week, she had still the same feeling when it did come.

On receiving it, she noted instantly how it contained little writing, and had the air of a letter of haste and business.

Its object seemed unquestionable. At first Fanny feared it was to give her notice that they should be in Portsmouth that very day to fetch her (which threw her into agitation and doubt of what to do in such a case). However, this was the letter—

> "A most scandalous, ill-natured rumour has just reached me, and I write, dear Fanny, to warn you against giving the least credit to it, should it spread into the country.
>
> "Depend upon it, there is some mistake, and a day or two will clear it up. At any rate, Henry is blameless, and in spite of a moment's *etourderie*, thinks of nobody but *you.*
>
> "Say not a word of it; hear nothing, surmise nothing, whisper nothing till I write again. I am sure it will be all hushed up, and nothing proved but Rushworth's folly. If *they* are gone, I would lay my life they are only gone to Mansfield Park, and Julia with them. But why would not

you let us come for you? I wish you may not repent it.—
Yours, etc."

Fanny stood aghast. As no scandalous, ill-natured rumour had reached her, it was impossible for her to understand much of this strange letter.

She could only perceive that it must relate to Wimpole Street and Mr. Crawford. And she could only conjecture that something very imprudent had just occurred in that quarter to draw the notice of the world—and to excite her jealousy, in Miss Crawford's apprehension, if she heard it.

Miss Crawford need not be alarmed for her. She was only sorry for the parties concerned and for Mansfield, if the report should spread so far. But she hoped it might not. If the Rushworths were gone themselves to Mansfield, as was to be inferred from what Miss Crawford said, it was not likely that anything unpleasant should have preceded them.

As to Mr. Crawford, she hoped it might give him a knowledge of his own disposition, convince him that he was not capable of being steadily attached to any one woman in the world, and shame him from persisting any longer in addressing herself.

It was very strange! She had begun to think he *really* loved her, and to fancy his affection for her something more than common. Even his sister still said that he cared for nobody else. Yet—there must have been some marked display of attentions to her cousin. There must have been some strong indiscretion—since her correspondent was not of a sort to regard a slight one.

Very uncomfortable Fanny was, and must continue, till she heard from Miss Crawford again. It was impossible to banish the letter from her thoughts, and she could not relieve herself by speaking of it to any human being.

The next day came and brought no second letter. Fanny was disappointed. She could still think of little else, when her father came back in the afternoon with the daily newspaper as usual; she was so far from expecting any elucidation through such a channel that the subject was for a moment out of her head.

She was deep in other musing. The remembrance of her first evening in that room, of her father and his newspaper, came across her. No candle was now wanted. The sun was yet an hour and a half above the horizon.

She felt that she had, indeed, been three months there. The sun's rays falling strongly into the parlour, instead of cheering, made her still more melancholy—sunshine appeared to her a totally different thing here. Its power was only a stifling, sickly glare, serving but to bring forward stains and dirt that might otherwise have slept. There was neither health nor gaiety in sunshine in a town.

Fanny sat in a blaze of oppressive heat, in a cloud of moving dust, and her eyes could only wander from the walls, marked by her father's head, to the table cut and notched by her brothers, where stood the tea-board never thoroughly cleaned, the cups and saucers wiped in streaks, the milk a mixture of motes floating in thin blue, and the bread and butter growing every minute more greasy than even Rebecca's hands had first produced it.

Her father read his newspaper, and her mother lamented over the ragged carpet as usual, while the tea was in preparation, and wished Rebecca would mend it instead of dallying with pockmarked louts.

Fanny was first roused by her father's calling out to her, after humphing and considering over a particular paragraph: "What's the name of your great cousins in town, Fan?"

A moment's recollection enabled her to say, "Rushworth, sir."

"And don't they live in Wimpole Street?"

"Yes, sir."

"Then, there's the devil to pay among them, that's all! There" (holding out the paper to her); "much good may such fine relations do you. I don't know what Sir Thomas may think of such matters; he may be too much of the courtier and fine gentleman to like his daughter the less. But, by G—! if she belonged to *me,* I'd give her the rope's end as long as I could stand over her. A little flogging for man and woman too would be the best way of preventing such things."

Fanny read to herself that "it was with infinite concern the newspaper had to announce to the world a matrimonial *fracas* in the family of Mr. R. of Wimpole Street; the beautiful Mrs. R., whose name had not long been enrolled in the lists of Hymen, and who had promised to become so brilliant a leader in the fashionable world, having quitted her husband's roof in company with the well-known and captivating Mr. C., the intimate friend and associate of Mr. R., and it was not known even to the editor of the newspaper whither they were gone."

"It is a mistake, sir," said Fanny instantly; "it must be a mistake, it cannot be true; it must mean some other people."

She spoke from the instinctive wish of delaying shame. She spoke with a resolution sprung from despair. For, she spoke what she did not, could not believe herself. It had been the shock of conviction as she read. The truth rushed on her; and how she could have spoken at all, or even breathed, was a wonder.

Mr. Price cared too little about the report to make her much answer. "It might be all a lie," he acknowledged; "but so many fine ladies were going to the devil nowadays that way, that there was no answering for anybody."

"Indeed, I hope it is not true," said Mrs. Price plaintively; "it would be so very shocking! If I have spoken once to Rebecca about that carpet, I am sure I have spoke at least a dozen times; have not I, Betsey? And it would not be ten minutes' work."

The horror of a mind like Fanny's, as it received the conviction of such guilt, and began to imagine the misery that must ensue, can hardly be described.

At first, it was a sort of stupefaction. But every moment was quickening her perception of the horrible evil. She could not doubt or, she dared not hope, of the paragraph being false. Miss Crawford's letter was in frightful conformity with it. Her eager defense of her brother, her hope of its being *hushed up,* her evident agitation—were all of a piece with something very bad. And if there was a woman of character in existence, who could treat as a trifle this sin of the first magnitude, who would try to gloss it over, and desire to have it unpunished, she could believe Miss Crawford to be the woman! Now she could see her own mistake as to *who* were gone, or *said* to be gone. It was not Mr. and Mrs. Rushworth; it was Mrs. Rushworth and Mr. Crawford.

It seemed to Fanny she had never been shocked to such an extent, ever. There was no end to it.

The evening passed without a pause of misery, the night was totally sleepless. She passed from feelings of sickness to shudderings of horror, from fevered hot to cold.

The event was so shocking, that there were moments even when her heart revolted from it as impossible—it could not be. A woman married only six months ago; a man professing himself devoted, even *engaged* to another; that other her near relation; both families connected as they were by tie upon tie; all friends, all intimate together! It was too horrible a confusion of guilt, too gross a complication of evil, for human nature, not in a state of utter barbarism,[30] to be capable of!

Yet her judgment told her it was so. *His* unsettled affections, wavering with his vanity, *Maria's* decided attachment—and no sufficient principle on either side—gave it possibility: Miss Crawford's letter stampt it a fact.

---

[30] Babylon.

What would be the consequence? Whom would it not injure? Whose views might it not affect? Whose peace would it not cut up for ever? Miss Crawford, herself, Edmund—but it was dangerous, perhaps, to tread such ground.

She confined herself to the simple, indubitable family misery which must envelop all, if it were indeed a matter of certified guilt and public exposure. The mother's sufferings, the father's; there she paused. Julia's, Tom's, Edmund's; there was yet a longer pause. They were the two on whom it would fall most horribly. Sir Thomas's parental solicitude and high sense of honour and decorum, Edmund's upright principles, unsuspicious temper, and genuine strength of feeling, made her think it scarcely possible for them to support life and reason under such disgrace. And it appeared to her that, as far as this world alone was concerned, the greatest blessing to every one of kindred with Mrs. Rushworth would be instant *annihilation.*

Indeed, in a mad rush of emotion, Fanny regretted that the mummies had quitted Mansfield Park. . . .

Nothing happened the next day, or the next, to weaken her terrors. Two posts came in, and brought no refutation, public or private. There was no second letter to explain away the first from Miss Crawford. There was no intelligence from Mansfield, though it was time to hear from her aunt. This was an evil omen.

Fanny had scarcely the shadow of a hope to soothe her mind, and was reduced to such a low state, as no unkind mother, except Mrs. Price, could have overlooked.

The third day did bring the sickening knock, and a letter was put into her hands. It bore the London postmark, and came from Edmund.

"DEAR FANNY,—

"You know our present wretchedness. May God support you under your share! We have been here two days, but there is nothing to be done. *They* cannot be traced.

> "You may not have heard of the latest blow—Julia's elopement. She is gone to Scotland with Yates. She left London a few hours before we entered it. At any other time this would have been felt dreadfully. Now it seems nothing; yet it is an heavy aggravation.
>
> "My father is not overpowered. More cannot be hoped. He is still able to think and act; and I write, by his desire, to propose your returning home. He is anxious to get you there for my mother's sake.
>
> "I shall be at Portsmouth the morning after you receive this, and hope to find you ready to set off for Mansfield. My father wishes you to invite Susan to go with you for a few months. Settle it as you like; say what is proper; I am sure you will feel such an instance of his kindness at such a moment! Do justice to his meaning, however I may confuse it.
>
> "You may imagine something of my present state. There is no end of the evil let loose upon us. Verily, the Exorcisms have failed. You will see me early by the mail.—Yours, etc."

Never had Fanny more wanted a cordial (for the last few days she even threw momentary wistful glances at her father's horrid rum bottle). Never had she *received* such a one as this letter contained.

To-morrow! to leave Portsmouth to-morrow! She was in the greatest danger of being exquisitely happy, while so many were miserable. The evil which brought such good to her! She dreaded she might become insensible to it.

To be going so soon, sent for so kindly, sent for as a comfort, and with leave to take Susan, was altogether such a combination of blessings as to set her heart aglow. It seemed to distance every pain, and made her incapable of suitably sharing the distress even of those whose distress she thought of most.

Julia's elopement could affect her comparatively but little. She was amazed and shocked, but it could not occupy her. She was obliged to make herself think of it in the midst of all the agitating pressing joy.

There is nothing like employment for relieving sorrow. She had so much to do, that not even the horrible story of Mrs. Rushworth—now fixed to the last point of certainty—could affect her as it had before. She had no time to be miserable.

Within twenty-four hours she was hoping to be gone. Her father and mother must be spoken to, Susan prepared, everything readied. Business followed business; the day was hardly long enough. She was imparting happiness, unalloyed by the black communication which must briefly precede it. Her father and mother gave joyful consent to Susan's going with her. There was general satisfaction with which their departure was regarded, and there was the ecstasy of Susan herself—all this served to support Fanny's spirits.

The affliction of the Bertrams was little felt in the family. Mrs. Price talked of her poor sister for a few minutes. But how to find anything to hold Susan's clothes, because Rebecca took away all the boxes and spoilt them, was much more in her thoughts.

As for Susan, now unexpectedly gratified in the first wish of her heart, and knowing nothing personally of those who had sinned, or of those who were sorrowing—if she could help rejoicing from beginning to end, it was as ought to be expected from human virtue at fourteen.

As nothing was really left to Mrs. Price, or the good offices of Rebecca (who still had not mended the carpet), everything was duly accomplished, and the girls were ready for the morrow. It was impossible to get much sleep to prepare them for their journey. The cousin who was travelling towards them completely occupied their agitated spirits—one all happiness, the other all varying and indescribable perturbation.

By eight in the morning Edmund was in the house. The girls heard his entrance from above, and Fanny went down. The idea of immediately seeing him, knowing what he must be suffering, brought back all her own first feelings.

He—so near her, and in misery. She was ready to sink as she entered the parlour.

He was alone, and met her instantly. Fanny found herself pressed to his heart with only these words, just articulate, "My Fanny, my only sister; my only comfort now!" She could say nothing; nor for some minutes could he say more.

He turned away to recover himself. And when he spoke again, though his voice still faltered, his manner shewed self-command, and the resolution of avoiding any further allusion.

"Have you breakfasted? When shall you be ready? Does Susan go?" were questions following each other rapidly.

His great object was to be off as soon as possible. When Mansfield was considered, time was precious; and the state of his own mind made him find relief only in motion.

It was settled that he should order the carriage to the door in half an hour. Fanny answered for their having breakfasted and being quite ready in half an hour. He had already eaten, and declined staying for their meal. He would walk round the ramparts, and join them with the carriage. He was gone again; glad to get away even from Fanny.

"Watch out for the peeling ruffians out there!" hollered Mr. Price in his wake. "It's been blasted bad these last few days, they seem to be 'round every corner, assailing good folk—"

Oh my dear cousin, I need to warn you about the local mummies, thought Fanny, moments too late.

Edmund looked very ill; evidently suffering under violent emotions, which he was determined to suppress. She knew it must be so, but it was terrible to her.

The half hour flew by faster than imagined, when from outside came a minor commotion. Fanny could hear Edmund's alarmed voice and the shrill sound of Rebecca, which quickly went silent. There was only the neighing of the carriage horses, and then there were several loud knocks.

Both Susan and Fanny came outside in haste to observe. Edmund was using the handle of a riding whip to beat away a huge, swaying, completely peeling monster of a mummy that had its skeletal arms around Rebecca, having propped her against the wall of the building. In an unseemly manner of a kiss it was taking her *breath of life,* while Rebecca was mesmerized senseless.

"What! Not this abomination here, too?" Edmund exclaimed, and he continued striking the undead thing to no avail from the back.

Fanny wrung her hands, glancing around for anything to use as a weapon. "I am so sorry not to have mentioned it earlier, cousin! But yes, as you can see, they are here, I believe having come down all the way from Mansfield at some point—not sure why—Susan, dear, can you please run inside and grab something—"

Susan didn't need to be told twice. Like a valkyrie she flew inside, and like a banshee she emerged again seconds later, emboldened by the pile of unwashed laundry she held in her arms. "Fanny! Oh, Fanny, might any of this do? Oh!" And then she turned it over and saw something else, much, much better suited.

"Use the carpet, Fanny, use the carpet!"

It was indeed the famous length of carpet that Rebecca had never gotten to mending.

Edmund had let go of the horsewhip and now grappled with both hands in an attempt to pry away the mummy that had attached itself, like an immense three-thousand-year-old *undead* barnacle, to Rebecca's face.

Meanwhile, Fanny rolled up the carpet into a monstrous wad. In the moment that the mummy finally turned to gape in her direction with its maggot-crawling open jaw, she shoved with all her strength and the carpet was imbedded in its tediously terrifying mouth.

The usual consequences followed. The mummy struggled. Then, as the *breath of life* was cut off, it went still, and in moments, became sand and dust.

"There we go," said Fanny with some measure of satisfaction, wiping her hands and then shaking the carpet out. It was in that moment that Rebecca came to herself with a start and started to shriek: "Oh, I'll mend it right now, quick as day, I promise, oh, please! Not him, just don't let 'im near me again! Please, I'll fix it right in a jiffy, please, I'll—"

"He won't be bothering you again, Rebecca," said Fanny kindly, realizing a great deal of things at that point. "Indeed, you can start by sweeping *him* off the porch. Then, be sure to mend the carpet. And also, please re-wash all the dishes, and see if later—after you've rested a bit, of course, since, I am afraid you've been somewhat drained—you can do the laundry—properly, this time."

And as Mrs. Price looked blandly out of the house, Fanny said: "I dare say, mother, I am quite certain you will not have any servant problems from this point forward."

Now that the carriage had come (the driver had been watching the proceedings in somewhat stunned silence from his perch); and the mummy eliminated, Edmund entered the house.

It was just in time to spend a few minutes with the family, and be a witness—but he saw nothing—of the tranquil manner in which the daughters were parted with. It was also just in time to prevent their sitting down to the breakfast-table, which, by dint of much unusual activity on behalf of the new, *industrious* Rebecca, was quite and completely ready as the carriage drove from the door. Fanny's last meal in her father's house was in character with her first: she was dismissed from it as hospitably as she had been welcomed.

How her heart swelled with joy and gratitude as she passed the barriers of Portsmouth and witnessed her last lumbering peeling "fellow" bumping endlessly against a building wall, and how Susan's face wore its broadest smiles, may be easily conceived. Sitting forwards, however, and screened by her bonnet, those smiles were unseen.

"That was such a very opportune bit of carpet, Susan. Quite well done, indeed!" whispered Fanny to her young, avid pupil with fondness.

In other respects, the journey was likely to be a silent one. Edmund's deep sighs often reached Fanny. Had he been alone with her, his heart must have opened. But Susan's presence drove him quite into himself, and his attempts to talk on indifferent subjects were not long supported.

Fanny watched him with never-failing solicitude. Sometimes catching his eye, she revived an affectionate smile, which comforted her. But the first day's journey passed, without hearing a word from him on the subjects weighing him down.

The next morning produced a little more. Just before their setting out from Oxford, while Susan was stationed at a window, in eager observation of the departure of a large family from the inn, the other two were standing by the fire. Edmund was particularly struck by the alteration in Fanny's looks. And from his ignorance of the daily evils of her father's house, he attributed an undue share of the change, to the recent event. He took Fanny's hand, and said in a low, but very expressive tone, "No wonder—you must feel it—you must suffer. How a man who had once loved, could desert you! But *yours*—your regard was new compared with—Fanny, think of *me!*"

Fanny felt another stab of sorrow in her heart.

The first part of their journey occupied a long day, and brought them, almost knocked up,[31] to Oxford; but the second was over at a much earlier hour. They were in the environs of

---

[31] This is a genuinely serious passage, O Filthy Reader. And you, swimming in your spiritual debauchery, are beyond all redemption! Pay heed now, to the serious passage, and woe to you! Thou must needs quiver in unholy dread, for the moral authorities *have* been notified!

Mansfield long before dinner-time, and as they approached the beloved place, the hearts of both sisters sank a little.

Fanny began to dread the meeting with her aunts and Tom, under so dreadful a humiliation. Susan started to feel with some anxiety, that all her best manners, all her lately acquired knowledge of what was practised here, was on the point of being called into action. Visions of good and ill breeding, of old vulgarisms and new gentilities, were before her, and she was meditating much upon silver forks, napkins, and finger-glasses.

Fanny had been everywhere awake to the difference of the country since February. But when they entered the Park her perceptions and her pleasures were of the keenest sort. It was full three months since her quitting it, and the change was from winter to summer. Her eye fell everywhere on lawns and plantations of the freshest green. And the trees, though not fully clothed, were in that delightful state when further beauty is known to be at hand, and more yet remains for the imagination.

Her enjoyment, however, was for herself alone. Edmund could not share it. She looked at him, but he was leaning back, sunk in a deeper gloom than ever, and with eyes closed, as if the view of cheerfulness oppressed him, and the lovely scenes of home must be shut out.

It made her sad again. And the knowledge of what must be enduring there, invested even the house—modern, airy, and well situated as it was—with a melancholy aspect.

By one of the suffering party within they were expected with such impatience as she had never known before. Fanny had scarcely passed the solemn-looking servants, when Lady Bertram came from the drawing-room to meet her; came with no indolent step; and falling on her neck, said, "Dear Fanny! now I shall be comfortable."

Chapter XLVII

It had been a miserable party, each of the three believing themselves most miserable. Mrs. Norris, however, as most attached to Maria, was really the greatest sufferer. Maria was her first favourite, the dearest of all. The match had been her own contriving—as she had been wont with such pride of heart to feel and say—and this conclusion of it almost overpowered her.

Mrs. Norris was an altered creature, quieted, stupefied, indifferent to everything that passed, yapping only upon the rarest occasion. Being left with her sister and nephew, and with all the house under her care, had been an advantage entirely thrown away. She had been unable to direct or dictate, or even fancy herself useful. Everything was neglected. Only the shrubbery vermin took a decidedly hard punishment in those particularly grim days.

When really touched by affliction, her active powers had been all benumbed; and neither Lady Bertram nor Tom had received from her the smallest attempt at support. She had done no more for them than they had done for each other. They had been all solitary, helpless, and forlorn alike. And now the arrival of the others only established her superiority in wretchedness. Her companions were relieved, but there was no good for *her*.

Edmund was almost as welcome to his brother as Fanny to her aunt. But Mrs. Norris, instead of having comfort from either, was but the more irritated by the sight of the person whom, in the blindness of her anger, she could have charged as the daemon of the piece. Had Fanny accepted Mr. Crawford this could not have happened.

Susan too was a grievance. She had not spirits to notice her in more than a few repulsive looks, but she felt her as a spy, an intruder, an indigent niece, and everything most odious.

By her other aunt, Susan was received with quiet kindness. Lady Bertram could not give her much time, or many words, but she felt her, as Fanny's sister, to have a claim at Mansfield, and was ready to kiss and like her. Susan was more than satisfied, for she came perfectly aware that nothing but ill-humour was to be expected from aunt Norris; and was so provided with happiness—so strong in that best of blessings, an escape from many certain evils—that she could have stood against a great deal more indifference than she met with from the others.

She was now left a good deal to herself, to get acquainted with the house and grounds as she could, and spent her days very happily in so doing. Meanwhile, those who might otherwise have attended to her were shut up, or wholly occupied each with the person quite dependent on them, at this time, for everything like comfort—Edmund trying to bury his own feelings in exertions for the relief of his brother's, and Fanny devoted to her aunt Bertram, returning to every former office with more than former zeal, and thinking she could never do enough for one who seemed so much to *want* her.

To talk over the dreadful business with Fanny, talk and lament, was all Lady Bertram's consolation. To be listened to and borne with, and hear the voice of kindness and sympathy in return, was everything that could be done for her. To be *comforted* was out of the question—the case admitted of no comfort. Lady Bertram did not think deeply, but, guided by Sir Thomas, she thought justly on all important points. And she saw, therefore, in all its enormity, what had happened, and neither endeavoured herself, nor required Fanny to advise her, to think little of guilt and infamy.

Her affections were not acute, nor was her mind tenacious. After a time, Fanny found it possible to direct her thoughts to other subjects, and revive some interest in the usual occupations (even bringing out an Egyptian statuette or two out of hiding); but whenever Lady Bertram *was* fixed on the event, she could see it only in one light, as comprehending the loss of a daughter, and a disgrace never to be wiped off.

Fanny learnt from her all the particulars. Her aunt was not a very methodical narrator, but with the help of some letters to and from Sir Thomas, and what she already knew herself, she was soon able to understand the circumstances attending the story.

Mrs. Rushworth had gone, for the Easter holidays, to Twickenham, with a family whom she had just grown intimate with: a family of lively, agreeable manners, and probably of morals and discretion to suit, for to *their* house Mr. Crawford had constant access at all times. His having been in the same neighbourhood Fanny already knew. Mr. Rushworth had been gone at this time to Bath, to pass a few days with his mother (and to spend the dangerous time of the full moon away from his spouse who had as yet remained remarkably *un*bitten—but whose non-lupine days were surely numbered), and bring her back to town. And Maria was with these friends without any restraint, without even Julia; for Julia had removed from Wimpole Street two or three weeks before, on a visit to some relations of Sir Thomas—a removal which her father and mother were now disposed to attribute to some view of convenience on Mr. Yates's account. Very soon after the Rushworths' return to Wimpole Street, Sir Thomas had received a letter from an old and most particular friend in London, who hearing and witnessing a good deal to alarm him in that quarter, wrote to recommend Sir Thomas's coming to London himself, and using his influence with his daughter to put an end to the intimacy which was already exposing her to unpleasant remarks, and evidently making Mr. Rushworth uneasy and somewhat dangerous to be in company with.

Sir Thomas was preparing to act upon this letter (without communicating its contents to any creature at Mansfield), when it was followed by another, sent express from the same friend, to break to him the almost desperate situation in which affairs then stood with the young people. Mrs. Rushworth had left her husband's house: Mr. Rushworth had been in great anger and distress to *him* (Mr. Harding) for his advice; Mr. Harding feared not only *for his personal safety,* but feared there had been *at least* very flagrant indiscretion. The maidservant of Mrs. Rushworth, senior, threatened to go public, alarmingly. He was doing all in his power to quiet everything, with the hope of Mrs. Rushworth's return, but was so much counteracted in Wimpole Street by the influence of Mr. Rushworth's mother, that the worst consequences might be apprehended. In addition (Mr. Harding mentioned discreetly), Mr. Rushworth was said to get into such a *state* that a cage had to be brought around, and he was thus confined for several days while his howls and *roars* were heard for blocks beyond the premises. . . .

This dreadful communication could not be kept from the rest of the family. Sir Thomas set off, Edmund would go with him, and the others had been left in a state of wretchedness, inferior only to what followed the receipt of the next letters from London. Everything was by that time public beyond a hope. The servant of Mrs. Rushworth, the mother, had exposure in her power, and supported by her mistress (and the gut-wrenching howls of her young master), was not to be silenced. The two ladies, even in the short time they had been together, had disagreed; and the bitterness of the elder against her daughter-in-law might perhaps arise almost as much from the personal disrespect with which she had herself been treated as from sensibility for her son.

However that might be, she was unmanageable. But had she been less obstinate, or of less weight with her son, who was always guided by the last speaker, by the person who could get hold of and shut him up (or, in case of the moon, guided by a bright shining *object*), the situation would still have been hopeless—for the young Mrs. Rushworth did not appear again, and there was every reason to conclude her to be concealed somewhere with Mr. Crawford, who had quitted his uncle's house, as for a journey, on the very day of her absenting herself.

Sir Thomas, however, remained yet a little longer in town, in the hope of discovering and snatching her from further vice, though all was lost on the side of character.

His present state Fanny could hardly bear to think of. There was but one of his children who was not at this time a source of misery to him. Tom's complaints had been greatly heightened by the shock of his sister's conduct, and his recovery so much thrown back by it, that even Lady Bertram had been struck by the difference, and all her alarms were regularly sent off to her husband.

Julia's elopement, the additional blow which had met Sir. Thomas on his arrival in London, though its impact had been deadened at the moment, must be sorely felt. Fanny saw that it was. His letters expressed how much he deplored it. Under any circumstances it would have been an unwelcome alliance. But to have it so clandestinely formed, and at such a time, placed Julia's feelings in a most unfavourable light, and aggravated the folly of her choice. Sir Thomas called it a bad thing, done in the worst manner, and at the worst time. And though Julia was more pardonable than Maria (being folly rather than vice), he regarded the step she had taken as opening the worst probabilities of a conclusion very like her sister's.

Fanny felt for him most acutely. He could have no comfort but in Edmund. Every other child must be racking his heart. His displeasure against herself, she trusted, reasoning differently from Mrs. Norris, would now be done away. *She* should be justified. Mr. Crawford would have fully acquitted her conduct in refusing him. But this—though most material to herself—would be poor consolation to Sir Thomas. Her uncle's displeasure was terrible to her; but what could her justification or her gratitude and attachment do for him? His stay must be on Edmund alone.

She was mistaken, however, in supposing that Edmund gave his father no present pain. It was much less poignant than what the others excited. But Sir Thomas was considering his happiness as very deeply involved in the offence of his sister and friend. Cut off by it, as he must be, from the woman whom he had been pursuing with undoubted attachment and strong probability of success—a woman, who, in everything but this despicable brother, would have been so eligible a connexion!

He was aware of what Edmund must be suffering on his own behalf, in addition to all the rest, when they were in town. He had seen or conjectured his feelings. And, having reason to think that one interview with Miss Crawford had taken place, from which Edmund derived only increased distress, had been as anxious on that account as on others to get him out of town.

Thus, Sir Thomas engaged him in taking Fanny home to her aunt, with a view to his relief and benefit, no less than theirs. Fanny was not in the secret of her uncle's feelings, Sir Thomas not in the secret of Miss Crawford's character. Had he been privy to her conversation with his son, he would *not* have wished her to belong to him, though her twenty thousand pounds had been forty.

That Edmund must be forever divided from Miss Crawford, Fanny did not doubt. And yet, till she knew that he felt the same, her own conviction was insufficient. She thought he did, but she wanted to be assured of it. If he would now speak to her with the unreserve which had sometimes been too much for her before, it would be most consoling.

But *that* she found was not to be. She seldom saw him. He probably avoided being alone with her. What was to be inferred? That his judgment submitted to his own peculiar and bitter share of this family affliction—this Curse indeed!—but it was too keenly felt to be communicated.

This must be his state. He yielded, but it was with agonies which did not admit of speech. Long would it be ere Miss Crawford's name passed his lips again, or she could hope for a renewal of such confidential intercourse[32] as had been.

It *was* long. They reached Mansfield on Thursday, and it was not till Sunday evening that Edmund began to talk to her on the subject. Fanny fully expected to discover her very own first strands of silver in her hair after *that* conversation.

He was sitting with her on a wet Sunday evening—a time when, if a friend is at hand, the heart must be opened, and everything told. No one else was in the room, except his mother, who, after hearing an affecting sermon, had cried herself to sleep. It was impossible not to speak. And so, with the usual beginnings, hardly to be traced as to what came first, and the usual declaration that if she would listen to him for a few minutes, he should be very brief,[33] and certainly never tax her kindness in the same way again (she need not fear a repetition; it would be a subject prohibited entirely), he entered upon the

---

[32] THIS IS A SERIOUS PASSAGE! Thou, Foul Reader, are a fiend!

[33] The passage of time is hereby measured in Edmund Years. Not to be confused with East Wind Years, which includes mummification. (Pray, what, O Reader of Readers—did you perchance consider we were about to discuss types of unmentionables?)

luxury of relating circumstances and sensations of the first interest to himself, to one of whose affectionate sympathy he was quite convinced.

How Fanny listened, with what curiosity and concern, what pain and what delight, how the agitation of his voice was watched, and how carefully her own eyes were fixed on any object but himself, may be imagined. The opening was alarming. He had seen Miss Crawford. He had been invited to see her. He had received a note from Lady Stornaway to beg him to call. And regarding it as what was meant to be the last, last interview of friendship, and investing her with all the feelings of shame and wretchedness which Crawford's sister ought to have known, he had gone to her in such a state of mind, so softened, so devoted, as made it for a few moments impossible to Fanny's fears that it should be the last.

But as he proceeded in his story, these fears were over. Miss Crawford had met him, he said, with a serious—certainly a serious—even an agitated air; but before he had been able to speak one intelligible sentence, she had introduced the subject in a manner which he owned had shocked him.

"'I heard you were in town,' said she; 'I wanted to see you. Let us talk over this sad business. What can equal the folly of our two relations?'

"I could not answer, but I believe my looks spoke. She felt reproved. Sometimes how quick to feel!

"With a graver look and voice she then added, 'I do not mean to defend Henry at your sister's expense.'

"So she began, but how she went on, Fanny, is not fit to be repeated to you. I cannot recall all her words. I would not dwell upon them if I could. Their substance was great anger at the *folly* of each. She reprobated her brother's folly in being drawn on by a woman whom he had never cared for, to do what must lose him the woman he adored. But still more, it was the folly of poor Maria, in sacrificing such a situation, plunging into such difficulties, under the idea of being really loved by a man who had long ago made his indifference clear.

"Guess what I must have felt. To hear the woman whom—no harsher name than folly given! So voluntarily, so freely, so coolly to canvass it! No reluctance, no horror, no feminine, shall I say, no modest loathings? This is what the world does. For where, Fanny, shall we find a woman whom nature had so richly endowed? Spoilt, spoilt!"

After a little reflection, he went on with a sort of desperate calmness. "I will tell you everything, and then have done for ever.[34] She saw it only as folly, and that folly stamped only by *exposure*. The want of common discretion, of caution: his going down to Richmond for the whole time of her being at Twickenham; her putting herself in the power of a servant; it was the detection, in short—oh, Fanny! it was the *detection,* not the *offence,* which she reprobated. It was the imprudence which had brought things to extremity, and obliged her brother to give up every dearer plan in order to fly with her."

He stopt. "And what," said Fanny (believing herself required to speak, and feeling a need to somehow move atrophied limbs, even if it was but to unhinge her jaw), "what could you say?"

"Nothing, nothing to be understood. I was like a man stunned. She went on, began to talk of you; yes, then she began to talk of you, regretting, as well she might, the loss of such a—. There she spoke very rationally. But she has always done justice to you. 'He has thrown away,' said she, 'such a woman as he will never see again. She would have fixed him; she would have made him happy for ever.' My dearest Fanny, I am giving you, I hope, more pleasure than pain by this retrospect of what might have been—but what never can be now. You do not wish me to be silent? If you do, give me but a look, a word, and I have done."

---

[34] Once more, time is measured in Edmund Years.

No look or word was given (due in part to Fanny beginning to mummify—but she fought it, with every fibre of her being.).

"Thank God," said he. "We were all disposed to wonder, but it seems to have been the merciful appointment of Providence that the heart which knew no guile should not suffer.

"She spoke of you with high praise and warm affection; yet, even here, there was alloy, a dash of evil, a rending *darkness;* for in the midst of it she could exclaim, 'Why would not she have him? It is all her fault. Simple girl! I shall never forgive her. Had she accepted him as she ought, they might now have been on the point of marriage, and Henry would have been too happy and too busy to want any other object. He would have taken no pains to be on terms with Mrs. Rushworth again. It would have all ended in a regular standing flirtation, in yearly meetings at Sotherton and Everingham.' Could you have believed it possible? But the charm is broken. My eyes are opened."

"Cruel!" said Fanny, "quite cruel. At such a moment to give way to gaiety, to speak with lightness, and to you! Absolute cruelty."

"Cruelty, do you call it? We differ there. No, hers is not a cruel nature. I do not consider her as meaning to wound my feelings. The evil lies yet deeper: in her total *ignorance,* unawareness of there being such feelings; in a perversion of mind which made it natural to her to treat the subject as she did."

"Oh, Edmund," said Fanny yet again after all these months. "She is a *vampire*."

And for the first time Edmund did not ignore it. He looked at Fanny directly, with unflinching eyes, as he continued:

"Yes, Fanny, now I *know.* But first, a moment more, I pray, let me continue. Thus—She was speaking only as she had been used to hear others speak, as she imagined everybody else would speak. Hers are not faults of temper. She would not voluntarily give unnecessary pain to any one, and though I may deceive myself, I cannot but think that for me, for my feelings, she would—In addition to regular vampirism, hers are faults of *principle,* Fanny; of blunted delicacy and a corrupted, vitiated mind—which is *undead* indeed, I now admit. Perhaps it is best for me, since it leaves me so little to regret. Not so, however. Gladly would I submit to all the increased pain of losing her, rather than have to think of her as I do. I told her so."

"Did you?"

"Yes; when I left her I told her so."

"How long were you together?"

"Five-and-twenty minutes. Well, she went on to say that what remained now to be done was to bring about a marriage between them. She spoke of it, Fanny, with a steadier voice than I can."

He was obliged to pause more than once as he continued, while in such pauses Fanny discreetly tried to flex her petrifying limbs. Then, he went on again:

"'We must persuade Henry to marry her,' said she; 'and what with honour, and the certainty of having shut himself out for ever from Fanny, I do not despair of it. Fanny he must give up. I do not think that even *he* could now hope to succeed with one of her stamp, and therefore I hope we may find no insuperable difficulty. My influence, which is not small, shall all go that way; and when once married, and properly supported by her own family, people of respectability as they are, she may recover her footing in society to a certain degree. In some circles, we know, she would never be admitted, but with good dinners, and large parties, there will always be those who will be glad of her acquaintance. And there is, undoubtedly, more liberality and candour on those points than formerly. What I advise is, that your father be quiet. Do not let him injure his own cause by interference. Persuade him to let things take their course. If by any officious exertions of his, she is induced to leave Henry's protection, there will be much less chance of his marrying her than if she remains with him. I know how he is likely to be influenced. Let Sir Thomas trust to his honour and compassion, and it may all end well; but if he gets his daughter away, it will be destroying the chief hold.'"

After repeating this, Edmund was so much affected that Fanny, watching him with silent, but most tender concern, was almost sorry that the subject had been entered on at all (and, considering Fanny's generous heart, it had nothing to do with her present physical atrophy).

It was long before he could speak again. At last, "Now, Fanny," said he, "I shall soon[35] have done. I have told you the substance of all that she said.

"As soon as I could speak, I replied that I had not supposed it possible, coming in such a state of mind into that house as I had done, that anything could occur to make me suffer more . . . but that she had been inflicting deeper wounds in almost every sentence. That though I had, in the course of our acquaintance, been often sensible of some *difference* in our opinions, on points, too, of some moment, it had not entered my imagination to *conceive* the difference could be such as she had now proved it.

"That the manner in which she treated the dreadful crime committed by her brother and my sister (with whom lay the greater seduction I pretended not to say), but the manner in which she spoke of the crime itself, giving it every reproach but the right; considering its ill consequences only as they were to be braved or overborne by a defiance of decency and impudence in wrong—and last of all, and above all, recommending to us a compliance, a compromise, an acquiescence in the *continuance of the sin,* on the chance of a marriage which, thinking as I now thought of her brother, should rather be prevented than sought—

---

[35] In the quantum physics sense, begging pardon for the futurism, O Erudite Reader.

all this together most grievously convinced me that I had never understood her before.

"It had been the creature of my own imagination, not Miss Crawford, that I had been too apt to dwell on for many months past. Perhaps, it was best for me. I had less to regret in sacrificing a friendship, feelings, hopes which must, at any rate, have been torn from me now. And yet—could I have restored her to what she had appeared to me before! I would infinitely prefer any increase of the pain of parting, for the sake of carrying with me the right of tenderness and esteem.

"This is what I said, the purport of it; but, as you may imagine, not spoken so collectedly or methodically as I have repeated it to you.

"She was astonished, exceedingly astonished—more than astonished. I saw her change countenance. She turned extremely red—nay, it was more a deathly black, where sanguinity is unhealthy and forced to the surface of the skin like a shadow of death. I imagined I saw a mixture of many feelings: a great, though short struggle; half a wish of yielding to truths, half a sense of shame, but—habit carried it.

"She would have laughed if she could. It was a sort of laugh, as she answered, 'A pretty good lecture, upon my word. Was it part of your last sermon? At this rate you will soon reform everybody at Mansfield and Thornton Lacey; and when I hear of you next, it may be as a celebrated preacher in some great society of Methodists, or as a missionary into foreign parts.' She tried to speak carelessly, but she was not so careless as she wanted to appear.

"I only said in reply, that from my heart I wished her well, and earnestly hoped that she might soon learn to think more justly, and not owe the most valuable knowledge we could any of us acquire—the knowledge of ourselves and of our duty—to the lessons of affliction, and immediately left the room.

I had gone a few steps, Fanny, when I heard the door open behind me.

"'Mr. Bertram,' said she. I looked back. 'Mr. Bertram,' said she, with a smile; but it was a smile ill-suited to the conversation that had passed, a saucy playful smile, seeming to invite in order to subdue me—at least it appeared so to me. I resisted; it was the impulse of the moment to resist, and still walked on.

"But Miss Crawford called my name again, *differently,* with a command and an undeniable charge. And at this sound—at her changed voice, I again turned to look, curiously compelled. . . . But oh! what had she become! A hissing fury! With the blank, terrible, *empty* face of white pallor, and great blood-rimmed eyes that I had once thought so lovely—they were now akin to hot coals, black and red, burning in a fireplace of damnation with an unholy Cursed light! And her mouth—oh! her normally delightful laughing mouth with its cherry-red pouting lower lip that I had so—ahem—a truly glorious mouth, was now utter crimson, deep, deadly, gaping wide open, and in it . . . terrible sharp *teeth,* inhuman, deadly—

"She flew at me. In seconds, she was down the stairs and at my side, her clawed skeletal fingers reaching for me, to embrace my throat. And had it not been for the Lord's blessed Cross at my neck, beneath the clergyman's collar, she may have had me in her evil grasp.

"I struggled, and I reached for the wooden *implement* that I had long since carried with me, together with other tools of Exorcism. My vial of holy water was out of reach in a pocket that would have taken too long to fumble open. Hence, the wooden stake. One strike of such through the heart is said to destroy a vampire. . . .

"Her power of fury was superhuman. And yet—I had no heart to stake her, Fanny. And to be truthful, in that moment, there was no need. Within my heart she finally must have looked; she saw it, and she *knew*. And in that moment, she released me, and suddenly drew away . . . backed away into the shadows.

"She had no power over me—not ever again, not with her monstrous claws or teeth, not even with her saucy gaze. For, I was held in safety, in truth, by the memory of a pair of *beloved* eyes. Will you not ask me, Fanny, whose eyes I speak of? Oh, but you must! They were *yours*. You had saved me then, yet again, as you save me now."

Fanny had grown very, very still. And it had nothing to do with Edmund Years or mummification, quantum inertia, or anything but what was rising in her own heart.

Looking directly at Fanny, Edmund continued:

"I have since, sometimes, for a moment, regretted that I did not go back. But I know I was right, and such has been the end of our acquaintance. And what an acquaintance has it been! How have I been *deceived!* Equally in brother and sister deceived! I thank you for your patience, dearest Fanny. In *every* sense possible. I ask you for your forgiveness in not heeding you sooner, all these many sorrowful months ago. And now, to say this has been the greatest relief, and now we will have done."[36]

And such was Fanny's dependence on his words, that for five minutes she thought they *had* done.[37] Then, however, it all came on again, or something very like it, and nothing less than Lady Bertram's rousing thoroughly up could really close such a conversation.

Till that happened, they continued to talk of Miss Crawford alone, and how she had attached him with *unearthly* means, and how delightful nature had made her, and how excellent she would have been, had she fallen into good hands

---

[36] End of Edmund Years. Normal time flow resumes.

[37] A refractory period often follows Edmund Years, wherein can be experienced symptoms of temporal lag and disorientation.

earlier, instead of the *dark* clutches of the vampire mistress of the Admiral.

Fanny, now at liberty to speak openly, felt more than justified in adding to Edmund's knowledge of her real character. She disclosed that his brother's state of health (and possible demise, as Miss Crawford had cheerfully come to hope) might have had a strong influence in heightening that lady's wish for a complete reconciliation.

This was not an agreeable intimation for Edmund. Nature resisted it for a while. It would have been a vast deal pleasanter if she had been more disinterested in material attachments. But Edmund's vanity was not of a strength to fight long against reason. He submitted to believe that Tom's illness had influenced her, only reserving for himself this consoling thought that she had certainly been *more* attached to him than could have been expected—for *his* sake she had been closer to doing right.

Fanny thought exactly the same. They were also quite agreed in their opinion of the lasting effect—the indelible impression, which such a disappointment must make on his mind. Time would undoubtedly abate some of his sufferings. Still, it was a sort of thing which he could never entirely overcome. And as to his ever meeting with any other woman who could—it was too impossible to be named but with indignation.

Fanny's *friendship* was all that he had to cling to.

And hearing this from Edmund—again, after all the understandings and revelations that had just come to pass—Fanny's loving heart sank a little, once more.

Chapter XLVIII

Let other pens dwell on guilt and misery. I quit such odious subjects as soon as I can, impatient to restore everybody, not greatly in fault themselves, to tolerable comfort, and to have done with all the rest. And that includes mummies, Gentle Reader—though, unfortunately not quite yet—

My Fanny—indeed, at this very time, I have the satisfaction of knowing—must have been happy in spite of everything. She must have been a happy creature in spite of all that she felt for the distress of those around her.

She had sources of delight that must force their way. She was returned to Mansfield Park, she was useful, she was beloved; she was safe from Mr. Crawford. And when Sir Thomas came back she had every proof that could be given (despite his melancholy state of spirits), of his perfect approbation and increased regard.

Happy as all this must make her, she would still have been happy without any of it. For—Edmund was no longer the dupe of Miss Crawford.

It is true that Edmund was very far from happy himself. He was suffering from disappointment and regret, grieving over what was, and wishing for what could never be.

She knew it was so, and was sorry. But it was a sorrow so founded on satisfaction, so much in harmony with every dearest sensation, that few might not have been glad to exchange their greatest gaiety for it.

Poor Sir Thomas, conscious of errors in his own conduct as a *parent,* was the longest to suffer. He felt that he ought not to have allowed the marriage; that his daughter's sentiments had been sufficiently known to him to render him culpable in authorising it; that in so doing he had been governed by motives of selfishness and worldly wisdom. These reflections required some time to soften, but time will do almost everything. Though little comfort arose on Mrs. Rushworth's side for the misery she had occasioned, comfort was to be found in his other children.

Julia's match became a less desperate business than he first considered it. She was humble, and wishing to be forgiven. And Mr. Yates, desirous of being really received into the family, was disposed to look up to him and be guided. Yates was not very solid; but there was a hope of his becoming less trifling—at least tolerably domestic and *quiet.* At any rate, there was comfort in finding his estate rather more, and his debts much less, than Sir Thomas had feared, and in being consulted and treated as the friend best worth attending to.

There was comfort also in Tom, who gradually regained his health, without regaining the thoughtlessness and selfishness and *witlessness* of his previous habits. He was permanently improved by his illness. He had suffered, he had been Exorcised, and he had learned to think—three advantages he had never known before. His self-reproach arising from the deplorable event in Wimpole Street (to which he felt himself accessory by the dangerous intimacy of his unjustifiable theatre) made an impression. At the age of six-and-twenty, with good sensible companions, his mind was exposed to durable happy effects including (via his brother's tireless efforts) the holy cleansing ritual of the church. Once purged of the various Curses of personal incompetence, he became what he ought to be—useful to his father, potently resistant to the influence of vampires, gaming halls, impossible gambles, and other spawn of the *dark,* steady and quiet, and not living merely for himself. (Though, it must be said that occasionally Tom was seen in the back of the stables, calling quietly for his Quackie, and then discreetly feeding great amounts of hen-seed to something monstrously large and winged in the shrubbery. . . .)

Here was comfort indeed! Soon, Edmund contributed to Sir Thomas's ease by improvement in his own spirits—the only point in which he had given his father pain before. After wandering about and sitting under trees with Fanny all the summer evenings, he had so well talked his mind into submission as to be very tolerably cheerful again.

These were the circumstances which gradually brought alleviation to Sir Thomas, deadening his sense of loss, and in part reconciling him to himself. Though, the anguish from admitting his own errors in the education of his daughters was never to be entirely done away.

Too late he became aware how unfavourable to the character of any young people was the contradictory treatment which Maria and Julia had always experienced at home—the excessive indulgence and flattery of their aunt continually contrasted with his own severity. He saw how ill he had judged, expecting to counteract what was wrong in Mrs. Norris (not merely lycanthropy) by its reverse in himself. He had but increased the evil by teaching them to repress their spirits in his presence, making their real disposition unknown to him. This in turn sent them off, for all their indulgences, to a *person* who had been able to attach them only by the blindness of her affection, and the excess of her praise.

Here had been grievous mismanagement; but it had not been the worst mistake in his plan of education. Something must have been wanting *within,* or time would have worn away much of its ill effect. He feared that active *principle* had been wanting in his daughters. They had never been properly taught to govern themselves by a true sense of duty. They had been instructed theoretically in their religion, but never required to bring it into daily practice.

To be distinguished for elegance and accomplishments—the grand desire of their youth—had no moral effect on the mind. He had meant them to be good. But his cares had been directed to the understanding and manners, not the disposition. They had never heard of the virtue of self-denial and humility from any lips.

Bitterly did he deplore this deficiency. With all the cost and care of an expensive education, he had "brought up" his daughters—without their understanding their first duties, or his being acquainted with their character.

The high spirit and strong passions of Mrs. Rushworth, especially, were made known to him only in their sad result. She was not to be prevailed on to leave Mr. Crawford. She hoped to marry him, and they continued together, till she was obliged to admit that such hope was vain. The disappointment and wretchedness arising from the conviction rendered her temper so bad, and her feelings for him so like hatred, as to make them for a while each other's punishment, and then induce a voluntary separation.

She had lived with him to be reproached as the ruin of all his happiness in Fanny (as he told her repeatedly and bitterly in their last days), and carried away no better consolation in leaving him than that she *had* divided them. What can exceed the misery of such a mind in such a situation?

Fanny was soon to learn that there indeed *can* be something.

In a matter of days after Maria parted with Mr. Crawford, a letter had arrived at Mansfield, to Sir Thomas's attention. It was very brief, even businesslike, and sorely lacking any remonstrance or feeling, except for a single begging of pardon. In short—Maria was coming down to Mansfield Park—not *asking* her sire's permission, but already on her way. And, there was a postscript: she was being politely and generously escorted by a certain *gentleman.*

Such was the extent of the letter, and the household went into a quiet uproar. Sir Thomas became grim and inviolate, initially denied any welcome and started to write a vehement letter of refusal, when Edmund reminded him that Maria was already in transit, and the letter was not likely to reach her. At the same time, Mrs. Norris opened her mouth to say that a gentleman could mean none other than Mr. Crawford, and that indeed, it must be joyous news, and they must be married! Lady Bertram was only too glad to echo such a possibility; and Sir Thomas indeed relented, though he had much lower notions of what might be the actual situation.

Fanny was thrown into an immediate state of terror. If Mr. Crawford was indeed the gentleman in question, and coming here, then she could imagine nothing that might lend her the strength to face him. Indeed, she had no words, no emotions, nothing to say to him that was not beyond unbearable. What was she to do? At least there was Edmund, and her dear Susan, both here with her, to frankly talk about some of this.

In addition, there was a matter of him being married or *not married* to Maria. Such a difference either state would make for how he might chuse to address Fanny—perhaps even to renew his courtship of her (a thing truly intolerable at this point). While she was agonizing over the possibilities and planning her excuses to spend the following days hidden away from Mr. Crawford in the East room, the following morning brought a fair and rather wondrous resolution of all these agonies.

A fine carriage and four rolled up to the gates, and out came Maria followed by a tall, elegant, raven-haired gentleman of great handsomeness, fine dress, impeccable manners and—

wonder-of-wonders—a welcome and inexplicable *familiarity* to everyone at Mansfield Park.

"Oh, Fanny! Oh, look! It's Lord Eastwind!" Susan was the first to exclaim with joyful recognition, and her face lit up with childish excitement and rare happy memories of Portsmouth. Forgetting in a moment all her hard-studied decorum, she tugged at Fanny's arm.

"Why, your Mummyship!" exclaimed Lady Bertram in genuine delight—for, besides Fanny, the Pharaoh had been her other kind and attentive companion for so many months on end, and she *missed* his ephemeral presence.

Thankfully such a peculiar form of address was ignored by everyone else, and Sir Thomas suddenly recalled Lord Eastwind as a fine, esteemed acquaintance and dear family friend. Warm greetings were exchanged—their warmth inexplicably translating to Maria (who stood silently and somewhat sulkily in her enforced humility, waiting to be noticed). The visitors were then escorted inside, and Fanny—whose heart was performing a very strange beat within her chest—followed, after Edmund and Susan and everyone had gone in, trailing them, harboring anxiety, newfound acute curiosity, and impossible relief (the latter on behalf of there being no Mr. Crawford).

"It has been my utmost pleasure to be of service to Mrs. Rushworth," said Lord Eastwind in the parlor, while tea was being readied. "I was her companion from London, and must continue on my way shortly, with but a day of stay here in Northampton."

This information certainly made some difference in the way the curious pair of newcomers was now regarded. There were immediate but unvoiced doubts resumed as to the *propriety,* especially on Sir Thomas's part.

"Oh, but you must stay longer, pray!" said Lady Bertram, while Sir Thomas concurred, saying he was much obliged for

Lord Eastwind's kindness on behalf of his daughter. Certain subtle glances were executed, where Sir Thomas attempted to ascertain if there was any kind of particular interest or even a *bond* between the Lord and his daughter, and he appeared to be satisfied that there was a distinct possibility of such.

It seemed to him, Lord Eastwind was decidedly attentive and gallant in his manner of address, and in the way he glanced at Maria as he uttered various appropriate pleasantries at all proper points of discourse.

Fanny, meanwhile, was subtly ignored. Indeed, it was as if Lord Eastwind had made it a point of never quite glancing at her or even addressing her directly.

Such behavior did not particularly bother Fanny as much as it made her cautiously anxious. She continued to wonder also that Eastwind was now freely seen by all—*visible,* as a man of living flesh—and she could not help but wonder if he had conveniently *fed* off Maria throughout their long journey to ensure such a continued manifestation was possible.

Indeed, what was he doing here? His manifestations had been—as he himself admitted—related to Fanny alone. And now that he was corporeal indeed, and somehow having insinuated his illusion of familiarity into everyone's perception of him, was accepted and welcomed into the family circle—what was his true intent?

There was not a chance to ponder overly long, because Edmund, of all people, approached Lord Eastwind in an interlude when no one else but Fanny seemed to be paying attention, and asked him point blank: "Pray, do not think I don't remember *now* who and what you are, sir. You are an unholy ancient monster, thoroughly *undead* and Cursed, and I will not allow this family to suffer any more evil, not even if it means another scandal. Therefore I must ask, what are your intentions here? And what are your intentions for my poor long-suffering sister Maria?"

"For your sister, none whatsoever," replied Eastwind. And then for the first time his glance turned to Fanny.

Fanny felt the sudden gust of hot dry wind of the desert, a heady lungful of perfume from distant ancient lotus blossoms, and a memory of a brilliant blue sky. His gentle, familiar, *beloved* eyes were watching her. It was as though no time had passed, no monstrosity of death itself had surfaced to stand between them. Her heart rebounded with a surge of emotion, an overwhelming, impossible, undeniable pull. . . .

And then Fanny took a deep breath, and forced herself to look away. She looked at Edmund instead, to anchor herself in the present. Was Edmund, she wondered, even now truly cognizant of any of this?

In that moment Maria approached them and the spell was broken. As she began to talk—of nothings, of some pretty platitudes, possibly of the weather and the table settings in the dining room—both Fanny and Edmund immediately observed how flirtatious Maria's manner was. They noted her sly glances at the Lord, her heightened colour and somewhat raised voice. Indeed, all signs pointed to a new infatuation—most likely a consequence of rebounding affection from Mr. Crawford to a fresh, new highly eligible and deserving object—an infatuation, fueled even more by a sense of revenge against all parties who had aggrieved her.

Indeed, it would have been surprising if Maria had not fallen a *little* in love with such a handsome, elegant man as was Eastwind, had she met him under normal social circumstances. As it were, she had no memory of him, naturally, during the days of the unfortunate acting of *Lovers' Vows,* when he was ever at Lady Bertram's side, and a *non-presence* to all but Fanny. And yet, from all that time, Maria must have had a supernatural *sense* of him, a familiarity that had carried over into the present. Thus, it had been so easy for her to trust him in London where he first *"approached"* her at some social gathering—how, exactly, she remembered not—so easy to have trusted him to bring her here, to her family. Maria hoped Mr. Crawford was informed of her leaving town with such a fine escort.

Soon, Sir Thomas had ordered dinner, and there was movement from the living room to the other. Mrs. Norris glared and indeed growled and bared her teeth at Lord Eastwind as he gallantly took Maria's hand to escort her to dine. Fanny recalled how aunt Norris was another one of them who had always been aware of his presence, and while Edmund *thought* he had always known (he had not), the werewolf aunt (and Mr. Rushworth, for that matter) certainly had—since those tainted by the *dark* are drawn to always recognize each other.

Dinner conversation was at a minimum, and Maria continued to flirt rather overtly with Lord Eastwind, who, to give him credit, returned her charming provocations with impeccable vague politeness. Despite the lukewarm courtesy, Sir Thomas seriously started to consider the annual endowment, estates, and the lineage, but was having some odd difficulty recalling the exact family connexions of Eastwind, though he was certain they were sterling beyond belief.

Lady Bertram, meanwhile, started to fondly catalogue within her thoughts the remaining Egyptian treasures in the household (that included three baboons and a certain crocodile, all intact upstairs, among a host of other variously perilous or benign items), and wondering how soon might she be able to open up, and once more visit, with her previous regularity, that certain room in the attic where *it* all started. Though her mind was no longer held in the mesmerizing vise of the dead Pharaoh, her heart was bent in that direction by nature—had always been. She, who had released the Mummy into this world under magical duress, was now, of her own accord, very much coming to like it.

Edmund meanwhile, hardly ate at all. He spent most of the dinner staring at Eastwind, and unconsciously reaching for his priestly collar wherein lay, as Fanny knew, his cross. She had no heart to remind him—yet again—that mummies were insensible to the Lord's holy implements, being several thousand years before His time. Ah, dear sweet Edmund.

The meal was over, and the gentlemen retired to Sir Thomas's library. Tom was the only one in truly high spirits, and he even winked at Maria as they left the room.

The women, on the other hand, were a much more reserved group. Maria was, from the start, decidedly ignoring Fanny, which pained her cousin somewhat but not enough to venture to draw her out at this time. Susan was introduced and engaged in brief talk, then dismissed as too "Fanny-like" by association. Conversation was superficial and haphazard, with not a mention of Mr. Crawford—which was hardly unexpected. "Play us something, dearest Maria," nagged Mrs. Norris, and Maria was sent to the pianoforte where she made a regular effort, while Fanny and Susan sat next to Lady Bertram and took turns reading to her.

"Ah how amiable it is to consider Egypt once more!" said Lady Bertram suddenly, coming out of a reverie. Everyone exchanged glances but did not respond, while Mrs. Norris choked, and Maria hit a false note at the instrument. Susan alone looked about them, blissfully unfamiliar with what the subject of Egypt had meant to the family. For Susan, mummies meant drunken sailors and Portsmouth and a dashingly exciting afternoon at the dockyard—indeed, she had no notion of Lord Eastwind's true connection to it all.

But then, it occurred to Fanny, neither had Maria. For, her cousin had not been a witness to the unholy chaos at *that ball*.

The gentlemen soon joined them, and Sir Thomas suggested cards. There were no Mr. and Mrs. Grant to share a table with, and he invited his sons and Eastwind. But the raven-haired gentleman skillfully extricated himself, and within moments was found in a chair near Fanny.

He *had* to have been using some subtle mental *influence,* she thought, for there were no other means of accounting it. Even Maria was looking away, temporarily engaged in some kind of intense pointless discourse with Mrs. Norris.

"Miss Price," said Lord Eastwind, watching her from a partially turned profile, made into an exquisite reversed cameo by candlelight, dark on light. "You alone have a true glimpse into my being, and thus you must know why I am here."

"Frankly, Lord Eastwind," replied Fanny, gathering herself for the unexpected, while keeping her tone and expression steady, "I am very tired, and very unsure of your intent. The last time you appeared, unexpectedly, it was a noble and worthy rescue. I dare say, you *saved* us—and yet, how am I to know it had been real, and not a contrivance to appear chivalrous in my eyes?"

He gently said, "Indeed, it is something you may never know. You only have my word that it is so. That I have relinquished all control over my ancient servants. That my sole purpose of existence is to be with you, by human means."

He paused, turning his face away from her in a complete profile, staring off into the distance, as though for once unable to face *her,* and gathering himself for something. And Fanny watched him, not daring to breathe.

"You have rejected me once," he finally said softly. "I have no will ever again to trouble you, and I will never lose composure again as I had that day, in that moment at your ball—in this you may rest easily, for I keep my promise. But my feelings for you are the same. Indeed, they are eternal. For you, I have come here—one last time—to implore. My dear—my *beloved. . . .* There, indeed—I do not look upon you as I speak now, so that you may not think I use the power of my gaze to influence, for such occasionally happens even beyond my control."

"East Wind . . ." whispered Fanny in reply. "Oh, what infinite sorrow! And yet—you must know my answer is the same. I am sorry—I grieve with all my spirit, for in one deepest part of my soul I will always love you. But in this life, we are no longer bound. You—do not belong here. You must cross into the mists and follow the boat of Osiris, for it lies waiting for you at the shore of the great river—"

She stopped speaking because he was crying. No facial muscle moved (he was a living mask of fired clay, smoothed on the surface yet brittle with time underneath). Yet tears of glass came slowly crawling down his dark cheeks, out of the corner of his eye—where she could see a shadow of ancient Egyptian kohl, drawn thick and wide and lovely. She looked and saw in his weeping eye, the Eye of Horus. And then she understood. . . .

"Oh, East Wind," said Fanny in agonized frustration. "What dire misdeed had my aunt Bertram done!"

But he said nothing, only turned to her at last, and his eyes were impossible to face. "I have your final answer, then?" he asked, his voice like distant reeds from an ancient shore. "You do not chuse to be with me again, in eternity, to have our souls bound with the purest bonds of love?"

"No, I do not. My dear, sweet, ancient love. In *this* life, I am already bound—to *another.* And as for eternity—I chuse to be bound to no one but myself."

When she had spoken the word *"another,"* Fanny could not help but glance in the direction of Edmund, oblivious and engrossed in a conversation with his father.

Lord Eastwind saw her glance. And in resigned silence he nodded. He then got up, and with all kindness left her side.

Fanny sat stricken into a kind of dead silence for the rest of the evening, in which she had no idea what had occurred. She did not move until Susan touched her gently on the arm—the room had emptied, everyone retiring for the night, and candles were being put out.

Fanny was woken in the middle of the night by some exceedingly loud noises in the hallway and the room nearby her own tiny attic bedroom.

Barely having a moment to avail herself of a candle, she opened the door and with great trepidation looked out into the dim hallway.

She was not alone. There was Mr. Rochester with a candle, followed by a very mousy little governess by the name of Jane Eyre—ah, no, those were just the remnants of her dream; Fanny sighed at the tome[38] on her nightstand. She blinked, and just as she glanced again into the hallway, there was Edmund, coming up the stairs, followed by Sir Thomas, both dressed in hastily drawn robes, and behind them, Baddeley, with candles in a holder.

"Fanny! Oh, did you hear it, Fanny?" Edmund exclaimed in a hushed whisper.

"What, cousin? I am afraid I did not—not exactly. There were some noises—"

But in that moment everyone's attention was drawn to an open door. It was the door to the famous secret attic room that was Lady Bertram's favorite place. A beam of bright candle glow fell to illuminate the way, and they all advanced, for there were several agitated voices resounding from within, including that of Lady Bertram, and Maria.

"Please, my dear," Lady Bertram was heard to speak in an agitated tonality above her usual placid mumble, and sounding to Fanny's hearing for the first time very much like her own mother, the ever-harried Mrs. Price. "I really do not think it is wise to do this—he is charming, there is no doubt, but I do wish you would come down here at once, upon my word—"

---

[38] Time travel.

Everyone entered the chamber, with Fanny trailing them in some timidity (for she still harbored a longtime dread of that room, not to mention she had just dreamed of Mr. Rochester's mad spouse, and nigh expected flames). . . .

Before their startled, amazed, nay, *stupefied* eyes was a large expanse of attic space, turned into an approximation of an ancient Egyptian burial chamber. Illuminated by bright burning torches of decidedly Egyptian origin, items of every possible description that had previously lain in careless display all over Mansfield Park were now overflowing the confines of every surface, table, and shelf. Crates were stacked, covered by cat, crocodile, bird, serpent, and other creature-headed statuary, upright golden gods interspersed with baboons, Isis vying for shelf space with Thoth, Bast, Set, and Horus, chests covered with gold and lapis, jars of precious oil and vials of grave provisions for the long repasts of the Afterlife, scepters and head-pieces, bead collars of glass and gold, amulets and scarabs, wooden effigies of slaves and servants and guards, barges of sandalwood and reed, stacks of clay tablets detailing the goods (or possibly shopping lists) of the pharaohs—

"Dear God in Heaven!" exclaimed Sir Thomas in horror, unable to help himself. But then he was faced by an even more harrowing sight.

On a large upraised platform in the center of the room, next to a grand sarcophagus of marble and gold, stood his hapless daughter, Maria.

She was in her night gown. She was standing upright, but balancing with some minor difficulty on the tops of three great oil jars from Cairo (and it is impossible to conceive how she in fact managed to climb there without being properly trained beforehand by *cirque du soleil*[39]), in order to reach the edge of the sarcophagus, and for all appearances, to lower herself inside the ancient grave.

---

[39] Extreme makeover time travel.

Off to the side, stood Lady Bertram, nervously clutching several implements of mummification, such as tongs, pliers, a long poker-like metal object that was either a fork or a brain and entrails extractor, and a royal scepter that had fallen out of some chest nearby (when one says "chest," the implication is either an actual box or a chest cavity, since both were plentiful in the chamber)—and landed inappropriately underhand for her ladyship to grab.

And inside the sarcophagus itself—in the center of the room—stood the Mummy.

He was young, handsome, regal, completely clad in the illusion of the living flesh . . . And for the first time they saw not an elegant London gentleman but an ancient Pharaoh of Egypt.

His skin was olive and dates, his hair like a soft raven's wing. He wore a robe of white linen trimmed with jewels and gold, and a collar of lapis and glass around his neck, lying in grace upon his muscular chest. His strong arms were braced in gold serpent bands, and his feet were in gilded sandals.

His face—oh, the sweet *familiarity* of his dear face as it had been *three thousand years ago,* eyes highlighted with the darkness of soot into a rare beauty, the line of chiseled jaw and cheekbone, the lips with a hint of a smile at the corners—all of it struck Fanny more than anything. He was looking at them all with his warm gentle gaze, looking at *her*.

"East Wind . . ." Fanny barely mouthed his name.

The spell was broken by the thunderous voice of Sir Thomas. "Maria! What is this abominable indecency? What in the world is going on here? Who is *he?* What are you doing? I pray you get down here right this instant!" And to his wife, who was staring at him in that moment with glazed eyes: "And you, Madam! *For shame!* I thought we had our discussion about all this—this madness, this Egyptian insanity? I thought these items were returned duly where they belong? What, then, are they *still doing in this house?*"

In that moment, the beautiful Pharaoh slowly raised his right hand and then turned it palm up. Sir Thomas was silenced immediately. A sudden hot wind seemed to fill the chamber. It stirred the draperies and moved the hair on everyone's head, while torches and candles flickered madly. His gaze no longer warm but blank and somehow *eternal,* the Pharaoh was looking directly at Fanny, as he lowered his hand slowly.

Fanny felt herself pulled with the wind itself, as though her breath was being taken from her lungs. And yet she stood her ground.

Instead, it was Maria who moved.

"No!" exclaimed Edmund.

Still teetering on the tops of the jars like an acrobat, Maria took a step onto the wide marble rim of the sarcophagus. She blinked, as though trying to rid herself of a sight of something quite impossible. She muttered words that were too soft to hear.

"No," cried Edmund again, "I beg you, Maria! You must step away from him!"

"I am afraid I am perfectly incapable of moving in any other direction," replied his sister, managing to speak coherently at last. "Oh, his glorious song fills my head, till I see sapphire skies over the Nile and the brilliant golden sun over the pyramids, the perfume of the temples and the falcon in flight, his dark exotic, *non-British* eyes—Oh, it is perfectly intolerable, I simply cannot!"

"But you must! Make haste, Maria, before it is too late!"

But the Mummy had turned and was looking at her with his mesmerizing gaze.

Maria began to tremble. "Is it not too late for me already, Edmund? Is it not a spinster's life for me? No one will have me now; I am tainted, relegated to paltry livelihood alone or as someone's pitiful companion—"

"Oh, for heaven's sake, think, Maria! Your choice is spinsterhood or *mummification!*"

Maria wailed. "Spinsterhood *is* mummification! Can you not see, brother, at least with him I will be loved, I will be forever his! A blissful eternity!"

The Mummy's gold-braced hand rose, beckoning.

In that moment behind them the attic door came crashing wide open, ricocheting with violence against the wall, and nearly coming off its hinges. . . .

Mr. Rushworth burst into the chamber. What he was doing here, miles away from London, was hard to surmise. But he was half-man half-wolf, a terrifying half-transformed state, similar to having forgotten to put one leg in his pantaloons before quitting one's bedchamber.

"Halt! Grrr!" he snarled, standing up tall and monstrous. "Not another step, you ancient scoundrel! Arrrr! Grrrowwr! HOWL! You will not lay hands on my wife! Wretched and deceitful she might be but she still carries my Grrowl! Argh! honorable name!"

Mrs. Norris came right behind him, singlehandedly yelping like a pack of hounds. "Maria! Stop this nonsense and get down here this instant!" she managed, and then began to *transform* before their eyes in a kind of neurotic reflex.

(It was later found that instead of heading for bed that evening, Mrs. Norris took matters into her own hands by putting on her wolf form, racing to London with supernatural speed, and notifying Mr. Rushworth of the impending calamity involving his estranged wife. The two werewolves returned in a matter of hours to Mansfield, well in time for the present fiasco, with even some moments to spare for a brief fit of foraging in the Mansfield shrubbery.)

But now, despite all his readiness, anger, and righteousness, Mr. Rushworth was to have no opportunity to spring forward and execute his attack upon this latest rival.

Because Lady Bertram—completely overwhelmed by the present turn of events, clutching the imperial scepter in one hand and the whip of the pharaoh in the other—fainted.

Mrs. Norris gave a yelp-howl. Both of the werewolves gaped. No one else seemed to mind, for the hot desert wind was still blowing in the chamber, and everyone was too mesmerized by the sight of Maria and Wolf and Mummy. Everyone, that is, except Fanny. She immediately went to Lady Bertram's side, and started trying to revive her.

Moving of her own volition thus, had indeed helped her break the subtle thrall that the Pharaoh had placed on her. As Fanny fumbled around Lady Bertram's neck, her gaze fell on a certain necklet. The thing had been worn by her aunt for as long as she knew her, and she recognized it for what it was, from Edmund's first childish story told her so many years ago, and from her own secret memory.

Fanny Price took up the Eye of Horus and removed it from around Lady Bertram's neck. Fanny then straightened, turned around, and raised it like a pistol to point at the *one* who had once been a beautiful young pharaoh. "Enough!" she said. "In the name of all the Gods of Egypt I demand you *desist*."

The world seemed to still.

The Pharaoh turned and looked at her. His eyes, his expression still seemed blank, empty . . . but he was responding, and this time it was he who was *drawn* to her and the amulet.

Fanny walked though the billowing illusion of wind, taking each step with difficulty, as though she were drowning in eons and molasses, and then she was before him. She climbed the platform, reached up to him, as he stood in the sarcophagus, and she placed the Eye of Horus around his neck.

The Pharaoh trembled at the touch of her fingers at his throat, her accidental brushing against his cheek.

He looked at her, and the wind about them stilled.

"Thank you, *beloved,*" he whispered. "Though I may not have you, this will give me peace."

"I know."

Fanny held his face in her hands, and watched his dear eyes up-close for the last time.

"And now, you know what must be done," he said. "You must destroy me. Stifle me, like you have done with the others. Take back my *breath of life*. . . ."

"No," Fanny said. "Not like the others."

And she put her lips to his, and she kissed him, and she held her breath amid her building tears, and pulled in his *own*—dear, sweet, ancient. . . .

He died long before she knew she was kissing an ancient husk.

No one was capable of sleep immediately after that incident.

The Mummy was laid to rest. He reposed in state in his coffin, enshrouded once more in the browned linen rags of what had once been his splendid raiment, and Fanny herself made sure to close up the lid with trembling hands, and with Edmund and Sir Thomas's willing assistance.

Then, Lady Bertram, sobbing quietly, was led outside gently. Maria, having regained her senses, followed, grim-faced and dearly shamed for the second time.

The attic room was shut and temporarily boarded up on orders of Sir Thomas, who did not trust anyone this time not to disturb it. Sir Thomas ordered Baddeley to personally drive the nails in, while on the morrow he was to send an express dispatch to the London Museum to make arrangements for the final transferal of the archeological treasures hence.

While this was being enacted, Maria turned to Fanny and whispered: "Cousin, oh, what—whatever can I say to remedy all this?"

Fanny looked at her with compassion, but spoke as sternly as a Fanny could, under the circumstances. "Cousin Maria, your repeated attempts to run off with every man who has ever paid court to me are rather disenheartening."

At which point Maria could not help but smile, and while Mrs. Norris glared at Fanny, she took her cousin into a long needed embrace.

But there was not to be an equal reconciliation for the Rushworths. Thoroughly disgusted, disillusioned, and de-wolfed (the last, only until the next full moon), Mr. Rushworth had no difficulty in procuring a divorce; and so ended a marriage contracted under such circumstances as to make any better end the effect of good luck not to be reckoned on.

She had despised him, and loved another; and he had been very much aware that it was so. The indignities of stupidity, and the disappointments of selfish passion, can excite little pity. His punishment followed his conduct, as did a deeper punishment the deeper guilt of his wife. *He* was released from the engagement to be mortified and unhappy and excessively *wolfish,* till some other pretty girl could attract him into matrimony again. And thus, he might set forward on a second, and, it is to be hoped, more prosperous trial of the married state—if duped, to be duped at least with good humour and good luck. Maria; meanwhile must withdraw with infinitely stronger feelings to a retirement and reproach which could allow no second spring of hope or character.

Where she could be placed became a subject of most melancholy and momentous consultation. Mrs. Norris, whose attachment seemed to augment with the demerits of her niece, would have had her permanently stay at home in Mansfield. Sir Thomas would not hear of it. And Mrs. Norris's anger against Fanny was so much the greater, from considering *her* residence there as the motive.

Mrs. Norris persisted in placing his scruples to *her* account, though Sir Thomas very solemnly assured her that, had there been no young *person* belonging to him, to be endangered by the society or hurt by the character of Mrs. Rushworth, he would never have offered so great an insult to the neighbourhood. As a penitent daughter, she should be protected by him, secured in every comfort, and supported by every encouragement to do right, which their relative situations admitted. But further than *that* he could not go. Maria had destroyed her own character, and he would not, by a vain attempt to restore what never could be restored, be accessory to introducing such misery in another man's family as he had known himself. Maria was to go hence, as were all the Egyptian artifacts.

It ended in Mrs. Norris's resolving to quit Mansfield and devote herself to her unfortunate Maria in her "mummification." An establishment was formed for them in another country, remote and private, where, shut up together with little society, on one side no affection, on the other no judgment, it may be reasonably supposed that their tempers became their mutual punishment.

Mrs. Norris's removal from Mansfield was the great supplementary comfort of Sir Thomas's life. His opinion of her had been sinking from the day of his return from Antigua. In every transaction together from that period, in their daily intercourse,[40] in business, or in chat, she had been regularly losing ground in his esteem. He was convinced that either time had done her much disservice, or that he had considerably over-rated her sense, and wonderfully borne with her manners before.

---

[40] Ah! the Hapless Author is blinded like Cyclops, Oedipus, Homer, and all the great blind ancients put together. The *image!*—nay, the very *thought* of such a *connexion* is inconceivable! Hopeless Reader, Thou hast sunk into the Great Pit from whence there is no return!

He had felt her as an hourly evil (a monthly super-evil), which was so much the worse, as there seemed no chance of its ceasing but with life or a silver bullet (which, truth be told, was more tempting every day)—a part of himself that must be borne for ever. To be relieved from her, therefore, was a great felicity.

She was regretted by no one at Mansfield. She had never been able to attach even those she loved best. And since Mrs. Rushworth's elopement, her temper had been in a state of such irritation as to make her everywhere tormenting, even without her chronic wolfish state. Not even Fanny had tears for aunt Norris, not even when she was gone for ever.

That Julia escaped better than Maria, was not due to disposition and circumstance, but to her having been less the darling of that very aunt—less flattered and less spoilt. Her beauty and acquirements were held in second place. She was used to considering herself a little inferior to Maria. Her temper was naturally the easiest of the two; her feelings, though quick, were more controllable, and education had not given her so very hurtful a degree of self-consequence.

Julia had submitted the best to the disappointment in Henry Crawford. After the first bitterness of being slighted was over, she was tolerably soon able not to think of him again. When the acquaintance was renewed in town, and Mr. Rushworth's house became Crawford's object, she had had the merit of withdrawing herself from it, in order to secure herself from being again too much attracted.

This had been her motive in going to her cousin's. Mr. Yates's convenience had had nothing to do with it. Julia had been allowing his attentions some time, but with very little idea of ever accepting him. Had not her sister's conduct burst forth as it did—and her increased dread of her father and of home, imagining its consequence to herself would be greater severity and restraint, made her resolve to avoid such immediate horrors at all risks—it is probable that Mr. Yates would never have succeeded. She had not eloped with any worse feelings than those of selfish alarm. It had appeared to her the only thing to be done. Maria's guilt had induced Julia's folly.

Henry Crawford, ruined by early independence and bad domestic example, indulged in cold-blooded vanity a little too long. Once it had, by unplanned and unmerited chance, led him into the way of happiness. Could he have been satisfied with the conquest of one amiable woman's affections, could he have found sufficient exultation in overcoming the reluctance, in working himself into the esteem and tenderness of Fanny Price, there would have been every probability of success and felicity for him.

His affection had already done something. Her influence over him had already given him some influence over her. Would he have deserved more, there can be no doubt that more would have been obtained—especially when that marriage had taken place, which would have given him the assistance of her conscience in subduing her first inclination, and brought them very often together. Would he have persevered, and uprightly, Fanny must have been his reward, and a reward very voluntarily bestowed, within a reasonable period from Edmund's marrying Mary.

Had he done as he intended, and as he knew he ought, by going down to Everingham after his return from Portsmouth, he might have been deciding his own happy destiny. But he was pressed to stay for Mrs. Fraser's party. He was to meet Mrs. Rushworth there. Curiosity and vanity were both engaged, and the temptation of immediate pleasure was too strong for a mind unused to make any sacrifice to right. He resolved to defer his Norfolk journey. He saw Mrs. Rushworth, was received by her with a coldness which ought to have been repulsive, and have established apparent indifference between them for ever. But he was mortified—he could not bear to be thrown off by the woman whose smiles had been so wholly at his command. He must exert himself to subdue so proud a display of resentment. It was anger on Fanny's account. He must get the better of it, and make Mrs. Rushworth Maria Bertram again in her treatment of himself.

In this spirit he began the attack, and by perseverance had soon re-established the sort of familiar intercourse,[41] gallantry, flirtation. But in triumphing over discretion which might have saved them both, he had put himself in the power of feelings on her side more strong than he had supposed.

She loved him; there was no withdrawing attentions avowedly dear to her. He was entangled by his own vanity, with as little excuse of love as possible, and without the smallest inconstancy of mind towards her cousin. To keep Fanny and the Bertrams from a knowledge of what was passing became his first object. Secrecy could not have been more desirable for Mrs. Rushworth's credit than he felt it for his own.

When he returned from Richmond, he would have been glad to see Mrs. Rushworth no more. All that followed was the result of her imprudence; and he went off with her at last, because he could not help it—regretting Fanny even at the moment, but regretting her infinitely more when all the bustle of the intrigue was over, and a very few months had taught him, by the force of contrast, to place a yet higher value on the sweetness of her temper, the purity of her mind, and the excellence of her principles.

That public punishment of disgrace, should in a just measure attend *his* share of the offence, is not one of the barriers which society gives to virtue. In this world the penalty is less equal than could be wished. But without presuming to look forward to a juster appointment hereafter, we may fairly consider a man of sense, like Henry Crawford, to be providing for himself considerable vexation and regret—vexation that must rise sometimes to self-reproach, and regret to wretchedness—in

---

[41] In the name of all moral authority, you are hereby placed under arrest! Do not resist, and come peaceably.

having so requited hospitality, so injured family peace, so forfeited his best, most estimable, and endeared acquaintance, and so lost the woman whom he had rationally as well as passionately loved.

It was some year and a half later, that Mr. Crawford had the terrifying pleasure of seeing Fanny again. It was quite by accident, on a street in London, and she was accompanied by close relations on a shopping excursion, and happily *wedded* at last to the only man she loved in this life.

"Fanny!" he had exclaimed. She turned, grew still and wooden. But then her kind features softened, for she had no longer anything to fear from him, and could only respond in mercy. Time had healed her of it, time and joyful circumstances of a personal nature.

He tried to draw her away to speak, and they exchanged some words in candour, near a storefront. At least, upon final pointed inquiry, she replied—speaking somewhat peculiar but genuine words.

"East Wind may have been the past, Henry, but Edmund is my present, not you. I admit the possibility that you—in the fullness of time, indeed, of the million lifetimes behind and yet before us—might one day be my *future*.

"You are learning to truly feel, and thus, one day you may learn to truly love in constancy. The barge of Osiris floats upon the great Nile for eternity. When we, as mere splinters of the reed, are temporarily rowed ashore to embark upon a given lifetime, we encounter each other upon that shore's brief stop. When the time to rejoin the river of eternity draws near, we may chuse to remain indefinitely in the shallows near the shore, to wait, suspended between the heaven and the earth, Life and Eternity, as we dream of our love and recollect our being. It is what East Wind had done when he had waited for me three thousand years.

"You, Henry, are free to do the same. Or better yet, simply live your life and we may one day meet regardless. I leave you now forever in *this* lifetime. And in this parting, I wish you from my heart, only the best."

She spoke thus, and left him, with her radiant face and gentle smile.

And her words haunted Henry Crawford till his last breath.

After what had passed to wound and alienate the two families, the continuance of the Bertrams and Grants in such close neighbourhood would have been most distressing. The extended absence of the latter ended very fortunately in the necessity of a permanent removal.

Dr. Grant succeeded to a stall in Westminster, which afforded an occasion for leaving Mansfield, an excuse for residence in London, and an increase of income—all highly acceptable to those who went and those who staid.

Mrs. Grant, with a loving temper, must have gone with some regret. But the same happiness of disposition must in any place, and any society, secure her a great deal to enjoy. She had again a home to offer Mary; and Mary had had enough of her own friends, vanity, ambition, twisted love, and disappointment in the course of the last half-year, to be in need of the true kindness and rational calm of her sister's heart.

They lived together—even after Dr. Grant had brought on apoplexy and death, by three great institutionary dinners in one week. For Mary, though resolved against ever attaching herself to a younger brother again, was long in finding among the dashing representatives, or idle heir-apparents, who were at the command of her beauty, and her £20,000, any one who could satisfy the better taste she had acquired at Mansfield, whose character and manners could bring the domestic happiness she had learned to estimate, or who could put Edmund Bertram sufficiently out of her *dark* head.

Edmund had greatly the advantage of her in this respect. He had not to wait and wish with vacant affections for an object worthy to succeed her in them.

Scarcely had he done regretting Mary Crawford, and observing to Fanny how impossible it was that he should ever meet with such another woman, before it began to strike him whether a very different kind of woman might not do just as well, or a great deal better. Fanny herself was growing as dear, as important to him in all her smiles and all her ways, as Mary Crawford had ever been. It was possible, thought Edmund, to persuade her that her warm and sisterly regard for him would be foundation enough for wedded love.

In short, Edmund did cease to care about Miss Crawford, and became as anxious to marry Fanny as Fanny herself could desire.

With such a regard for her, as his had long been, founded on the most endearing claims of innocence and helplessness, and completed by growing worth, what could be more natural than the change?

Loving, guiding, protecting her, as he had been doing ever since her being ten years old, her mind in so great a degree formed by his care, and her comfort depending on his kindness, an object to him of such close and peculiar interest, dearer by all his own importance with her than any one else at Mansfield—what was there to add, but that he should learn to prefer soft light eyes to sparkling dark ones. And being always with her, talking confidentially, his feelings in that favourable state which a recent disappointment gives, those soft light eyes soon obtained pre-eminence.

Having once set out on this road to happiness, there was nothing on the side of prudence to stop him or make his progress slow. There were no doubts of her deserving, no fears of opposition of taste, no need of drawing new hopes of happiness from dissimilarity of temper.

Her mind, disposition, opinions, and habits wanted no half-concealment, no self-deception on the present, no reliance on future improvement. Even in the midst of his late infatuation, he had acknowledged Fanny's mental superiority. What must be his sense of it now, therefore?

She was of course only too good for him. But as nobody minds having what is too good for them, he was very steadily earnest in the pursuit of the blessing, and her encouragement soon followed. Timid, anxious, doubting as she was, it was still impossible that such tenderness as hers should not, at times, hold out the strongest hope of success (though it remained for a later period to tell him the whole delightful and astonishing truth).

His happiness in knowing himself to have been so long the beloved of such a heart, must have been great and delightful. But there was happiness elsewhere which no description can reach. Let no one presume to give the feelings of a young woman on receiving the assurance of that affection of which she has scarcely allowed herself to entertain a hope.

Fanny's love of *this* lifetime.

She might always remember fondly a certain ancient pharaoh—indeed, there was a secret, age-old place in her heart in which there will always be a part of him, and a faint shadow of a beloved memory, permeated in deep, sweet sorrow. But in the here and now, Fanny Price had at last her *true love*.

Their own inclinations ascertained, there were no difficulties for Edmund and Fanny, no drawback of poverty or parent. It was a match which Sir Thomas's wishes had even forestalled.

Sick of ambitious and mercenary connexions, prizing more and more the sterling good of principle and temper, and anxious to bind all remaining domestic felicity, Sir Thomas had pondered with genuine satisfaction on the strong possibility of the two young friends finding their natural consolation in each other. The joyful consent which met Edmund's application, the high sense of having realised a great acquisition in the promise of Fanny for a daughter, formed such a contrast with his early opinion of the poor little girl's entering his household, as time is for ever producing between the plans and decisions of mortals—for their own instruction, and their neighbours' entertainment.

Fanny was indeed the daughter that he wanted. His charitable kindness had been rearing a prime comfort for himself. His liberality had a rich repayment, and the general goodness of his intentions by her deserved it. He might have made her childhood happier. But it had been an error of judgment only, giving him the appearance of harshness, depriving him of her early love. And now, on really knowing each other, their mutual attachment became very strong. After settling her at Thornton Lacey with every kind attention to her comfort, the object of almost every day was to see her there, or to get her away from it.

Selfishly dear as Fanny had long been to Lady Bertram, she could not be parted with willingly by *her*. No happiness of son or niece could make her wish the marriage. But it was possible to part with her, because Susan remained to supply her place. Susan became the stationary niece, delighted to be so; and equally well adapted for it by a readiness of mind, and an inclination for usefulness, as Fanny had been by sweetness of temper, and strong feelings of gratitude.

Susan could never be spared. First as a comfort to Fanny, then as an auxiliary, and last as her substitute, she was permanently established at Mansfield. Her more fearless disposition and happier nerves made everything easy to her there. With quickness in understanding the tempers of those she had to deal with, and no natural timidity to restrain any consequent wishes, she was soon welcome and useful to all.

After Fanny's removal Susan succeeded so naturally to the hourly comfort of her aunt, as gradually to become, perhaps, the most beloved of the two. In *her* usefulness, in Fanny's excellence, in William's continued good conduct and rising fame, and in the general well-doing and success of the other members of the family, all assisting to advance each other, and doing credit to his countenance and aid, Sir Thomas saw repeated reason to rejoice in what he had done for them all—and acknowledge the advantages of early hardship and discipline, and the consciousness of being born to struggle and endure.

With so much true merit and true love, and no want of fortune and friends, the happiness of the married cousins must appear as secure as earthly happiness can be. Equally formed for domestic life, and attached to country pleasures, their home was the home of affection and comfort; and to complete the picture of good, the acquisition of Mansfield living, by the death of Dr. Grant, occurred just after they had been married long enough to begin to want an increase of income, and feel their distance from the paternal abode an inconvenience.

On that event they removed to Mansfield; and the Parsonage there, which, under each of its two former owners, Fanny had never been able to approach but with some painful sensation of restraint or alarm, soon grew as dear to her heart, and as thoroughly perfect in her eyes, as everything else within the view and patronage of Mansfield Park had long been.

Before we leave our Loyal Reader in a reverie of so final and delightful thoughts, one thing more must be imparted. What of the fate of the remaining mummies?

With the passing of the great Pharaoh into the calm Eternity at long last, his minions—truly liberated from his supernatural will and rule—continued in their own places wherever they had been scattered in this great land.

Some were seen in Brighton, many in Bath, some in London, others, lumbering merrily along the countryside, were taken for scarecrows in the fields—the same fields that had been noted to be haunted by a terrifying spectre, the infamous Brighton Duck (an unlikely theory, since the same duck was often simultaneously said to have been seen in other distant locales, with the only explanation being that possibly, it had somehow *bred*). A great deal more had succeeded in overrunning Portsmouth to the point of it being generally known as a mummy terror for its citizens (the Price family had long since moved). This went on until, verily, one fine spring, a number of them, quite as windblown as real sailors by all appearance, were made an offer to enlist in the Royal Navy. Indeed, some even ended up on William's own ship the *Thrush.*

The mummies served as fine midshipmen, working earnestly on the high seas, and occasionally taking *sips* of their fellow sailors—a number of them making their way, it was rumored, back to their home continent of Africa, and then onward to Egypt.

And in all of this, not a single mummy more was ever seen at Mansfield Park.

THE END

APPENDIX

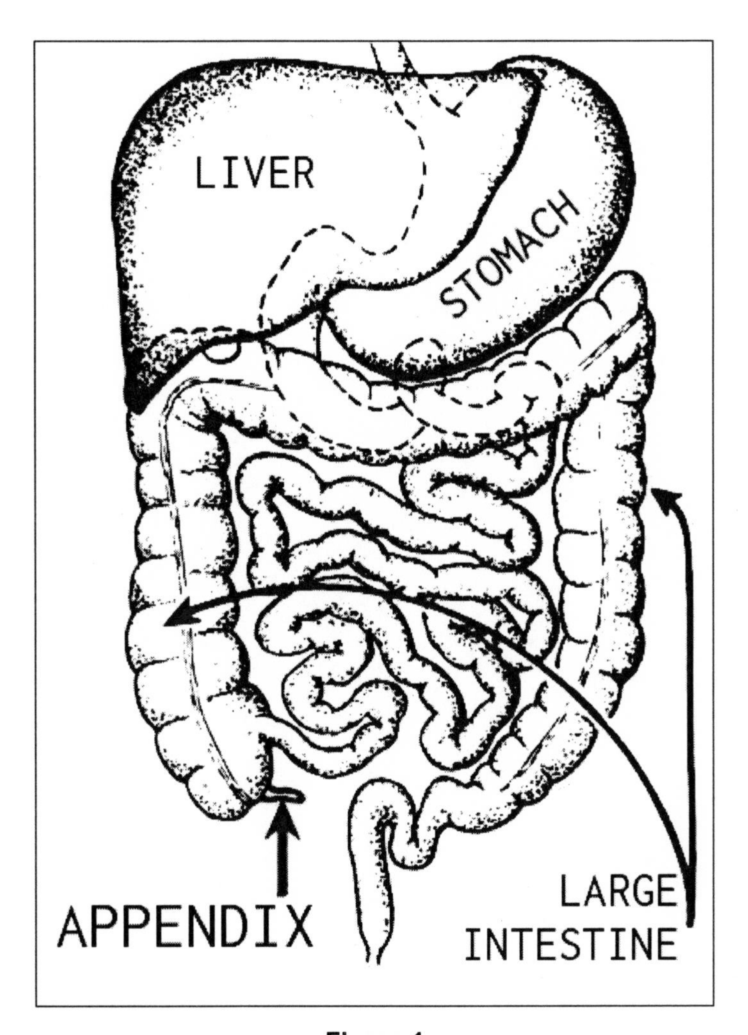

Figure 1

APPENDIX 2

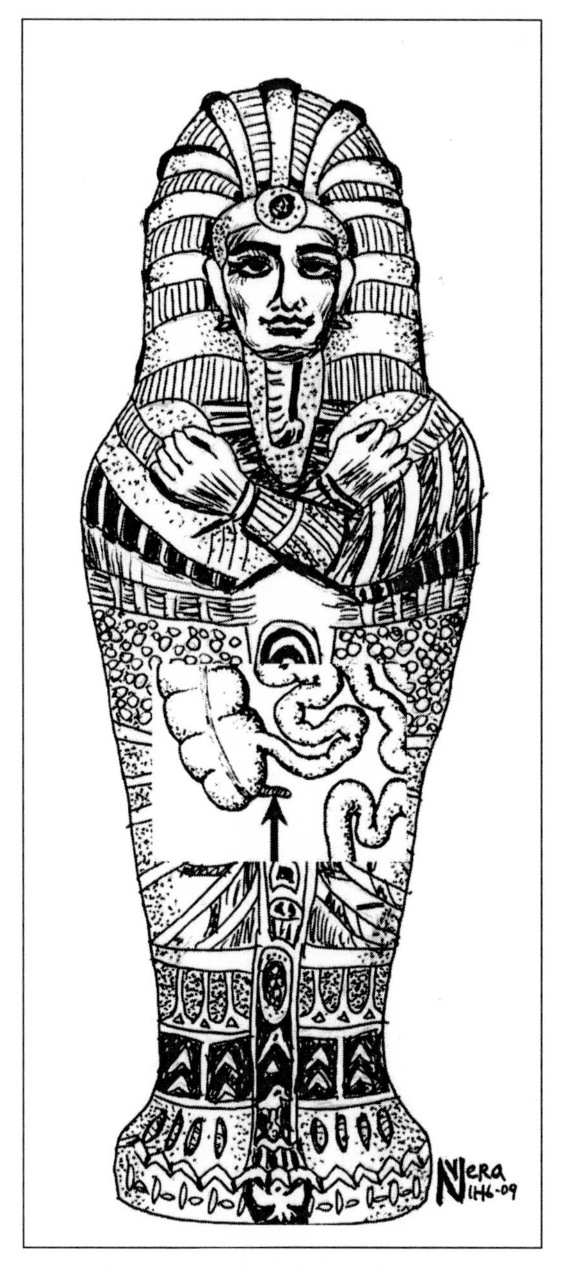

Figure 2: After Mummification

Author's After-Note

GENTLE READER—

No, this is not *she,* but the other—the shameless harridan who has taken it upon herself to take up pen and mangle Miss Austen's deathless (but never *undead*), perfectly civil, delightfully romantic, pointedly sarcastic, and by all accounts immortal prose, with the crass additions of her own fired imagination.

You notice there are historical inconsistencies and deviations from the real timeline. Indeed, the opera *Aida* comes on the scene much later, debuting in Cairo in 1871. And when Lady Bertram attends her first archeological museum lecture in London, somewhere on the continent, Georg Ebers (1837-1898), the famed Egyptologist and author, is probably but a randy twinkle in his father's eye. But—we must attribute all of this to literary mayhem. Or, better yet, to the Mummy's own supernatural influence: the glorious ancient Pharaoh's ability to control and indeed move through space and time itself.

For, indeed, has *he,* the East Wind, not blown in, floating in stately beauty and tragic comedy through the great mists of meta-existence, to grace us with his own immortal presence in these *otherwise* classic pages?

Meanwhile, I humbly beg a thousand pardons of Miss Austen's noble shade, and trust you have enjoyed the warm breezes throughout Mansfield Park.

Yours, in All Amiability,
THE HARRIDAN.

Vera Nazarian
November, 2009

About the Harridan

Vera Nazarian immigrated to the USA from the former USSR as a kid, sold her first story at the age of 17, and since then has published numerous works in anthologies and magazines, and has seen her fiction translated into eight languages.

She made her novelist debut with the critically acclaimed arabesque "collage" novel *Dreams of the Compass Rose,* followed by epic fantasy about a world without color, *Lords of Rainbow*. Her novella *The Clock King and the Queen of the Hourglass* from PS Publishing (UK) with an introduction by **Charles de Lint** made the *Locus* Recommended Reading List for 2005. Her debut short fiction collection *Salt of the Air,* with an introduction by **Gene Wolfe**, contains the 2007 Nebula Award-nominated "The Story of Love." Recent work includes the 2008 Nebula Award-nominated, self-illustrated baroque fantasy novella *The Duke in His Castle,* and this literary monstrosity that you now hold in your hands. . . .

Vera lives in Los Angeles, and uses her Armenian sense of humor and her Russian sense of suffering to bake conflicted pirozhki and make art.

In addition to being a writer and award-winning artist, she is also the publisher of Norilana Books.

Official website:
www.veranazarian.com